DESERT WARRIORS

Vicky continued to stare at the men, who were too far off to be properly identified. But she could tell that they were men of the desert, and that they carried rifles and spears, and that they were slowly increasing in number, and spreading out so as entirely to surround the oasis. Her heart beat fast because from behind the men there now came sound, drifting on the wind. It was principally the sound of many hooves, many tramping feet, and of clanking accoutrements. There were a great many people out there. But there was also a kind of singing sound, a mournful dirge which rose and fell with a regular cadence, punctuated by short, sharp snaps. Those were sounds she had heard before, in the slave kingdom of Zanzibar.

'Oh, my God,' she muttered. 'Those are Touaregs. And that is a slave caravan . . .'

Victoria's Walk

CAROLINE GRAY

SPHERE BOOKS

A *Sphere* Book

First published in Great Britain by Michael Joseph Ltd 1986
First published in paperback by Sphere Books Ltd 1988
This edition published by Sphere Books 1995

Printed in England by Clays Ltd, St Ives plc

Sphere Books
A Division of
Little, Brown and Company (UK)
Brettenham House
Lancaster Place
London WC2E 7EN

Victoria Lang found herself responsible for twelve bewildered and frightened people cast into an utterly alien environment – she took the only course open to her, and walked them back to civilisation.

PROLOGUE

The black orderly stood to attention. 'Major McClarrie has returned, Governah, sah! He wishes to see you, Governah, sah!'

Sir Francis Hodgson raised his head so suddenly he disturbed the flies which had clustered on the crown of his thick black hair, and peered across his desk at the blue-clad policeman. 'Well, glory be,' he said. 'Show him in, Fazal. Show him in.'

Relief seemed to gush from his shoulders to mix with the sweat which was already soaking the white drill tunic he considered it necessary to wear to his office. Outside, the rain teemed down, in a steady, monotonous downpour, drumming on the roof above his head with sufficient intensity to start a headache. But the headache was already present, because of the heat. The rain made no difference to the heat: rather it intensified it.

It was November, in Kumassi. That it happened to be November 1898 was not relevant. Every November in Kumassi ranked as bad as every other. It rained, and the mud-hut town – only a generation ago the capital of the Ashanti Empire – seemed well on the way to dissolving into filth and stench: it had been raining since June. The fortress was more substantially built, as it contained the seat of the British West African administration, and the houses within the compound were built of seasoned timber, yet they too seemed to dwindle before the weather. All West Africa was regarded as a white man's graveyard. Kumassi, a hundred miles from the coast and buried in the heart of the most unpleasant forest in the world, had to be the bottom of the grave pit itself. Barely acceptable in

1

the dry season, in the wet season it was a living hell. And if the office itself was dry, the Governor had but to look out of the window, across the rooftops, to see the forest, on three sides, and the swamp on the fourth, where the waters would have risen more than a foot during the past week, the mosquitoes and tsetse flies would be breeding, the alligators would be wallowing, the baboons and hyenas would be seeking higher ground . . . and the Ashanti, proudest and most warlike people in all Africa since the eclipse of the Zulu, would be squatting in their mud huts . . . and doing what?

Only Major McClarrie would know that.

Sir Francis stood up as the door opened, wiping sweat from his neck with a linen handkerchief. He was of no more than average height and powerfully built, with almost no neck and blunt, ruddy features. He looked what he was, an ebullient and totally dedicated representative of the greatest empire the world had ever known, now virtually at its zenith. Only a man this ebullient could possibly hold down such a governorship in such a place; only a man utterly dedicated to the white man's burden would have considered bringing his wife to the white man's graveyard, where white women were not supposed to survive a month. Lady Hodgson had survived far longer than that.

And today, despite the rain, was obviously going to be a good day: McClarrie was back.

'McClarrie!' Hodgson said, and extended his hand.

The tall Scot, hatchet-like features burned almost mahogany by the sun, thin frame trembling with malaria, paused to salute and then to remove his sun helmet before taking the offered fingers. He wore a khaki uniform which had seen better days, and his boots were mud stained. He had clearly come straight to the Governor without pausing to bathe or change. He had not shaved in several days.

'My God, man,' the Governor said. 'I had not expected you back. Five weeks . . . I thought of fever.' He looked through the window at the swamp and the jungle; he had actually thought of many worse things than that.

'Aye,' McClarrie said. 'It was slow work, to be sure.'

2

'Whisky!' Hodgson opened his cabinet and poured three fingers for them each; he knew better than to offer water. 'And sit down, man, sit down. You saw Kuno?'

McClarrie slowly lowered himself into the chair before the desk. He took the tumbler and sipped, sighed with pleasure. 'I saw the black devil. But not the Stool. He says he does not know of it.'

Hodgson also sat down. He wished he did not know of the Golden Stool himself. It was, to him, nothing more than a legend. But Whitehall had dictated that it should be obtained; a High King of the Ashanti could only be endowed with the umbrella of office while seated on the Golden Stool. Thus, Whitehall considered, if the Golden Stool were to be removed from the Ashanti there could never again be a High King to challenge British rule. A simplistic approach, but who was to say the Colonial Office was not right? The Ashanti were a simplistic people.

Supposing the Stool actually existed.

'He was lying, of course,' McClarrie said, sipping some more whisky. 'But I had only four constables with me.'

'And what of the reports?' Hodgson asked.

'That there's something brewing? It's possible. But they'll wait for the signs to be right. There are still Ashanti warriors who can remember Sir Garnet Wolseley marching through their forests and burning their kraals. That was only twenty odd years ago.'

'Wolseley had white troops,' Hodgson growled. 'I have native levies.'

'Good men,' McClarrie said. 'If well led.'

'But not the same as the Brigade of Guards, eh?' Hodgson remarked. 'They won't give me a man, you know, McClarrie. Not a single damned regular. I have written and telegraphed and implored, and the answer is always the same: there are too many other commitments. India, and now this South African business . . . but the truth of the matter is, they know that to send even a company of white troops out here and have half of them die of fever would bring down the government. So we are left to face an impossible situation. You say the Ashanti remember Wolseley? He had white soldiers. I'll bet there are some of their old men who also remember McCarthy. He went up against them with just native levies, and what do you suppose happened to him?'

'They cut off his head and made it into a fetish,' McClarrie said. 'I know. They showed it to me.'

Hodgson slowly put down his glass. 'You have seen McCarthy's head?'

'His skull,' McClarrie said. 'Fashioned, you might say, Sir Francis. But there's the point. It's deteriorating. The climate even gets at preserved bones, I reckon.'

'My God!' Hodgson looked quite distressed. 'You *saw* the thing?'

'It's a powerful fetish, Sir Francis. And fetishism is what those people live by. Now it's falling apart. They'll not start trouble until they've a replacement.'

'My God!' Hodgson said again. 'You were *there*, McClarrie. In their midst. With only four policemen.' He peered at his subordinate, as if to make sure he really did still have a head.

McClarrie gave a humourless grin. 'It's not my head they want, to replace McCarthy's, Governor. Not yours, neither. It has to be a woman.'

Hodgson leaned back in his chair so hard he nearly fell over. 'A woman? How on earth . . .?'

'Logic, Sir Francis, in their eyes. Logic. The British sent McCarthy against them, and they cut off his head. Nobody quite remembers how McCarthy got beat, but they remember he *was* beat. Then we were afraid of them, for a while, and whenever we got too big for our breeches, they marched into battle bearing the skull aloft, and we were beat again. Until Wolseley settled matters. Now you know, Sir Francis, and I know, that Wolseley beat them because he was the best general in the British Army, and because he had regulars armed with repeating rifles, and because he had artillery. They won't accept those facts – they cannot, and still be Ashanti warriors. They know there had to be another reason. It's taken them twenty years to find one, but their fetishmen have at last come

4

up with the answer. They waved McCarthy's head at Wolseley, and got beat. Because McCarthy was a man, and Wolseley was working for a woman – at last, someone has told them we've a queen on the throne.'

'Holy Jesus!' Hodgson said.

'So they want a white woman's skull to mount as their battle fetish. Then they figure they can throw us right out of West Africa.'

'A woman,' Hodgson muttered. 'A white woman. Can you imagine . . .?'

'I've *seen* what they do to their own, when the blood lust takes them, Sir Francis. I don't have to imagine. But I reckon you don't feel all that much when your head's been cut off. Now, they'd like Queen Victoria's head best, of course, but lacking that . . .'

Hodgson gave him a disgusted glance. 'Your sense of humour escapes me, McClarrie. My God, when I think . . . Sylvia!'

'I doubt Lady Hodgson is in any danger, here in Kumassi,' McClarrie pointed out. 'They won't start a war until they have their fetish, and they'd have to start a war to get at your wife, now wouldn't they?'

'Well, then . . . the only other white women in the entire colony are down on the coast.'

'What about the missionaries?'

Hodgson frowned.

'There are four mission stations up there,' McClarrie reminded him. 'Each run by a husband and wife.'

'God, I'd forgotten them. They're not even English!' Hodgson again spoke with disgust.

'They're white. And they're also subject to British law, in a British colony. Call them in, Sir Francis.'

'They could already have been murdered,' Sir Francis moaned. 'One of them, anyway.'

'I doubt that, Sir Francis. They're low on the list, simply because they've been there some time. Kuno seems convinced that some strange white woman is suddenly going to pop up out of the bush. Well, we know that the odds on that happening are

5

several million to one. But because the fetishmen say it *will* happen, Kuno is prepared to wait. On the other hand, he isn't going to wait forever. So if you just make sure there are *no* white women at all in that bush, there's your best chance of avoiding an Ashanti revolt right now. Call those missionaries in as quickly as you can and tell them to stay here until you've solved the business.'

'And how do you suggest I do that, McClarrie?'

'Raise yourself an army, even a native army, and find that Golden Stool.'

'It'll take time,' Hodgson groaned. 'A year . . . we'll never get any worthwhile force together before the next wet season.'

'You'll have time,' McClarrie asserted. 'If you make sure there are no white women up in that bush. There never should be, in my opinion. But certainly not until King Kuno and his bully boys have been laid to rest.'

'My God,' Hodgson said. 'What a mess! All I need now is to be told that damned Arabian bandit who calls himself Zobeir ibn Rubayr is around . . .'

McClarrie gazed at the ceiling and cleared his throat.

'You're not serious?' Hodgson shouted.

'Well, sir, there's a rumour amongst the Ashanti that Zobeir Pasha is making for the Western Sahara, with as many of his Dervishes as he could rescue from Omdurman. It's a fact he wouldn't want to stay in Egypt or the Sudan until Kitchener goes home.'

'Why he wasn't captured and hanged . . .' Hogdson growled. 'But, God damn it, man, if he starts slave-raiding down into the Fulani and Ashanti country, that'll stir them up even if they don't manage to get hold of a female skull. Christ, McClarrie, what are we going to do?'

McClarrie finished his whisky, and stood up. 'We could try praying, Sir Francis,' he suggested. 'For something to turn up.'

6

CHAPTER 1

'At last!' Major General Sir William Dobree gazed at the official-looking sheet of paper he held in his hand. 'By Jove, I thought they'd forgotten I existed.'

'Good news, is it, dear?' inquired his wife, from the far end of the long breakfast table, also busy with her mail.

'An appointment.' Dobree laid the paper down beside his coffee cup with the air of a magician who has extracted an unusually large rabbit from his hat, and beamed along the table. He was a very large man, over six feet tall and with immensely broad shoulders; his features, suggestive of an aggressive bloodhound, matched his physique, and seemed to hang above the cloth.

'Oh, Daddy!' exclaimed Mary Dobree. 'You're not going to fight a war with someone?'

Mary, Dobree's eldest daughter, was aged fifteen, and already possessed the family height. But not, fortunately, her father's looks. If her face was necessarily long and basically sombre, she had inherited a certain sharpness of feature from her mother, the first Lady Dobree, and was quite pretty. Her hair, long and thick and black – her father's hair – was secured in two pigtails.

'War?' Dobree inquired. 'The British don't fight wars nowadays. We leave that sort of thing to the Frogs and the Germans.' A professional soldier, he clearly did not include under the heading of 'wars' the several colonial campaigns on which he had served.

'I'm so pleased for you, William,' Lady Dobree said, continuing to open envelopes, the contents of which were

7

apparently far more interesting than any communication from the War Office. 'Aldershot, is it?'

'Ah . . .' Dobree cleared his throat. 'Cape Town.'

'Cape Town?' cried Elizabeth Dobree, Mary's younger sister: she was thirteen, and a carbon copy of her sister in every way save size.

'Cape Town,' muttered Lieutenant David Whiting, who sat on the other side of the table, facing the girls. (Baby Charlie was not yet permitted to join the family and had a small table to himself in the far corner of the room, where Nurse Brown could stop him throwing things, or limit the damage if he did.)

David Whiting was the General's aide-de-camp. He had to be tall to be acceptable to this family. Unlike his superior, he was slim, but had good, firm features and crisp yellow-brown hair, with which he wore a small matching moustache. In his crimson uniform jacket with its gold braid he looked every inch a soldier. He was very much a part of the family, having been Dobree's aide-de-camp for four years, ever since the General had picked Whiting to accompany him to India in 1895, and he thoroughly enjoyed his life. However, he was only too aware that at thirty-one, and still a lieutenant, his career was passing him by. But if the General was being sent to South Africa . . . there were all manner of rumours circulating about what was happening there – the suggestion of incipient crisis which had persisted since the Jameson Raid of a few years before suggested a situation where rapid promotion might be possible.

'Cape Town,' Lady Dobree remarked. 'What a long way to go! Will you be away for very long?'

General Dobree cleared his throat again. Although Alison was his second wife, and twenty years his junior, simply because she was the most beautiful woman he had ever known – and thus his most prized possession after his rank and uniform and decorations – he was a little afraid of her, although he would never have admitted as much to anyone. But he had made a successful career of never allowing fear to interfere with what he considered his duty – or his own best interests. 'We,' he said, deliberately pausing for a moment before continuing, 'will be away for three years.'

'You mean we can come with you?' screamed Mary Dobree. 'Three years! Cape Town! Oh, my darling Daddy!' She got up to throw both her arms round her father's neck and kiss his cheek.

'Three years? In Africa?' Elizabeth also hurried to the head of the table.

'Three years, three years, three years,' bawled three-year-old Charlie, hurling a spoonful of scrambled egg at the wallpaper.

'Now, Master Charles, please,' Prudence Brown begged.

'Rather exciting,' murmured David Whiting.

But Dobree continued to look at his wife, who was slowly desisting from arranging the pile of letters into those to be answered, those to be considered, and those to be consigned to the wastepaper basket – they were all either invitations or bills. Having done that, she equally slowly raised her head to meet his gaze. '*We*,' she said, following his example in pausing, 'are going to South Africa? All of us? Really, William . . .'

When Alison Dobree said, 'Really, William,' the General, who many years before had earned the Victoria Cross by single-handedly repulsing a charge of Afghans in the Khyber Pass, felt distinctly uneasy. But he reminded himself that this was at least partly because when aroused – and he had only ever seen her aroused by *dis*pleasure – she was even more beautiful than usual. And she was a beautiful woman. Tall, slender, elegant in every movement, with perfectly carved if slightly bold features, cool blue eyes, silky golden hair which at this hour of the morning had not yet been arranged in its usual fashionable pompadour but lay in glorious profusion on the shoulders of her crimson silk undressing gown . . . it was always incredible for Dobree to remember that only an hour before she had been lying in bed next to him, and would do so again tonight. He had never been absolutely certain why. Of course, when he proposed, six years before, he was a dashing brigadier, several months short of forty, wearing that precious crimson ribbon on his breast, amongst others, with a baronetcy and a substantial personal income both inherited from his father, which allowed him to be independent of his service pay. And far more than being merely an eligible bachelor, he was an

9

eligible widower, greatest of challenges to any woman. On the other hand, he already had a family by his first wife, and Alison, at eighteen, was the most sought after debutante in London. Yet she accepted his proposal. When, some time after the marriage, he asked her why, she gave one of those smiles of hers which were even more disturbing than her frowns, and replied, 'Because, dear William, you are the first man to have proposed marriage to me who is actually taller than I am.'

She was joking, of course. Or was she? He simply did not know her well enough to be sure, even after five years. Their wedding, in the early spring of 1894 – it would soon be their fifth anniversary – was the event of the pre-London season. Their first six months were blissfully happy, as indeed were all the months since, at least as far as the world was able to observe. If she remained disdainfully cool and uninterested in matters of the flesh, that was neither more nor less than he would expect of a very well-born young Englishwoman – and uninterested or not, by the end of six months she was pregnant. But that was when the rot set in. With singular thoughtlessness, only a month after they toasted with champagne the prospect of an heir, the War Office despatched General Dobree to India, where there was the usual recurring spot of bother with the Afghans, who seemed to resent British attempts to take over their country. William Dobree had earned his military fame on the North West Frontier; he could hardly refuse to return when needed, especially as the command was accompanied by promotion to Major General.

But he could hardly take a pregnant wife with him, either. She would join him, in due course. However, the problem lay in the interpretation of that phrase. By the time Charles was born it was well into 1895: by the time he was weaned it was nearly the middle of 1896. And General Dobree's tour of duty was due to be completed at the end of 1897. Eighteen months can either be a very long time or a very short time. That also was a matter of interpretation. It was really, in the opinion of Lady Dobree, too short a time to expect her to travel to India and set up a home, only to have to pack it all up and return to England again as soon as it was done. Besides, take little Charlie to India? That was absurd.

William Dobree, handicapped by having to carry on the controversy at a distance of several thousand miles and through the medium of an irregular mail service, surrendered, which he would never even have considered as an alternative when faced with a horde of rampaging Rajput warriors. He duly returned at the beginning of the previous year, and they spent an utterly blissful twelve months together – again, in the eyes of the world. Save that they were almost strangers. Alison, then in her twenty-fourth year, had her own circle of friends in Town, and considered that her marriage, followed by her pregnancy, followed by feeding Charlie, had extracted her from society for too long. They spent the Season of 1898 at the Dobree town house in Cadogan Square, and it was with great difficulty that he managed to cajole her into coming down to the country estate at Lower Wissing in Devon for the winter months. But the 1899 Season would soon be upon them again, and she was undoubtedly looking forward to it – as was London, judging from the pile of invitations beside her plate.

But he was damned if he was taking himself off to Africa for another three years of separation. Last summer he had, in fact, done some serious thinking about the situation, and reached the conclusion that the only hope for his marriage was to get Alison out of England and to some place where she would be all his, all the time. He had actually applied for an overseas posting where it was possible to take wives and children, and while he had been thinking of a colonial governorship, a military command was certainly preferable. It was simply a matter of sticking out his chin and leading from the front, as he had done so often and so successfully against the Afghans.

'We will all go,' he said firmly. 'My dear, you will love it. A sea voyage, then Cape Town, one of the most beautiful cities in the world. I stopped there once, en route to India, when the Canal was in some sort of bother. It was perfection.'

'I think it sounds just wonderful,' Mary exclaimed. 'How long will the voyage take, Daddy?'

11

'Oh, well . . . several weeks, I should think.'

'Hurrah!' shouted Elizabeth Dobree. 'I've always wanted to take a long sea voyage.'

Alison Dobree gave her a glance which would have shrivelled most people. She heartily disliked her two stepdaughters, another fact which had not escaped her husband, and which effectively undermined the domestic bliss most people supposed they enjoyed. There were faults on both sides, he knew. Mary and Liz resented their stepmother. She was too young, too pretty, and they could both remember too well their real mother. This antagonism had been evident from the moment their father announced his engagement, but he had assumed that a *fait accompli* situation, and time, and intimacy, would change things. They hadn't, because there was no intimacy. Alison felt the girls did not treat her with a proper respect and, instead of trying to break down the barriers, had adopted an attitude of ignoring them as much as possible – which seemed to suit them equally – leaving their upbringing entirely in the hands of the redoubtable Mrs Chandler. Something else which might be cured by a prolonged period away from the distractions of London.

Predictably, Lady Dobree's glance was wasted on Elizabeth, who only resisted the temptation to put out her tongue because of the presence of her father.

'I cannot possibly take little Charlie to Africa,' Alison said, equally firmly.

'Now don't be absurd,' Dobree said, flushing as he found himself on the end of one of the famous gazes, and reminding himself that it was necessary to be tactful as well as firm. 'This isn't just Africa. It's Cape Town. The most healthy climate in the world. It's simply splendid down there. It will do Charlie the world of good.'

'While he gets shot at by natives and things,' Alison remarked, icily.

'There are no natives shooting at anyone at this moment.'

'Then why are you being sent there?' she demanded, triumphantly.

'I am to command a division stationed in Cape Province,'

Dobree explained, glancing at his letter again.

'And why is there a division stationed there? Simply because we are about to go to war with the Boers,' Alison pointed out. 'Everyone says so.'

'Of course we aren't going to war with the Boers, no matter what the papers say,' her husband declared. 'Really, my dear, can you imagine two tiny little tinpot republics taking on Great Britain? The presence of a sizeable British force at the Cape is just to remind them of what they *would* be taking on if they ever got uppity again. I do assure you, this will be the trip of a lifetime.'

Lady Dobree continued to gaze at him, but at least she knew him well enough to understand he was a man who seldom changed a decision, especially one taken as publicly as this. 'Very well,' she said. 'As the place seems to attract you so much, and if you are quite sure we will be in no danger, from any source, Willie . . .' She knew he hated being called Willie in front of the children and even more in front of David Whiting. '. . . of course we shall travel to South Africa. We shall come down in September.'

'Ah . . . we are leaving at the end of next week.'

Alison's head came up again.

'Orders, I'm afraid, my dear. There is a transport waiting in Southampton to carry me and my staff to Cape Town as rapidly as possible. She sails on Saturday week. That is the fourth of March. Today is Wednesday, the twenty-second of February. Ten days,' he repeated, pleased with his arithmetic.

Alison Dobree pushed back her chair and got up. 'I would like a word with you, William,' she said, and gave Mary a cold stare. 'In private, if you would be so kind.'

She led the way into her private sitting room, stood in front of the fire, and waited. Dobree closed the door behind him.

'William,' she said, in as reasonable a tone as she could manage, 'now you know I cannot possibly be ready to leave in ten days.'

'Why not?' He began to fill his pipe with great deliberation, clearly aware that he was about to engage in one of the most severe battles of his career. 'Because you will miss Ascot?'

'Ascot? The thought never crossed my mind.' Indeed, she was telling the truth; she had been thinking only of the Duchess of Westminster's spring ball. But now she did think of Ascot, and grew angrier still. 'I merely know that it is quite impossible. There is the packing, and the . . . well, the organisation, and –'

'Stuff and nonsense! It isn't as if we were emigrating, my dear.' Dobree sat down and crossed his legs. 'Both houses will be maintained by the staff while we are away. I am only taking Pressdee, apart from David, of course. You will take Nathalie and Nanny and Mrs Chandler. It is just a matter of telling them to pack the necessary clothes and going down to Southampton by next Friday. I will meet you there.'

'You will . . . where are you going?'

'I am leaving for London on Saturday. I must be at the War Office for briefing on Monday, and I thought I'd spend Sunday at my mother's, saying goodbye.'

There was no mention of her saying goodbye to her parents, she thought. That was clearly impossible as they lived in the Isle of Man, which was a journey of several days, there and back. She would have to write. But in any case, saying goodbye to parents was quite irrelevant, at this moment. 'You are gallivanting off to Town, leaving me here, to see to everything?'

'I shall leave David with you, my dear. *He* will see to everything.'

'David,' Alison said contemptuously. He was a dear boy, but so confused by having the wife of his employer six years younger than himself and England's premier beauty into the bargain, that he had been too frightened to attempt to flirt with her. She would have slapped him down, of course, but that he had never even tried seemed adequately to reflect his ability. 'William, don't you think you are being a trifle unreasonable? I know you have to catch this beastly boat next Saturday, but surely there is no need for me to do that. There is too much to be done. I could so easily follow you out in September.'

'I wish you to come with me, now.'

Her chin came up. 'Why?'

14

'Because you are my wife, and I love you.'

'Because you think if I don't come now I won't come at all. Isn't that the true reason?' She gasped at her own boldness.

Dobree struck a match and puffed once or twice. 'If you insist.'

'William! How could you!'

'You raised the point, my dear. I have spent less than half my married life in your company. I wish to be sure we are never separated again. So I would be most grateful if you would stop acting like a silly little girl and put your heart into the adventure. Because it *is* an adventure, for us all. And we are all going together, on the *Doncaster*, on Saturday week.'

Alison Dobree stared at him for several seconds. 'And that is your final word on the matter?'

'Yes,' William Dobree said.

Alison stamped up the stairs to her suite and banged the door shut.

'Oh, madame!' Nathalie Prudhomme cried. 'I've 'eard the strangest thing.'

'It is true,' Alison said. 'I am going to Africa.'

'Oh, madame.' Nathalie rolled her eyes. She was a Provençale and in the strongest possible contrast to her mistress she was dark and solidly built instead of fair and elegant. But she had a marvellous ability to dress hair.

'Oh, don't worry,' Alison told her. 'You are coming too.'

'Oh, madame!' Nathalie cried. It was difficult to decide whether she was delighted or appalled.

'So there is a great deal to be done,' Alison said. 'Clothes to be sorted out, Charlie's things to be seen to . . . you'll send Nanny to me immediately, please. Oh, and Nathalie . . . I'll have to have a word with Mrs Chandler.'

'Of course, madame. I will send 'er up right away.' Nathalie hurried from the room, obviously in a state of great excitement.

Alison stood at the window and allowed herself a few moments of positive seething. Cape Town! Some colonial village where they probably didn't even drink tea. And apart from the invitation to the Duchess of Westminster's, and Ascot, and Wimbledon, and Henley, and the Palace garden parties, she had an invitation from Lady Warwick, and another from Lady Keppel, and even one from the dreadful Langtry creature. She hadn't been able to decide whether or not to accept that one . . . but of course the Prince would be there. As if it mattered, now. How could life be so *unfair?* And a sea voyage! She loathed sea voyages. Her mother had taken her, in the year of her engagement, to France just to polish up her French, and she had been seasick both coming and going on the Channel packet, while the main reason that she had seen so little of her parents since her father had retired from the High Court Bench had been the necessity of a sea voyage to reach Douglas, the town on the Isle of Man where they now lived. That was a matter of hours. William was talking of weeks!

And then, Africa. She knew nothing about Africa, except that by definition it had to be hot, and full of black people always throwing spears and things, and lions, and snakes, and spiders . . . she hated spiders even more than she hated the sea.

'Ahem,' said Prudence Brown. Prudence was in her late thirties, a solidly plump, utterly calm woman with blunt features and quiet brown eyes, blue uniform gown spotless and freshly pressed as ever, brown hair neatly coiled beneath her starched cap.

'Oh, Nanny,' Alison said. 'You've heard . . . well, you were there.'

'Yes, milady. I shall see to Master Charlie's belongings immediately. I'll make up a list, shall I, and let you see it before I actually get down to packing?'

'Oh, Nanny, you are a treasure.' Alison wondered if Nathalie could be trusted to make up a list of what *she* should take. Almost certainly not.

'I'll start right away,' Prudence said. 'And . . . Mrs Chandler is waiting to speak with you.'

'Of course. Do have her come in.' She was so relieved by Prudence's massive calm that she neglected to observe the slight hesitancy in her reference to the governess. Actually,

Alison preferred to see as little of Mrs Chandler as possible. The governess had been firmly in charge of the girls long before Alison had become Lady Dobree, and she had been very happy to let the arrangement continue. Mrs Chandler apparently ruled Mary and Elizabeth with a rod of iron; indeed, she appeared to be the only human being of whom they were in any way afraid. She also appeared to have taught them everything they needed to know, in order that they could both make an advantageous marriage – the sooner the better. But most important of all, she stood between them and their stepmother, like a jetty separating the turbulent ocean from the calm waters of a harbour.

Actually, Alison herself was a little afraid of the governess – with reason. Mrs Chandler was a large woman whose jutting chin only matched her jutting bosom, and who sailed, rather than walked. She wore pearls. Alison had never seen her without that rope round her neck. As if it was her only worthwhile jewellery, she was clearly determined never to lose sight of it.

'Mrs Chandler,' Alison said 'you'll have heard the news, no doubt. Isn't it exciting? Now, there is so much to be done, in so short a time . . .'

'If you will excuse me, milady,' Mrs Chandler said. 'I have something for you.'

'For me?' Alison took the envelope. 'What can it be?' She adored surprises.

'My resignation,' Mrs Chandler said.

Alison raised her head. 'Your *what?*'

'I am afraid, milady, that, reluctantly, I am forced to leave Sir William's service.'

'But . . . why? Now? You can't, Mrs Chandler. You simply can't!'

'I'm afraid I cannot go to Africa, milady,' Mrs Chandler said.

'But . . . have you ever been there?' Wild thoughts rushed through her mind that there might be some kind of warrant out for the governess, issued by the Cape authorities for her having bullied a baboon.

17

'Good heavens, no, milady. But what would my husband say? He'd never permit it.'

'You mean you have a husband?' Alison spoke without thinking; she had not been aware of it before. She knew that Mrs Chandler invariably took every other weekend off and went away for several weeks in the summer and at Christmas, but she never thought too deeply about the matter.

'Of course I have a husband, milady,' Mrs Chandler asserted, offended.

'Oh, I am so sorry,' Alison protested. 'I'm so upset about the whole thing . . .'

'And so you should be, milady. My Harry always says: Africa, it's behind God's back.'

'Oh, come now.'

'Death and disease, black people and black animals,' Mrs Chandler declared. 'And it is hot.'

Alison gulped. The woman had just admirably summed up her own feelings on the place.

'As for taking two young girls out there, to say nothing of Master Charles . . .' Mrs Chandler continued.

'I'm sure you're right, Mrs Chandler.' More than that Alison could not say: she dared not be disloyal to her husband before a member of the staff. 'But in view of the . . . the possible disadvantages of the place, don't you see that we shall need you more than ever? Surely your husband . . . we could find him a position. What does he do?'

'My Harry is retired, milady.'

'Well, then –'

'He will never go to Africa, milady. He never leaves England. Never has done and never will do.'

'But surely he can't object to your seeing something of the world? We . . . we'd arrange a passage home every summer, and –'

'I am sorry, milady. I will not go to Africa.' Mrs Chandler's tone suggested that the moon or even China could be considered, but Africa definitely could not.

'We should, of course, also increase your salary,' Alison ventured in utter desperation.

'I am sorry, milady. My mind is made up. If you wish, naturally I shall remain here until you have found a replacement or until you depart. Will you excuse me, milady? It is time for the girls' first lesson.'

She closed the door behind her.

Alison stormed into her husband's study.

'How nice to see you, my dear,' William Dobree remarked, somewhat wearily. 'What has happened now?'

Alison threw Mrs Chandler's letter on his desk. 'I didn't even know the creature was married.'

'Shall I, er . . .?' David Whiting sidled towards the door.

'I'm sure that won't be necessary, David,' Dobree said, reading. 'Well, my dear, she is a Mrs, you know. Hm. Silly woman. It really does surprise me how people take on these absurd prejudices.'

'What are we going to do about it?' Alison asked, speaking quietly with great self-control.

'Do? Well, as she seems to feel so strongly about it, we shall have to let her go.'

'I meant about the girls, William. Obviously they cannot now accompany us. If you insist upon my coming to Africa, we will have to find them a school where they can board. I have heard there is a very good college for young ladies down in Cheltenham.'

William Dobree leaned back in his chair. 'Alison, my daughters are not being sent to any boarding school. You know my feelings on that subject. Girls should be brought up at home.'

'But William . . . the whole idea was absurd from the beginning. What about Mary's coming out? You could be ruining her life.'

Dobree refrained from wondering, at least aloud, why she hadn't raised that objection before this moment. He merely said, 'My dear Alison, we will be home in time for Mary's eighteenth birthday. I should think that having spent three years in South Africa she will appear more attractive, rather than less. As for their schooling, I have no doubt that we shall

19

find a suitable replacement for Mrs Chandler at the Cape.'

'The Cape? You mean a *black* woman?'

'My dear Alison, there are probably more white women living in Cape Town than black.'

'But . . . what happens until we get there?'

'Well, I think you can look after them yourself for that period.'

'I? Now you know that is quite impossible.'

'Oh, come now. How much looking after do they actually need? They're both almost adults. I think it would be a very good thing. I don't expect you to give them lessons, my dear. Just well . . . be a mother to them. You *are* their mother, you know. I think this voyage is going to bring us all much closer together. I should like that very much. Anyway, there is simply no alternative. I don't see how you can possibly find a replacement for Mrs Chandler here in England, in ten days. Now, my dear, David and I simply have to get these files into order . . .'

Alison stamped back to her bedroom, and hurled herself on to the bed. She discovered to her consternation that she was weeping. It was not an habitual weakness. But this . . . Mrs Chandler quitting was just the last straw. The whole idea . . . she hated decisions, upheavals, at the best of times. The only conscious decision she had ever taken in her life was to marry William, and that had been a decision made in order to avoid having to make other decisions. She had been surrounded by suitors, most of them eager and amorous young men. She had opted for a man twenty years her senior, because surely, as he already had a family, he would be less interested in the earthy side of life, about which she knew nothing and had no desire to find out, as well as being able to provide her with a title and a home and the style of living she craved. And it had turned out very well – until now. If William was, regrettably, still interested in the earthy side of life, she had negotiated that hurdle by lying very still and keeping her eyes tight shut – he was usually very quick about it. And Mrs Chandler had prevented her from becoming involved with the girls, especially over the past couple of years when all the unpleasantnesses she remembered from her own girlhood had started to happen. She simply had no idea how to cope with someone else's menstrual problems and had no desire to find out, especially when she heartily disliked both the young persons in question. Of course William didn't understand about these things, but really . . . and indeed this was the principal cause of both her grief and her anger: she had never known William to be so dogmatically determined. He had never actually opposed her in anything before, not if she dug in her heels and used her frowns and her smiles to best advantage. But this time . . .

'Ahem,' said Prudence Brown.

Alison rolled over and sat up, aware that she must look a sight.

'I have that list . . . oh, milady!' Prudence actually looked at her mistress for the first time.

Alison sniffed, and accepted the use of Prudence's handkerchief.

'Is it because of Mrs Chandler, milady?'

'She has left me with an impossible situation, Nanny.' Alison blew her nose. 'You know that.'

'I suppose the whole thing has been rather sudden, milady. But . . . can she not be replaced?'

'Oh, yes,' Alison said. 'Sir William says we will be able to replace her when we get to Africa. That is weeks, perhaps months away. And it will be some strange woman talking some foreign language . . .'

Prudence looked doubtful, but preferred not to argue. 'Could you not replace Mrs Chandler before you leave England, milady?'

'You mean here? We leave in ten days, Nanny. And I am stuck down in the back of beyond . . . oh, I am sorry.' Prudence had been born and bred in Little Wissing. 'But you know what I mean.'

'Why don't you have a talk with Mrs Payne, milady?' Prudence suggested.

Alison frowned. Mrs Payne was the vicar's wife. 'Why?'

'She might be able to suggest someone, milady.'

'Mrs Payne: You mean, someone from around here?'

'I'm sure she will do the best she can, milady,' Prudence said. 'Shall I send Nathalie to you? And tell Martin to prepare the trap?'

Rowena Payne was a small, birdlike creature in early middle-age, who was overwhelmed to have Lady Dobree come to call. 'Why, it is such a pleasure,' she exclaimed. 'And may I say how lovely you looked in church last Sunday, milady? As you look lovely today as well, of course. One lump, or two?'

'I do not take sugar, thank you, Mrs Payne,' Alison said.

'Ah,' said Mrs Payne, who had a sweet tooth. But she put the sugar bowl aside, and gave her guest a bright smile. 'That is very sensible.'

Alison was never one to beat about the bush. 'I have come to see you, Mrs Payne,' she said, 'on the recommendation of my Charlie's Nanny, Prudence Brown –'

'Oh, Prudence,' said Mrs Payne. 'Such a nice girl.'

'Because I am faced with a rather serious problem,' Alison continued, 'which Prudence thought you might be able to help me solve.'

'Oh dear,' Mrs Payne said, her mind clearly racing the gamut from a possible pregnancy on the part of one of the Dobree girls to something far worse.

'I shall tell you about it,' Alison said, and did so.

If Mrs Payne was disappointed that there was a total absence of scandal in what Lady Dobree had to say, she concealed it well. 'I never liked that Chandler woman,' she confessed. 'Too uppity by far.'

'Quite,' Alison agreed. 'However, you can see my predicament.'

'Oh, indeed, milady. And Prudence thought I might be able to help,' mused Mrs Payne. 'Why, do you know, milady, I might have the very answer.'

Alison frowned at her, unable to believe her ears. 'You mean you, and Prudence, both know of a suitable replacement for Mrs Chandler, available at ten days' notice? Here?' This must be her lucky day.

'As a matter of fact, I do,' Mrs Payne said. 'And clearly

Prudence was thinking along the same lines. The lady I have in mind is a schoolmistress . . .'

'Oh, that would be splendid!'

'She is also the widow of a missionary.'

'A widow, oh, how superb! I mean,' Alison added hastily, 'while I am very sorry about her condition, we really do not wish any more trouble with husbands, do we?'

'Of course we don't, milady,' Mrs Payne agreed.

But Alison's frown had returned. 'A missionary. C of E, I hope?'

'Oh, indeed, milady. And do you know what is the most remarkable thing of all? She knows Africa. That was where she and her husband were missionaries.'

'Mrs Payne!' Alison cried. She could almost have hugged the woman. 'But that is perfect. You mean she has been to Cape Town?'

'Well . . . I suppose she must have. She and her husband had a mission in some place called the Kenya Territory. I suppose that's quite close to Cape Town. I mean, it's all Africa, isn't it?'

'Of course it is,' Alison agreed. 'I don't suppose she would have any references?'

'I imagine she could obtain one, from the headmaster of the Etheridge School. But I would be willing to vouch for her myself.'

'You know her?'

'Oh, indeed, very well. I would describe her as most capable, and very pleasant with it.'

'My dear Mrs Payne,' Alison said. 'Rowena . . . may I call you Rowena?'

'I should be flattered,' Mrs Payne agreed, wondering if there could possibly be a reciprocal invitation on the way.

Alison didn't think of it. 'This person sounds an absolute paragon. But . . . will she really be prepared to leave England and go back there?'

'I am sure of it, milady. It has all been rather tragic, you see, and as a result of her misfortunes, Mrs Lang – that's her name, you see – Mrs Lang is having rather a difficult time of it at the moment. You know that missionaries don't make a lot of

23

money, and what with doctor's bills and hospital bills and things consequent upon her husband's illness and death, she was left without a penny. As she is a qualified teacher, my husband and I got her a job teaching the Preparatory Form at the Etheridge School, but . . .'

'You mean she's not here in Little Wissing?'

'No, no, milady. But Etheridge is only just down the road, on the other side of the Manor, in fact. And as I was saying, I know she hates it there and would love to return to Africa. It can do no harm to talk with her, anyway. Shall I send a message over to Etheridge, asking her to call on your ladyship?'

'I think that would be very satisfactory, Mrs Payne. Oh, very. Now let me see . . . she'd be about forty, I suppose?' She couldn't actually suggest that a woman old enough to be a friend of Mrs Payne's, and a widow, might just be too old for a safari, but it was an important point.

'Ah, no,' remarked Mrs Payne.

Alison raised her eyebrows.

'She really is quite young, milady. Thirty years of age.'

'Thirty? Good heavens. But you said she was a friend of yours.'

'So she is, milady,' Mrs Payne said, refusing to take offence.

'Thirty,' Alison said again, unaware of having been tactless. 'Why, that's even younger than David Whiting. Still . . .' She gave a bright smile. 'I suppose she's seen a lot of life. Oh, yes, I would like to see her. If you would be so kind . . .'

'There is just one thing, milady,' Mrs Payne said, nervously.

Alison's frown returned. 'She's not black, Mrs Payne? Tell me she's not black.'

'Oh, good heavens, no, milady! Nothing like that. But, Mrs Lang, well . . . she's an American.'

From the expression on Lady Dobree's face Mrs Payne decided it would, after all, have been far preferable for Victoria Lang to be a Zulu.

'An *American?*' Alison asked, in scandalised tones.

'A very nice American,' Mrs Payne ventured.

'There is no such thing,' Alison asserted. She had only

met two American women in her life, and one had been that ghastly Vanderbilt person who had successfully upstaged her last season by wearing jewellery not even she could match. 'Think of the accent!'

'Ah . . . Victoria has a very pleasant accent. She comes from New England, you know.'

'Victoria?' Alison was interested. 'Is that her name? After Her Majesty?'

'Well . . . I imagine so,' Mrs Payne said.

'Hm.' Perhaps the creature had some redeeming features after all, Alison thought. But all the same, an American! 'I must say, I am disappointed, Rowena. I had thought all of our problems were solved. But really, an American . . . I cannot imagine what the General would have to say if I entrusted his daughters' upbringing to an American.'

'But . . . you said you were going to employ a Cape woman, if all else failed, milady,' Mrs Payne pointed out. 'That is, presumably, either a British or a Dutch colonial. Well, what are Americans, historically, but British colonials?'

Alison regarded her thoughtfully. That point had not occurred to her. And did it really matter if Mary and Elizabeth started speaking through their noses? It might be rather amusing.

'I'll ask her to call, shall I?' Mrs Payne suggested.

CHAPTER 2

From the high road, which connected the village of Little
Wissing to Etheridge, which was somewhat larger, the drive
into the Dobree Estate curved through banks of damply
beautiful rhododendrons, and was overhung by a colonnade of
huge limes and trees. Here was every sign of that landed gentry
whose wealth and solid conservatism was the backbone of
England's prosperity. As she guided the pony and trap over the
gravel, gloved fingers tight on the reins, Victoria Lang's mouth
twisted in a wry smile; her forebears had come from a
background very similar to this, and their descendants still
lived very much in this style, outside Plymouth, Massachusetts. All except one.

Victoria reminded herself that now was not the time to dwell
on the past, and certainly not to feel bitter. It was necessary not
even to appear excited, however rapidly she had asked for the
afternoon off on getting Mrs Payne's message. That message
seemed like a nod from the gods to remind her they still
recognised her existence – and over the past couple of years she
had occasionally doubted that. But this Lady Dobree would be
looking for solidity and good sense, calm and purpose. That
was what she must have.

Thus Victoria had dressed with great care in her very best
outfit; it was in fact her only good outfit. She wore a pale green
tailored linen costume – the colour set off the titian of her hair to
perfection – over a white waistcoat and shirt, with a dark green
tie. Her hat was a straw with a dark green ribbon, and the
flaming tresses which she regarded as her greatest asset were
carefully pinned up to leave her neck exposed. That the whole

was presently concealed beneath a voluminous cape and a thick blanket – it was a mild February, but still February – was all to the good, in Victoria's opinion. She would emerge as something to look at.

In fact, she *was* something to look at, and for more than just the hair or the gown, even to the casual observer. Victoria Lang was not conventionally beautiful, or even pretty, but she was most attractive. She had small, firm features, dominated by a wide mouth beneath a delightfully retroussé nose, and a flawless complexion, though this was ruined, as far as fashion was concerned, by the lavish scattering of pale brown freckles induced by prolonged exposure to the African sun. One needed to come closer to see the true beauty of her green eyes, which could either sparkle or freeze, but which in repose allowed a glimpse into an ocean's depths of feeling and resolve. It was that resolve which had got her into so much trouble. And had kept her there, until now.

The face and the hair went well with the body below. Victoria was only five feet four inches tall, and was slimly built. But, again, any suggestion of fashionable willowness was distorted by a larger than usual bosom, something she had never been able to account for, but which had certainly attracted both James Lang and the Kikuyu of the Kenya Highlands. That her arms and shoulders, and even the tops of her breasts, were also spotted with freckles was a secret known only to herself since James's death. It was not a secret she ever proposed to share again. This had nothing to do with either women's rights or prudery; she just knew there could never be another James. Come to that, she did not really want there to be another anybody, although she had, during the past year, occasionally dreamed of some knight in shining armour appearing to sweep her up from her truly miserable and lonely existence and carry her off to parts unknown. Or better still, parts known: she had been happy in Africa.

How odd that the knight in shining armour should turn out to be the knight's lady, with two unruly stepdaughters to be managed. Mrs Payne had told her the situation, and had asked if she thought she could handle it. Victoria never doubted that she could. But she would have said yes in any case, if it meant returning to Africa.

The drive rounded a lawn studded with Grecian statues and arrived before the terraced front steps, where a dignified-looking individual in a black tail-coat was waiting. 'You will be Mrs Lang,' he said. 'I heard the hooves.'

'And you?'

'I am Bestwick.' He handed her down, snapped his fingers, and a groom appeared to lead the pony away.

'I've an appointment with Lady Dobree,' Victoria said, just a little breathlessly. Not even Pa, with all his solid affluence, had a butler quite like this one. And the house in Plymouth would have fitted into one wing of this four-storeyed, many-windowed, multiple-chimney-potted edifice.

'Of course. This way.'

She was not being taken through the oaken front doors. Well, that made sense; she was here as a member of staff. Bestwick led her along the terrace to a side door, and thence into a small office, clearly his own: an open door gave access to a pantry where a footman was fussing about with some wine bottles.

'You may sit down, Mrs . . . ah . . . Lang,' Bestwick said majestically, indicating a straight chair in the corner. 'May I take your coat?'

Victoria gave him the coat and duly sat down, resisting a strong temptation to kick him on the ankle. She watched him sit behind his desk and whistle into a speaking tube. 'Ah,' he said, 'Prudhomme. Mrs Lang is here. Is her ladyship free?'

He listened.

'Very good, ' he said at last and replaced the speaking tube. 'Someone will be down for you in a moment, Mrs Lang. Now, if you will excuse me . . . I have things to do.'

'Certainly,' Victoria replied.

He raised his eyebrows and left the room. As he left the door open and the footman remained in the pantry, she had to resist another temptation, to explore, and forced herself to remain sitting as still as she could. She was beginning to wonder if she had done the right thing. This atmosphere was most strange. But if it was going to take her to Africa . . .

28

The door to the hall opened. "Allo,' said the dark young woman.

Vicky got up. 'Hello.'

'I am Nathalie,' Nathalie said. 'I am Lady Dobree's maid. Lady Dobree is presently 'aving tea. You would like a cup of tea?'

'Oh, please,' Vicky said. Tea with Lady Dobree; that sounded splendid. She was about to be treated as a human being, after all.

'I will show you,' Nathalie said, and led her into the great hall. 'That is the grand staircase, yes? But we will use this one.' She went through a side door to a smaller hall, where there was another, smaller staircase. Vicky followed her up to the first-floor gallery, from where she could hear the clink of cups and saucers. But Nathalie did not go that way. 'I will show you the schoolroom,' she said.

Vicky made no reply. She was not going to be treated as a human being, after all. But then she had been hopelessly over-optimistic in the first place.

Nathlie went to the end of the gallery and opened a door. 'Mrs Chandler,' she said. 'This is Mrs Lang.'

Mrs Chandler regarded Vicky as Goliath had undoubtedly regarded David. 'How nice,' she remarked. 'You'll want to meet the girls. Mary and Elizabeth.'

Vicky gazed at them. They somehow seemed older, and they were certainly bigger, than she had expected: the girl Mary was considerably taller than herself. But they were the reason for her being here. She produced a bright smile. 'Good afternoon.'

They stared at her.

'Do please say something,' Mrs Chandler commanded.

'Good afternoon, Mrs Lang,' Elizabeth said.

'She's not . . . good lord!' Mary burst out laughing. 'You're an *American!*'

Vicky knew she was flushing, and glanced at Nathalie, who was in the same unfortunate position of not being British in this most English of households.

'That will do, Mary,' Mrs Chandler said. 'I am sure Mrs Lang will look after you admirably.'

'I will make tea,' Nathalie said reassuringly, and led Vicky from the room. Now here, the French girl thought, was someone she could like instantly. Those girls . . . 'They 'ave too much,' Nathalie remarked, perhaps to herself, but clearly knowing what Vicky was thinking. They climbed another flight of stairs. 'This is the family floor,' Nathalie said.

But they were not family. They climbed another flight of stairs, and Vicky began to puff. 'Up 'ere is where we live,' Nathalie opened a door. 'I've my own sitting room,' she pointed out. 'Lady Dobree is very good to work for.'

She was trying to establish a point. Vicky sat down and watched the French girl placing the kettle on the tiny gas ring: she had one exactly like that in her bedsitter in Etheridge. Perhaps she would after all be better off staying there, teaching the first form. But the Dobrees were going to Africa, Mrs Payne had said so.

'You 'ave the most lovely 'air,' Nathalie remarked, spooning tea into a pot. 'If you will take off your 'at, I will dress it for you.'

'Will you?' The suddenness of the approach took Vicky by surprise; she hadn't had her hair dressed since leaving Plymouth, Massachusetts. 'Do you think I should? I mean, take off my hat. Lady Dobree . . .'

Even as she spoke, a bell rang. 'Ooh, là là,' Nathalie exclaimed, and turned down the gas. 'She is ready for you. I will show you.'

Vicky sighed, licked her lips thirstily, and followed her mentor down another flight of stairs and along a corridor, pausing as they encountered a tall, blond young man in a blue military undress uniform.

'Oh, Mr Whiting,' Nathalie said. 'This is Mrs Lang. She is 'ere about the position of governess.'

'How do you do?' David Whiting said, and then frowned as he peered at her. 'How do you *do*, Mrs Lang.' He held her hand.

'I'm very well, so far,' Vicky assured him, gently freeing herself.

''Er ladyship is waiting,' Nathalie said, hurrying on. ''E likes you,' she said, in a loud whisper.

'Who is he?' Vicky whispered back as they arrived before a closed door.

"E is the General's – 'ow do you say? Adjutant, eh? 'E is very nice.'

No doubt, Vicky thought. But also a looming problem, even if she was prepared to like him. Which she wasn't; in no way did he remind her of James.

Nathalie lightly knocked on the door, then opened it. 'Mrs Lang, madame.'

Vicky gazed at Alison; Alison gazed at Vicky. Lady Dobree had been sitting down, but now she stood up. 'Good heavens,' she remarked, and Vicky's heart commenced a very rapid slide towards her boots – she was clearly not what Lady Dobree had been expecting. But then this tall, blonde, utterly beautiful and incredibly young woman was not what *she* had expected, either.

'Madame?' Nathalie inquired.

'You're not ... well ... I had expected someone a little taller,' Alison remarked lamely. Clearly she had been thinking something else.

Vicky raised her eyebrows; if she wasn't going to get the job anyway, she saw no reason to be too subservient. 'Mrs Payne didn't say that size went with the position, milady.'

'Ah.' Alison glanced at Nathalie as if seeking support, then waved her hand. 'Thank you, Nathalie. That will be all.'

'Yes, madame.' Nathalie closed the door behind her.

'Please sit down, Mrs Lang,' Alison said, doing so herself.

Vicky perched on a straight chair, allowing herself a quick glance around the sumptuously furnished boudoir.

Alison continued to stare at her. 'You are ... quite fit?' she inquired, anxiously.

'Milady?'

'Those ...' Alison flushed. 'Well ... spots.'

'Freckles, milady. From the sun.'

'Of course. How silly of me. Africa. My word,' Alison remarked, 'I won't get those, will I?'

'Not if you always wear a hat and a veil out of doors, milady.'

'But you didn't.'

'It wasn't always practical to do so, milady.'

'Ah. Wasn't it? I thought missionaries spent all their time in churches and such things.'

'Not all their time, milady. Running a mission means running an entire community. And then, sometimes it is necessary to build the church before you can go inside.'

Alison shot her a quick glance, suspecting she was being ridiculed. And then dismissed the idea as impossible. 'I never thought of that,' she said. 'Still, you know Africa. That is the important thing, I suppose. Tell me about Cape Town.'

'I have never been to Cape Town, milady,' Vicky said, wondering when she was going to be asked to leave.

'Never been to Cape Town? Why ever not?'

'Because I was in Kenya, milady.'

'Out in the . . . the *veldt*, isn't it called?' Alison was pleased both with her knowledge and her pronunciation. 'Yes, yes, I understand that. But surely it was possible to get into town, sometimes?'

'Into town, milady, but not Cape Town. It is approximately two thousand, seven hundred and fifty miles from where my husband and I were to Cape Town. That is only a little less than from here to New York. And that is as the crow flies. The actual journey would be well over three thousand miles.'

'Oh,' Alison said, frowning. 'But you *were* in Africa?' She was determined to establish this point.

'Yes, milady.'

'Hm. I think you should tell me something about yourself. Mrs Payne says you come from New England.'

Vicky's heart slowly began to climb again. Did she possibly still have a chance? 'Plymouth, Massachusetts,' she said. 'Where the Pilgrims landed.'

'Did they? How terribly interesting.'

'My family weren't with them,' Vicky hastily added. 'My father is a judge.'

'*Is* he?' For the first time Alison looked animated. 'Why, so is mine. Or he was.' She frowned. 'Yours still is?'

'I'm an eldest child,' Vicky explained.

'Oh.' Alison still looked confused. 'But . . . if your father was a judge, is a judge, well then . . . I mean . . . how can you be a schoolmistress? And a missionary?' The two clearly could not be related, in her world.

'I suppose I was a disappointment to my parents,' Vicky confessed. The realisation that this superb creature actually had a background no better than her own was pumping confidence back into her arteries. Even if Lady Dobree was not quite so dense as she appeared, she certainly had a very limited concept of the world. 'I wanted to *do* something instead of just sitting around waiting to be married. Can you understand that, milady?'

Alison apparently could not even understand the question.

'So,' Vicky went on, 'I went off and qualified as a schoolmarm. That didn't make anyone too happy. But it might have been smoothed over, except that James came along.'

'Your husband?'

'Yes.'

'The missionary?'

'That's right, milady. He wasn't actually on a mission in New England, of course. He was completing his theological studies at Harvard, and happened to be in Plymouth on vacation.'

'Doesn't it cost a lot of money to attend Harvard University?'

'It does,' Vicky agreed. 'But James had won a scholarship offered by the Church. He was tremendously intelligent.'

'And he carried you off to Africa,' Alison remarked, clearly not considering that to have been a very intelligent act.

'Why, yes he did. Father wouldn't give his consent, you see. So we eloped.'

'Good heavens! Why would your father not agree to the marriage?' In Alison's eyes, a graduate of Oxford or Cambridge, the English equivalent of Harvard and Yale, would necessarily have to be acceptable as a husband.

Vicky smiled wryly. 'James had no money and he was Anglican. Father is Presbyterian.'

'Good heavens,' Alison said again, Vicky could not be sure which of them she was condemning. 'But you *are* Anglican?'

'I was married to an Anglican missionary,' Vicky said with

33

careful accuracy. 'And I teach in an Anglican school.'

'Of course you do,' Alison said, reassured. 'But Mrs Lang, Victoria . . . do you mind if I call you Victoria?'

'Not at all, milady.' Vicky thought that Alison could call her whatever she liked, so long as she offered her the job.

'What on earth possessed you to elope? I mean, to leave a good home, good family, ah . . . pleasant surroundings, I imagine . . . to go to Africa?'

'I loved James,' Vicky said.

Alison gazed at her, once again obviously confronted with something beyond her ken. 'I see,' she remarked. 'And then your husband fell ill, and died . . . I am so sorry about that, Victoria. And so you came back here.'

'I brought James back, milady. He had contracted enteric fever and the doctors said his only hope was to return to England. So we came back.' She sighed. 'But he died all the same. Just over a year ago.'

'My dear, how miserable for you,' Alison remarked. 'Yes, well, I think I understand, No, I don't. Why have you remained in England? In, well, straitened circumstances, when you could have gone back to this Plymouth place, and your family?'

'I didn't want to do that, milady,' Vicky said, looking at her very hard. 'They made me leave in the first place.'

'Oh dear, how sad. And you and Mr Lang had no children?'

'No, milady. We were just too busy. And then James became ill.'

'Yes. You must tell me about that when we have the time,' Alison said. 'Perhaps during the voyage.'

Vicky opened her mouth, closed it again, opened it again. 'Are you offering me the job?'

'Well,' Alison said. 'I have to be frank with you, Victoria. You are not the person I had in mind for the position. Oh, please, I am sure you are a very good schoolmistress and would make an ideal governess, in the right circumstances, but, well . . . I had really anticipated employing an Englishwoman, and in addition, well, I'm not really sure you'll fit in to the pattern of our household, if you see what I mean.' She flopped her eyelashes once or twice. Vicky quite understood. Apart from Nathalie, who obviously didn't count, there was no adult in this household under five foot ten, and the girls would soon arrive at that height, most certainly. 'On the other hand,' Alison went on, 'I simply must have *someone* to supervise the girls, at least until we reach Africa. Would you be prepared to come along on a . . . shall we say probationary basis? If it were to become necessary to replace you after our arrival . . .' Her tone indicated that she had no doubt that *would* be necessary, 'we should of course pay your passage home. Back to England,' she hastily added.

Once again Vicky had a momentary thought that she'd be much better off with the first form at Etheridge. This woman clearly existed inside a cocoon of wealth and privilege which ended about three inches in front of her nose, and everyone and everything which was outside of that was required to dance exactly to her tune, no matter how humiliating or inconvenient they might find it, or be written off as irrelevant. She had, in effect, just said, 'I'll take you because I'm stuck for anything better, but the moment I do find anything better, you're out!' So why not tell her to go climb a tree, and feel like a human being again?

Because she was being offered a round trip to Africa, free. Even if it was a part of Africa of which she knew nothing, and even if it involved her in trying to cope with two unpleasant young women and being treated like dirt while she did so. And even if she was put on the first boat back, she would have had not less than three months of travel, away from the horrible children she had to cope with every day. But best of all, she would have returned to Africa.

'I should be happy to come along on that basis, milady,' she said.

'Well, then,' Alison said, 'you'd better come along and meet Sir William.'

Alison led her along the upper hall, down the main staircase, and into her husband's study. 'William,' she said. 'This is Mrs

Lang. Victoria. She will be looking after the girls until we get to Africa.'

William Dobree raised his head slowly, and then hurriedly got to his feet. 'Mrs Lang,' he said, clearly finding the afternoon suddenly brighter. 'Victoria.'

'Sir William,' Vicky acknowledged.

His mouth fell open and Alison hastily hurried on. 'And this is Lieutenant Whiting, my husband's aide-de-camp.'

'We've already met,' Vicky said.

'Indeed we have,' David Whiting said, like his employer, clearly enjoying what he was looking at.

Unlike his employer, however, he was not disturbed by Vicky's accent. Dobree had sat down again, and was now gazing at his wife. 'You never said anything . . .'

'I think,' Alison said, speaking more loudly than usual, 'that it would be a very good idea if Victoria could move in as rapidly as possible, so that she can get to know the girls and their routine before we actually depart. Don't you agree, William?'

William gazed at Vicky.

'Can you move in right away, Victoria?' Alison asked.

'Well . . . I have to hand over the first form . . . but Mrs Payne said she'd step in until they found a replacement. I could come in on Saturday, milady.'

'That would be most convenient,' Alison said. 'Well, Victoria, I'm sure you have a great deal to do, and time is so short. We shan't keep you any longer. I shall expect you on Saturday afternoon.'

Vicky realised she had been dismissed. But there hadn't been any proper discussion, no mention of a salary, or hours; and she couldn't just leave England without paying her bills . . . she felt utterly embarrassed and humiliated, but had no choice. 'If I could have a word, milady,' she said. 'Well . . . about arrangements.'

Alison gazed at her with raised eyebrows.

William Dobree came to her rescue. 'Of course, Mrs Lang,' he said. 'Victoria. I quite understand. It is terribly short notice, isn't it? Would fifty pounds be sufficient to square everything away?'

36

'Fifty . . . oh . . .'

'An advance against your salary,' Dobree said, opening his drawer and taking out an enormous packet of huge five-pound notes, from which he counted ten, and folded them neatly in half. 'There we are.'

'You're very kind, Sir William,' Vicky said. 'But . . . well . . .'

'We shall pay you two hundred pounds a year, and all found,' Dobree said. 'Will that be satisfactory?'

'Satisfactory?' Vicky asked faintly. That figure was beyond her wildest expectations.

'I'm glad you're pleased,' Dobree said, standing up again to squeeze her hand. 'I'm sure we're going to get along very well.'

'Perhaps, David, you would be good enough to show Victoria out,' Alison suggested, coldly.

'Oh, of course.' He hurried forward and opened the door.

'And I shall see you on Saturday afternoon, Victoria,' Alison said.

'I'll be here, milady. And again, thank you.'

Alison watched the door close. 'Well,' she said, happy to be able to move on to the attack. 'She seems to have made an impression. Two hundred pounds a year, and all found?'

'That's what we are paying Mrs Chandler.'

'Yes, but she's a trifle more experienced, wouldn't you say? With children,' she hastily added. 'Was it wise to give this woman that money? Fifty pounds? To someone like that, fifty pounds is a fortune.'

'She obviously hasn't a penny, and no doubt has outstanding bills.' Dobree sat down again. 'You didn't tell me she's an American.'

'I must have forgotten.' Alison smiled at him. 'Shall I go down and tell her you've changed your mind about employing her?'

'Oh, I didn't mean that, my dear, it just came as something of a surprise.'

'She is a qualified schoolteacher,' Alison reminded him. 'Which is more than Mrs Chandler is.' That she was now contesting her own previous point about Vicky's inexperience, was irrelevant beside the power she suddenly felt in her grasp. 'And I am assured by Mrs Payne that she is a very competent person. I cannot say I really like the woman, mind you, and she's so tiny I don't really know how she's going to cope, but if she is unsatisfactory, in *any* way, I intend to send her home from the Cape.'

'Oh, come now, she's not all that tiny,' Dobree said, clearly remembering.

Alison had gone to the door. She paused, her hand on the knob. 'Do you suppose she . . . well, pads her bodice? I have heard some women do.'

'I am sure she doesn't,' Dobree said positively.

'I see,' Alison said, and closed the door behind her.

'I must say, it's a bit of a change, or it will be, having you around instead of Mrs Chandler, Victoria,' David Whiting said as he escorted Vicky down the great staircase. 'Do you mind if I call you Victoria?'

'It's my name, Mr Whiting. Why should I be so great a change to Mrs Chandler?'

'Well, she's such an old dragon, and you're . . . well . . .' He flushed.

'I'm a young dragon, Lieutenant Whiting. That's what I'm being employed to be, isn't it?'

'But it's not really what you are, is it? I say, why don't you call me David?'

'Do you think I should?'

'Well . . . I suppose not in front of the General or Lady Dobree. But when we're in private . . .'

'I'll try to remember,' Vicky agreed. 'Because I don't suppose we will be in private very often, will we?'

Bestwick was waiting with her cloak, and the groom had the trap at the steps.

David did not seem the least abashed by her putdown. 'Are you sure you can get home all by yourself?' he asked. 'It'll be dark in an hour.'

'I can manage, thank you.' Vicky seated herself, waited while he tucked the blanket around her skirt – he had fallen so

38

completely and heavily she supposed she could allow him that little pleasure.

'Of course, you've lived in Africa,' he said, as if that experience must have left her capable of coping with anything she could possibly encounter in the English countryside. 'Well . . . I am looking forward to Saturday. I could come and fetch you, if you wished.'

'So am I looking forward to Saturday, Lieutenant Whiting,' she said. 'But I think it would be best if I found my own way. Good night.' She smiled at Bestwick, flicked the whip, and walked the pony down the drive.

On the road she could let him trot, feel the cold breeze whistling past her cheeks. She didn't know whether she was standing on her head or her heels. For one thing, she had fifty pounds in her reticule; she had never had fifty pounds at one time in her life before. Two hundred and fifty dollars. Suppose she were to abscond . . . but she knew, and they knew, that she wasn't going to do that. She was going to be paid two hundred pounds a year. Even supposing she didn't last a year, that was still sixteen pounds, thirteen shillings, and fourpence a month. And she was going to Africa! With . . . she wrinkled her nose. An employer who had an eye for the ladies, that was obvious – but who could hardly stray very far when married to such a wife. Well then, with an employer's wife, who clearly should never have strayed from the pages of a fashion magazine, but who from this moment forth was going to be the most important person in *her* life, that was obvious. She would just have to be borne. And with an employer's secretary who was clearly desperate . . . well, who could blame him? living as he did in an almost entirely female household, and such good-looking females too. But if he thought she was available for even the mildest flirtation she would have to slap him down, very hard. She had no wish to be involved with the Dobrees, or any of their offshoots, in any way more than was necessary. Which brought her to the girls. They were to be her responsibility, and she was not the sort of person ever to give less than her best. But obviously there were going to be some tough times ahead; anyone who was to take over from such a well-established institution as Mrs Chandler was likely to have a rough ride until she could establish herself in turn. Even if the girls had been absolute paragons – and Rowena Payne had told her they were quite impossible – they would seek to discover in which areas they could take advantage of their new mentor. That was human nature. Therefore it would be essential to establish herself as positively and quickly as possible.

How? She sat up in her narrow bed that night, brooding. She had to accept, initially at any rate, the fact that the girls would actually matter less than the Dobrees themselves. She suspected that, while Alison Dobree was her immediate boss, in the end the stepmother would matter less than the father. It was he who needed analysis, in all his responses to the varied stimuli that she was going to provide. Thus . . . the General was a soldier, a well-known one and something of a hero. But he was also a man in early middle age, who, Vicky calculated, was probably somewhat in awe of the events going on around him, particularly the development of little girls into young women: she was not only an avid reader of philosophy but an avid student of human nature. She could perceive in him a touch of mental incest added to a very real love, with a certain confusion of loyalties between new wife and old children, and a personal philosophy that only physical success mattered. It occurred to her that she was setting out to tread a very narrow path indeed, with precipices on both sides, and no certainty that her summing-up of the situation was right. But it was all she had to go on.

And anyway, she had the comforting feeling that she must only survive until they were actually steaming out of Southampton Harbour and then they were stuck with her until Cape Town. And although this was hardly the attitude she would like any employee of hers to possess – and therefore was an attitude of which she was half ashamed – she could remind herself that in devoting so much of her life to James and his ideals and principles, she had not allowed herself to be selfish for too long. She had even subdued her own religious upbringing to his faith. This had not actually been difficult, as she had never held any very firm doctrinal beliefs – except in

40

Christianity as such – but that very fact had made her over aware that she was acting a role and therefore being insincere, at least to herself. But before her conscience overwhelmed her, it had become a matter of nursing, and feeling the growing desperation of knowing that there was no happy end in sight; of watching the man she adored dwindling into nothing; of understanding that though her life had barely begun, it was already well on its way to being over. That whatever her crimes, real or imagined, expiation was going to be a long and slow and perhaps eternal process.

It was not a feeling she had easily overcome, or indeed overcome at all. Even this little jaunt was a sort of last fling, before an eternity of nothingness, as far as she could see. But if it was going to be a last jaunt, she had better make the most of it. She owed the Dobrees nothing. They were making use of her, and Lady Dobree had been quite explicit in stating that as soon as they could find anyone better, she would cease making use of her. So then, she would be what they wanted, until she was on that ship for Africa . . . and then, she thought, she could thumb her nose at the lot of them.

Next day came the sheer pleasure of bicycling around Etheridge, settling the various accounts which had steadily grown over the year. Most of the merchants had allowed her a generous credit because James Lang had been an Etheridge lad. His elderly father still lived in the old family home; he had often suggested that his daughter-in-law move in with him, but Vicky felt she would be smothered in such surroundings. However, she visited him twice a week and, indeed, visiting him to tell him she was going away for a while was the only sad moment of her departure.

The people of Etheridge were united in their commiseration for her unhappy fate. They had been prepared to respect her desire to mourn her husband, even for as long as a year, to the despair of the young men of the village, for whom the widow Lang was the most exciting thing that had happened in a long time and who continued to call and invite despite her unchanging refusals. On the other hand, they all had livings to earn, and as the year wore on, Vicky had become increasingly aware of a certain hesitation on the part of her various creditors when she had assured them that the funds they sought would be available in the near future – without any clear idea of when that future was going to arrive. She had always had the comforting feeling that if her life ever became absolutely desperate, there was always Pa . . . but an exchange of letters not long after James's death – presumably, on her parents' side, intended to be sympathetic – had left her sure that, though Pa would certainly bail her out to prevent her, for instance, being sent to gaol, the act of mercy would be accompanied by such demands for total surrender and abasement for her earlier defiance that she might as well go to prison.

So she had stuck it out, and suddenly, here she was, with ten five-pound notes in her hand and the man on the other side of the counter gaping at her.

The headmaster was less than happy about the situation. But when she announced that she was leaving anyway, he realised there wasn't much he could do. And Rowena Payne *had* agreed to take the class herself until a replacement could be found. 'I am being utterly, viciously, selfish,' Vicky confessed to the vicar's wife. 'Don't you agree? And don't you think that is terrible of me?'

'I think Shakespeare wrote something about taking the flood tide or forever regretting it, my dear girl,' Rowena said. 'I cannot pretend *I* would find anything exciting about rushing off to Africa . . . but if you can manage to hold the position, why, General Dobrée is a very wealthy man. That Chandler woman was there for eight years, to my knowledge. You could be looking forward to a totally secure life.'

In which to grow grey and grim, Vicky thought, sadly. But she smiled as brightly as she could. 'So I'm forgiven?'

'I don't think there is anything you should ask forgiveness for,' Rowena said. 'Just go, and live, and laugh. And be happy.'

Which was surely all she had to remember to do, she kept telling herself as she rode in the hired pony and trap, this time with a driver to take it back again and her two suitcases neatly

42

stacked beside her. The few household items she had managed to save from the wreck of her married life, or accumulate during the past year, had been packed in a box and left with Rowena.

This time Bestwick was waiting with two footmen to carry her bags and instead of Nathalie there was Prudence Brown. Here was a known and friendly face, and a welcoming one. 'Mrs Lang,' Prudence said. 'How good to have you at the Manor.'

'Prudence.' Vicky kissed her on the cheek. 'Mrs Payne told me this was all your idea. I am so very grateful, believe me.'

'I was just happy to be able to help, Mrs Lang – both you and Lady Dobree. I'll show you to your room.' She led the way to the attics. 'Normally her ladyship would allow you to fit these rooms out exactly as you wish,' she explained. 'But as we are leaving in a week . . .'

'Of course,' Vicky agreed. 'I quite understand.'

'Are you looking forward to it?' Prudence asked.

'Oh, tremendously. I adore Africa. Well, East Africa, anyway. I don't know about the South. But I'm told it is even more lovely and a much better climate.'

'That's what we all hope.' Prudence waited while a footman brought the suitcases in and Vicky tidied up. 'Her ladyship thought it might be a good idea if you were to eat with the girls,' she said. 'I suppose becoming a part of the family needs to be accomplished just as quickly as possible.'

'Of course,' Vicky agreed.

'So I wondered if you would like to change . . .'

'No,' Vicky decided. She would still have to see her ladyship some time this evening, she presumed. 'I'll stay as I am for the time being.' She peered into the mirror to make sure her hat was still on straight and none of her pins had come unstuck.

'You have such beautiful hair,' Prudence commented. 'My lucky charm,' Vicky smiled. 'Is Mrs Chandler, um . . .?'

'No, no,' Prudence said, understanding. 'Mrs Chandler left this morning. Her ladyship felt that there should be only one governess in residence at a time. I think she was very happy to see Mrs Chandler go. They never got on particularly well, and

43

her ladyship felt she had been rather let down by Mrs Chandler's attitude over this move.'

'Even if she had a husband she couldn't leave?'

'I'm afraid her ladyship finds it difficult to recognise that any of us have lives of our own, outside the family,' Prudence explained. 'She demands total loyalty, and, I may say, as long as she receives it she is the best of employers. I suppose what it comes down to is that this is no place for a married woman. But as none of us are . . .' She paused.

'I quite understand, Prudence,' Vicky said.

'Shall we go down and meet the staff before supper?' Prudence suggested. 'I know they all wish to meet you.'

'Surely. But shouldn't I call on Lady Dobree first, to let her know I'm here?'

'She will know you are here, Mrs Lang,' Prudence said. 'And she'll send for you when she wishes to see you. Oh, by the way, here is a complete timetable for the girls' day. You'll have to make up your own for the boat journey, of course, but her ladyship felt that would act as a guide for the next week.'

'How thoughtful of her,' Vicky murmured, glancing at the closely written sheet of paper. The time was just past six, and she observed that it was marked as a preparation period for the girls, before their supper. Presumably that was why there was no sign of them, for which she was heartily thankful: it gave her an opportunity to settle down a little.

She placed the timetable on her dressing table, to be studied and perhaps amended at her leisure, and accompanied Prudence down to the servants' hall, where it seemed a large number of people had assembled to meet her. Apart from Bestwick and his footmen, there was Cook, and the housekeeper, and two upstairs maids and two downstairs maids, and a scullery maid and a boot boy, and Martin the head groom as well as two stable boys . . . the General's valet, Pressdee, had apparently accompanied him to London. 'But the fair one has stayed here,' Cook explained. 'He's to supervise the packing up. Him!'

From which Vicky gathered they had no great respect for David Whiting. But, she gathered, they weren't all that impressed with her, either. They greeted her courteously enough, and made encouraging remarks, as well as some commiserative ones about her imminent departure – they were all staying here to continue staffing the Manor until the General's return – but when Prudence indicated that it was time to go to the children's dining room and she went to the door, she overheard an arch whisper from one upstairs maid to the other, 'She'll not last the week, poor little thing. Those terrors will eat her for breakfast.'

Prudence had heard the comment too. 'Mrs Chandler was very strict,' she said, as she led the way upstairs.

'And apparently needed to be,' Vicky agreed, grimly. Prudence preferred not to offer an opinion on that, and a moment later Vicky's apprehensions disappeared as they encountered Nathalie, who burst into a stream of greetings.

''Er ladyship says you must come and see 'er, after supper,' she said.

'I shall do so,' Vicky promised. She accompanied Prudence into the children's dining room, where Charlie Dobree was running back and forth, Elizabeth was lying on her stomach on the floor, sketching, and Mary sat in a straight chair, tilted on its back legs, reading a book.

'Master Charles,' Prudence said. 'Now stop that this instant. Go along and wash your hands.'

There was a bathroom immediately alongside the dining room, and into this Charlie disappeared without question, followed by Prudence; clearly, she had *him* under control.

Mary and Elizabeth both raised their heads to look at their new governess.

'I think a good wash would be an excellent idea, don't you?' Vicky said, pleasantly.

'My hands are perfectly clean, thank you, Lang,' Mary said.

Vicky realised that her first crisis was upon her even sooner than she had expected. But she was determined to keep her temper, no matter what the provocation, while being absolutely firm. And she understood that it was necessary to be more than firm, at least for this one occasion; if she showed the slightest weakness now she might find herself in an irretrievable position.

She ignored Mary for the moment and knelt beside Elizabeth, taking her hand and turning it over. It was stained with crayon. 'You certainly need to wash yours,' she said. 'Off you go.'

Elizabeth hesitated, then scrambled to her feet and ran into the bathroom.

'I told you,' Mary Dobree began as Vicky straightened and approached her.

'What is that you're reading?' Vicky asked, once again pleasantly.

'It's a novel.'

'I understood the hour before supper was a preparation period.'

'Mrs Chandler didn't set us any preparation. Anyway, tomorrow is Sunday.'

'So it is,' Vicky agreed. 'What's the name of the book?'

'Nothing that would interest you,' Mary said.

Vicky took the book from her hands, read the title.

'It's all the rage,' Mary said.

'*The War of the Worlds*,' Vicky commented. 'Yes, I have heard of it. Does your father know you read Mr Wells?'

'Well, really, Lang, I read what I please.'

'No, no, Mary,' Vicky said. 'From now on, you read what *I* please. And I do not consider horrific novels of this nature to be suitable for a fifteen-year-old girl. I shall confiscate this.'

'You . . . you wouldn't dare!'

'I have just done so,' Vicky said, quietly, placing the book on the table. 'And Mary, you will refer to me as *Mrs* Lang. Remember that.'

Mary stared at her. 'You're only temporary,' she declared. 'Old Chandler said so. You're going to get the boot, the moment we reach Cape Town.'

Vicky smiled, with her lips. 'But until we get there, Mary, I am going to be the one with the boot. Now go and wash your hands.'

Mary gave her another long stare, but while she had planned

this early confrontation, she had not sufficiently prepared herself for such determination, and did not know how to continue. She went into the bathroom.

Vicky sighed with relief.

The meal was a quiet affair, served by one of the footmen. The girls at least had perfect table manners, Vicky was pleased to note, even if Charlie didn't. But Charlie was Prudence's problem.

She endeavoured to make conversation, but Mary merely glowered at her, and although Elizabeth's first response was cheerful, a glance from her sister turned her quiet as well. Prudence and Vicky continued to exchange commonplaces.

'Well,' Vicky said brightly, when the dessert had been removed, and with a quick smile at the worried Prudence, who was clearly expecting another clash of wills. 'What is the normal form after supper?' She looked at Mary.

'It's in the timetable,' Mary said.

'I'm sure it is. But the timetable is in my room.'

For the first time, Mary's face relaxed into a smile. 'Then you'll have to go and look at it, won't you, *Mrs* Lang?'

Vicky gazed at her. There was a great temptation to order the girl to go and fetch it but she was determined to behave absolutely correctly in every way. Leaving the timetable had been her decision, and her mistake.

Prudence attempted to help. 'I think there is usually an hour's reading before bedtime,' she said.

'That sounds an admirable arrangement,' Vicky said. 'But I will go and fetch the timetable. You will remain here, Mary, Elizabeth, until I return.'

Mary shrugged.

Elizabeth giggled.

They were obviously conspiring in some direction or another. Things were going to be even more difficult than she had supposed, Vicky thought, as she climbed the stairs. But if they wanted to play it hard, then they would have it played hard. She'd make sure they did everything, but everything, according to that timetable, and on the dot of each appointed hour. And she'd make one or two changes as well, just to tighten things up.

She reached the attic level, hesitant in the gloom, for the electricity did not reach up here and the hall was lit by a single large candle in a holder on the wall. She went to her own door, and found that it was slightly ajar. She frowned. She was positive she had closed it before going down to the servants' hall. But presumably one of the maids had come upstairs to tidy things up and even perhaps to turn down the bed. That was nice of them; she had not expected to be looked after in any way.

She stepped into the doorway, pushing the door in front of her, and was struck a resounding blow on the head.

CHAPTER 3

The blow itself quite dazed her. She was aware of having cried out as she fell to her knees, and then on to her face, becoming soaked as she did so in some dreadful sticky liquid seeping down from her head. Blood! She screamed before she could stop herself, sitting up and clawing at her face, and her hair, which was sodden with the stuff.

'Oh, my God!' she screamed again, while the room seemed to revolve around her and she had the oddest feeling that her entire head had been opened up.

People arrived from every direction, carrying lanterns and candles; Nathalie, Prudence, a footman, David Whiting . . . and Lady Dobree. The room and the corridor became filled with light, and chatter, and exclamation, while David knelt and raised Vicky into a sitting position, cradling her head on his shoulders regardless of the damage being done to his smoking-jacket.

She gazed around her, and realised the enormity of what had happened. The bucket which had been wedged on the top of the open door had struck her head before falling beside her; it had given her a good thump but had apparently not actually broken the skin of her scalp, thanks to her hat, which had been knocked off by the blow and lay beside her in a sodden crumpled mess. Certainly there was no blood. Instead, there was a dreadful concoction of treacle, ink, mud and water which had been contained by the bucket, soaking her hair, her blouse, her jacket, her underclothes, staining her face and hands . . .

'Good Lord,' Alison commented. 'You are a terrible sight, Victoria.'

49

'Those girls,' Prudence said. 'Oh, those girls.'

'They are so naughty,' Nathalie commented.

'My God!' David commented. 'they really should be thrashed, you know.' He was contemplating the state of his jacket.

The maid and footman were clearly only preventing themselves from laughing with an immense effort.

'You don't mean Mary and Elizabeth did this?' Alison asked. 'Good heavens!' For a terrible moment Vicky thought she was going to laugh too, but she also managed to suppress her amusement. 'Nathalie, you had better draw a bath for Victoria, right away. Nanny, will you attend to the girls for tonight, please? I'm afraid . . . well . . . I would like to have a word with you, when you are slightly more presentable, Victoria. Come along now.' She chased the other servants away.

Nathalie fussed, and Vicky, still dazed, found herself sitting in a tin tub in the middle of her bedroom, with no clear idea of undressing or getting there at all. She looked at her clothes lying in a heap in the far corner, and felt hands massaging her scalp and washing her hair. Immediately she knew who it had to be, and was grateful for it, and for the fact that they were alone.

'Oh, those girls,' Nathalie said. 'They are so wicked. They should be flogged. And such hair . . .' Lovingly she rinsed Vicky's hair again and again, stretching it down her back: unpinned, Vicky's hair brushed her buttocks. 'But all of you is so beautiful,' Nathalie said. 'All of you. Such breasts . . . I 'ave breasts like yours, Victoria. But the rest of me . . . pouf! I would like to wash the rest of your body, Victoria.'

Victoria made no objection, let her get on with it. She was past feeling. Or she was too deeply embedded in feeling to be aware of any particular one. Physically she felt a wreck; her head was throbbing and she felt vaguely sick. But that was despair. Every time she allowed herself to think of those two little hoydens smiling at each other she could feel the tears dribbling out of her eyes. But she couldn't afford to despair. They had thrown down the most blatant challenge to her. She must either crawl away into the night, her head bowed forever more, or she must meet them head on. She had to meet them head on.

And her only good outfit, ruined. This time the tears were of pure anger.

Nathalie helped her to stand and then step from the tub, and wrapped her in a towel, gently patting and massaging her dry. 'You will make some man very 'appy,' the French girl sighed. 'But you are angry. Oh, you should be angry. But what can you do?'

'What would Mrs Chandler have done?' Vicky asked, speaking for the first time since the disaster, and surprised at the evenness of her voice.

'Mrs Chandler . . .' Nathalie frowned. 'I do not know. I do not know 'ow she managed it, but they were afraid of 'er.'

'Yes,' Vicky breathed. 'They were afraid of her.' She dressed herself in one of her daywear skirts and blouses, omitted the tie, allowed Nathalie to gather her hair in a long, damp, red-gold tress and secure it with a green ribbon, then went down to Lady Dobree's sitting room. She just wanted to get into bed and stop thinking, for a while. But she couldn't do that. There were too many things to be faced . . . beginning with that arrogant blonde woman. She was surprised, and slightly concerned, at how angry she felt, and how her sense of outrage embraced this entire household. Yet oddly, for all her emotional exhaustion, she also felt a peculiar tingling sensation, of being very alive. She had never known such a feeling before, that she could remember. Could Nathalie have had anything to do with it? Because she had never been bathed before, either, since she had been a little girl. But that was an even more disturbing thought, not to be explored until her mind was again at rest, if that ever did happen. More important, she felt no weakening of the resolve to make it to that ship, and then Africa.

Alison and David Whiting were having an after-dinner brandy.

'My dear Victoria.' David was on his feet to hold the door for her; he had changed shirt, jacket and tie. 'I can't tell you how sorry I am . . . about everything. If I had my way . . .'

'I have promised you that the whole escapade will be

51

reported to the General, David,' Alison said severely. 'Certainly I can do no more than that. Are you quite recovered, Victoria?'

'Quite, milady,' Vicky lied. She had not been invited to sit down and thus remained standing in the centre of the room, rather, she felt, as if she were the guilty party. Her anger grew.

'Well, I can only say that I entirely agree with Lieutenant Whiting,' Alison said. 'They really have gone too far this time. Why, they might have seriously hurt you. However, it is a matter for their father. Unfortunately, as you know, we shall not be seeing the General again until Friday or Saturday, and I do not see how you can hope to get through the next week, under the circumstances. Believe me, this upsets me more than it upsets you. I shall have to try to get Mrs Chandler back for the last few days, I suppose, and I really do not care for the thought of that. But I do have her address.'

Vicky frowned at her, feeling as if she had been kicked in the stomach. 'Am I being dismissed, milady?'

'I have no alternative,' Alison pointed out.

'But . . .' She couldn't believe her ears. She had been prepared to accept almost anything in order to survive until they were on the boat – and she was not even going to survive one night.

'Oh, don't worry. Under the circumstances, and with our now owing you a new gown, you may keep the fifty pounds. I am sure the General would wish you to have that.'

'But I haven't done anytthing to be dismissed,' Vicky gasped, hating herself for begging.

Alison gazed at her, eyebrows arched.

Vicky licked her lips. 'If . . . if I give you my word, milady, that such a thing will never happen again, that Mary and Elizabeth will from this moment treat me with the greatest respect, will that not suffice?'

'My dear Victoria,' Alison said, as she might have spoken to a backward child. 'If wishes were horses, then beggars would ride. I'm afraid that Mary and Elizabeth will *never* treat you with respect again, after tonight. It is unfair, but they are like

52

that. They take after their father. Physical triumph is what matters.'

'I understand that, milady. I still think I deserve a chance to set things right.'

'By Jove,' David said. 'You know, Alison . . .'

'Oh really, David,' Alison snapped. 'How can she . . . what can you hope to do to change the situation now?'

Vicky drew a long breath. There was only one thing she really wanted to do. And after everything, to do it might get her the sack. But as Alison had just confirmed, her original estimation of the General was accurate. Therefore surely her only chance of survival lay in being even more physically successful than the girls. Quite apart from the satisfaction to be had. 'I have been appointed their governess, milady. Therefore, as long as I hold that position, I am *in loco parentis*, am I not, at all times?'

'Why . . . *in loco* . . . why yes, I suppose you are.'

'Therefore their punishment should be left to me, not their father.'

'Well, of course I never interfered with Mrs Chandler in any way,' Alison admitted. 'But you . . .'

'Perhaps you could tell me what General Dobree might decree as a punishment, were he here, milady.'

'Well . . . if he were here now, I have no doubt at all that he'd probably thrash the pair of them. And serve them right. Unfortunately . . .' She sighed. 'After a week . . .'

'The matter will be dead and buried,' Vicky said. 'So with your permission, milady, I will withdraw and resume my duties. *In loco parentis*.'

Alison stood up. 'You cannot be serious.'

'I am very serious, milady,' Vicky told her. 'It is not something I ever supposed I would have to do, but then the experience I have had this evening is not one I ever expected to undergo, either. And as we are all agreed that the culprits should be severely punished, I intend to punish them. Severely.'

'By Jove,' David said. 'But you know . . . Mary, well, she's a big strong girl. Do you not suppose her ladyship or I should, well . . .' He flushed in embarrassment.

'I shall not require any assistance, thank you, Mr Whiting,' Vicky said. 'However, if her ladyship would like to be present in a supervisory capacity, I have no objection.'

'Who, me?' Alison cried. 'Oh, Good Lord, no! It's just that . . . well, I do hope you know what you're doing. Even if the General . . . well, I really cannot imagine what he may say about it.'

'I am sure the General will understand *our* situation, milady,' Vicky, determined to associate her mistress in the event. 'However, if you do not wish to be present, I must ask you not to interfere in any way. There may be some noise,' she explained.

Alison's eyebrows took on their familiar arch.

'Very good, milady,' Vicky said. 'Now, if you will excuse me.' She closed the door behind her, and discovered that she was sweating harder than ever before in her life. She had spoken the exact truth when she told them that she had never in her wildest nightmare anticipated anything like this. But that had been the coward in her. She had known there would be a confrontation, and victory or defeat. She had just not allowed herself to consider that the confrontation could be so sudden, or so brutal. Therefore she had to outmatch them, or, as she had recognised in the bath, sneak away into the night. As for the General . . . but she was following her instincts. They were all she had.

She went back up to her bedroom, where Prudence was supervising an upstairs maid and a footman in cleaning the mess off the floor, while Nathalie sat on the bed and watched them.

'Soon be done,' Prudence announced cheerfully, and then lowered her voice to a whisper. 'I can't tell you how sorry I am about this, Mrs Lang. I really never supposed even those two would go this far.'

'Everything is just fine, Prudence,' Vicky said. 'But I feel I should have a word with the girls, after everything that has happened. Can you tell me where they are?'

All the heads in the room turned to stare at her.

'Ooh, là là.,' Nathalie commented.

'Ah . . . I sent them to bed,' Prudence said. 'I thought it best.'

'Of course, that was entirely the right thing to do.'

'They should have been flogged,' Nathalie remarked.

'I agree with you.' Vicky went to her dressing table and picked up her hairbrush, which was long and thick and heavy.

'Ooh, là là.!' Nathalie exclaimed. 'I must come with you.'

'No,' Vicky said definitely.

Nathalie looked disappointed.

'Ah . . .' Prudence had been staring at her with her mouth open. 'Would you like *me* to come with you?'

'No, no, Prudence, you have done enough for one evening. And thank you all so much for looking after my room.' She went outside, aware that they were still staring after her, and supposing, with some pleasure, that tonight was not one the Dobree household would ever forget. Then she went down the stairs to the family bedrooms. She was again conscious of the tingling sensation, and now recalled that she *had* experienced something like it before, once, during her early days in Kenya, with James, on the occasion that the mission had been surrounded by Kikuyu warriors. The Africans had not actually appeared antagonistic to them as individuals, but had a grievance against the British administration and were literally up in arms, while the missionaries had been the only white people for some miles. James had never believed in resorting to weapons, although he kept a rifle to protect them from marauding wild animals. That night he had gone outside, unarmed, to talk with the chiefs. She had been alone in the tiny house, and she had taken down the rifle and loaded it and then stood at the window, determined to defend herself and him to the last, even though she had never fired a gun in her life. And standing there, she had felt herself tingle, her heart pounding and her nipples hardening at the thought that in a few minutes she might be fighting for her life, much less her honour. She hadn't had to, of course. James had talked them out of whatever they had been proposing to do.

And how she would like to have James at her elbow now. But then, what were two teenage girls after a Kikuyu war party?

She opened the door of Elizabeth's room without knocking. There was a hasty rustling sound, and the electric light went off. Vicky turned it on again. 'Still awake, I see,' she said. 'What are you reading?'

Elizabeth half sat up and pretended to yawn. 'Shakespeare.'

'Shakespeare, Mrs Lang,' Vicky said.

'Shakespeare, Mrs Lang,' Elizabeth repeated, uncertainly, frowning at her, 'You . . .'

'I have had a bath,' Vicky agreed, 'and washed my hair, and am perfectly clean again. And you have had your fun, which was nice for you, wasn't it? Now I'm afraid you must pay for it. Get out of bed.'

'Me?' Elizabeth held the sheet to her throat.

'You.' Vicky reached out and removed the sheet from the girl's fingers.

Elizabeth stared at the hairbrush. 'You can't hit me. You . . .'

'Out,' Vicky said.

Elizabeth crawled out of bed and stood beside it, a trembling wisp of white linen nightdress. 'I'll scream,' she threatened. 'I'll scream.'

'I'll be disappointed if you don't,' Vicky said. 'But it's not your turn yet. Go in to your sister's room.'

Elizabeth hesitated, then ran for the door. Clearly she felt safety was just along the corridor.

'Walk,' Vicky commanded. 'Don't run.'

Elizabeth checked herself, and stepped outside, Vicky at her elbow. From further down the corridor there came a rustle, but whoever it was had withdrawn round the corner. Not that Vicky had any doubt who it was. She opened the door to Mary's room. Here there was no attempt to switch off the light. Mary sat up in bed reading *The War of the Worlds*, which Vicky had forgotten to remove from the dining table. 'Good heavens,' she remarked, as her sister and Vicky entered. 'You must have done some scrubbing.'

'I see you're reading the book I confiscated,' Vicky observed, locking the door and pocketing the key.

'It's my book,' Mary said. 'You have no right to confiscate it. You have no right to do anything at all. You're out. Everyone says you're out.'

'Because you made up that trap for me,' Vicky said.

Mary tossed her head. 'Yes,' she said. 'Because we made you look like the fool you are.'

'I see,' Vicky said. 'Well, I am so pleased that you are prepared to confess your crime. Unfortunately, as you see, I am not out, as you put it. I am still in, and I did warn you that until I actually get the boot, I possess it, and intend to use it. Out of bed.'

'She has a hairbrush,' Elizabeth gasped.

As Mary could now see. 'You wouldn't dare,' she snapped. 'You wouldn't *dare*. You . . . you colonial savage.'

'Please endeavour to be polite,' Vicky said. 'I was intending to give you six strokes for the bucket and the bang on the head. Then I decided to add three strokes for your disobedience in reading that book. Now I think I will add three strokes for your insolent remarks. I do recommend you consider what else you wish to say, very carefully.'

'You . . .' Mary glared at her, then looked at Elizabeth. 'Get help. Call stepmama. Call David.'

Elizabeth ran to the door. 'It's locked,' she shouted.

'Out of bed,' Vicky commanded. 'And bend over.'

'You touch me, and I'll . . .'

'No, no,' Vicky said, standing very close to the bed. 'You resist me, and I'll break your nasty little neck.'

Mary stared at her, then threw back the covers and leapt out of the bed, obviously intending to burst past her and gain the door. But Vicky caught her arm. Mary turned towards her, swinging her hand in a slap. Vicky avoided the blow without difficulty, and exerted all her strength. Mary's only normal exercise consisted of guiding her pony round and round a paddock; Vicky had not only spent four years in Africa, quite literally helping to build a mission church and house and run a small farm with her own two hands, but during the past year she had had to be entirely self-sufficient, from cutting her own firewood and carrying it up to the stairs to the fireplace in her room, to carrying her own laundry down. Mary gasped and fell on her face across the bed. Vicky retained hold of her arm, twisting it behind her back, and began to apply the brush, aiming from buttock to buttock.

'Aaagh!' Mary screamed, legs kicking desperately, but helpless because of the pressure on her arm. 'Help! Help me, Liz. Help!'

Vicky ignored Elizabeth, who continued to bang on the door, and swung her arm, time and again, the brush head crashing into the quivering linen beneath her, while she counted aloud. When she reached twelve, she released Mary, and stood up, panting, blouse soaked with sweat, her own muscles jumping. By then Mary was howling tears of pain and outrage, and she subsided on to her knees against the side of the bed.

Vicky stood straight, walked round the other side. 'Now then, Elizabeth,' she said. 'Your turn.'

Elizabeth stopped banging on the door, and slowly turned. 'No,' she whispered. 'No, please. Please, Mrs Lang. It was all her idea.'

'I believe you,' Vicky said. 'So I only propose to give you three strokes. But you will have to have them. You did help her. Come along now.'

Elizabeth stared at her, cast a glance at her sobbing sister, and then slowly crossed the room.

'Bend over,' Vicky commanded, and when she obeyed, hit her three times. Elizabeth exploded into tears, and fell across the bed, body writhing.

'There,' Vicky panted, and picked up the book. She went to the fireplace and threw it in, watched it catch fire and poked it once or twice. 'Believe me, I regret having to do that. But I will be obeyed. When you are eighteen, Mary, I will personally buy you a new copy of that book. And any other that you may choose.'

'You . . .' Mary was still on her knees, still crying and rubbing her bottom. But she had managed to raise her head. 'I am going to have you sent to gaol. I will have Papa do that.'

Vicky realised that it was entirely possible that could happen. So she preferred not to take up the point. But she had never felt so satisfied in her life. She unlocked the door, replaced the key. 'You will both go to bed and to sleep, now,' she said. 'No lights. And I will see you tomorrow morning for breakfast, at seven-thirty.'

'Seven-thirty?' Mary shouted. 'Breakfast isn't until eight.'

'I will arrange with Cook to have yours ready half an hour earlier than usual,' Vicky told her. 'We have a lot to do.'

'But we don't have anything to do, until church at eleven,' Elizabeth wailed. 'We don't have lessons on Sundays.'

'Starting tomorrow, we do,' Vicky said. 'Both before and after church. Good-night, girls.'

She went outside and, closing the door behind her, looked along the corridor to where Alison Dobree and David Whiting stood together; they had clearly been listening.

'You did it,' Alison said. 'You really did it.'

'I intended to do it, milady,' Vicky said.

'By Jove,' David said. 'I do so admire you, Victoria. Really I do. That's what these girls have needed for a long time.'

'I don't know what's going to happen,' Alison said. 'I really don't. But . . .' She gazed at Vicky for several seconds, then threw back her head and gave a peal of laughter.

William Dobree opened the door of the cabin on board the *SS Doncaster* which had been allocated to him as an office for the voyage. He had only reached Southampton an hour ago, well pleased with himself and the command he had been given, if a little apprehensive of Alison's reaction to his being so late, when she and the children had arrived yesterday afternoon; now he had found himself in the middle of an outsize domestic crisis. 'My dear,' he said, ignoring the other people waiting in the corridor. 'Do please come in.'

Alison stepped into the room, clearly not in the best of tempers at having been kept waiting, and glanced at her stepdaughters, who stood together against the bulkhead, holding hands. They had done a lot of holding hands over the past week.

Dobree put his arm round her shoulders. He had, of course, welcomed his wife earlier that afternoon, as soon as he had boarded, but had then been swept up in his daughters' stream of tearful complaints, and thus they had not had a chance to be alone. Now he knew he would have to feel his way very carefully, although as there were faults on both sides his position was a strong one. Much depended on how strong he wished it to be – he had spent a good deal of the past week thinking less of Alison than of Victoria Lang. But either way it was simply a matter of being as masterful with his wife as he was with everyone else.

'What do you think of the ship?' he asked.

'Well . . .' Alison was also aware that they were both sparring for an opening. 'It's not very big, is it?'

'Well, possibly she's not the *Great Eastern*,' Dobree acknowledged, giving her another kiss, 'but she's seven thousand tons. Ample enough to carry us to the Cape. Oh, my dear, I have missed you so.'

'I have missed you too, William,' Alison murmured, possibly genuinely, he felt, on this occasion.

He sat her on the bunk which also served as a settee, and decided to charge. 'Now then, what's all this about your Mrs Lang giving my girls a tanning?'

'*My* Mrs Lang?' Alison inquired, eyebrows arched. She had worked out her strategy with great care.

'You employed her,' Mary snapped. 'And you took her side when she assaulted us.'

Alison looked at the General.

'Mary,' William Dobree said. 'I must ask you to be quiet, unless someone addresses you. You have had your say. Now I wish to hear another point of view.' He smiled at his wife. 'But you did employ Mrs Lang, my dear.'

'I was under the impression you employed her,' Alison pointed out. 'I think she is under that impression as well. In any event, we had no choice, as you well know.'

'What exactly happened?'

Alison shrugged. 'The girls dropped a bucketful of treacle

60

and various other unpleasant things on Victoria's head, and she gave them a good spanking.'

'Ha!' Mary commented.

'It was only a joke,' Elizabeth protested.

'The bucket hit her on the head,' Alison pointed out. 'It could well have done her a serious injury, had she not been wearing a hat. I don't blame her in the least for being angry.'

'She was angry, was she?' Dobree inquired. 'When she attacked the girls?'

'Well . . . I am perfectly sure she was angry. But she didn't show it. She seemed remarkably cool.'

'But don't you think, leaving the question of the beating itself aside for the moment, that the punishment was excessive? Twelve strokes? My God! Mary tells me she couldn't sit down in church next day.'

'Is that why you were squirming about like that?' Alison inquired. 'Good heavens. Well, William, Victoria seemed to have it worked out. She's very methodical. It was six for the bucket, three for Mary's being found reading a book Victoria had forbidden, and three for impertinence.'

'I see,' Dobree remarked.

'And Lizzie only got three, for being an accomplice rather than a principal,' Alison added.

'I see,' Dobree said again. 'Then you approve of what Victoria did?'

'I think that is something we should discuss in private, William,' Alison said.

'You're probably right. I just wanted the girls to hear what you had to say.' He looked at Mary. 'Do you agree with everything your stepmother has told me?'

'I . . .' Mary flushed, but it was mainly anger. 'Anyone would think *we* had done something wrong.'

'I suspect most people do. Now take your sister on deck and try to behave yourself.'

Alison watched the door close. Strategy was over, and tactics were about to begin. She had, in fact, seldom enjoyed a week more, even though she had known it would end in crisis. But to have the girls, once they realised their new governess was not immediately going to be dismissed and imprisoned for assault, so absolutely baffled, and scared; to have the entire staff staring at her with new respect for having employed such a creature . . . and to have Victoria's very experienced assistance while packing up . . . it had all been more an exciting adventure than the calamity she had anticipated.

Of course, now the creature – because she was a creature – would have to go. But she had served her purpose. Alison did not think the girls would ever be the same again; she even felt capable of coping with their moods herself – especially with William around all the time – until she could find a proper governess in South Africa. It was just a matter of establishing that William's support would be forthcoming.

'I'm not sure I approve of what Victoria did,' she said. 'But obviously she had to do something, or leave. As you know, I never interfered in any way with Mrs Chandler's methods . . .'

'Which never included corporal punishment, to my knowledge,' Dobree interrupted.

Alison shrugged. 'I have no idea. I am sure they must have done, if perhaps not so formally or vigorously as Victoria used it. Of course I had no idea what she was going to do . . .' She gazed at her husband with her enormous blue eyes; the man who would dare call those eyes liars would deserve a flogging himself. 'However, I must say that the girls certainly deserved punishment. It was a beastly thing to do, especially to a . . . well, a foreigner. She is a foreigner, you know, even if she speaks English, and they don't have our sense of humour. And then, after it happened, I felt I simply had to support her, at least until I could see you. You do realise that none of this would have happened if you hadn't gone off and left me all alone . . .'

'Yes, yes,' Dobree said wearily. He got up to sit beside her on the settee and hold her hands. 'And how have things been with you, personally, this past week?'

'Oh, perfect,' Alison said. And smiled. 'Well . . . I suppose you could say we have been enjoying an armed truce. Everyone has been waiting on the arrival of the great white chief.'

He raised his eyebrows.

'Oh, that is how they think of you, William. On the other hand, as I have indicated that, failing any directive from you, I proposed to support Victoria's action, the girls have been excellently behaved.'

'I see,' William Dobree said. 'I had meant, did you miss me?'

'Of course I did.'

Perhaps her reply was a shade too quick in coming, but it was what he wanted to hear. 'My darling girl. If you knew how much I missed you.' He took her in his arms, gently massaging the bodice of her gown while he kissed her mouth.

'William!' she snapped, pushing him away. 'You'll have my hair down. And you're crushing my bodice. William!' Her voice rose an octave as his left hand slid down her thigh to raise her skirt past her boots. 'Whatever are you doing? Someone might come in.'

'No one is going to come in,' Dobree said, uncovering her stocking. 'My dearest girl . . .'

'*William!*' She stood up, retreating across the cabin. 'You simply cannot come at me in an office. And in the middle of the afternoon! There is a time and a place for everything, as I am sure you know. Anyway, I had supposed you wished to discuss Lang.'

William Dobree sighed, and returned behind his desk. Once he was seated, Alison cautiously resumed her seat. 'What about Lang?' he asked. 'Isn't the incident closed?'

'That is up to you. However, if you consider she was unduly harsh, or may become a disruptive element, I have no doubt I can keep the girls in order until Cape Town, providing you will promise to support me on all occasions.'

He frowned. 'You wish to let Victoria go?'

'Well . . . do you seriously mean to sit there and have your daughters beaten black and blue whenever this creature feels like it?'

Dobree gazed at her for some seconds. Then he smiled. 'Perhaps I had better have a word with her.'

'I told her to wait outside.'

'Then would you ask her to come in?'

Alison's turn to raise her eyebrows. 'You wish to see her alone?'

'I think it would be best.'

Alison shrugged, got up, and opened the door. 'Will you come in please, Victoria,' she said, and looked back at her husband. 'Do be careful, William,' she said, and closed the door behind her.

Vicky stepped inside and stood before the desk. She knew she was herself looking like a delinquent schoolgirl at this moment, because she very nearly felt like one. And hated herself for it. But she was more nervous than she had ever supposed she would be. Throughout the week she had been subjected to a great deal of varied opinion, from that of the girls themselves, their whispered, 'Just wait until Father hears about it,' to Bestwick's pontifical, 'It won't do, Mrs Lang, I'm afraid it won't do,' to Housekeeper's, 'Someone should have taken a hairbrush to those two brats a lot sooner,' and Prudence's silent sympathy, and Nathalie's bubbling, 'I'll support you, Vicky. To 'is face.'

Most difficult, of course, had been Lady Dobree and David Whiting. David, while endeavouring to flirt with her despite her patent non-interest, especially in her uncertain circumstances, had kept reassuring her that he would most certainly put in a good word for her. As if she wanted a good word. She wanted only an understanding of the situation. While Alison had said, 'Well, Victoria, I simply have no idea what the General is going to say. I did warn you of that. We are just going to have to wait and see.' But she had laughed on the night itself.

Unfortunately, she was not laughing now. And neither was the General, although his face was not as severe as it might have been. 'Sit down, Victoria,' he said.

Victoria perched on the bunk opposite the desk, trying to remind herself that her entire attitude, and all her actions, had been governed by the estimation she had formed of this man's character and frame of mind on the occasion of their first and only meeting. If she had misjudged him, she would be dismissed without further discussion.

'As you probably realise,' Dobree began, 'I have heard exactly what happened from every possible angle. Would you care to add anything?'

'No, Sir William,' she said.

'It is your normal custom to take hairbrushes to your charges?'

'No, Sir William. Is it yours?'

The question took him by surprise. 'I have never laid a hairbrush on anyone in my life.'

'Which has probably been a big mistake,' Vicky remarked. 'However, I had never used a hairbrush either, before last Saturday night.'

'Did you enjoy using it?'

Vicky met his gaze. 'Yes, Sir William. at the time. I enjoyed using it. I had never been so . . . well, humiliated in my life.'

'And so you struck back at my children in blind rage.'

'It was not blind, Sir William.' And it was not all rage, she thought. But that was a subject she was afraid to pursue.

Dobree placed his elbows on his desk, and looked more like a bloodhound than usual. 'You then burned Mary's book, I believe. Wasn't that rather medieval?'

'I hated burning that book, Sir William. It was a horrible thing to do. But as I had forbidden your daughter to read it, and she had so flagrantly disobeyed me, I had no choice. If I am to be their governess, they must obey me.'

'I find you an uncommonly forceful young woman,' he mused. 'One might almost describe you as insolent.'

'I would prefer the word honest, Sir William. I did what I considered to be both necessary and fair and, as I do not intend to apologise for it, I think I had better leave this ship now.' She was burning her boats. But she had to believe he would not let her drown.

'You did what you considered to be necessary and fair,' he mused, again. 'Suppose I were to act on the same principle, Victoria, and put you across my knee and tan your pretty little behind, here and now? That may well be necessary, and it would probably be fair.' He smiled at her. 'And I have no doubt that I should enjoy it, too.'

Vicky sat bolt upright. She had never been addressed like that, in such terms, in her life. Nor had she ever been threatened with physical violence before, not even by the Kikuyu. If he had wanted to surprise her in turn, he had more than succeeded. She felt a sense of shock, a sudden awareness that her analysis of his character might have been *too* accurate – and had not carried her far enough.

She kept her face composed and her voice even, although she could feel the heat in her cheeks. 'I'm afraid I should scream for help, Sir William.'

'As did Mary and Elizabeth, I believe. But none was forthcoming.'

'I should then charge you with assault.'

He nodded. 'That is what the girls wish me to do with you.'

She glared at him. 'I would also scratch out both of your eyes while you were attempting to carry out your threat.'

'Ah. My girls never considered doing that. But then, they have not had the advantage of living in Africa.'

He was laughing at her. She stood up. 'I think I had better go.'

He nodded. 'It's what my wife thinks should happen, certainly.'

Vicky sighed. As she had suspected, Alison's apparent support had been pure expediency. 'You owe me a week's wages, Sir William, but I owe you fifty pounds. I'm afraid I no longer have the fifty pounds.' She looked down at her new gown. 'So . . .'

'So don't you think you should at least work off your debt? I have also paid for your passage.'

She stared at him, uncertain of exactly what she was hearing. *Was* he laughing at her, or was he much more sinister than she had ever imagined?

'We could say, perhaps, ten shillings a stroke. That would require a lot of strokes, wouldn't it? I should hate to damage you. Perhaps we could think of something different, for which you could be more highly paid. What about twelve and six for bare flesh?'

Vicky drew a long breath. 'You are a toad, Sir William Dobree,' she said. 'And . . . more than that. You are married to just about the most beautiful woman in the country, and . . .'

'Beauty is so often skin deep, Victoria,' Dobree remarked, apparently not offended.

Once again she stared at him. Now she was more angry than insulted. Here went all of her dreams, cascading down the drain of a man's lust.

'And I accept', he went on, 'that I was quite unpleasantly rude, just then. I wanted to observe your reaction. I am impressed, Victoria. You are a young woman of uncommon courage and, shall I say, probity. Or was that an act?'

He was trying to mend his fences. 'No, Sir William,' she said quietly. 'It was not an act. Nothing for me is for sale, except my skill as a schoolmistress, such as it is. Now, I think I had better get off this ship before she casts off.' There were bangs and crashes from above her, and the ringing of bells. 'I shall repay your fifty pounds, as best I can.'

'I should like you to stay,' Dobree said.

Vicky shook her head. 'No, sir.'

'As governess to my children.'

'Because you suppose that once we are at sea . . .'

'Because I think that you will be good for them. And because I would like to watch you at work.' He smiled. 'I would just like to watch you.'

She licked her lips. He certainly had the gift of undermining total resolve. 'Sir William . . .'

'I shall not lay a finger on you, improperly, throughout the voyage, Victoria. Or after we reach South Africa, without your consent. I give you the word of an officer and a gentleman. However, I would feel gratified were you to remember our little conversation, and consider that it could be a means to a most lucrative, and indeed pleasant, future for you. My understanding is that at present you have no future at all. So do think about it, Victoria. Meanwhile, you are my children's governess.'

Another smile. 'The situation is not without certain historical precedents.'

She didn't know what to say. She so desperately wanted to make this voyage. And she believed his word; he belonged to the class which would sooner die than break a promise, whatever private vices they might indulge. But just to surrender . . . 'You . . . you are . . .'

'A man who is perhaps slowly realising that he has made a considerable mistake in choosing a partner for the latter half of his life. As I said, one can be fooled by a beautiful face. However, it is not a mistake I can correct, legally, or would even consider trying to correct. You must be very certain on that point: Alison is the mother of my only son. But it is none the less a mistake I mean to alleviate, as much as possible. I need, I have to have, a woman who will respond to me. I propose to find such a woman, and I think you are supremely suitable for the position. If it is not to be you, Victoria, it will most certainly be someone else. Why throw away the advantages, and I promise you they will be considerable, in every sense, which could be yours, at least without considering them very carefully? You have the voyage to do that. Now come . . .' He got up and held out his hand. 'Let us join the family on deck to wave goodbye to old England.'

CHAPTER 4

To the sound of booming sirens, cheers, the beating of drums and the jangling of bells, the *SS Doncaster* was pulled away from the Southampton dockside by her attendant tugs. She was an old ship and in addition to her two funnels she had two masts and could carry a considerable amount of canvas, both for steadying and as an aid to propulsion when the wind was fair.

Handkerchieves and scarves were waved, people shouted farewells into the wintry night. In addition to the staff of several officers, together with their wives, the ship was carrying well over a hundred other ranks as replacements – and these had not been allowed to take their wives with them. Thus the farewells had been tearful. But then, the officers' wives were also feeling tearful; only the General's wife had been allowed to take her children.

And the General's wife was feeling as tearful as anyone, for no good reason, except that she was leaving England. 'Shall I ever return?' she wondered, leaning against her husband.

'You will return in three years,' he said reassuringly, and put his arm round her shoulders. As if to balance himself against the movement of the ship, he put his other arm round Vicky's shoulders, as she was standing on his other side. David Whiting, who had been obviously screwing up his courage to do just that himself, sidestepped as if she were on fire.

Vicky didn't feel tearful at all. She wasn't sure what she felt. It was a curious mixture of elation over her triumph – she knew that Mary and Elizabeth were only a few feet away, watching; of apprehension that she might have jumped with both feet into a situation of which she had no experience and insufficient understanding – in that she had pushed her way into the middle of another family's lives and traumas; and of self-disgust, that she had so accurately discerned William Dobree's character, and so shamelessly taken advantage of it. She should have slapped his face and walked off the ship. She had not done so; she was determined to make this trip, come hell or high water. But she had refused him, and intended to go on refusing him. Indeed, she had no business allowing his arm to be round her shoulders, even if she could pretend it was simply an act of policy, to let the girls see just how their complaints had backfired.

'I think I should go below, Sir William,' she said softly. 'The cold is really intense.' Which was true enough; unlike Lady Dobree, she was not wrapped in a fur coat.

He gave her a little squeeze. 'Of course, Victoria. I shall see you tomorrow.'

Because, even if he would like to get her to bed, she still had to eat in the Second Class Dining Saloon with the rest of the staff and those of the non-military passengers unable to afford First Class fares. Just as her cabin was down in the deepest bowels of the ship, only a few feet above the waterline. And she was sharing it with Nathalie. And, indeed, that was a relief; however much she was prepared to accept Sir William's word as an officer and a gentleman, it was reassuring to know there was no way he could hope to break that word.

It also kept her immune from any ideas David Whiting might have. Because, having charged ahead with total determination to achieve her goal of getting on this ship, she was also now realising that she had placed herself in a quite ridiculously difficult situation, as far as he was concerned. She had no idea of what she was going to do about it, even supposing there was anything she *could* do about it.

It was so easy to start making excuses for the General. Alison Dobree was certainly about the coldest fish she had ever met. And Sir William did love his daughters, probably as much as he loved his wife. But from none of them could he obtain the love he wanted. So, as he had said with perfect frankness, he also

70

needed to love someone else with an even greater intensity, at least physically. How happy Alison would be, were she simply able to give him what he wanted. Vicky was not at all sure what that was, as James had actually wanted very little more than to hold her naked in his arms – she had no doubt that a man like William Dobree would wish a lot more than that.

And he had fallen for her. Or he had supposed she might be the person he was looking for: she thought she understood him well enough to be sure he would not actually allow himself to fall until he was sure of that. On the other hand, she was equally sure that he was an entirely honourable man, according to his lights – which did not include his sexual desires for a member of the lower classes – and that were she to surrender she might indeed be setting herself up for life. As a married man's mistress? That was an impossible thought. She was along for the voyage, there and back. She would tell him so, when they reached Cape Town.

But he was only the greatest of her problems. Alison Dobree, for instance, might prefer not to see anything in life which could neither interest nor be of advantage to her; her husband's peccadilloes perhaps came under both heads. And Alison was certainly aware that Sir William had his eye on the new governess.

Then there was David Whiting, a most charming young man, who had fallen for Vicky quite as heavily as the General, but, lacking the General's worldliness, was afraid even to attempt to hold her hand unless she invited him. And she wasn't going to do that.

Then there were the girls. She no longer had any apprehensions about keeping them disciplined, certainly not with William Dobree's power behind her – but that was hardly the right attitude for a governess. It was not in her nature to approach any task without a determination to do her very best to succeed, and she had an idea that both Mary and Elizabeth could turn out to be quite nice young women, with a little encouragement. They certainly did not lack in character. But clearly it was going to be a hard struggle, made harder by the constant recollection that as she would undoubtedly be leaving their lives forever on arrival in South Africa, was it truly worth worrying about?

Then there was even Nathalie. Nathalie was a treasure. But she was as smitten as either Sir William or David. Vicky, who, if she had never been to Cape Town, had visited both Nairobi and Zanzibar, where despite British efforts the slave trade still flourished, was no more disposed to be morally critical of others than she was to assume rigid religious attitudes – providing those lonely or frightened souls who sought unusual personal relationships left her alone. She could see that Nathalie was a girl who simply had to adore someone, and she obviously thought nothing of either David Whiting or Pressdee the valet – the thought of Sir William had clearly never entered her head – and so Vicky had been elected. It could hardly be a lasting emotion, she was sure, as the French girl would soon realise there were more than a hundred unattached young men down in steerage . . . but for the time being she promised to be something of an embarrassment. After supper she was waiting in the little cabin to brush Vicky's hair, and stroke her shoulders, and comment on the freckles and the beauty beneath. 'It is so exciting,' she said. 'You and me, setting out together . . .'

'It is indeed,' Vicky agreed, donning a heavy flannel nightdress. 'Which bunk do you wish?'

'It is your choice,' Nathalie said.

'Well,' Vicky said, 'do you suffer from sea sickness?'

'Sea sickness?'

'*Mal de mer.*'

'Oh, but I have never been to sea, Vicky.'

'Then how did you get to England from France?'

'By the Channel. On a packet ship.'

'And you think that wasn't exactly the sea. It's a point of view. But it can be pretty rough, in the English Channel. Were you sick on that crossing?'

'Oh, yes. It was terrible. The boat rolled so.'

'Then you had better have the lower bunk,' Vicky decided,

72

immediately erecting the ladder and clambering into the upper. She had never been sea sick in her life.

And indeed there was the answer to all her immediate problems. The weather could hardly be described as bad, in fact it was splendid, with a fresh easterly breeze which enabled the sails to be set and the engine revolutions reduced, and the *Doncaster* seemed to go bounding down the Channel towards Biscay. But bounding was the operative word, and she also rolled from time to time. When Vicky climbed down from her bunk the next morning, having slept soundly, Nathalie was incapable of movement, save to position her head over the chamber pot Vicky had thoughtfully left beside her. 'Oh, dear,' Vicky said. 'Aren't you feeling well?'

Nathalie groaned and showed the whites of her eyes.

'You'll be all right in a day or so,' Vicky said cheerfully. 'I'll bring you down some breakfast.'

A promise which elicited an even more heartfelt groan.

Only Prudence was present in the Second Class Dining Saloon, along with one of the sergeants. 'Poor Pressdee is not going to survive,' Prudence remarked.

After breakfast they went up to the First Class deck together, to find things even worse at this exalted level. Charlie was all right, and anxious to be up and doing; Prudence's day commenced immediately. But both girls refused to leave their bunks, and when Vicky looked in on the Dobrees to warn Alison that Nathalie was *hors de combat*, she found Sir William, in a brocade dressing gown, holding a chamber pot for his wife, who looked as different from her normal soignée self as could be imagined, with her magnificent golden hair scattered on her shoulders and hanging down on each side of her face, and her lace nightdress soaked with sweat.

'Oh, Victoria,' Sir William said. 'Thank God you're up, at any rate. Would you mind summoning Nathalie? I've been ringing since dawn, but there has been no reply.'

'Nathalie isn't feeling well,' Victoria said, deciding against telling him she had disconnected the bell before turning in.

'Oh, good Lord . . .' He hastily turned back to his wife as she

73

retched and vomited. 'Well, look, I just have to get up and see how the men and horses are. You'll have to take over here for a while. Are the girls all right?'

'The girls are feeling sea sick, Sir William,' she said. 'But they are all right. Shall I wait outside while you dress?'

'I'll dress in the other cabin,' he said, for his sleeping cabin adjoined his office.

Vicky took the bowl, allowed him to give her shoulder an intimate squeeze, and put her arm round Alison's shoulders. The door closed behind the General.

'Is Charlie all right?' Alison muttered.

'Charles is as right as rain, milady,' Vicky said. 'Prudence is with him, and he isn't even feeling sick.'

Alison raised her head to stare at her. 'I loathe you,' she remarked. 'Why cannot you be sea sick like everyone else?'

So much for that, Vicky decided. She had no reply to make, could not even risk taking offence, certainly not if it entailed acknowledging that her mistress had a reason for feeling as she did. 'I am sure I appreciate my good fortune, milady,' she said. 'Shall I bring you something to eat?' Because Alison was vomiting green bile.

'Just get out,' Alison muttered. 'Get out and leave me alone, you . . . you creature.'

Vicky obeyed, but none the less returned with a packet of salt biscuits, which the Head Steward recommended for sea sickness. She then obtained another for the girls, and another for Nathalie, and then, exhausted by climbing up and down stairs and ladders, washed out their chamber pots and left them all to it, collapsing in a deck chair on the after well deck.

There was no way she could be sacked now, or, if she could be sacked, they still had to accept her presence as far as Cape Town, and then ship her back again. And she was thoroughly tired of the lot of them; not even Nathalie seemed grateful for her efforts. All she wanted to do was enjoy the movement of the ship, and feel the fresh air on her face, and watch the heaving whitecaps . . . and remember, when she had first made this voyage, with James. They had still been honeymooning, and

74

Cape Town had only been a stage on their journey. They had actually disembarked at Zanzibar, when she had first come into contact with the immense mystery, and tragedy, that was Africa. She had been shocked by what she saw and learned, and heard whispered, and more than a little frightened. Tales of harems and eunuchs, impalements and blood feuds, had not been part of the scene in Plymouth, Massachusetts. But James had been at her shoulder to reassure her, and guide her, and make everything come right. For four short years.

On board the *SS Doncaster*, despite the large numbers of men present all the time, at least half of whom were interested in the titian-haired American beauty, from her point of view there could only be Sir William or David to take her arm on this occasion. And they both had problems enough, with the men and the horses. It was, she supposed, a measure of William Dobree's abilities both as a man and a general, that although he held such an exalted rank, he nevertheless concerned himself with every detail of the men and animals under his command, and took a personal interest in their well-being. Not that he neglected his family, and spent some time each day with his daughters. Less so with Alison, whom he clearly suspected of malingering, after the first few days. In fact Vicky, however much she disliked the woman, knew that she wasn't. She had never seen anyone so absolutely prostrated by sea sickness – Alison Dobree could not even keep down warm soup, and Vicky became very concerned for her health. She felt that the girls were the ones malingering, in that they would come on deck every morning, once Biscay was behind them, and enjoy the fresh air, but the moment Vicky approached them with a suggestion of lessons they were overtaken by violent nausea and had to lie down. However, she never mentioned this to Sir William. If they didn't want to learn, she didn't want to teach them. As far as she was concerned, they could stay sea sick until they reached Cape Town.

Nathalie soon recovered, but was fully occupied with caring for Lady Dobree. 'I don't know what to do,' she told Vicky. 'Everything that goes in comes out again.'

'Well, keep forcing it in,' Vicky recommended. 'She must get her sea legs soon, or she'll die.' But that opinion also she did not confide to Sir William.

After a week of changeable weather, the wind dropped completely. The sails were furled, and the engine revolutions increased as they chugged into a calm sea, leaving a cloud of black smoke behind them to overhang the white of their wake. Now, at last, even Alison was well enough to emerge on deck and sit in a deck chair, wrapped in coats and blankets, face pale but determined, manner distinctly cold, to everyone, but especially to the husband who had inflicted this purgatory upon her. Vicky she never appeared to notice at all.

'I think the old boy made a mistake in forcing her to come,' David remarked to Vicky, standing beside her on the well deck at dusk, to watch the sun slowly drooping towards the western horizon. He had taken to coming down here to look for her most evenings, as of course she was not supposed to venture up into First Class except when on duty. It would have been rather amusing, she supposed, if it were not so potentially embarrassing. Perhaps it was the romance of a sea voyage, but he was considerably less diffident than she had first thought, and she had an idea he might even be working himself up to kiss her, or attempting to do so. Was he then utterly unaware of his employer's interest, and indeed his proposal? Then what would his reaction be were she to tell him? But that, she supposed, might be to go wading in very murky waters.

'She simply is not a traveller,' he went on. 'Although,' he added with one of his flushes, 'I am glad he made the mistake, of course. Had he not, well . . . you wouldn't be here either.'

'And I would rather be here than anywhere else in the world,' she sighed without thinking.

'Would you, Victoria? Would you?' His hand crept along the rail towards hers.

Hastily she corrected her mistake. 'Of course,' she said. 'I am remembering my honeymoon; we made this same journey.'

'Oh,' he said, thrusting his hands into his pockets.

'Lieutenant Whiting, Mrs Lang,' said Captain Brian,

pausing behind them as he returned his evening inspection of the ship. 'Enjoying the weather?'

'There is nothing more beautiful than the sea, Captain,' Vicky said.

'In its best moods,' the Captain agreed. 'But I shall be happy to leave those fellows behind.'

She frowned in the direction of his pointing finger; she hadn't observed the low humps on the horizon before.

'Those are the Canary Islands, Mrs Lang. Reefs and rocks. Best avoided.'

'But as you know they're there . . .'

'Oh, they present no danger, in good conditions. Alas, the glass is falling. We could have a blow in the next twenty-four hours.'

'Do you mean the ship could be endangered, sir?' David demanded.

Captain Brian smiled. 'Good heavens, no, Mr Whiting. This ship, why, I have driven her through a hurricane on the North Atlantic run. No, no. But it will be uncomfortable, I fear.' He winked. 'Not all of our passengers seem to be at home on the deep, eh?'

Here we go again, Vicky thought, as the skies began to fill with clouds and the wind dropped still further, next day. She had been on the point of forcing the issue with the girls to make them start lessons – mainly through boredom – but decided to postpone the idea until the storm was past. Sir William was certainly worried, and paced the upper deck behind the bridge, hands folded behind his back, giving a stream of orders to David. Vicky was summoned to join him there, and he barked at her, 'Tell me what I've forgotten. You must have been in a storm at sea before.'

'Why, yes, Sir William. Ah . . . the horses will undoubtedly panic.'

'I've assigned extra men to their stalls.'

'Well, then, once they're taken care of, we always found that for human beings the best course was simply to proceed as normal.'

77

'We?' he asked.

'My husband and I, Sir William,' she explained.

'Ah. I'd forgotten him.' He went below, mentally damning the dead missionary. He had no doubt that could Victoria just forget about her husband, she would succumb to his offer. And, equally, he had no doubt that would be the experience of a lifetime – and he had bedded women of almost every race and colour in the course of his army service. But Victoria . . . quite apart from her looks and her considerable figure, she possessed at once an air of innocence combined with her streak of what could be called severity, all overlaid with a determination to succeed, which he thought would be irresistible.

Alison was dressing for dinner, her hair being pinned up by Nathalie. 'My dear,' he said. 'How good to see you feeling so much better.' She had not put in an appearance at dinner before.

'I seem to have got used to this beastly motion,' she agreed. 'Will the sea remain calm from now on?'

'Ah . . . I'm afraid not.'

She turned her head so sharply Nathalie gave an exclamation and nearly jabbed a pin into her mistress's scalp. 'What do you mean?'

'When it is this calm, it often means there is going to be a bit of a blow. In fact, the Captain is expecting one.'

'A blow? You mean a storm?' Alison's voice rose an octave.

'Just a gale of wind, my dear. That is Captain Brian's estimate, and he has been up and down this coast several times. Indeed, I remember that the last time I did it there was a bit of a blow. Nothing the least alarming. Rather, well . . . invigorating.'

'Nathalie,' Alison Dobree said. 'Do get out.'

'But, madame, your 'air . . .'

'Oh . . . damn my hair,' Alison shouted.

Nathalie hurried from the cabin.

'There is no point in getting upset, my dear,' Dobree said, reassuringly. 'These things do happen, at sea. But this ship is certainly able to withstand a gale of wind, believe me.'

'You', she said, pointing, 'insisted I come along on this

cooped-up floating coffin. Do you know how ill I have been these last ten days? I thought I was going to die. I . . .'

'I knew you weren't well, my dear,' he protested.

'Did you? I can't imagine how. You have hardly spent enough time in here to know I was on board.'

Dobree sighed. She was clearly in a mood. 'Well, I do have my duties to attend to and . . .'

'You mean that if I am not in a fit condition for you to . . . to . . .' It came as something of a shock for her to realise she had never actually put it into words before.

'To make love to,' he suggested.

'Love? Is that what you call it?' she remarked, bitterly. 'It has never appeared to be a very loving act to me.'

'That is because you have never allowed yourself to enjoy it,' Dobree pointed out, patiently. 'However, my dear, believe me, I have not stayed away from you because I love you any the less, or desire you any the less, for being unwell. To be frank, the sight of you being sick, and even more, the smell of it, made me feel ill myself, and I had to consider the effect on the morale of the men, were it to become known that their commanding general was prostrated.'

'Do you really expect me to believe that?' she stormed, her brain a seething mass of alarm at the thought of the approaching bad weather. 'Isn't the real reason that you've found enough to occupy your time with that . . . that American savage?'

He regarded her with genuine surprise. 'That is entirely untrue, Alison,' he said. 'I think you owe Mrs Lang, and myself, an apology.'

'Ha,' Alison remarked.

William Dobree had not won the Victoria Cross for nothing. 'I insist upon it,' he said.

But Alison, having discerned that her husband had after all a considerable share of the average man's weaknesses, was not disposed to surrender. 'I shall not,' she declared. 'She should have been sacked in Southampton. And you know that.'

'I know nothing of the sort,' Dobree snapped, at last beginning to get angry himself. 'I do know that perhaps I should follow her example with the girls, and put you across my knee.'

'Just try it,' she suggested, and pulled the pins from her hair, without indicating whether she intended to use them as weapons. 'I shall not, after all, come down to dinner tonight, William. Have them make me up a tray.' She smiled at him. 'You can send it up with Mrs Lang. We may as well give her something to do.'

'Here we are, milady.' Vicky placed the tray on the table in the day cabin of the General's suite. If she disliked intensely being used as a lady's maid, she realised there was little she could do about it, and she had the pleasure of understanding that, as Dobree had put it, her ladyship was upset about the prospect of a storm.

But Alison did not look particularly upset. She had changed her gown for a negligée, and lounged on the settee berth. 'What rubbish are they serving us tonight?' she demanded disagreeably.

'Chicken broth, to begin with, milady. Followed by smoked ham.'

The *Doncaster* had carried a stock of live animals from Southampton, but after ten days at sea the chef was down to his last few chickens. Thus it had become time to break out the smoked food.

'My God, what a banquet,' Alison remarked.

'There is some nice wine as well, milady,' Vicky said, pouring a glass.

'Well, that's something. Is there really to be a storm?'

'I believe so, milady.' Vicky waited to be dismissed.

'But I suppose you have been through so many storms at sea you are not in the least concerned.'

'I think everyone has to be concerned about storms at sea, milady. But they are seldom dangerous to well-found ships.'

'Oh . . .' Alison sat up, violently, drank some wine. 'Get out. I can serve myself.'

'Yes, milady.' Vicky reached for the door handle.

'Wait,' Alison commanded. 'Are you my husband's mistress, Lang?'

Vicky turned, slowly.

'Don't trouble to deny it,' Alison said.

'I do deny it, milady,' Vicky said, speaking with careful composure. 'Your husband has never laid a finger on me, improperly.' She stuck out her chin. 'No man ever has.'

'Indeed? Were you not married? Or is that also a lie?'

'It is not possible for a husband to touch his wife improperly, milady,' Vicky pointed out.

'You would think that. Well, do not suppose I am fooled by your lies. Go on, get out.'

Vicky hesitated. She really wanted to slap Alsion's face, but supposed that would be going a shade too far. Certainly, she felt tempted immediately to find Sir William and tell him she accepted his offer. But that was too irrevocable. She contented herself with saying, 'Milady, you can depend upon it, that were I Sir William's mistress, I would not be dancing attendance upon *you*. Good-night.'

She closed the door behind her and leaned against it, panting with anger. But it was not only anger, of course. She could honestly put her hand on her heart and swear that the General had never touched her . . . but he had made plain his wish to do so and she was still on this ship. More than that, he had made plain his desire to betray his wife, with *someone* . . . and she had not betrayed him. And what if she did really wish to be persuaded it might be worth while? How dreadful of her. Indeed, how guilty of her. Because the thought was there, all the time, twisting in her mind, and building on additional thoughts that would have been present anyway, that why should such a languid, insincere, self-centred creature as Alison Dobree enjoy so much which she had done so little to deserve, while she . . . truly, she was setting out to plunge directly into hell. All because of a determination to see Africa once again.

'She is frightened,' Nathalie said wisely, as they lay in their bunks and listened to the slurping of the waves against the ship's hull. Only gentle waves at the moment, but there had been none at all last night. 'But I am frightened too. Will it be very bad, Vicky?'

'No,' Vicky told her, 'it will not be bad at all. It will be exciting, Nathalie. Exhilarating. You will never forget it.'

'Ooh, là là,' Nathalie said. 'I do not wish to be exhilarated, that way.'

She was even less exhilarated next morning, by which time the wind had risen. Vicky suggested she remain in bed; clearly everyone else who could was going to. The exceptions, as usual, were Prudence and herself. By now the wind was coming in sharp gusts, each gust accompanied by a heavy rain squall, which made it quite impossible to go on deck. The seas had become lumpy as well and the ship occasionally lurched without warning; keeping Charlie from falling down left Prudence fully occupied – the little boy seemed quite impervious to sea sickness.

Vicky made her usual visits with biscuits and tea and soup, and was pleased to note that the girls seemed genuinely frightened; she told them that it was likely to get worse before it got better. She and Alison exchanged no conversation at all, Alison not even replying to Vicky's 'Good morning, milady'. Perhaps, Vicky thought, she is ashamed for her outburst of last night. But she doubted it.

She saw little of the General or David, who were making their rounds to check that all was well below. The other officers had their duties as well, and only one of the ladies, Mrs Mainwaring, the wife of the adjutant, stout and fortyish and very composed and dignified, appeared at all. Numbers in Second Class were also again limited, with Pressdee once more prostrated, and only a handful of the non-service men and women – making their way to the Cape for a variety of business and domestic reasons – putting in an appearance. Because, as Vicky had warned the girls, it did get worse before it got better. By that night the wind was blowing above forty knots, which made it more than just a gale, and the seas were enormous, crashing into the bows, flying high into the air as spray which even came down well aft, and also flooding along the decks. Vicky, venturing out into the aft well deck for a breath of fresh air at dusk as usual, was immediately driven below again to avoid a soaking.

The storm continued for three days, reducing the Second Class dining establishment to just Prudence and herself. But on the third evening the wind at last dropped below thirty knots, and the seas began to subside. There were no more people for dinner that night, but after the meal, David, for the first time since the blow had begun, managed to come down to find her, looking very smart in his duty uniform of red jacket and blue trousers, with a blue peaked cap, but also extremely weary and somewhat concerned. 'I wish I had more confidence in the old man,' he confessed.

'In the General?' Vicky was shocked, having assumed David regarded the General almost as a second father.

'No, no, in Captain Brian. I'm positive he doesn't have any idea where we are, although he pretends he does.'

'But . . . what about his instruments and things?'

'Do you know anything about navigation?' David asked.

'I'm afraid not. How seamen tell their position out of sight of land has always seemed magic to me.'

'Well, I'm not a seaman, but I've done a lot of yachting,' he said. 'We use a chronometer to tell us the exact time difference between where we think we are and Greenwich, which gives us our longitude, and a sextant to measure the height of the sun, or one or two selected stars, above the horizon, which gives us our latitude. Where the longitude and latitude lines cross, that is the position of the ship. Unfortunately, you have to be able to see the sun or the stars to measure their height, and because the sky has been totally overcast for the past three days, the captain hasn't been able to take any sights at all. That would be bad, but there now seems little doubt that our chronometer has been malfunctioning since we left Southampton, so he's not too sure of our longitude either. In addition to all that, because of the weather he hasn't even been able to take soundings to establish whether or not we've been pushed closer to the African shore than we should be. With the wind so strong from the west I would say that is very likely. The result is that he's operating entirely on dead reckoning, that is, his calculations of drift and windspeed, rather than actual observations, and those calculations could very well be wrong.'

'Well,' she protested, 'he is a very experienced master, and this is a very empty ocean.'

'It isn't all that empty, you know. There's the Cape Verde Islands, just for example. He swears they're still several hundred miles to the south of us, but he doesn't *know*, and here we are, crashing along like a runaway coach in a fog . . .'

She squeezed his hand, the first time she had ever done that. 'We'll survive,' she said.

He flushed. 'I'm sorry, Victoria. It's just that . . . to think of anything happening to you, well . . .'

She squeezed his hand again. 'Nothing has ever happened to me, David. So probably your best bet is that nothing will happen to me this time, and the Captain will bring us safe through.'

'Oh, Victoria, you are such a brick. I say . . .'

He was getting worked up. But she had done her bit, and she was even less inclined to flirt with him while he was apparently scared stiff. 'I'm going to turn in,' she said. 'Why don't you do the same?'

She felt her way down the companion ladder to the lower deck, where the Second Class cabins were, hanging on to the handrail for dear life as the ship lurched from side to side. She reached her cabin and pulled the door open, replacing it on the hooked latch; this left it able to rattle, but she did not like closing and locking doors at sea in bad weather – they could jam.

'Oh, Vicky,' Nathalie groaned. 'Oh, Vicky, I am so ill.'

'It'll soon be over now,' Vicky assured her. 'The wind is dropping all the time.'

Undressing was a long, slow business, as she had to hold on with one hand, even when sitting down to remove her boots. But finally she got everything off, leaving her clothes strewn around the cabin, and dropped her thick flannel nightdress over her head. It was the sort of weather when flannel seemed most appropriate, and she had worn this one since the storm began.

'Oh, Vicky,' Nathalie groaned. 'Could I 'ave a glass of water?'

'Surely.' Vicky filled it from the tap on the washbasin, handed it to her, waited, holding on and swaying to and fro, while she drank it.

'I am so thirsty, all the time,' Nathalie said.

'That's the vomit. I wish there was something I could give you.'

'You are a treasure,' Nathalie said, lying back with a sigh. 'So strong. I do not know what I should 'ave done without you. I will tell you, though, when they decide to come back, I will travel by train, even if I 'ave to cross Africa.'

Vicky smiled, and kissed her on the forehead. 'I have an idea you may not be the only one. Good-night, now.' She could switch off the electric light from her bunk, so she placed the ladder and clambered up, hand over hand, every lurch of the ship threatening to throw her against the bulkhead. She got one knee on to the mattress and gave a grunt of relief . . . and was hurled into space as there was an ear-splitting crash which brought the *Doncaster* to an abrupt halt.

Vicky never knew what she hit on the way down. She discovered herself lying on the carpeted floor of the cabin, with things still falling on top of her, amongst them Nathalie, who was uttering a continuous high-pitched scream. And the light had gone off, so that it was utterly dark for a moment. The bulb glowed again, and she could sit up, discovering in the process that both her right shoulder and her left hip were most painful, suggesting she had been thrown to and fro as she fell. She gazed at the utter chaos; it seemed as if everything in the cabin had been torn loose, excepting only the bunks. The drawers had fallen out of the bureau and their clothes were scattered, the ladder had collapsed, the basin had half torn itself out of the bulkhead, the cabin door had burst free of the latch and was swinging backwards and forwards . . . and the corridor outside was filled with men and women, shouting and screaming. Elbowing her way through them was Prudence, a Brünnhilde-like figure in a dressing gown, with her brown hair in two long

85

plaits. 'Mrs Lang,' she shouted. 'Vicky, are you all right?'

Vicky saw other people staring at her, and realised that the skirt of her nightdress had risen around her thighs. Hastily she pulled it down and scrambled up. Nathalie clung to her arm, weeping and moaning. '*I'm* all right,' Vicky gasped. 'But what happened?'

'We must have hit something,' Prudence said. 'I think –' She was interrupted by the jangling of an alarm bell.

'That's the call to boat stations,' someone shouted. 'Quickly, to the upper deck!'

'Water!' screamed someone else.

Prudence and Vicky stood together in the cabin doorway and watched a thin stream of water seeping across the floor of the corridor, in the same moment as they realised that the ship had a list to port.

'Oh, my God!' Vicky muttered. Her brain seemed numbed by the implications of catastrophe.

'Master Charles!' Prudence snapped. 'I'll see you on deck, Vicky. And hurry, do.' She ran back into the corridor, once again pushing people left and right.

Vicky wondered at her dedication to duty, even as she turned back into the cabin.

Nathalie had let her go and slumped to the floor again, swaying and moaning. 'I must get back to the bed,' she groaned. 'Oh, I 'ave broken a rib. I know it. You will 'ave to fetch the doctor.'

Vicky knelt beside her, thrust her fingers into the French girl's nightdress, massaged her ribs. Nathalie screamed in pain, but Vicky could find no evidence of anything broken. She grasped Nathalie's shoulders and shook her. 'You're only bruised,' she said. 'Now, listen to me. We are going to drown if we don't get on deck. We must hurry.'

'Drown?' Nathalie asked. 'Drown!' she screamed.

Vicky slapped her face, as hard as she could; Nathalie gasped and fell over. Vicky located her dressing gown amidst the rubble and wrapped the stricken girl in it. Then she found her own and pulled it on. She couldn't find any slippers. She pulled Nathalie to her feet and pushed her at the door.

'Aaagh!' Nathalie screamed as the water, now ankle deep, surged around her.

Vicky half pulled and half carried her towards the now steeply sloping stairs. Most of the other people had already left and they were unimpeded as they made their way upwards, passing only two stewards who were checking the cabins to make sure they had all been evacuated. Their ears were filled with the constant jangling of the alarm bell and a terrifying grinding and grating from beneath them, and, worst of all, a frantic neighing and stamping from forward, where the horses were confined.

They reached the First Class Saloon, which was empty, and thence gained the promenade deck, which was absolutely packed with people, shouting and screaming, rushing to and fro, knocking each other over, cursing at each other, begging for help, issuing irrelevant commands. But as Vicky and Nathalie arrived there were several crisp cracks as revolvers were fired into the air, and the panic was momentarily stilled.

'Now listen to me,' William Dobree bawled, using a speaking trumpet and standing on the lower rungs of the bridge ladder, the better to be seen. He was an odd sight, for over his brocade dressing gown he had strapped his service revolver. But his face was composed and very strong. 'This ship has struck a rock, but the pumps have been manned and there is no immediate danger. Listen to me,' he shouted, as the noise began again. 'Purely as a precautionary measure, we are swinging out the lifeboats. Women and children will go to the boats. There is nothing to be afraid of. Each lifeboat will be fully crewed, and you will be in no danger. Soldiers fall in on the upper deck and await orders. Ladies, kindly report to the boats. Now then, there must be no panic. Move in an orderly fashion.'

The calmness of his voice had a soothing effect. But as the deck lights had been switched on Vicky could see that he had taken the precaution of mounting at least one armed soldier beside every boat.

'Come on,' she told Nathalie. 'Women and children. That means us.' She pushed her way into the throng, making for the nearest of the boats; they had not actually been allocated a place in any of them. Then she heard her name called.

'Vicky!'

She turned, and looked at the General, who had come down from the ladder.

'Vicky!' He held her shoulders, and brought her against him. 'Listen to me. I want you to go with my wife and family in number one boat.'

She gazed at him. 'Very well, Sir William. But shouldn't you do that?'

His smile was twisted. 'I cannot leave the ship, as long as a single member of my command remains on board.'

'But . . . if there is no danger . . .'

'Vicky . . .' He held her tightly against him. 'This ship is going to sink, very soon,' he whispered in her ear. 'Half her bottom is torn out. There is no hope for it.'

'Then you *must* get into a boat . . .'

'Vicky,' he said again. 'There are six boats. Each will carry twenty-four people. That is one hundred and forty-four. There are two hundred and ninety-five souls on board.'

Her head jerked. 'Oh, my God,' she whispered. 'Oh, my *God!*'

'So I want you to go with my wife and children, Vicky. Look after them. God knows, they are not capable of looking after themselves. Do this for me, Vicky, I am begging you.'

'But . . . you . . .?'

He kissed her on the mouth. 'I am going to think of you, for as long as I can. Hurry now.'

CHAPTER 5

For a moment Vicky stood absolutely still, almost unaware of the people jostling around her, of the noise, or even of their danger. She had not been kissed on the lips since James had done so, the day before he had died. She felt a sense of shock, and also one of humility. She had dismissed this man as a lecher – but even lechers could be heroes, and know their duty.

He held her arm, took Nathalie's as well, and pushed them through the crowd. 'Make way there,' he shouted. 'Make way.'

'Over here, General Dobree,' David Whiting called. He stood by the rail, still wearing his uniform – because, Vicky realised, it was actually less than an hour since they had sat together in the Second Class Dining Saloon. But he also had a revolver strapped to his waist, and looked ready to take part in an old-fashioned battle. He was guarding the approach to the number one lifeboat, which had already been swung out, and was filled with people; Vicky saw Alison, clutching a shouting Charlie against her, Prudence nearby, her, Mary and Elizabeth, all wearing nightclothes and looking utterly shocked and almost incredulous of what was happening. Then there were several other women, all wives of the officers who had made up Sir William's staff, and six seamen, clutching the oars.

'You'll take two more,' Sir William shouted.

'We're full,' one of the women objected. 'Lower away.'

'Halt there,' William Dobree snapped at the sailor manning the falls. 'Lower this boat before I say so and I'll put a bullet through your brain. Over you go, Victoria.'

He lifted her to sit on the rail. She swung her legs over, clutching at the skirt of her nightgown as it flew in the breeze.

David held her other arm to steady her.

'Oh, not *her*,' Mary Dobree remarked loudly. 'Put her with the crew.'

William Dobree ignored his daughter. 'Now, Victoria,' he said.

Vicky looked down, at the surging dark water, some twenty feet beneath her. Only twenty feet, where the height from this deck was usually forty. The *Doncaster* was sinking, and fast. Two of the seamen were reaching out for her. She thrust herself forward and they caught her arms as she felt herself falling, spread her across the gunwale while two of the women seized her legs and tumbled her, breathless, into the boat.

'Don't leave me, Vicky,' Nathalie screamed. 'Oh, please don't leave me.'

Vicky, trodden on by the women, jostled as they squirmed and shuddered and shouted, turned her head in alarm.

'Nobody's going to leave you, Nathalie,' Sir William said, and held her round the waist to swing her also on to the rail.

'Aaagh!' Nathalie screamed, legs kicking as she looked down, but already two of the seamen had grasped her as well, and she was dragged on board to land beside Vicky.

'Lower away,' Sir William commanded.

The men hesitated. 'We must have an officer in command, sir,' one of them said. 'That's the rule. Each boat must have an officer in command.'

Dobree turned his head left and right, seeking someone to send, but as he did so the ship gave a terrifying lurch and there was another grinding sound from beneath them. Then the lights went out, plunging them into total darkness. Instantly there was a fresh chorus of screams and shrieks of fear.

'David,' Dobree snapped. 'Get on board.'

'Me, sir? I can't leave you.'

'This is an order, David. You've done some sailing in your time. Take command of that boat, now.'

'Sir, I must respectfully . . .'

'God damn it!' Dobree shouted. 'That is my wife and children there. Get on board, sir, or I will have you cashiered!'

David hesitated only a second longer, then grasped the falls and swung himself into the stern of the boat.

'Lower away,' Dobree ordered.

The ropes ran through the blocks.

'William!' Alison shouted. 'William! Come with us. For God's sake, come with us.'

'Daddy!' shrieked Mary and Elizabeth. But already the boat was plunging down into the darkness, striking the water with a splash and a jar which threw the people on board about; the General's face was lost above them.

'Pull,' David commanded. 'Pull away.'

'We must stay by the ship,' Alison shouted. 'We must stay.'

'We must get away from her,' David insisted. 'Or we could hit the rocks ourselves. Pull, God damn you.'

He had not said, or we'll be sucked under when she goes, Vicky thought. But the men understood that well enough, thrust their oars into the water and heaved their backs to drive the boat away from the lee of the ship and into the still turbulent seas. The two girls screamed, and some of the other women called out the names of their husbands. Vicky held the sobbing Nathalie close as the boat surged into the darkness. Within seconds the *Doncaster* itself was lost to sight.

'Check your oars,' David commanded. 'But keep the bows up to the wind.'

For the seas, smaller than they had been at the height of the storm, were still big enough to send spray flying over them all, and even green water slurping over the bows, to a constant chorus of cries from the women sitting forward. But the boat lost way, pointing into the wind, and the motion became less violent. It was impossible to tell how far from the sinking vessel they had gone.

'Where is the ship?' Alison cried. 'Oh, where is the ship?'

'Over there, ma'am,' replied one of the men. Vicky stared into the darkness. She could not see anything, but she could still hear the dreadful noises, and the screams of the people left on board and those still trying to gain the lifeboats.

'You'll stay here, David,' Alison said. 'You'll stay here, until we find the General.'

'Of course,' David agreed, and left the tiller to crouch in the bottom of the boat, shading the wind with his body while he struck a match and lit the oil lamp with which every lifeboat was provided. It glowed immediately. 'Send this up to the bow,' he said. 'Careful now, don't drop it.'

The lantern was passed from hand to hand, while Vicky felt a sudden surge of confidence, seeping across her fear. Only a little earlier she had supposed him afraid, and she had always considered him something of a wet. But his voice was calm and confident, and he seemed to know what he was doing. Just as he had been quite right to doubt the Captain's instruments and his ability. They could only have struck a rock because they were off course.

And now *she* was the one afraid. As with the bucket falling on her head, she had never envisaged anything like this ever happening to her. She had been in several storms at sea. The first time she had been frightened, the second time less so, and after that she had taken gales in her stride, with total confidence in both captain and his instruments. But this . . . out in an empty ocean in a small boat with twenty-four terrified people . . . but there were only twenty-three terrified people. Thank God for David Whiting.

'Now they'll know where we are,' David said, as Mrs Mainwaring, in the bow, placed the lantern on the short foredeck and held it there. 'There's one of the others.'

Another light began to bob on the water, and then another. By now lanterns had also been rigged on the *Doncaster* itself, delineating the outline of the sinking ship.

'It's so far away,' Alison complained. One thing about being totally terrified, Vicky thought: it left no room for sea sickness. That would come later. But it was terribly cold, for the latitude. No doubt that too was a combination of shock and fear, and insufficient clothing.

'We're being carried away from her,' David agreed. 'Pull, lads, take us back up to the ship.'

'What about those rocks?' someone asked.

'We didn't hit any drifting down,' David reminded him. 'We'll hardly hit any going back now. Besides, they're well below the surface, or we'd see breakers. They won't trouble us, we don't have enough draught. Pull, now.'

Reassured, the men obeyed, and the boat began to move back towards the glowing lights. Which suddenly went out again, at the same time as there was a tremendous noise, like a train racing out of control.

'What's happened?' Alison shouted.

Mary Dobree screamed.

'It's a squall,' David snapped, and leaned on the tiller. 'Keep pulling, lads. we must maintain her bow to the wind.'

Any idea of regaining the ship was abandoned, and the boat turned directly into the wind and rain, which came rushing out of the Atlantic to smash at them. A wave broke on the bow, and Mrs Mainwaring gasped as the lantern was torn from her grasp and went overboard. But it no longer mattered; the teeming rain had blotted out all the other lanterns as well. Now the seas were again very big. The boat rose high in the air, and then fell with a crash into the following troughs. Water flew over the bows and slurped over the sides, while the wails of the terrified women rose even above the whine of the wind.

'We're taking a lot of water,' one of the seamen gasped, as he pulled on his oar.

'We must bail her out,' David shouted. 'Vicky, where are you?'

'Here,' she said; she was only a few feet from him.

'Take this.' He pushed a bailing can into her hands. 'Who else is there?'

'I will help her, Mr Whiting,' Prudence volunteered, crawling aft. The water was already up to their thighs as they knelt, but they thrust their cans in and began emptying them over the side, hampered by the other women who were trying to draw their feet up to stop getting wet and by the oarsmen to either side, who were pulling as hard as they could to keep the boat from turning broadside on to one of the steep waves which were assaulting them.

Vicky had no idea how long the squall lasted. She threw water over the side, was met by more coming in, which, added to the now pouring rain, soaked her to the skin – but at least she could open her mouth and let the fresh water splash on to her lips. She was hit in the face by an oar clutched in a man's fist, and trodden on by a woman falling off her seat, but ignored them all and kept going, because there was nothing else to do, and because anything was better than doing nothing. Only dimly she became aware that the rain had stopped, and that there was less water coming on board.

'Relieve Mrs Lang and Miss Brown,' David said. 'Come along, ladies, we're all in this together.'

Two of the other women took the bailing cans from Vicky's and Prudence's fingers; Vicky's arms felt like lumps of lead. 'Nathalie,' she said. 'Are you all right, Nathalie?'

Nathalie groaned from the bilges, where she was lying in a sodden heap, half in and half out of the water. Vicky pulled her straight.

'Where's the ship?' Alison shouted from the bow. 'Where's the ship? Where's my husband?'

They peered into the darkness; there was nothing to be seen in any direction, and the sky was again totally overcast.

'She's gone, lady,' one of the seamen said.

'Be quiet,' David snapped. 'We seem to have lost sight of her for the moment, Alison.'

'We must find her,' Alison screamed. 'We must find Sir William.'

David steadied himself as he stood up, to stare into the darkness. Then he looked down at the little compass embedded in the transom of the lifeboat, its betel light giving off a faint glow. He chewed his lip. To search for the ship meant pulling back out into the Atlantic, as they had clearly been swept to the east by the squall. For all his reassuring words to the seamen, there was always the risk of encountering the reef; he couldn't be sure all the heads were sufficiently far below the surface not to take the bottom out of even a lifeboat. But at the same time he couldn't abandon the General, and his comrades, as long as there was a chance they could be alive. 'We'll hold her here,' he decided.

'Here?' Mary Dobree cried. 'What about Father?'

'We can do nothing until daybreak, Mary,' David said.

'None of us can. We have to make absolutely certain where we are, first, otherwise we might just go rowing off in entirely the wrong direction. We'll hold our position here, until daybreak. It can't be too far off.'

It was, in fact, several hours off. The longest several hours Vicky had ever experienced up to that time. Their only solace was that there was no more rain and that the wind, and therefore the sea, steadily dropped. The men rested on their oars, only pulling to the west every fifteen minutes or so, when told to do so by David, who continued to peer into the darkness and every so often cupped his hands and called out . . . but there was never a reply.

The sodden women huddled against each other and shivered and sobbed, only occasionally crying out. Prudence went forward again in search of Charlie, and Vicky sat against Nathalie, with her arms round the French girl, so that they could exchange body heat. Nathalie was again being sick, and in fact there were several women vomiting, from the noises. Dawn! Vicky kept thinking, dawn! But what would dawn bring, save despair?

The darkness faded, but it seemed to grow colder. She raised her head and looked up, and realised that the skies had quite cleared; it was going to be a beautiful morning. She looked aft. Amazingly David still wore his cap, and apart from the salt stains on his red jacket might have been ready for inspection, save for the light growth of beard on his chin. And he stared into the dawn as well.

She held on to Nathalie's shoulder and stood up, every bone and muscle seeming to be glued to every other. There was only the occasional whitecap now, the sea having settled down to a quiet blue-green, and the wind dropped to hardly more than a dozen knots. It was a steadily warming wind, too, as the sun rose above the eastern horizon, a majestic red ball which seemed to seek and then find the lifeboat, and send its rays directly over the tiny floating object. Because they were alone. The realisation took some time to penetrate her consciousness. As she slowly turned her head she expected constantly to see one of the other lifeboats, or the *Doncaster* itself, or at least the reef they had struck. But there was nothing. Absolutely nothing.

'Jesus Christ!' remarked one of the sailors, also looking around him.

Other heads were raised.

'Where's the ship?' Alison asked. 'Where's the ship?' She might have been a cracked gramophone record, Vicky thought, and now her voice rose an octave. 'Where's my husband?'

David sighed. 'The ship must have foundered during the squall,' he muttered.

One hundred and fifty-one men, supposing all the lifeboats had been filled, Vicky thought. But none of the other lifeboats were to be seen, either. And there had also been quite a few horses. And the remaining chickens. And the ship's cat. But she kept thinking of the soldiers, drawn up on the deck, waiting there with perfect discipline until the water had closed over their heads. William Dobree would have been standing in front of them, reassuring them to the last.

As Alison was now realising. 'Oh, my God!' she screamed. 'They're drowned. Oh, my God!'

But William Dobree had not been thinking of his wife when he took his last breath, Vicky thought; he had been thinking of *her*. She felt ready to burst into tears.

'Calm her, for God's sake,' David snapped, and Prudence put her solid arms round her mistress's shoulders, passing Charlie for the moment to his stepsister Elizabeth, who seemed totally bemused.

Everyone else looked at each other. The dawn was serving to make the enormity of their plight the more obvious. Fourteen women, two girls, and a little boy, all wearing sodden and in some cases torn nightclothes, their hair loose and damply plastered to their scalps – even Alison looked like a rag doll, but she was at least securely clad, for over her satin nightdress and its matching silk negligée she wore her fur coat. The rest of them . . . Vicky looked down at herself, and thanked God for having chosen a flannel nightgown, but she had lost the cord for her dressing gown and the sailors were staring at her. Again she thought, thank God for David Whiting.

'Gone,' Mrs Mainwaring said. 'All gone.'

'Shouldn't we see the other boats, Lieutenant?' asked one of the seamen.

'We must have become separated during the night,' David said.

'Or they sank in that squall as well,' someone muttered.

'They're not there,' one of the women wailed. 'Nobody's there. What are we going to do, Mr Whiting?'

David stared at Vicky, who stared back.

'William,' Alison moaned, rocking against Prudence as if she was a child. 'William.'

The other women wept silently; they had each lost a husband.

The seamen gazed at David.

Who squared his shoulders. 'Well,' he said. 'We must do the best we can. Now then, this lifeboat is fully equipped, I have no doubt . . .'

'The other boats,' said one of the seamen. 'If they're still afloat, they can't be far.'

'They're probably just over the horizon,' David agreed. 'They'll turn up, I have no doubt.'

'They might hear you, Mr Whiting, if you was to fire your gun.'

David frowned, and then nodded. 'That's a good idea.' He drew his revolver, and fired twice into the air. One of the women screamed. 'Now let's all be quiet,' he said. 'Listen.'

'I'm so thirsty,' Elizabeth said in a loud whisper.

'Me too,' Mary agreed. 'And . . . Prudence . . . how do we go?'

Prudence looked at Vicky.

'Hallo,' David shouted, flushing with embarrassment. 'Hallooooo.'

There was no response. Meanwhile the sun rose higher and they could feel themselves begin to steam. It was going to be a hot day.

'Ah,' David commented, holstering his revolver. 'I'm sure they heard the shots, and will be rowing this way. Meanwhile . . .' He surveyed the bedraggled company before

97

him. 'First of all, as I was saying, this is a well-equipped lifeboat. There is food and water in this locker.' He tapped the wooden box beneath the transom. 'Now, who has the key?'

'Only officers have the keys to the boats' supplies,' said one of the men.

'Ah,' David said again. 'Well, then, we shall just have to break it open. I would prefer not to shoot the lock, because I might puncture one of the water cans. Your knife.' He looked at the nearest seaman, who promptly handed over the knife which hung from his waist. David inserted the blade into the hasp of the padlock and began to exert pressure.

'I simply have to go,' Mary told Prudence, still in a loud whisper.

'We all do, miss,' said one of the women.

David stopped working to gaze at Vicky in something close to panic.

Vicky sighed. She just wanted to close her eyes and pretend she wasn't there. But Sir William had asked her to look after his family. She made herself think. 'You'll have to call all the men aft,' she told David, 'and tell them not to look.'

'Oh, quite,' David agreed. 'Come on, chaps. Leave your oars. In fact, you can ship them.'

'Ladies to the bow,' Vicky said, as cheerfully as she could, while trying to drag Nathalie up.

'Just leave me 'ere,' Nathalie groaned. 'I am going to die.'

Vicky decided to abandon her for the moment. She made her way forward, clambering over thwarts, falling against people. 'All right,' she said, brightly. 'Who's first?'

'I suppose you've done this sort of thing before as well, Lang,' Alison remarked.

'No, milady, I have never been shipwrecked before,' Vicky told her. 'But what we have to do seems obvious. You first, Mary, as you seem the most desperate. Sit over the bows and pull your skirts up.'

'You must be quite mad,' Mary said. 'Pull my skirts up, in front of . . .' She looked aft, at the men, who were ostentatiously turning their backs.

'No one is going to look at you,' Vicky promised her.

'Well . . . I'll fall in.'

'No, you won't,' Vicky assured her. 'Prudence and I will hold your hands.' She looked at Prudence, who nodded, plump cheeks filled with embarrassed determination.

'Oh, really,' Mary said. But as Vicky had estimated from her own condition, the girl was desperate, and crawled forward to do as she was directed, hitching up the skirts of her nightdress and dressing gown and then extending her hands so that Vicky and Prudence could grasp each one.

The nightdress promptly collapsed around her again, the hem trailing in the water.

'Oh, God damn it,' Vicky said. 'Liz, come here and hold your sister's skirt.'

Liz handed Charlie to one of the women and obediently came forward.

'If you imagine for one *moment* that I am doing that, you are mistaken,' Alison announced.

'Suit yourself, milady,' Vicky said. 'But it's now or not at all for the next twelve hours.'

'Oh, you . . .' But Alison allowed herself to be persuaded to follow one of the other women, although they had another task to persuade her to take off her mink coat. Mary held her stepmother's skirts for her, and Vicky discovered that Lady Dobree had legs just as perfectly shaped as the rest of her, sheathed in the palest of translucently white skins. How Sir William must have supposed he had achieved the ultimate in wives, when marrying this!

' Only you left, Elizabeth,' Vicky said, when all the women had been accommodated, including a weeping and retching Nathalie and a bemused Charlie.

'I can't. I simply can't,' Elizabeth protested, looking aft. Because the men, if apparently intent upon relieving themselves, with considerably less trouble, were nevertheless casting surreptitious glances forward.

'You must,' Vicky insisted. 'If this is as intimate as we have to get, you've nothing to worry about.'

Elizabeth sighed, and obeyed.

'Now,' Vicky said. 'Who's going to help me hold Prudence's wrists?'

'Oh, you go next, Mrs Lang,' Prudence said.

'Very well.' Vicky looked around. 'We still need a volunteer.'

'Well,' Mrs Mainwaring said. 'I'll . . .'

'Oh, I will do it,' Alison announced. 'After all, I employed you, didn't I?'

She grasped one of Vicky's wrists, and Prudence grasped the other, while Mrs Mainwaring held her skirts, and Vicky sat over the gunwale, realising for the first time how very difficult it was to do something like that in such circumstances, aware that twenty-three other people were at least listening. Then there was a sudden scream from Mary, and Alison let go. Vicky all but tumbled overboard and was only saved by Prudence's grip on her right wrist. She swivelled right round, frantically kicking her legs to keep them out of the water as she still sat on the gunwale, watching a huge grey shape, at least as long as the lifeboat, it seemed, sliding past only two feet from her bottom.

'Jesus Christ!' remarked the sailor who had made the same comment earlier.

Vicky felt inclined to agree as Prudence tumbled her into the bottom of the boat.

'Ah, he's already breakfasted,' said one of the other men.

'Oh, *God!*' Alison screamed.

One of the women burst into tears.

'That was a bloody stupid thing to say,' David snapped.

'I was thinking of the horses, sir, honest I was,' the man protested.

'All right,' David said. 'He won't trouble us, anyway. Just ignore him, ladies, and he'll go away.' He had prised open the lock, and now revealed three small casks of water, and two of biscuits. 'Now then,' he said. 'You and you, take these casks forward. One cup of water per person. Remember, one cup. And one biscuit. I'm sorry, ladies, but that is the ration until we reach land.'

'Land!' Nathalie shouted. 'Oh, where is it?'

'Not far,' David said reassuringly. 'Have your breakfast.'

Vicky sat beside her, as far as possible from the bow. She was still shivering, could still see those inert shark eyes staring up at her, coldly unfeeling but part of the most dreadful, deadly machine on earth.

'I'm sorry I let you go, Lang,' Alison said. She sat immediately in front of them, with Prudence and Charlie; Mary and Elizabeth were next. 'I was really frightened.' She sounded surprised, as if she had never actually been frightened before in her life.

'Forget it, milady,' Vicky said. 'I guess maybe he wasn't hungry, at that.'

'I don't like biscuits,' Charlie announced as the sailors reached them, 'unless they have jam on them. I'd rather have porridge.'

'There isn't any porridge, dear,' Prudence said. 'And these are very special biscuits. Just try one for today.'

'They'll break his teeth,' Alison grumbled, peering at her food.

'They're *awful*,' Mary said.

'Try nibbling,' Vicky suggested.

'Oh, go away and leave me alone,' Mary snapped.

'She hates you,' Elizabeth pointed out, not very helpfully.

Vicky left them to it and clambered aft to sit beside David.

'Are you all right?' he asked.

'You tell me. I can't see the colour of my hair, but I'm sure it's white.'

'It looks fine to me,' he said. 'So do you. It was my fault; I never saw that blighter coming until he appeared. I thought they were always supposed to show a fin or something, as they circled before attacking.'

'They only behave like that in books,' she said. 'David . . . what are we going to do?'

'Ah,' he said. 'I hate to admit it, Vicky, but I suspect we're the only survivors. When that really sinks in to those women . . .' He sighed. 'But it's my duty to make sure that we do survive. So . . . there's a mast secured there –' he pointed to the spar, strapped to the starboard gunwale, 'with its sail already bent on. I propose to step it as soon as everyone has eaten and then head due east. The wind is still out of the west so we should make good time. And we know there's land over there.'

'But how far is it?' Vicky asked. 'Can we really do it?'

'Of course we can. It can't be much more than fifty odd miles, by my reckoning. We *were* too close. Look at the colour of the water.'

Vicky looked over the side with an effort; she was afraid of seeing that shark still there, waiting for his next meal. But he seemed to have gone for the moment. And the water was no longer the deep blue of the ocean but distinctly tinged with green.

'We must be well over the continental shelf,' David said.

Vicky nodded. 'I'm glad Sir William made you come along.'

'So am I,' he agreed, and smiled at her. 'Vicky, I'm sorry Alison and the girls are being so difficult. It's just that they're terrified out of their wits and trying not to show it. Nothing like this has ever happened to them before.'

'Oh, yes,' Vicky said, 'I know that. And they've just lost a husband and father. Don't worry, I won't bite them. I won't even let them fall overboard.' She went forward again. Why should I hate them? she asked herself. He wasn't thinking of them when he drowned, he was thinking of me. She didn't suppose any woman could be offered a greater compliment than that.

The seamen stepped the mast, happy to be able to ship the oars. The sail was sheeted home, and instantly the lifeboat seemed to awaken, sweeping to the east at a good speed, judging by the wake bubbling away from the stern and the little flurries of spray from the bows.

'I would estimate we're making four knots, at least,' David said buoyantly. 'Why . . . we'll be there by tomorrow morning.'

'Where?' asked Mrs Mainwaring.

'Ah, well, Africa.' He gave another bright smile. 'That's where we're supposed to be going, you know.'

'Isn't he amusing?' Mary confided to Elizabeth. 'You'd think he was in the Navy, really you would.'

Nathalie stared over the side. 'I'm going to die,' she moaned. 'Oh, I know it.'

One of the women still wept, from time to time.

'Charlie,' Alison begged. 'Do sit still. Come and sit beside me.'

'I'm bored,' Charlie said. 'And it's so hot.'

Because suddenly it was, as the sun rose and seemed to hang directly above their heads. Now the flannel became a positive oven, and Vicky could feel sweat trickling down her shoulders. The men had completed the bailing and the bilges were now dry; even her bare feet were hot.

'Pretend we're on a picnic,' Prudence suggested. 'Come on, let's swat all the flies.'

'There aren't any flies,' Charlie pointed out, devastatingly.

'Then we're very fortunate, aren't we?' Prudence countered, illustrating why she was such a treasure as a nanny. 'I know what we'll do: we'll play trains. Wagon.'

'Numbskull,' Mary Dobree said.

'It wasn't your turn,' Charlie shouted. 'Why do you always have to spoil anything? It wasn't your *turn*.'

'All right,' Mary said. 'I withdraw numbskull. You say something beginning with "n".'

'I can't think of any,' Charlie shouted, and burst into tears.

'I know,' Prudence said. 'We'll give Mummy a turn. Milady?'

'Oh, Prudence,' Alison sighed. 'Prudence . . . are we . . .?'

'Of course, milady,' Prudence said. 'Mr Whiting says everything will be all right.'

'Noodlegut,' Mary suggested.

'That's not a word,' Elizabeth objected. 'That's slang.'

'I didn't mean it as a word,' Mary told her. 'I was thinking of David. He's a noodlegut. Fancy having him in charge of us.'

Elizabeth giggled. 'You'd better be careful what you say. If he's the captain, he could have you flogged.'

Thank God for David, Vicky thought, and closed her eyes.

It was the best thing to do, and as the day wore on most of the women followed her example, sinking down into the bilges to sit leaning against each other, heads on the gunwale. They were all exhausted from lack of sleep, anyway, and in addition were suffering from shock and from a physical endeavour far beyond anything they had ever experienced. They were afraid, and thirsty, and as the day wore on, hungry. But it was the thirst which was the most difficult to bear.

'David!' Mary called. 'When can we have another drink?'

'Not until this evening, I'm afraid, Mary.'

'Oh, you are just ridiculous,' she snapped.

'This evening,' he repeated firmly. 'Or when we sight land. There'll be a drink for everyone when we sight land.'

'I'm so thirsty,' Elizabeth wept. 'So thirsty.'

'Well, stop complaining,' Alison told her. 'I'm sure David is doing the best he can. If you'd talk less you wouldn't feel it so. David . . .' She directed her voice aft. 'This land we're coming to . . . there won't be any stupid formalities about getting ashore, will there? I mean, Charlie has simply got to have a hot bath right away. So have I,' she added as an afterthought.

David gazed at Vicky with his mouth open.

'I'm sure of it, milady,' Vicky said.

The afternoon wore on. Even the children at last subsided into silence, as the sun grew hotter and hotter. Vicky made her way aft to sit beside David; she could see him drooping over the tiller. 'You must be exhausted,' she said. 'Can't you hand over the helm?'

'To whom?'

'Well . . . I'll have a go.'

'I don't really think . . . have you ever helmed a boat?'

She shook her head. 'But you can't sit there until you collapse. We'll need you when we reach land.' She forced a smile. 'To arrange hot baths and things.'

'Um,' he said. 'Well . . . try it.'

He waited for her to grasp the tiller, and then released it. She was unprepared for the pressure, and the helm went up, causing the boat to swing to starboard and a wave to slurp against the side, sending spray flying inboard. There was a chorus of shouts and complaints from the women.

'Oh, really, David,' Mary called. 'Now is no time to be playing games with your lady friend.'

'Bring her back,' David said quietly. 'You'll soon get the hang of it.'

As she did, after about ten minutes of surging about. 'Say,' she remarked, 'it's rather fun.'

'The best fun in the world,' he said, sleepily, and closed his eyes, having sat in the bilge to rest his head against her knee. She wondered if he really meant what he said.

Alison came aft, Charlie having gone to sleep in Prudence's arms. People grunted and grumbled as she held on to them to climb over the thwarts. The silk and satin really left very little to the imagination, but she had apparently decided to ignore the risk of anyone looking too closely at her – just as she had spent her life ignoring everything else which could possibly be unpleasant – and allowed her long white legs to gleam in the sunlight as she crossed each seat in turn: the heat had forced her to abandon her mink.

'Please don't wake David, milady,' Vicky begged. 'He's exhausted.'

Alison sat beside her on the transom. 'Victoria Lang to the rescue,' she remarked.

'I'm doing the best I can, milady,' Vicky said. 'Would you like to have a go?'

'Me?' Alison's eyebrows, the only remaining immaculate part of her, made that famous arch. 'Thank you, no.'

Well, then, be quiet, Vicky thought. But she didn't say it.

Alison gazed at the sea. 'Do you think Sir William is dead, Victoria?'

Vicky turned her head in surprise. 'I have no idea, milady.'

'If he is not dead,' Alison said, 'then where is he?'

'He could be anywhere. That squall . . .'

'I think he's dead,' Alison said. 'In fact, I know it. I'm a widow.' She made a brief noise which could have been a laugh. 'Just like you, Victoria.'

Vicky sighed. 'If Sir William is dead, milady, then there are twelve widows on board this ship. Prudence and Nathalie are the lucky ones.'

Alison did not speak for several moments, then she asked, 'Were you his mistress, Victoria? Surely you can tell me, now.'

105

'I was not his mistress, milady.'

'But he wanted you to be,' Alison persisted. 'For God's sake, I saw how he looked at you.'

Vicky sighed again. But what did it matter? 'Yes, milady,' she said.

'And you refused him? Why?'

Vicky turned her head to look at her. 'Because . . .' It was too absurd to be sitting here in a nightdress after having spent some fifteen hours in the company of seven men, still wearing that same nightdress, and now say something like, "I am a respectable woman". 'I guess I didn't love him, milady,' she said.

'Love,' Alison said bitterly. 'My God! He wanted *you*, when . . .' Her voice tailed away.

'When he already had you. But a man needs to do more with a woman than just look at her, milady. And shall I tell you something? I'm sorry now that I didn't say yes to Sir William. He was a very brave man.'

Alison stared at her, then without a word she got up and made her way forward again.

Vicky awoke David at dusk, so that he could dole out another ration of biscuits and water. Then it was time for another toilet drill, which left her utterly exhausted. At least this time there were fewer complaints – and no sharks to be seen. Then she went aft again, and sat in the bilges at his feet.

'You are being the most perfect brick,' he told her.

'They're all being perfect bricks,' she answered. 'I at least have some experience of living rough, while they have none. Even Alison is being a brick, I think.'

'Yes,' he said, thoughtfully, and she wondered if he *had* been asleep that afternoon.

'David,' she said, 'where exactly in Africa do you think we'll come ashore?'

'Oh, God knows. If the skipper was right in his position, then we're about five hundred miles north of Cape Verde. But I'm damned sure he wasn't right. So . . .'

'There's going to be nothing there, then?'

'Not a lot. Nothing good for us, at any rate. Are you scared?'

'Aren't you?'

'Not as long as you're around. Is that silly?'

'Believe me, the feeling is mutual, as regards you. But David, what are we going to do?'

'You mean, when we get ashore?'

She nodded. 'They all think our troubles will be over. But . . .'

'You and I know they'll just be beginning. For example, it's going to be the edge of the Sahara Desert.'

'Only the edge, David. When I was in Kenya, I spoke with men who had crossed the desert.'

'Unfortunately, we don't have a caravan, and we don't know where the oases are.'

'These men weren't with caravans, and they were far from oases. They were escaped slaves, some of them. David, it can be done.'

'Cross the desert?' he asked. 'This lot? With water for maybe two days? And a few biscuits?'

'Hush,' she said. 'If the men I spoke with were telling the truth, it can be done, with nothing. There is life in the desert, David, and water – if you know where to look. And in any case, we don't have to cross the desert itself, I'm certain. David, I teach Geography. I'm sure I can remember the physical map of West Africa. Cape Verde is in the tropical rain belt. That stretches about one hundred miles north of the cape, then there are about two hundred miles of open grassland, where there is water and food. Then there is the desert. But even that is a slow process, a slow changing of the grassland into the wilderness. I'm sure, if we were to head south, we would come to food and water in a day or two. If . . . if we went on rationing the biscuits and water we have, we could make it.'

He chewed his lip, staring into the darkness. 'You're still talking about walking several hundred miles, Vicky, before we get near any civilisation. And even if we get through the desert, there's the tropical rain forest, and snakes and wild animals, and the Ashanti . . .'

'What is the Ashanti?' she asked.

'The natives down there. They're officially under British rule, but I wouldn't rely on it. And they're a fairly unpleasant people, or they can be, when they feel in the mood. But just the walk . . . several of these women have no shoes. *You* have no shoes.'

'I have tough feet,' she said. 'And what's the alternative? We can't just sit on the beach and wait to be rescued. We'd bake, and we've only enough water for a couple of days, and no ship is going to close this shore, anyway.'

He sighed. 'You're right, Vicky – as always.'

'They won't like the idea,' Vicky said. 'You'll have to *make* them do it, David. You're in command. You simply have to make them.'

'Yes,' he said, and grinned. 'My first independent command. I've dreamed of that. Sixteen women and a little boy.'

'And six men,' she reminded him.

'They're probably the worst of our problems,' he said thoughtfully. And looked down at her. 'Vicky . . . did you really . . . well . . .' His face was lost in the darkness.

'I didn't think you were quite asleep,' she said.

'I didn't mean to eavesdrop,' he apologised. 'I couldn't help it, sitting right there. And when you told her you had refused . . .'

'I did refuse, David. I wasn't prepared to become anybody's mistress. Not even a general's. And not even for a fortune.'

'You're *such* a brick,' he said. There was silence for a few minutes, but she knew he was working up his courage, and then his arm went round her shoulders. 'Vicky . . . if we come through this mess . . .'

'When, David,' she told him. 'It has to be when.'

'When,' he agreed.

'Let's talk about it then.'

'Makes sense,' he agreed again, but he was disappointed. She rested her head on his shoulder, and listened to the gentle slurping of the water, and swish as it passed the hull, the occasional sough of the breeze, the rumble of distant thunder, steadily growing louder as the night grew darker.

Thunder! 'Oh, God,' she said, sitting up. 'Not another storm?'

'I've been listening to it too,' he said. 'But there's not a cloud in the sky.'

She looked up. He was right; every star was visible, although there was no moon. 'Then what is it?' she asked. 'Do you think . . .?'

'Yes,' he said. 'I think it's surf.' He stood up, peering into the gloom.

Others had heard the noise too. People began to sit up and chatter. 'That's surf, that is, Mr Whiting,' said one of the seamen.

'Surf?' Alison called. 'David, what does that mean?'

'It means we've reached land,' David replied.

'Land!' someone shouted.

'Land!' someone else screamed.

There was such a chorus of noise accompanied by sudden movement that the boat rocked dangerously.

'Please settle down,' David said. 'Come on, now, ladies.'

The racket subsided.

'I can't see anything,' Alison complained, peering to the east.

'You'll see it at dawn,' David promised her.

'But that's hours away. Why can't we go in now?'

'Because there may be rocks in the surf. A reef. As a matter of fact . . . unstep the mast, you fellows,' he decided. 'We'd better not get any closer until we can see what we're doing. We'll just drift about here until daybreak.'

The seamen obeyed, while the women muttered at each other and tried to get out of their way.

'You said we could have a big drink of water when we sighted land,' Mary Dobree reminded David.

Vicky squeezed his hand.

'Ah . . . I think we'd better wait until we get ashore,' David said. 'It won't be long now.'

'Oh, you . . . you liar,' she shouted.

Gradually the excitement subsided, and the boat was quiet again. But now people actually slept, the sleep of relief.

'Well,' Vicky whispered. 'We got to stage one.'

'Yes,' he said. His arm was back round her shoulders.

'We are going to make it, David,' she said. 'I know we are.'

'We must,' he said, and looked down, while she was looking up. Their lips touched, and hers parted, while she felt the stubble of his beard tickling her chin. His tongue came against hers. No, she told herself, this mustn't happen. We have problems enough without adding personal feelings. But she didn't move, and felt his other arm go round her to hold her closer yet, because with the boat drifting he could release the tiller.

How comforting he felt, and how long it was since she had been held in a man's arms. She realised that for all her fine words, she could give herself to this man right now, if they didn't happen to be hunched on a narrow transom with twenty-two people within touching distance. So no doubt she should thank God for the narrow transom and the twenty-two people.

She dozed in his arms, and had an erotic dream, and awoke to find her left breast cupped in his hand, through the nightgown. Another first in more than a year. But she didn't want to move. This was as attractively compelling a man as she had ever known, once he took off the over-civilised veneer imposed by Eton and Sandhurst.

David Whiting? He would want to marry her. He already did. She wondered what Lady Dobree would say to *that!*

The hand left her breast, and he sat up; she realised that the darkness was fading.

Other people were stirring.

'Now, then,' David said. 'There is a lot to be done before we go in. First of all, toilet drill and breakfast.'

They moved like a well-oiled machine now, and even with some eagerness, although Mary still wished to grumble. 'There *is* going to be proper food and something decent to drink, once we get ashore?' she asked.

Everyone ignored her; they were too busy looking for a first glimpse of the land. As was Vicky, her heart seeming to slow. Because they couldn't see any land at all. In front of them the calm sea, for the wind had dropped even more during the night, stretched for perhaps two miles, glinting as the sun rose above the horizon to send its light swathing past them. But then the sea seemed to get higher, rising up and up and up. She couldn't see over the top of the rise, but even from behind she could see that it curled up there, while she listened to the enormous crashes that came from beyond, and watched the spray tossed high into the air further still in the distance.

'Jesus Christ,' remarked the sailor fond of that expletive.

Vicky looked at David, watched his mouth settle into a hard line.

'Is that a reef?' she asked in a low voice.

He shook his head. 'No. According to the pilot book there is no reef on this coast. But the book also says that landing for small boats is impossible because of the continuous, heavy surf . . . unless the crews are experts.'

'Are ours?'

'I don't think any of us have tried it before.'

'Oh, my God,' she said. 'Can we do it?'

He looked down at her. 'We have to do it, Vicky. Or stay out here and die of thirst.'

She realised that he had known what he was up against from the moment he had made his decision to steer east. And had confided his apprehensions to no one, indeed had given a superb exhibition of total confidence. Maybe, she thought, they did teach something of value at Eton and Sandhurst.

Now he was looking from face to face, as all the faces were looking at him. 'It might just be a little bumpy going in,' he told them. 'So I want you to listen to me very carefully. I want all the women to sit in the bilges, as close amidships as you can. And I want you all to hold on to each other. You too, Vicky,' he said.

The women slowly obeyed, sitting shoulder to shoulder in the bottom of the boat. Alison, face pale but determined, held Charlie in her arms, Prudence beside her ready to grab the little boy should anything happen. Mary and Elizabeth held hands. Vicky sat next to Nathalie, took the French girl's hand in hers.

'I am so frightened,' Nathalie said. 'I am sure we are all going to die.'

Vicky didn't reply; the French girl was only uttering what was uppermost in everyone's mind, even if most of them were not aware of the extent of the danger. They could still see that the surf was very high. And they did not know what lay beyond.

'It's going to be tricky, Mr Whiting,' remarked one of the crew.

'It's simply a matter of keeping sufficient way on the boat, and thus controlling her at all times,' David assured him. 'Now, then, lads, pull slow and easy until I give the word. Then I want you to give us everything you've got. All right?' Again he looked from face to face, trying to instil something of his own determination into their spirits. He nodded. 'Give way.'

The oars dug into the water, and the lifeboat moved forward. Crouched in the bilges it was impossible to see for sure what was happening. Vicky's eyes were on a level with the gunwale, and she could only see the calm water, first flowing by, then seeming to move with them and gather pace. She could feel it picking up the lifeboat and sending it surging forward.

'Now!' David shouted. 'Now! Give way! Row as hard as you can.'

The men panted and thrust their oars into the water while David strained on the tiller to keep the boat straight. The lifeboat gained even more speed, and now seemed to be going up and up and up, straight for the sky, while the roaring sound surrounded them and blotted out even thought. Vicky stared at foaming water to either side, her stomach suddenly left behind as they surged down a deep green valley, with another mountain rearing in front of them. But the roaring still surrounded them, and now caught them up again as, even with the best efforts of the oarsmen, the boat began to slow in the approach to the next swell. She looked aft – and had to check a scream. The mountain of foaming surf they had just swept through was towering above them, ten, fifteen feet in the air, curling over, about to smash down on them.

David had seen it too. 'Pull,' he bellowed. 'Pull, God damn you to hell! Pull, you bastards!'

Vicky gasped in surprise at his bad language, the vehemence in his tone. But it was too late. The wave was now hanging immediately above them, and then it broke.

CHAPTER 6

Vicky was aware of being crushed beneath several tons of water as the wave landed on the boat. She seemed to go straight down, still seated in the bilges, knowing she had let go of Nathalie's hand, feeling other arms and legs hitting her own. Then she was going up again, rolling over and over. Her eyes were open, and she looked into a world of tumultuous green and white, streaked with red-gold; she realised that her hair was clouding about her face. Her lungs were bursting, and she was seeing stars before her eyes when her head broke the surface and she could gasp for breath, twisting from side to side, seeing nothing but foaming white water for a moment, then an arm, sticking up several feet away. Instinctively she turned towards it, thanking God that James had insisted she learn how to swim, and then went down again as the undertow got to her.

To her amazement her feet struck sand. She straightened, and found her head was actually out of the water. She was gazing out to sea, taking huge breaths . . . and staring at another monster wave, even higher than the last, towering above her, toppling over.

'Oh, God!' she gasped, and took another breath, before the water crashed on to her. Once again she struck the bottom, this time with her whole body, was swept up and again rolled over several times, hitting the sand again and again. All the breath was knocked from her lungs and she inhaled salt water, gasped and choked as her head again broke the surface, found herself kneeling, but being dragged backwards by the force of the undertow.

But she was only in three feet of water. She couldn't possibly

114

drown in three feet of water! She hurled herself forward, fell full length in the foaming surf, struggled back up again, digging her fingers into the sand, which oozed away from her. Then she was struck a violent blow on the back, and once again was rolled over and over. But this wave, having already broken, was an assistance. It drove her further up the beach and left her there, scattered on the sand. She gasped, and rolled on to her back, gazing up at the bright blue of the early morning sky, feeling as if she had just been trampled on by a horse. She listened, to the roaring of the surf . . . and then to a scream. At least one scream.

Panting, still dizzy, she pushed herself up, stared at the great waves breaking on the beach, sending clouds of spray high into the air – and at people, struggling to survive, as she had done. She scrambled to her feet, ran down to the water's edge, seized an arm and pulled one of the women clear; she did not even know her name. Then she ran to and fro, heart pounding, a succession of terrifying thoughts racing through her mind, with David uppermost – and gasped in horror as she saw a little body floating face down.

She flung herself into the surf, was bowled over by the next wave, but regained her feet, clutching Charlie in her arms. She didn't know if he was dead, could think of nothing to do save grasp him by the ankles, hold him upside down, and shake him as violently as she could. Water gushed from his nose and mouth, and he gave a cry of fear and discomfort. She staggered up the beach, still holding him by the ankles, laid him on the sand. 'Breathe,' she begged. 'Breathe!'

Charlie began to cry.

'Vicky . . .' Prudence came up the beach, tripping and falling to her hands and knees as her sodden nightgown wrapped itself round her legs; her pigtails flopped together in front of her face. 'Oh, Vicky! He was knocked from my arms. Oh, Vicky . . . is he . . .?'

'He's alive,' Vicky told her, and went back down the beach. She saw two sailors dragging at something, realised they had hold of Mary Dobree, all arms and legs and drifting dark hair and swirling nightgown, pulling her clear, saw too Elizabeth floundering in the shallows immediately behind her sister. But she was alive and would gain the shore. She saw another body rolling over in the surf and ran to it, recognising it as Mrs Mainwaring. She seized an arm to pull the woman out, tripped and sat down heavily in the shallows, got up again, tugging Mrs Mainwaring behind her. But the woman wasn't making any effort to help. Vicky ran out of breath, knelt beside her and rolled her on to her back. She looked down on those normally composed features, which were now twisted in the agony of fighting for life, unsuccessfully.

'Oh, God,' she gasped, realising that for the first time that Mrs Mainwaring was unlikely to be the only one.

There was Nathalie . . . 'Nathalie!' she screamed, her voice lost in the roaring of the surf. But Nathalie was nowhere to be seen.

And David! She got up again, and saw the lifeboat, submerged to its gunwales, but kept from actually sinking by its kapok bags. It was still some forty feet from the shore, and clinging to it was a blur of red.

'David!' she screamed, and ran into the water. She had reached waist depths when the next wave knocked her down. She went under, had her arm seized to drag her back to the surface, discovered one of the seamen standing beside her. He was the one whose sole contribution to the shipwreck so far had been 'Jesus Christ'. She thought that if he were to say that now she'd kick him in the groin.

'You'll drown, Mrs Lang,' he said.

'David!' she screamed at him. 'Lieutenant Whiting!'

David was still alive, and the boat was coming closer, while he continued to cling to it. She realised that he couldn't swim. And he was a yachtsman. But lots of sailors couldn't swim. Only last night she had wondered at the confidence with which he had steered them towards the shore, knowing of the ordeal which awaited them. What then could she make of the courage of a man who had accepted that ordeal as their only chance, knowing that if he went overboard he was finished?

'David!' she shrieked, and discovered that she had been joined by several of the men, while even Alison was standing ankle deep in the surf, willing David to make the shore. Alison! Vicky hadn't given her employer a thought to this moment, but Alison had survived, however effete she might like to appear, and stood there like some primeval goddess, wet hair plastered to her neck, wet clothes plastered to her body, silhouetted against the rising sun behind her.

But now was not the time to start thinking about Alison. Only David mattered. 'Let go of the boat,' Vicky shouted at him. 'We'll pull you out. Form a chain,' she told the men. 'Form a chain.'

Someone grasped her right hand, another her left. The sailor who had been first to join her went ahead, cautiously pushing into the water. Vicky was second, then another man, then the others, stretching back to the shore; Alison watched them.

David saw them coming, and released the boat. He disappeared beneath the surface, but came up again immediately; his feet had touched the sand. More confidently he came towards them, and Vicky watched another of the huge waves rearing above his head. 'Look out,' she screamed, and then lost her voice in horror. Because carried in the tumbling surf was the boat, rolling over and over, bearing down on the helpless figure beneath it.

They watched the wave break. The lifeboat disappeared in the foam for a moment, as did David. Then the boat came back up, smashed into several pieces from hitting the sand, bobbing about. And so too did the red jacket.

'There!' Vicky screamed. 'There he is!'

The seaman let her go and plunged into the water. None of the others seemed disposed to help him, so she herself followed. David's head came up, his fair hair drifting, his face suffusing. The seaman grabbed at him to raise him higher, and David screamed with pain and went under again. Now Vicky was also up to him, seizing his other arm, feeling him writhing and fighting her. 'David,' she begged. 'It's Vicky. We're trying to help you.' She endeavoured to pull him towards the shore, but another wave broke on them and drove her away. Again she was tumbled over and over, but felt a sudden freedom she did not understand, as she came back up, standing, shaking water

117

from her hair as she saw him again, in the shallows, the seaman still beside him. Once again the man dragged at the officer, and once again David jerked convulsively, and screamed. But he was out of danger now. Vicky stumbled through the shallows and fell to her knees beside him, gasping and spitting. 'Is he alive?' she shouted.

The seaman stared at her as if he was seeing a ghost.

'Is he alive?' she screamed again, and put her arms round David's head to cradle it and lift it from the ground. He moaned and moved his head against her breasts. Her naked breasts. But at the moment it didn't register. She watched air bubbling from his nostrils together with the last of the water. 'Oh, thank God,' she cried. 'Thank God!'

'He's alive, ma'am,' the sailor said. 'But he's hurt awful bad. But you . . .'

'Victoria,' Alison said, standing above her. 'I really must protest.'

Vicky raised her head, frowned at the woman. Alison was taking off her dressing gown. My God, Vicky thought, she's gone nuts.

'You'll have to use this.' Alison said.

Vicky looked down at herself, and leapt to her feet in panic. She was naked. She could vaguely remember losing her dressing gown when she had first gone in – it had not seemed important. She could also remember hearing a ripping sound when she had first been rolled up the beach, to suggest that her nightdress had been torn. That hadn't seemed important either. But it had been ripped right off her when she had been trying to help David. 'Oh, my God!' she gasped.

'Quite,' Alison agreed. 'My dear, people are staring at you. You really are quite indecent.' She wrapped the silk dressing gown round her; if it was a tight fit at the bust it was far too long and trailed on the sand. 'This really is *most* inconvenient,' Alison remarked, looking down at herself. 'This satin is quite absurdly sheer. But William did like me to wear it.'

Vicky could only stare at her, watch her stroke damp yellow

curls away from her neck; Lady Dobree, she thought – being Lady Dobree.

She dropped to her knees beside David again and gazed up at the sailor, who had been staring at her in turn but now had the grace to blush. He was a young man, certainly younger than herself by a good many years, she estimated; big and strong, he had a friendly face which even after two days had not sprouted much in the way of bristle. 'What's your name?' she asked. She thought it was important to know that, as he obviously now knew her so very well.

'Bream, ma'am,' he said. 'Harry Bream.'

'Well, Bream, you have to help me,' she said, and grasped David's arms.

Immediately David, still only half conscious, moaned and writhed. But his eyes were open. 'Vicky,' he muttered. 'Vicky,' he shouted.

'I'm here, David,' she said. 'I'll take care of you.'

'Ma'am, he's bad,' Bream said.

'He seems to have broken his leg,' Alison remarked.

Vicky looked down at David's legs, which were still submerged. But even through the water she could see the horrible shape of his left which seemed bent at right angles to itself. 'Oh, my God!'

'Jesus Christ!' Bream added, reverting to type.

'We must . . . oh, God,' she gasped again, and seized his shoulders. 'David . . .' She didn't know what to say. 'We must get him up to the beach. Milady . . .'

Alison raised her eyebrows, hesitated, then took one of David's wrists. Bream took the other and they dragged him clear of the water, while he writhed and shouted. 'No!' he screamed. 'Oh, God!'

'Just hold on,' Vicky begged. 'Hold on.' She tried to tear his trousers, found she couldn't. Bream leaned forward with his knife, and began to cut the blue serge, exposing the leg from the ankle to the thigh.

'Oh, really,' Alison commented, as she looked at his white drawers. And then lower. 'Ugh!'

119

They could all see the splintered shin bone pushing its way through the blue-tinged flesh, while blood oozed on to the sand.

'We must set it,' Vicky gasped.

Alison and Bream gazed at her.

Vicky scrambled to her feet, holding the dressing gown close, and stared at the people on the beach. She didn't know how many there were, whether they too had seen her naked, and she didn't care. They were people, and they could help. 'Help us,' she shouted at them. 'Listen . . .' She pointed at the sailors. 'You, and you . . . find the oars. They must be around somewhere. Bring in the remains of the lifeboat. I need two pieces of wood. For God's sake, *do* something!'

They began to move, uncertainly, but yet responding to her vehemence. She dropped to her knees again. 'David . . . it's going to be awfully painful.'

He nodded, panting.

'He's going to have to be held, ma'am,' Bream said.

'I'll help you, Victoria,' Prudence volunteered, kneeling beside her; she had given Charlie into the care of one of the other women.

'Oh, what a mess,' Alison commented, but she too dropped to her knees beside David's head. 'Can you do it, Victoria?'

No, Vicky thought. I can't. The pain is going to be unbearable. She drew a long breath. 'Yes, milady,' she said. 'If you'll help hold him. Bream, you help her ladyship.' But she needed other people to hold his leg, as well as Prudence. 'You . . .' She looked at one of the women who had come closer.

'Oh, my heavens,' the woman said, staring at David's leg. Then she fell to her knees and vomited.

'Someone,' Vicky screamed.

Mary Dobree knelt beside Bream. She too had lost her dressing gown but she still had her nightdress. Her black hair clouded her face, but the face itself was determined. Vicky had never doubted her courage.

'He's going to fight us,' Alison pointed out. David was already fighting, twisting to and fro.

'Ma'am . . .' Bream bit his lip.

Vicky gazed at his curled fist. And he was a big fellow. He

120

could do someone a lot of damage with that fist. But the alternative . . . 'Yes,' she said. 'Do it.'

Bream hesitated, then crawled up to kneel beside David's head. Alison gazed at him in surprise, then looked at Vicky.

'You can't do that,' she protested.

'It's best,' Vicky said. 'Otherwise . . . we don't know what might happen.' She couldn't bring herself to confess that she would be unable to do it with David screaming.

Bream inhaled, chose his moment as David's head was jerking forward in agony, and hit him on the chin with all his force. David's head jerked back, and he struck the sand to lie still.

'You have maybe five minutes, ma'am,' Bream said.

'Where in God's name is that wood?' Vicky screamed. 'You, Bream, give me your belt.'

Bream obeyed without question. Vicky unbuckled the heavy military belt round the waist of David's red jacket. It still carried both the revolver holster and the cartridge pouch, and she gazed at them in bewilderment, never having actually touched anything like that before. Alison took the belt from her fingers, slid both holster and pouch off, and returned the belt, without saying a word.

'I found this, ma'am,' a man said from above her, and she looked round at an oar.

'Only one? Well, break it,' she told him.

'Break it?' He was astonished.

'I need two lengths, so break it into two pieces.' Bream took the other end, and between them they managed to break the oar. The lengths were uneven and splintered, but they could be trimmed later. Vicky knew if she didn't do it before David woke up she was not going to have the determination to do it at all.

'Help me,' she muttered.

Prudence knelt beside her. The other man and Mary sat on David's good leg, while Bream and Alison, shoulder to shoulder, put all their weight on the arms they had stretched above his head. Vicky panted, and while Prudence pressed down on David's thigh, slowly brought the shattered leg straight. Without warning, David gave a scream of the purest agony, semi-conscious as he was. His body writhed and twisted despite the four people holding it.

'God!' he screamed. 'God!' His voice broke.

Vicky forced the broken bone back through the skin, while blood bubbled over her fingers. She looked around in desperation, then tried to tear a strip off of Alison's dressing gown, but the silk was too strong for her.

Bream stripped off his shirt, and tore it into lengths. He handed them to her and she bound up the wound. Then she placed the two pieces of wood one on each side of the leg, trying not to listen to the screams and moans, trying to ignore the writhing, twisting body beneath her, and secured them with the two belts, drawing them as tight as she dared without actually cutting off the circulation. She wept and panted as she worked.

'He'll not survive the pain,' the other sailor said, and indeed David seemed about to strangle on his own escaping breath.

'Bream is your name, is it?' Alison asked. 'Well, Bream, I think you had better hit him again.'

Bream looked at Vicky, then swung his fist again. Once more David's head hit the sand, and he lay there, unconscious.

But Vicky was there before him, in a dead faint.

She dreamed she was running through the corridors of hell, pursued by devils in the shape of ravenous sharks and overturning lifeboats, and chasing James, who kept appearing and disappearing again . . . only sometimes it wasn't James, but David. Only the heat was constant, seeming to grow and grow, to be intending to draw every last drop of moisture from her body. But the devils were merciful, and one of them was actually dripping a little water on to her mouth.

She opened her eyes, gazed at Nathalie. 'Nathalie?' she whispered in bewilderment.

The French girl smiled. She had hardly smiled since first boarding the *Doncaster*. But now she was back on dry land. 'Oh, Vicky,' she said. 'I am so 'appy you 'ave woke up.'

'I thought you were drowned,' Vicky muttered.

'I was rolled up the beach,' Nathalie said. 'Oh, I was

frightened. I was terrified. And then . . . *voilà*, I was left on the beach.'

'But . . .' Nathalie was holding the cup to her lips. 'We've found water? How marvellous.' It tasted like nectar.

'The casks came ashore,' Alison said. She knelt on Vicky's other side, and Vicky could only gaze at her in astonishment. Quite incredibly, she once again looked almost as immaculate as before the shipwreck. Her hair had dried, and she had fluffed it out and tied it on the nape of her neck with a length cut from the end of the dressing gown cord. Her satin nightdress might have been an evening gown, save for the tantalising way it clung to thigh and knee, shoulder and breast. Nor did her face reveal any particular emotion, not even discomfort at the heat. 'The biscuit barrels came ashore as well,' she said. 'Wasn't that fortunate? Victoria . . . Prudence tells me you saved Charlie's life.'

Vicky tried to think. 'I happened to see him, milady,' she admitted.

'Nonetheless, I am eternally grateful to you. And for helping David, of course, poor fellow. You really are turning out much better than I had supposed possible. Now . . .'

Vicky heard laughter, and sat up, blinking. The sun was already high, although it could still only be early in the morning, and blazed down on the empty beach. Only a little distance away Mary and Elizabeth were emptying a cask of water over each other's heads, chattering happily. Close by, Charlie was playing in the sand with what appeared to be half a dozen biscuits.

Vicky leapt to her feet, knocking Nathalie over, and ran at them. She snatched the cask from Mary's hands, held it up, and shook it. It was all but empty.

'What the devil do you think you're doing, you stupid fool?' Mary demanded, scrambling to her feet.

Alison also stood up. 'Victoria? Have you lost your senses?' Her tone indicated that she was considering a reappraisal of Vicky's worth.

Vicky looked around. There was a small group of women

seated together a few yards away, whispering together. The sailors stood by the shore, some picking at the remains of the lifeboat, others dragging bodies together to arrange them in a ghastly, silent row. David lay by himself, moving restlessly, but apparently still unconscious.

'Victoria!' Alison said sharply, coming closer. 'What is the matter with you?'

'It is the sun, and exhaustion,' Nathalie said gloomily, picking herself up and dusting herself off. 'She 'as gone mad.'

Vicky panted in sheer panic. David, the rock on whom she had built all her hopes of survival, was out. She did not even know if he would survive. But she did know that these people were not going to take orders from her. Therefore . . . their only hope of survival now lay in Alison Dobree. She simply could not afford to antagonise the woman. 'Milady,' she said, 'We are shipwrecked. We have only this little food and water on which to survive, until we find some more. That may not be for some time.'

'Oh, stuff and nonsense,' Alison declared. 'I am as upset as you by what has happened, my dear woman. By those who . . .' She glanced at the bodies. 'Who did not survive. But we must be positive. We are, as you say, shipwrecked. That isn't the end of the world. People have been shipwrecked before, and have survived. I have read *Coral Island*. Have you ever read *Coral Island*, Victoria?'

Vicky sighed. 'Yes, milady. That is a novel. And it is set on an island which just happens to be teeming with water and wild life, and trees, and shelter. This is an open beach.'

Alison looked left and right, and then up at the dunes which masked the eastern skyline. 'I agree it is a bit empty here, yes. But I am sure there are lots of trees and things just over there. And even here we should be able to gather sufficient firewood to light a fire, and –'

'Having found this wood, milady,' Vicky said patiently, 'how do we set it alight?'

'Well . . .' Alison frowned. 'Surely someone has matches?'

Vicky looked at the men, who had been listening to the conversation. The men looked back.

Alison snapped her fingers. 'I know. We hold a piece of glass so that the sun can shine through it, and it makes a fire. I've read all about it.'

'Do you have a piece of glass, milady?'

Alison stared at her, and then looked down at herself. Normally she wore at least a locket round her neck, with glass covering the two small likenesses of her parents. But she had been in bed, and her only jewellery was her wedding band and her diamond solitaire engagement ring. None of the other women were better equipped. She looked at Nathalie and Nathalie shrugged. 'Oh, *really*, Nathalie,' Alison remarked, clearly wondering how any lady's maid could have been so imcompetent as to allow herself to be shipwrecked without a piece of glass. 'Does *no* one have any glass?' she asked.

They gazed at her.

'We could rub two sticks together,' Mary said.

'That's right,' Elizabeth agreed. 'Mrs Chandler taught us how to do that.' She glanced at Vicky, who had not dealt with the subject of survival.

Vicky felt this absurd conversation had gone on long enough, even supposing that lighting a fire was essential to their survival. 'Two sticks,' she said, allowing some contempt to creep into her tone. 'You find us two sticks, Mary, and the paper to catch the spark. When you produce a spark.'

'Oh, well,' Alison sighed. 'So we may not be able to light a fire. But we can always wave when the ship comes.'

'Milady,' Vicky said, trying to stop herself from shouting. 'There isn't going to be a ship. No ship would approach this coast within a hundred miles, if it could avoid doing so. There is nothing for a ship to come close in for, quite apart from the chance of hitting a rock. There is nothing *here*. The *Doncaster* was off course. And it will be another four weeks at least before anyone even suspects something may have happened to her and thinks about looking. We are the only survivors.'

The people around her seemed to shift their feet, uneasily; she was putting into words what they had all suspected, and feared.

'Well,' Alison said, 'just what are you trying to say? Apart from being horribly gloomy?'

'That if we are going to survive, milady, we have to depend on ourselves and what we already possess. Nothing more.'

'And you have an idea of how we can do that?'

'Yes, milady. We have to walk to civilisation. Or at least, to where food and water can be obtained.'

'Walk?'

'That's desert out there, ma'am,' remarked one of the men. 'I've been up to those dunes to have a look, and there ain't *nothing* out there. Not even a tree. Nothing but rock, and sand.'

'I know that,' Vicky said. 'But it doesn't stretch all that far. We shall simply have to walk across it, using our existing supply of food and water. If we head south by east, we shall come to grassland – in a few days.'

'A few *days?*' Mary shouted.

'*Walk*, for a few days?' Elizabeth cried.

'How *can* we walk, for a few days?' Alison asked, as she might have remonstrated, gently, with a senile aunt, 'It's just not possible. How can *you* walk, Victoria? You have no shoes; neither does Nathalie.'

Nathalie peered at her feet, apparently realising that fact for the first time. 'Ooh, là là,' she commented.

'And besides, how can you expect Charlie to walk?' Alison continued. 'And David? I don't think David will ever walk very far again, after such rough and ready surgery. I'm not blaming you, Victoria. You did the best you could. You did very well, as a matter of fact,' she added magnanimously. 'But now we simply have to look facts in the face. There is no point at all in behaving hysterically.'

Vicky took one of her long breaths. 'Milady,' she implored, 'we have to leave this place, and find somewhere better. No matter how unpleasant or difficult it may be, no matter if we have to carry Charlie and David every step of the way. Because if we stay here, we are going to die. We have food and water for only another . . . oh, maybe a day and a half, after all that's been wasted. So . . .'

126

'And you say this other food and water is several days away,' Alison reminded her. 'I don't really see what we will be achieving, apart from obtaining sore feet.'

'We will be doing *something*, milady,' Vicky said desperately, 'instead of just sitting here waiting to die. Anyway, I believe it is possible to survive in the desert. I have spoken with men who have crossed the entire Sahara, on foot and without any supplies at all. I think I can remember how it is done.'

'She thinks she can remember how it is done,' Mary sneered.

'All right,' Vicky shouted, finally losing her temper. 'You stay here and rot. I'm going. If just one person will come with me to help carry Lieutenant Whiting. I'm going to walk to safety.'

'I'll come with you, ma'am,' said Harry Bream. She realised he would wish to follow her anywhere, hoping for another glimpse of her body. Or maybe more. That was a problem. But it had to have low priority until she got them moving. 'Thank you, Bream,' she said, and looked at Prudence.

Prudence sighed. 'With respect, milady,' she said, 'I agree with Victoria. It is better to do something which might succeed, rather than just sit around, when we know that is going to lead nowhere.'

'I will come with you, Vicky,' Nathalie decided.

Alison looked from one to the other. 'Oh, very well,' she said. 'If that is what you all really want to do. You men?' She looked at the other sailors.

'Whatever you say, ma'am,' one of them replied. 'You're the boss.'

'Oh?' Alison said, realising for the first time that she *was* the boss, with David *hors de combat*. 'Well . . .' She looked at Vicky. However full of ideas the American woman might be, if she was the boss it was time to contribute something to the plans being made. 'Before we can do anything, we have to bury those unfortunate people.'

Vicky nodded, and walked across the sand, to look down on Mrs Mainwaring and the five other women, as well as one sailor. Drowned people seldom look very pleasant, and these had been out of the water for several hours. Vicky's nostrils dilated, but she had seen death often enough before, in Kenya.

Yet she could not help reflecting on the whim of fate, in selecting just these and, for instance, leaving the Dobree family intact. But then she realised that fate had nothing at all to do with it. These women had all been in their early middle age; as the wives of army officers, they had been surrounded by servants and batmen to do any work which involved physical strain. Around them had been constructed the enormous physical and social fortress that was the British Army where, so long as an officer did not actually steal the mess funds and never turned his back on an enemy, he was cared for from Sandhurst to retirement. And officers' wives had even less temptation to let the side down. Even their peccadilloes, supposing they ever risked any, would always have been carefully swept under the carpet for fear of disgracing the regiment. Faced with the stark fact of death or life, in a matter of a few tumultuous seconds, they had lacked the strength of will to make the supreme effort. That the Dobrees had survived *en bloc* was due entirely to their youth and beauty – which had attracted the seamen to pull them from the sea before anyone else. And in Charlie's case, to her being in the right place at the right time. The real whim of Fate was that even four of the other women had survived.

She was being brutal and hard, even in her thoughts. Those had been wives and mothers, good and brave women who loyally supported and obeyed their husbands, either on a hundred and one warring frontiers, or remaining at home to keep the fires burning. That they had surrendered to the raging sea could be no disgrace on any of them. But it was necessary to be hard and brutal, and in more than just her thoughts, if she was going to drive the survivors to safety.

'Will you please dig a large pit?' she said to the waiting men.

'Right away, ma'am,' Bream said. 'Come on, you fellows.'

'Above the high water mark,' Vicky said.

'Oh, yes, ma'am.' They hurried up the beach and began digging at the sand with their knives.

Vicky turned to the women. 'Will you help me take their clothes off, please?'

'Do *what?*' Alison asked, eyebrows arched higher than Vicky had ever seen them.

'She's mad, without doubt,' Mary remarked.

'Vicky,' Prudence said uneasily. 'Surely . . . well, that's obscene.'

'Yes, it's obscene,' Vicky shouted. 'But *we need* those clothes. Some of us need their shoes. We are going to need their things even more in the desert, believe me. We have to have shelter, and we're all damn near naked as it is. We have to have those clothes.'

'Oh,' Alison said, 'really, Victoria, there is no need to swear. But surely you must see that we cannot wear clothes which . . . well, have been on dead bodies? I mean, the thought is too horrible for words. Oh, borrow a pair of shoes by all means. But you're welcome to keep my dressing gown, you know, even if it is a little long for you. Certainly until we get, well . . . wherever it is we're going.'

'Thank you, milady,' Vicky said. 'I really am most grateful. But we still have to have those clothes. We can wash them in the sea before we use them. But we have to have them.'

'With your permission, milady,' Prudence said, understanding that Vicky must have a very good reason for insisting upon so unpleasant a procedure, 'if you'll keep an eye on Master Charlie, I'll help Victoria.'

'I will 'elp too,' Nathalie said, obviously determined to be a tower of strength now she had regained dry land.

'Oh . . . very well,' Alison said. 'Come along, girls. You mustn't look at this. And Victoria, do make sure the men do not approach.'

Vicky, already kneeling by Mrs Mainwaring, pushed hair from her eyes without replying; the men were going to have to bury the poor things.

Slowly they dragged the nightdresses and dressing gowns from the inert bodies. One of the women wore stockings, and four had either slippers or boots. That was a stroke of fortune.

'Vicky,' Prudence asked. 'Do we really have to have these clothes?'

'Yes,' Vicky said.

'I'd be grateful if you'd tell me why. I mean, I can understand that we need shoes for Nathalie and you . . . but we do all have things to wear.'

'Prudence,' Vicky said. 'The only way we are going to survive in the desert is by avoiding heatstroke. That is when the sun just absorbs all the moisture in your body. Then you just can't move. We're not going to have the water to replace what we use, so we have to try to avoid sweating as much as we can.' She saw Prudence look down at the sweat rolling down her arms. 'I know we can't stop sweating altogether, but we can minimise it. That means that during the hottest hours of the day, we have to keep as still as possible and shelter from the sun. The Bedouin know this. They don't move in the heat but keep absolutely quiet, hibernate, wrapped up in their *haiks* and *burnouses*. But they have to be completely covered. Because, you see, the air outside them will actually get hotter during the day than that trapped in their clothing, however hot *that* may be. So they have to be covered all over, especially their heads. And what can we do? Take off our nightdresses and wrap them round our heads? Even if the sailors weren't there, we'd just bake ourselves.'

'Good Lord,' Prudence commented, obviously allowing her imagination to run wild.

The men had finished digging the grave.

'You mustn't go down there,' Alison called to them. She sat with her children close to the four surviving women. What they were saying, about her in particular, Vicky supposed, did not bear consideration. But she had six naked bodies, absurdly white and unmarked, stretched on the sand in front of her. She could only thank God that there were no insects on the beach and that it was still only about ten o'clock in the morning – although already the sun hung in the sky like a malevolent deity, and they poured sweat from their exertion.

'What about 'im?' Nathalie asked distastefully.

'We can't cover our heads with anything of his,' Prudence said thankfully.

'We need his clothes, to make up the stretcher for David,'

Vicky said grimly. She unfastened the seaman's belt and dragged on his trousers.

'I don't think I will ever be the same again,' Prudence confessed.

'You've done very well,' Vicky said. 'Now take these clothes into the shallows and thoroughly wet them, again and again.' She felt very close to hysterics herself.

'Yes,' Prudence said thankfully, and obeyed, clutching the nightdresses in her arms.

'Bream,' Vicky shouted.

The sailor took a couple of steps towards her, and checked. 'Lady Dobree said . . .'

'You have to come here, Bream,' Vicky said. 'You have to take the bodies to the grave. But please . . .' She didn't know exactly how to phrase it, felt herself flushing. 'Be nice about it.'

The sailors came down the beach, and hefted a body each, carrying them up the slope. The first man to reach the grave merely dropped his load, sending arms and legs scattering.

'For God's sake,' Vicky shouted, on the verge of tears, 'place them in. Don't just throw them!'

The bodies were placed in the grave, then they went back for the last woman and the man.

'Joey was my mate,' said one of the men. 'He was a great fellow.'

Nathalie began to weep.

Vicky pushed herself to her feet; her stomach felt light. She went towards the women, swallowing the saliva that kept filling her mouth. 'They're ready, milady,' she said. 'Would you say something?'

'Me?' Alison asked. 'You're the parson's wife.'

'Well . . . would you come and stand?'

'Yes,' said one of the women, and others got up also.

'I suppose we must,' Alison said. 'You're sure they're properly covered up?'

'Yes, milady,' Vicky said, and led them back to where the grave had indeed been filled in. Prudence hurried up the beach, carrying the soaking nightdresses, her own dripping wet.

The sailors smoothed the earth.

131

'Shouldn't they have some kind of marker?' Elizabeth asked.

'Yes,' Vicky said. 'Have all the oars come ashore?'

'Yes, ma'am,' Bream said.

'Well, fetch one and stick it in at the top.'

'Yes, ma'am.' He hurried off.

'Anyone would think *she's* running things,' Mary whispered to her step mother, loudly. 'You must *do* something, Mother.'

Alison arched her eyebrows.

Bream returned and thrust the oar into the sand.

There was a moment's silence, then Vicky said, 'Have mercy on these thy dead children, oh God, and receive them into your bosom with our grateful thanks. Amen.'

'That wasn't a very good service,' Mary remarked.

'And now we start walking, is that it?' Alison demanded.

'Oh, really, Mother,' Mary protested. 'It is far too hot. And I have a headache.'

Vicky realised that she also had a headache. In fact, they must all have headaches, due to a combination of over-exertion and fear, too much heat, hunger and thirst. But trust Mary to put it into words and make them aware of it.

'Anyway, I'm too exhausted to move.' Elizabeth flopped on the sand. 'And I feel sick.'

'You look sick, too,' Mary said, brutally.

Alison looked at Vicky, almost as a dog might look at its master.

'No, milady,' Vicky said. 'We don't start walking until this evening.'

'This evening?' Mary cried. 'That's not going to take us very far.'

'Yes, it is, Mary,' Vicky said. 'Because we are going to walk all night.'

They stared at her.

'And rest during the day,' she explained.

'But . . . how will we know where we're going, in the dark?'

'The stars will show us the way to go,' Vicky said. 'We're going south-east. That's simple enough.'

'In the darkness,' Alison said. 'It sounds perfectly dreadful.

There could be snakes and horrible things like that.'

'Yes, milady,' Vicky agreed. 'There may well be snakes. But they'll be less dangerous at night than in the day.'

'Oh, really, Victoria, the things you tell us. That is quite absurd. Why, everyone knows that in the dark . . .'

'Milady,' Vicky said, with great patience, 'snakes are cold-blooded creatures.'

'I know that,' Alison said. 'That's what makes them so unpleasant.'

'Therefore,' Vicky went on, ignoring the interruption, 'they do not gain their energy as we do. We eat, and then our digestive systems send the food into our bloodstreams, and we have the energy to move, and run, and fight, and think.'

Alison arched her eyebrows. Clearly the subject of human digestion was too distasteful to be considered in detail.

'Snakes are different,' Vicky went on. 'They take their energy direct from the sun. Therefore, when there is no sun, they have no energy. A snake is most dangerous at noon, least dangerous at midnight. That is true.'

They gazed at her, unwilling to believe so simple a biology lesson.

'Why don't we just follow the beach?' Elizabeth wanted to know.

'Because there will be nothing to eat or drink on the beach,' Vicky said, 'save salt water.'

'And there is going to be fresh water to drink in the desert?' Mary demanded.

'I believe so,' Vicky said. 'If we look for it.'

'But what are we going to do for the rest of the day?' Prudence asked, hoping to head off what could become an interminable discussion. 'If we're not leaving here now?'

'We are going to behave like the Bedouin,' Vicky reminded her. 'We are going to rest and keep as cool as possible. That's what the extra clothing is for. We must dig a series of pits in the sand. They don't have to be deep, although it'll help if you get down to the damp sand. The pits just have to be big enough to take two bodies each. I'm afraid we have to lie down in pairs because we don't have sufficient spare nightdresses to go

133

round. Then we get into our pits, cover ourselves with the spare clothing, and keep as quiet as we can. Oh, we'll all have a drink of water and a biscuit first,' she hurried on, before they could understand what she was telling them.

Mary understood right. 'You must be quite mad.' she commented.

Vicky ignored her. 'Bream,' she called.

'Yes, ma'am,' he said, coming forward.

'Will you and one of the others hand round the water and biscuits? Same as at sea, one cup and one biscuit per person.'

'Yes, ma'am,' Bream said.

'Mother, *do* something,' Mary hissed. 'She's telling everybody what to do.'

Alison looked up at the sun; it was nearly noon now, and extremely hot. And she was as exhausted as anyone, emotionally and physically – all she wanted to do was lie down and close her eyes, preferably somewhere cool. 'Are you sure you know what you're doing?' she asked.

Vicky shrugged. 'I believe so, milady. At least I have an idea. Do you have a better one?'

They gazed at each other.

Once again Prudence sought to avoid a crisis. 'I'll dig a pit for us, milady,' she said, dropping to her knees. 'And we can have Charlie with us. Come along, Charlie, let's dig in the sand.'

'It's too hot,' Charlie objected. 'And I'm too thirsty.' He had just had his cup of water.

Prudence was already digging.

'That's splendid,' Vicky said. 'Mary and Elizabeth, you dig a pit for yourselves. Ladies . . .' She looked at the other four women; they had never actually been introduced.

'I'm Joanna Cartwright,' said the one who was obviously the eldest, perhaps fifty. She was the woman Vicky had dragged from the surf. Now she glanced at the short, stout woman beside her, the one who had been sick when asked to assist with setting David's leg. 'Alice Marker. We're old friends. Alice and I will share a pit.'

'Good,' Vicky said. 'And you?' She looked at the other pair.

'I'm Phyillis Smart, Mrs Lang.'

'Margaret Pilling, Mrs Lang.'

'Could you share?' Vicky asked.

The women, both about forty, and remarkably alike in their thinness and general lack of colour, looked at each other, and then nodded. 'Yes.'

'Thank you. Now . . .' She looked at Nathalie.

'Vicky,' Nathalie whispered, anxiously. 'There are five sailors.'

It was difficult to decide whether she was terrified or anticipatory.

'Well, they'll have to go three and two,' Vicky decided. Bream had reached her by now, and she gratefully sipped a cup of water, allowing the liquid to seep slowly down her throat. 'How much is left?'

'There's a whole barrel unopened, Mrs Lang,' Bream said. 'Enough for two days.'

'Biscuits?'

'Nearly a full keg of those, too. Maybe sixty.'

'And seventeen people to be fed. Hm.' They would need more than two a day if she was to keep them walking. 'All right, Bream. You fellows do as I said, and cover yourselves up. Here.' She handed him three of the still wet nightdresses. 'Make sure your heads are covered.'

'I think I'll soak these again,' he decided. 'For coolness,' he hastily added.

'Why, that's an excellent idea. Ladies,' she said, standing above the women, who were all busily scraping at the sand, using their beautifully kept hands and nails for this utterly unnatural purpose. 'If you wet the nightdresses again they'll be that much cooler.' She gave a nightdress, or a dressing gown, to each pair, which left just the one for Nathalie and herself.

'Victoria.' Alison came towards them. She had of course left the digging to Prudence, and none of *her* nails were broken. 'Is there anything we can do about our complexions?' she asked. 'I mean, look at my arms. Well, look at your own arms. They're all red. And my face is burning, all the time. That's from lying about in that lifeboat, of course. I just know I'm going to get those dreadful freckles, just like you. As for the girls . . .'

Vicky sighed. 'Just keep covered up, milady. As much as possible.'

'Oh. Yes, I suppose that might help.' She regarded Vicky with a speculative expression, obviously considering whether to demand the return of her dressing gown in exchange for her nightdress; the dressing gown had sleeves, which Vicky had pushed back to the elbows, whereas the nightgown was sleeveless, and shoulderless as well. But she decided against it – presumably, Vicky thought, because the garment would have to be washed before she could possibly wear it again – and returned to Prudence and Charlie.

'Do you suppose *anything* will make her realise how serious our position is?' Vicky wondered aloud.

'What about 'im?' Nathalie asked, concentrating on essentials.

'We're going to have him with us,' Vicky said. 'Give me a hand. We have to get that red jacket off: the serge must be like an oven for him.' She knelt beside David, who continued to move restlessly, moaning and muttering.

'I can't make out what 'e's saying,' Nathalie grumbled.

'He's delirious anyway, so it doesn't matter.' When they had taken off the jacket, Vicky held a cup of water to his lips, went down to the sea to wet the nightgown and with it wiped the sweat from his forehead and cheeks, his neck and shoulders.

'Do you think he'll be able to make the journey?' Nathalie asked.

'He has to make it,' Vicky said. 'Now come on, let's dig.'

By the time they had made their own pit, almost everyone else was in place, a series of little white humps half buried in the damp sand. Vicky even thought she heard a giggle of laughter coming from Mary and Elizabeth's foxhole, and definitely made out a 'Really, Charlie, stop that!' from Alison. But for the moment all was well. They were obeying her, simply because they were too exhausted and shocked to do anything else. There would be problems ahead . . . so many problems. She stood up and surveyed the beach. Then she walked to where she had splinted David's leg and found his revolver holster and cartridge pouch. She unclipped the pouch, counted twenty-five bullets. It took her several moments to work out how the gun opened, but at last she found the catch and watched the bullets jerking out on to the sand. Only two of the cartridges were spent. That left twenty-nine, which seemed an enormous number. Supposing she knew how to fire the thing. But David would soon be himself again – he had to be.

She reloaded the gun with six bullets, then went down close to the water, to where she had stripped the dead sailor, found his belt lying on the sand, with its knife still in its sheath. All the men had knives at their waists. Something to remember.

She picked up the knife and the belt and went back to where Nathalie sat and watched her. 'Let's get him into the pit,' she said.

Between them they dragged David down to the pit, placed him in the middle.

'I'll soak this again,' Nathalie volunteered.

Vicky nodded, lay down beside him, gazed at his beard-stubbled face, which moved constantly, now and then giving a little whimper of agony. Soon he would be wide awake, and aware of his pain. And he would have to be carried, every step of the way . . .

Nathalie was back, holding the dripping nightdress above her as she slid down into the pit on David's other side. The nightdress lay across their heads and faces, and blessedly cooling water dripped down Vicky's neck.

'Vicky.' Nathalie's hand came across David's body to hold Vicky's fingers. 'Vicky. Are we going to make it?'

'Yes,' Vicky said.

Nathalie was silent for a few minutes. Then she said, 'Vicky, do you love 'im?'

'I think . . . maybe,' Vicky said.

Nathalie sighed, and subsided into silence.

CHAPTER 7

Vicky slept heavily. She had not realised how exhausted she was, both emotionally and physically . . . with nothing but exhaustion, emotional and physical, to look forward to. She felt, she *knew*, there was a great number of things she should sit down and think about, very carefully, but she didn't want to do that – she was afraid of losing her own resolution. Of being afraid.

She was awakened by David, groaning and moaning. 'God,' he whispered. 'Oh, God.'

'David.' She squeezed his hand.

'Vicky? Is it really you? Oh, thank heavens. I thought I was in a grave.'

'You're safe, David. And I am here with you.'

Nathalie appeared to be still asleep.

'Oh, Vicky . . .' He writhed as the pain washed over him.

'You've broken your leg,' Vicky told him. 'I think the lifeboat was thrown on top of you by the waves. You were lucky – you could have been killed. I set the bone as best I could, but I know it must hurt terribly. Oh, David, it's all been such a mess.'

'You set it, Vicky? *You?* My God, you are a treasure! Vicky . . .' Another spasm of pain struck at him. The nightdress above them had long since dried, and although it kept out the worst of the sun it could not repel the light. She could see the beads of sweat on his face, the desperate twistings of his mouth as he endeavoured not to cry out. She couldn't watch that, knowing what he must be feeling. She took his hand, and placed it on her breast, inside the dressing gown.

'Vicky,' he gasped. 'Vicky.' But his fingers had closed, and a moment later his hand was sliding up and down her body, from her stomach to her neck, while she lay as still as she could, and sweat poured out of her. The next time his hand went down it slid between her legs, and she shuddered but still did not move. Sometimes he hurt her, when a spasm overtook him and his fingers involuntarily dug into her flesh, but mostly he was gentle, and gradually some of the urgency left his movements. Presumably one could even get used to the pain.

The heat was leaving the sun, and there was so much to be done. She raised herself on her elbow. 'David . . . I have to go.'

'Go?' His fingers tightened again. 'Oh, Vicky . . . don't leave me. Vicky!'

'I'll be back,' she promised. 'But I have to get us organised.'

'Us? You mean others got ashore?'

It was difficult to decide whether he was happy or sad about that. 'Yes,' she said. 'There are seventeen of us.'

'Oh. Lady Dobree . . .?'

'Oh, yes. And her children. I'll leave you with Nathalie. Nathalie, are you awake?'

'Yes,' Nathalie said in a very deep voice; she had obviously been awake for some time.

'Look after him,' Vicky commanded. She did not specify whether Nathalie was to allow him to caress her as well. That would have to be her decision.

She moved the covering nightdress and crawled out, retied the dressing gown, and blinked in the still glaring sunlight. But the sun was drooping towards the horizon, and the heat was starting to dwindle. And she was covered in sand, stuck to her body by her own sweat.

For the first time she was aware of how hungry she was. Until now there had been too much stomach-churning horror and fear and excitement for her to feel like eating. Now her stomach rumbled and her mouth constantly filled with saliva. But she just had to bear it in silence; if she started to complain the rest of them would just disintegrate.

She went down the beach and knelt in the shallows, resisting the temptation to take off the dressing gown, allowing the water to break over her, and then appreciating the cool of having the

139

sopping silk nestling against her overheated body. She stayed there for several minutes, before getting up and walking up the beach, pulling the cord of the gown tight around her waist.

'Do you know that I actually slept?' Alison emerged from her grave, and tried to fluff out her hair. 'Ugh!' she said. 'It is absolutely stiff with salt and sand. Nathalie? Where is that girl? She simply has to do something about it.'

'Nathalie is very busy, milady,' Vicky explained, 'looking after Mr Whiting. And in any case, there is nothing she can do about the salt in your hair. As for sand, you're covered in it from head to foot.'

Alison looked down at herself. 'Good Lord,' she commented. 'So I am.'

'Why not have a bathe in the sea,' Vicky suggested. 'It'll at least refresh you.'

'A bathe? In the *sea?*' Alison peered at the waves from which she had so narrowly escaped only a few hours earlier, then glanced to where the men were also beginning to emerge. 'In front of *them?*'

'Keep your clothes on, milady,' Vicky advised. 'I did. And the cooler you can make yourself the better.'

'Ah,' Alison said. 'Prudence, did you hear that? Charlie, come along, we're going to have a nice bathe in the sea.'

'I'm thirsty,' Charlie complained. 'And hungry. I want some pie. I want apple pie.'

Alison looked at Vicky.

'There'll be a biscuit for you when you've had your bathe, Master Charlie,' Vicky promised. She went to where the men were getting up. 'I think you should all go and have a wash off and a cool down,' she told them. 'Go up the beach, away from Lady Dobree. Then we have to prepare to move. How many oars are there left?'

'Three, ma'am,' Bream replied.

'All right. We can use two of them to make a stretcher for Mr Whiting. You can use poor Joey's trousers and shirt, and I can let you have two of the nightdresses. Oh, you can also use Mr Whiting's red jacket.' She looked down at the dressing gown,

140

which trailed on the sand at her feet. 'You can use some of this as well.'

They gazed at her, uncertain of her meaning.

'Cut some off,' she said. 'Bream, use your knife to cut off the hem, as evenly as you can, up as far as the middle of my calf.'

'Yes, ma'am,' Bream said. He worked with great concentration, slowly uncovering her feet and ankles, watched by his mates.

'Well done,' Vicky said, when he was finished. 'Now I shall even be able to walk. Next, divide that into strips, and three of you begin work on the stretcher as soon as you've had your bathe. Remember, it has to be good and strong.' She selected one of the strips of satin and used it to copy Alison in tying back her hair; it was so long it was becoming a nuisance. 'Now, Bream, you and . . .' She looked at the fifth sailor. 'What's your name?'

'Curly Joe, ma'am.'

'Curly Joe, you and Bream have your dip, then I want you to serve out the water, one cup each, and one biscuit each.'

'Yes, ma'am,' Bream agreed.

The girls and the other women were also awake by now, and making their way down to the water. Mary was complaining, as usual, but as long as they were constantly kept busy there should be no problems. Vicky could only hope that applied to the men, too.

Nathalie had folded the nightdress, and David was trying to sit up. 'Lie back, David,' Vicky said, kneeling beside him. 'Nathalie, would you collect all the spare nightclothes and give them a rinse?'

'Yes, Vicky,' Nathalie said, and left.

'You seem to have things under control,' David said.

Vicky shrugged. 'So far.'

He gave a shudder of pain, and embarrassment. 'Vicky . . . about this afternoon . . . I should be horse-whipped. My God, I don't know what came over me.'

'Don't apologise,' she said. 'You were in pain. And in any case . . . maybe I enjoyed it!'

141

'Vicky,' he said. 'My Vicky.' He reached for her again.

She didn't resist, but she bit her lip. 'David . . . in about half an hour, we're leaving here.'

His fingers fell away as he frowned. 'To do what?'

'To walk, remember? South. To the forest and civilisation.'

'You persuaded them to do that, Vicky?'

She smiled. 'Let's say I shouted them into it.'

'But . . .' He looked down at himself.

'I'm not leaving you behind,' she told him. 'We're going to carry you. They're making the stretcher now. But David . . . I don't believe any of them are happy about the idea of the journey. I'd be grateful if you could . . . well, give me support whenever the going gets rough.'

'Of course you can count on me, my darling girl.'

'I knew I could. And maybe you could also give me advice from time to time.'

'I'm afraid you probably know more about what you're doing than I do.'

'Well, leave the desert to me. It's the people . . .' She gazed at him.

He nodded, while his face twisted to a fresh spasm of pain.

'It's not her ladyship, believe me, or the girls. They mean well, even if they don't show it. It's well . . . the men.'

Again he nodded. 'Have you got my revolver?'

'Yes. Do you want it?'

'I think you had better keep it. Carry my belt across your shoulder like a bandolier. I don't know that if it was necessary I would be in any condition to shoot, if I was in the midst of a bout of severe pain.'

'Oh.' She found it incredible that he could speak so dispassionately about something so horrific. 'David! Surely it won't come to anything like that?'

'I'm afraid it could, if . . . if anything should happen for them to lose faith in you, or if the sun affects them, or anything like that. But Vicky . . .' He grasped her arm. 'You must promise me something.'

'Of course. Name it.'

'Promise me that if there were to be a mutiny, or anything

142

you could not quell immediately with a few words, and you had to use the pistol, you will shoot to kill. Remember that.'

Her turn to frown. 'I couldn't do that. And surely . . .'

'You said you'd promise. Vicky . . .' His grip tightened. 'Man is the most dangerous animal on the face of this earth. If those men turn against you for any reason whatsoever, from wanting more water than you can allow them, to wanting to rape you and Alison and the girls, they are going to be more deadly than a pack of wolves. Remember that. If you let them get the upper hand, you're finished, all of you. They'll have you stretched on your backs in seconds, and when they're satisfied, they'll murder you just the same. You must remember that.' His grip relaxed, and he flushed. 'I'm sorry to be so unpleasantly explicit. But if it happens, that's how it will happen. So give me your word.'

She promised, because she knew he was right. She knew that was the unthinkable fear which had lurked at the edges of her mind all day, the fact that they had seen her naked, the expression in Bream's eyes, that they had seen Alison wearing only a sheer nightgown, that they had watched the girls' arms and legs being exposed . . . even that they had had to see and touch the naked bodies of the drowned women.

And above all, the way they had looked at her as Bream had cut the hem from her dressing gown. those had been the expressions of wolves, slowly developing a hunger. And yet, she had done that deliberately, to keep their interest, their devotion, she hoped. But now she understood what a narrow path she was walking, between success and disaster. Their devotion would last only for as long as they felt sure she alone could save them. Should they lose that belief, then, as David had said, where the women would merely complain and sulk, the men would become angry animals.

She had tried to tell herself that she was being prudish as a schoolmarm, that she was mentally accusing those five seamen – who had up to now worked so hard and so well – of animal desires, when the only male member of the party who had so far revealed any such desires was David himself. But she couldn't rid herself of the feeling, or of the awareness that not only were they all big, strong men, but also that they each carried a sheath knife on their belts. There was no way she could make them give those up without revealing her apprehensions, and risk provoking the very confrontation she feared; nor dared she risk revealing her fears to any of the women, not even Prudence or Alison, who appeared blissfully unaware that there was the slightest risk of the seamen ever doing anything other than what they were told, or of their being treated with less than the respect they had been accorded on board ship.

The burden was hers alone. With David's support. Much as she hated to do it, she obeyed his instructions, which necessitated switching belts. She gasped with distress at his groans of pain when she released the military belt, replacing it as quickly as she could with the dead seaman's to hold the splints in place; the pain was obviously excruciating. Once he was again secured, she threaded the holster and the cartridge pouch and the sheath knife through the military belt and, as he had suggested, looped it over her right shoulder, across her chest and back to her left thigh, like a bandolier. It took some time to settle it properly, but at last she seemed to get it right: the holster resting on her thigh, reversed, the knife hanging just over her right shoulder and the cartridge pouch in the middle of her back. The weights caused the belt to draw very tight and cut into her shoulder; while it helped to keep the dressing gown closed, it also left very little to the imagination. But she realised that was a minor worry as she watched the women struggling up the beach, all soaked to the skin and, apparently unaware that they were exposing raised nipples and dark vee patches to the gaze of the men.

She hurried towards them, anxious to get them as busy as herself. 'Those without shoes,' she said, 'see if we have anything to fit you.' She had already selected a pair of slippers for herself. She did not suppose they would last very long as they were made of felt, but they had good soles and would be better than nothing.

Mary gazed at her, and then burst out laughing. 'Desperate Dan, the bandit man!' she shouted.

Elizabeth also laughed, and even Prudence had to smile.

'My dear Victoria,' Alison remarked, 'you look quite ridiculous. You should see yourself. And you've managed to tear my dressing gown. It's ruined.'

Vicky kept her temper. 'I'm afraid your dressing gown *is* ruined milady,' she agreed. 'You may take its cost out of my wages. And I'm sure I do look ridiculous. But are you suggesting we leave the gun behind? Or would you prefer to wear it yourself?'

'*Me?* Good Lord, no! But . . . who are you going to shoot?'

Perhaps you, one of these days, Vicky thought. In the backside. But she smiled. 'If we see any game, milady, we will be very glad of the gun.' She hurried on before anyone thought to remind her that it had been she who had convinced them they could not light a fire. 'Now please listen to me, everybody. Gather round. Bream, is that stretcher ready?'

'Yes, ma'am,' Bream said, and waved the other men forward. 'Good as we can make it.'

They were seamen, and even lacking the proper tools had put together a very strong-looking bed, splitting various materials to tie to the oars, and criss-crossing the rest beneath and above to form a serviceable mattress; the remaining strips of satin were waiting to be used to strap David in.

'That's fine,' Vicky said. 'Now, here's how we're going to march. Two men will carry Mr Whiting, two more will hold themselves in reserve, and the fifth will carry the water barrel. You can switch around every half an hour. Understand?'

They nodded, exchanging glances.

'You'll go first,' Vicky said. 'The ladies will follow behind.' That way at least the men would not be staring at them every step of the journey.

'Yes, ma'am,' Bream agreed. 'But how do we know where to go?'

'You're sailors,' she reminded them, and pointed at the setting sun. 'Keep that over your right shoulder. When it gets

145

dark, you must keep the Pole Star over your *left* shoulder. Remember now. But I'll tell you if you're going off course.' She gave them her most encouraging smile. 'We're not trying to find a small harbour mouth, or a particular beacon, just to move in the general direction.' She turned to the older women. 'Now, ladies, will you four go next, carrying the biscuit barrel? I should think you could manage fifteen minutes each and then start again. It's not all that heavy, unfortunately. Carry it on your shoulders.'

The women hesitated, then Joanna Cartwright nodded, hefted the barrel on to her shoulder, and set off after the men, followed by the other three women.

'Milady,' Vicky said, 'if you are agreeable, perhaps you, Prudence, Nathalie, Mary and Elizabeth could take turns at carrying Master Charlie.'

'Oh, well, yes,' Alison said. 'I should think we can do that.'

'I want to walk,' Charlie declared. 'Why can't I walk?'

'Why, you're welcome to walk,' Vicky told him. 'For just as long as you feel like it.'

'What are you going to carry?' Mary inquired.

'Myself, and this gun, and this remaining oar,' she said.

'What are you going to use that for?' Elizabeth asked.

Possibly paddling somebody's rear end, Vicky thought, but she continued to smile at them. 'I have no idea. But I certainly don't mean to leave anything behind which could possibly come in handy. Now lead on. I'm going to bring up the rear, just to make sure nobody drops out.'

'Oh, yes,' Mary said. 'And if there is any trouble we get into it first.'

'There is not going to be any trouble, Mary,' Vicky said evenly, 'unless you intend to start it. Are you content with my arrangements, milady?'

'I suppose so,' Alison said doubtfully, and came closer to stand beside Vicky and lower her voice to a whisper. 'Tell me why we are walking south-east. Wouldn't it make more sense to walk due south?'

'I think east of south is best, milady,' Vicky said. She couldn't risk trying to explain why, in case she was wrong. But although it was a long time since she had looked at a map of West Africa, she was sure that there was a river which made a great bend to the north some distance from the coast. It was called the . . . She tried to remember. The Senegal! All her hopes were pinned on that river: surely the grassland would extend to the north of it for a greater distance than elsewhere in the desert. If she was wrong . . . but then, if she was wrong about anything, they were all as dead as the people they had buried on the beach.

Alison looked as if she would have liked to argue the point, but thought better of it.

'All right, then,' Vicky said. 'We walk for half an hour, and then we rest for five minutes. Then half an hour again. All night. Ready?'

Everyone was remarkably cheerful as they turned away from the beach. The heat had now left the sun, although it was still quite bright, and they obviously believed they were not all that far away from succour. She had made them believe that. But her heart sank as they topped the dunes and saw before them an apparently endless stretch of stony desert. There was not the slightest suggestion of any vegetation to be seen, not even a stunted tree. Nor was it in the least flat. Almost right away the lead sailor slipped down an unsuspected dip and dropped his end of the stretcher, to the accompaniment of shouts from his companions and a moan of pain from David.

'For heaven's sake, look where you're going,' Vicky shouted, hurrying to the front of the column and getting them started again.

'Silly oafs,' Mary remarked. It was comforting to feel, Vicky thought, that whatever they felt about *her*, the Dobrees were at least as anxious as she was to help David survive.

The afterguard were happy at this stage; Charlie was still walking. But only for a while. By dusk he was fast asleep in Prudence's arms, as they plodded onwards, kicking stones, going up and down. Vicky had no means of telling the time, as the only watch the party owned, David's hunter, had stopped in the water. But she reasoned that they were taking one step a

147

second, or sixty steps a minute, or eighteen hundred steps every half an hour. So she counted her steps, from one to eighteen hundred, and then called a halt.

'Really, Victoria,' Alison said. 'I'm sure we're not the least tired. Don't you think we should continue a bit longer while we can see?'

She had been carrying Charlie for five minutes. Prudence and Nathalie, who had been burdened with the child for considerably longer, had both sunk to their knees.

'No, milady,' Vicky said. 'We'll rest for five minutes, as we decided. We'll be tired, soon enough.'

'At least', Prudence said, 'there are no bugs. I thought all hot countries were full of bugs.'

Why, so did I, Vicky thought. There had certainly been bugs enough in Kenya. On the beach she had been so grateful for their absence it had not occurred to her to wonder why, and she had never doubted that there would be bugs once they left the seaside. But there was nothing – this was a totally lifeless world. Could it be, she wondered, that even bugs needed water and vegetation to survive?

But she had more important things to worry about. There were calculations to be made. If she was right, as each step had to be approximately a yard, they had actually just walked a mile. That seemed right, too, looking back at the dunes, and she could still hear the roar of the surf. So, they would average two miles an hour. They had left the beach about four, she estimated. If they walked until eight tomorrow morning, that would be thirty-two miles. Sixteen hours! Could she possibly keep them moving for sixteen hours, with just five-minute breaks? And suppose they did do thirty-two miles. If they could keep that up it would still take them six days to cover the two hundred miles she estimated separated them from the grassland. Her heart seemed to stop. Six days! That was quite impossible. Apart from the fact that as they became weaker and more exhausted they would necessarily travel at a slower pace, they only had water for two days at the outside, and biscuit for less than that.

She was leading them all to their deaths!

Then she remembered that she had to plan, and hope. And above all, remember. She got them back to their feet again and off they set, while she concentrated. It had been a black man, a Sudanese, called Sejm, who had appeared at the mission begging for food and shelter, and concealment. He was an escaped slave, a runaway from a caravan out of Ethiopia commanded by no less a personage than the infamous Zobeir ibn Rubayr, the most feared man in Africa, a man whose power was so immense that he had from time to time fought pitched battles with British and French soldiers and never been beaten. He was a disciple of the Mahdi, who fifteen years before had murdered General Gordon in Khartoum, and out of the ruins of the Mahdist Empire following the British victory at Omdurman a year ago, had carved an empire of his own, a slave trading empire, which he ruled with an iron hand. Zobeir even sent his men into the Kenya territory to seek the runaway, and James and she had to keep Sejm hidden as the slavers had scoured the bush, praying for the appearance of a detachment of the Queen's African Rifles on one of their irregular sweeps through the highlands.

It was during those traumatic days that Sejm talked to her of his experiences, and she listened as a child will listen to a story-teller. Oh, if only she had listened more carefully. But she could remember a great deal of what he had said. Sejm told her that the desert was not all sand, or even mostly sand, as was supposed by those who had never seen it. There was the Great Sand Sea, of course, stretching south from the Libyan Desert, and that was virtually impassable. But further west the desert contained great lakes, such as were found in the Tibesti region, and high plateaux, and even fabulous cities. More important, he told her that while there were considerable areas of what he called stony desert – such as they were certainly in now – these stony deserts seldom stretched for more than forty or fifty miles. The main part of the desert was not completely arid, but supported primitive and limited forms of life, and was criss-crossed with underground rivers and streams, several feet below the surface. Where the desert flowers sprouted, especially in the bottom of apparently dry river beds, or wadis,

Sejm said there was water to be found, if one were prepared to look hard and long enough. And every so often these underground streams bubbled to the surface as oases. Oh, what would she give to see an oasis! But just some flowers in a wadi would be sufficient.

By midnight they were exhausted, and complaining. And by then the temperature had dropped dramatically, as the treeless land lost its heat. That only a few hours before they had been sweating and attempting to shelter from the sun seemed incredible as now they shivered in their inadequate clothing, their discomfort increased by a strong wind which had sprung up to whistle across the desolate landscape and whip the dust into little eddies, and wanted only to huddle close to one another for warmth.

To get them moving again after their halt was difficult. Vicky and Prudence had to go from one to the next, shaking and even kicking them awake. They staggered onwards, falling over stones and over each other as they made their way, David groaning with pain as his stretcher lurched from side to side, and Charlie wailing with hunger and general discomfort. It was the longest night Vicky had ever known; it made their time on the lifeboat seem like a holiday. But she drove them on until after dawn, which revealed them in all their misery: a long straggling line of tattered scarecrows, wandering, it seemed, aimlessly towards an eternal doom. Only the fluttering banners of Alison's golden hair, the black of Mary and Elizabeth's, the dark brown of Nathalie's, and presumably, she supposed, the red-gold of her own, made them appear any different to walking corpses.

Still she kept them moving, until they came across a sandy patch in which they could dig. Then it was necessary to bully them to do even that.

Alison sat on the ground, sipping her water and slowly chewing her biscuit, legs stuck out in front of her, careless of the glances of the other women or even of the men, although her silk nightdress was beginning to tear. Her fair arms and face were now pitifully sunburned from her previous day's exposure. 'Victoria,' she gasped. 'This is impossible. On one cup of water

150

and a single biscuit it simply cannot be done.'

'It has to be done, milady,' Vicky said. 'If we stop now, we will all die.'

'Aren't we going to die, anyway? Charlie, and the girls . . . they have to have more . . .'

'Everyone has to have the same, milady,' Vicky told her. 'And we are not all going to die. Why, do you realise we've come more than thirty miles from the beach? We could see the grassland at any moment.'

'*Will* we see the grassland soon, Vicky?' Nathalie asked, as she and David settled into the hole Vicky had dug.

'Just pray,' Vicky said, and gazed into David's stubbled face. 'Are you all right, my darling?'

He forced a smile; even beneath the beard his face was grey with pain. 'You've never called me that before.'

'Maybe I never felt like that before. Tell me how *you* feel.'

'I adore you,' he said. 'But I feel damned guilty, being carried. Christ, if I could only walk. Maybe this evening . . .'

'Maybe in a couple of days' time,' Vicky told him, 'you'll walk.'

Getting them moving that evening was an even more lengthy task; Vicky did not know what she would have done without Prudence. Now their slippers, even the shoes of those fortunate enough to possess them, were beginning to fall apart; their nightdresses were torn and barely decent, as were the men's trousers from the number of times they had fallen down. They stank of sweat and they could feel it everywhere on their bodies, seeking every valley, making their limbs slippery against each other. Their bellies rumbled constantly and their tongues seemed able only to stick to the roofs of their mouths. Their hair was stiff with dirt and their heads ached and swung, causing the ground to seem to tremble beneath their feet, and absurd mirages, of streams of water cascading across the parched earth, to rise before their eyes. The only salvation was that they were too exhausted to quarrel, even the girls. It was all Vicky could do to encourage them, but encourage them she did, while she silently prayed. 'Tomorrow morning,' she told them, 'tomorrow morning we'll have crossed the stony desert. And we'll find water. I know we will.'

They had to, because there was only half the barrel left, and that evening they ate the last of the biscuits. At least, she thought, as the barrel was discarded, the women had been relieved of one of their burdens. And surely Sejm had not lied to her. By tomorrow morning they would certainly have walked more than fifty miles.

They staggered on throughout the night, once again afflicted by the freezing midnight cold, yet showing a determination Vicky had not suspected they possessed, but which she had nevertheless been counting on. Because even she had not realised it could be as bad as this, the constant placing of one foot in front of the other, every muscle a rivulet of pain, the blisters which were forming everywhere, the open cuts and bruises on their feet and knees, where they had fallen. She almost dreaded the appearance of dawn, for what it would bring. And she was right. It brought . . . nothing but more stony desert, although she felt that there was a change in the colour of the dirt over which they tramped. It seemed somehow darker.

'Green fields,' Mary said bitterly.

'This evening,' Vicky said. 'I know it. Let's dig in and rest for one last day, then we'll be there. It can only be another few miles.'

And if it wasn't, then they would all die. That was obvious, and even Alison made no comment this time, just dropped to her knees and began to dig. Even Alison, ruining those magnificent nails, scratching those beautiful knees, arching that splendid back, so nearly visible through the tattered silk, to scrape at the earth. Even Alison.

Vicky knelt beside Nathalie and began scraping at the sand herself, then reared back on her heels as there came a scream, and then another, a most unearthly sound, expressive of all the horror and disgust a human being could feel. She leapt to her feet, as Alison, Prudence, Mary and Elizabeth also scrambed up, to stare at Margaret Pilling, standing and screaming wildly, while Phyllis Smart rolled on the ground, half in and half out of the pit she had been digging, moaning and crying, her body jerking convulsively.

'Oh, my God!' Vicky seized the oar and ran forward, looked down on the horde of scorpions, poisonous tails waving like banners, disturbed by the women's fingers. 'Get her away!' she shouted at the men who had approached, and began hitting the scorpions with the blade of the oar, thumping it down again and again, killing some, driving the remainder back, pausing only when she ran out of breath, sinking to her knees in horrified misery. Bream picked up the discarded oar and continued the work, until the creatures were all dead or driven back under rocks and into crevices.

Vicky remained kneeling for some time, until Nathalie came to her. 'You must see to her, Vicky,' the French girl begged. 'She is very bad.'

Vicky sighed, and got up, and joined the women, who were clustered round Mrs Smart. She had lost consciousness, and her face was a brighter red than anyone else's, while already both her hands and wrists were swelling as if someone was pumping air into them.

'God,' Margaret Pilling was muttering. 'Oh, God.'

'Can she have some water, Vicky?' Prudence asked. She was pillowing the stricken woman's head on her lap.

Vicky nodded, and sank to her haunches again, overcome with despair. She had been wrong, after all. Perhaps she had been right in her memory of the topography of the land. But she had been catastrophically wrong in supposing these women could walk across it. As David had said, 'That lot?'

And yet it could just as easily have been Nathalie and her digging into the midst of a scorpion's nest.

'Victoria,' Alison said, moving some distance away from the group.

Vicky got up and joined her.

'She is badly hurt, Victoria,' Alison said. 'I don't think we can expect her to be able to walk for some time.'

Vicky nodded.

'Well,' Alison went on, 'I don't see how we can carry another sick person. Do you?'

'No, milady.'

'Well?'

Vicky raised her head to gaze at her. Alison was probably a huntswoman in her leisure moments. If her favourite horse were to fall and break its leg she would, no doubt weeping, command it to be put down. But she couldn't be thinking that about Phyllis Smart, surely. The trouble was, Vicky couldn't prevent the thought from crossing her own mind. Her responsibility, and she had voluntarily assumed it, was the preservation of these people's lives, or at least as many of them as could be saved. There were sixteen lives still at stake, as opposed to one.

But that was a thought she should put out of her mind.

'Well, milady,' she said. 'I think we just have to sit here until she gets better.' She found a smile. 'I guess we could all do with a rest.'

'While we die of thirst?'

'If you have any better ideas, milady,' Vicky told her, 'be sure to let me know.' She went back to the anxious group of people. 'We've a bit of a problem,' she said. 'We have to wait for Mrs Smart to recover from that poison.' She hurried on before anyone could say, 'or dies'. 'But we were going to rest here anyway. So dig your pits –' she forced another smile – 'keeping your eyes open for scorpions. And remember, the fact that there are scorpions here, any form of life, means that we must be coming to the end of the stony desert. Our goal is just over there.' She pointed south.

They stared at her.

Then the seaman Curly, spoke. 'Come off it, lady,' he said. 'You know we've had it. There isn't hardly any water left, there isn't any food at all, and we've a dying woman over there. So what if we're within a few miles of this oasis you've been promising us? We ain't never going to get there while we're lumbered like this.'

'Yes, we will,' Vicky said, desperately trying to project a confidence she didn't feel. 'I never promised it was going to be easy. I never even promised all of us would make it. But most of us will make it, if we're determined to do so.'

'All right,' Curly said. 'So we've got one thing straight, anyway: we won't all make it.' He flung out his hand, pointing at Phyllis Smart. 'She can't make it, and he –' he pointed at David – 'he can't make it either, on his own. So let's dump them and get on. We'll make one hell of a sight better time not carrying *him*. You're the one with the gun, lady. Put the pair of them out of their misery.'

'I'm going to try to forget you said that, Curly,' Vicky told him. 'Now, I've said what we're going to do. We're going to dig in until this evening. Get to it!'

'To hell with that,' Curly said. 'You've been running this expedition long enough, and you haven't done so well at it. *Women*, telling men what to do! That ain't natural. We'll take over now. *I'll* take over. I'll decide what's to be done next.' He grinned at her. 'And first thing, we'll split up, and let each man doss down with a woman, eh? What's the use in dying miserable, seeing as how we're going to die anyway?'

Vicky licked her lips and took a step backwards. The other men were all facing her now, even Bream, although he hung to the back. She glanced at the women. They seemed petrified, even Prudence. They would follow a lead, but they knew they stood no chance against five strong men armed with knives. She was the only one of them with a weapon, with the means to quell this mutiny.

Out of the corner of her eye she saw David frantically attempting to release the satin straps which bound him to the stretcher. In another few moments he would be getting himself killed, trying to help her.

She drew a long breath, and the pistol from the holster. 'You just put that idea out of your mind,' she said in a low voice.

Curly grinned at her. 'Or you'll shoot me, Mrs Lang? You? All right, go ahead and shoot me.' He stepped towards her. 'Because if you don't, I'm going to squeeze those breasts of yours.'

She gasped, took another step backwards, and squeezed the trigger. She hadn't aimed the gun and the explosion took her by surprise. The bullet slammed into the ground between Curly's feet, and he checked.

'Stop right there,' Vicky said, trying to capitalise on her advantage.

'Vicky,' David shouted warningly. She had disobeyed him already, by not shooting to kill. Shoot to kill? She didn't know if she could do that; she had never actually killed anything larger than a scorpion in her life – even the chickens she had cooked in Kenya had been slaughtered for her by James.

Curly grinned. 'You stop me,' he suggested, and ran at her. She brought up the gun, but could not force herself to fire. Instead she stepped backwards a third time, felt the earth crumbling beneath her feet, and fell into space. She went straight down, too shocked even to scream, in the midst of a small avalanche of stones and dirt. Then she hit something with a jar which drove all the breath from her body. She realised she was lying across a tree trunk, which protruded from the shallow cliff face, but before she could decide what that meant, she had slipped from it and fallen another five feet or so, landing on the ground with another breathtaking thump.

She lay on her back and gazed up at the sky, gasping for air, while the earth seemed to be heaving beneath her. She couldn't see any people, because the cliff top above her overhung, but she could hear their voices.

'Christ, what's happened to her?' Bream was shouting.

'Ah, she must've fallen into one of those goddamned ravines,' Curly said. 'Maybe she's broken her neck.'

'I must get down there,' Bream said.

'Not you, son,' Curly said. 'You've a shade too much feeling for that one. Dusty, you go get her. See if she's alive, anyway. And remember she has a gun. But don't knock her about too much. If she *is* alive, I want a feel of those breasts.'

Vicky listened to scrabbling earth as the man called Dusty started to climb down. She sat up, still dazed, looked left and right. She was indeed in a ravine, a dry river bed, she estimated, hardly more than a dozen feet across with banks perhaps twelve feet high. As with so many of the ravines they had encountered, they had not even suspected it to be there when they had elected to pitch their camp. And on the way down she had hit a tree growing out of the side of the escarpment. She knew that was important, even if she couldn't spare the time to work out why, as she watched Dusty climbing and sliding down the steep slope. Desperately she looked left and right, but couldn't see the revolver, which had been thrown from her grasp when she hit the tree.

'Now, then, ladies,' Curly was saying from above her. 'There's going to be a change of plan. You, Lady What's-her-name, come here. You're the one I want. I've been looking at your body, dreaming of your body, ever since we left the ship. Maybe before.'

'Now look, Curly,' someone said, 'we can all have one. Me, I like that dark-haired little bitch.'

'You'll have her, Jimbo. But we'll take them one at a time, or they might just get ideas. The girls will keep. Nothing like a virgin for dessert, eh? This beauty is the one to start with.'

'God damn it, you bastard,' David shouted. 'You . . .' there was a crisp sound, and a groan.

'I'm waiting, your ladyship,' Curly said. 'Or would you like me to shave the boy a little? Like his balls?'

Vicky rolled over to move herself from the wall of the ravine, where Dusty was sliding down. She was aware of any number of emotions, but the one uppermost was that all this was happening because she had disobeyed David's instructions, had in fact broken her word to him. Promise me, he had said, that if you have to shoot, you will shoot to kill. If they get on top of you, you're done.

She had promised, and had been unable to do it. They were on top now, and she and all the women were done. And one of them had just hit David, perhaps killed him. She felt the same sort of desperate anger as when the bucket had fallen on her head.

Alison was being Lady Dobree. 'If', she was saying, 'I don't fight you, but let you do as you wish with me, will you promise to spare Charlie and the girls?'

She might have been on the battlements at Cawnpore, Vicky thought. With the same effect she might have had on Nana Sahib.

'You let me do what I want with you, milady,' Curly replied, 'and maybe, just maybe, we won't cut your breasts off. Now strip. I want to look at you. I want to feel that body.'

Vicky watched Dusty land on the bottom of the ravine, just six feet away.

'Hey, Curly,' someone said, 'make her dance. Make her dance naked and shake her belly. I ain't never seen a ladyship dance, naked.'

'That's a good idea,' Curly agreed. 'You heard the man, ladyship. Dance. And shake that belly. I want to see your breasts jump.'

Dusty had regained his balance and stood gazing at Vicky. 'Don't give me any trouble,' he said. 'Or I'll have to force you.'

'It's my breasts Curly wants,' Vicky said, listening to the stamping of feet above her. Alison Dobree, dancing before a pack of wolves, trying to keep them from her children. The woman certainly had guts. So should they all. Guts and anger. She drew up her legs as Dusty approached, allowing the dressing gown to fall to either side to expose her from the waist down. 'I've got to get this belt off,' she said.

'You do that,' Dusty agreed, enjoying the view. 'But we have to make it quick or Curly's going to start wondering what we're doing. He's getting all worked up.'

From above them, Curly was saying, 'All right, that's enough of that. Get down on your knees, ladyship, and spread your legs. Come on now, show me your arse, or I'll put one of those scorpions on you . . .'

'I guess he's preoccupied for the moment,' Vicky breathed, reaching over her shoulder to close her hands on the haft of the knife. She drew the weapon and thrust it forward in a single movement, launching her body behind it. Dusty was only a few feet away, and had not bothered to draw his knife once he had seen she no longer held the revolver; totally surprised, he took the point in the middle of the chest. He uttered an unearthly scream, and fell backwards, blood gushing over Vicky's hands and staining her dressing gown as she fell with him.

'What the hell is that?' Curly shouted.

'It's that American bitch,' someone said.

'That was Dusty's voice. Let's get down there,' snapped someone else.

'No!' Curly shouted. 'You and you, stay with the women. You, Bream, make a move and I'll cut your balls off. You come with me, Jimbo.'

Vicky pushed herself away from the man and struggled to her feet, watching the blood pouring from Dusty's chest. She must in fact have struck straight into his heart, for although his eyes were open, and staring at her, she knew he wasn't seeing her, was already dead. She still felt nothing but anger. They *were* animals, wolves, as David had described them, and if she didn't destroy them they would destroy her and everyone else. But she couldn't fight them without the gun. She looked left and right, and saw it, lying amidst a curious little patch of wild flowers, their pinks and blues incongruous against the drab brown of the earth. She ran towards it, picking it up as Curly and the other man, Jimbo, reached the bottom of the ravine. She faced them, panting, the revolver thrust forward in her right hand, using her left hand to brush the flies from about her face. *The flies!* But she couldn't think about them, now.

'Now, woman,' Curly said, 'you know you don't understand how to use that thing. Put it down and I'll go easy on you. Put it down!' He advanced, his seaman's knife thrust forward. Vicky levelled the pistol, and fired. She actually aimed at his groin, but was unprepared for the kick and hit him in the left shoulder. He half turned beneath the impact, uttering an indeterminate exclamation. Vicky squeezed the trigger again, aiming at his knees now, and hit him in the small of the back. He fell to his knees, and her third shot struck him in the head; his scalp seemed to dissolve as blood flew, and his body hit the ground like a sack.

'Oh, Jesus Christ!' screamed Jimbo, and ran at the slope down which he had come, scrabbling at the earth.

Vicky's fifth bullet missed him, but her sixth hit him in the thigh, and he slid back down the slope, shrieking in agony.

The hammer clicked on the empty chambers. Vicky broke the gun, watched the spent cartridges spill on to the ground.

She reached into the pouch, and reloaded, slowly and carefully, tongue between her teeth.

The man rolled from side to side, pawing at his thigh, watching her. 'Help me, ma'am,' he begged. 'You've broken my leg. For God's sake help me! No!' he screamed, as she came closer.

Vicky took very careful aim, and shot him through the head.

The whole sequence had taken little more than a minute. But now it was necessary to climb the slope and deal with the others. For the moment there was silence above her. Everyone up there had heard the shots and the screams; they were waiting to see who would emerge.

She thrust the pistol back into the holster and began to climb, digging her fingers into the earth, reached the tree, which had suddenly become so important, like the flowers. She rested on it, listening, catching her breath. She was still only aware of a white hot anger, a total determination to finish this, once and for all, now.

'Christ, something must've happened,' the fifth man was saying. 'You go down and take a look, Harry.'

'*You* go down and take a look, you mean,' Bream countered.

'Well . . . keep watching these bitches. And if any one of them so much as twitches, use your knife.'

Vicky pushed herself up until she was standing on the tree trunk, body pressed against the wall of the ravine. She drew the revolver and looked up, watched a face peer down. He didn't see her at first, but he gazed at the three dead men.

'Oh my God,' he remarked, and leaned over further. Vicky shot him through the chest.

He gave a scream and came tumbling down, almost hitting her. He landed on the floor of the ravine, twisted and turned, and tried to sit up. Vicky looked down on him, and fired again, and then again, hitting him each time, watching his body jerk beneath the impact. She realised she was becoming quite an expert.

His body jerked one last time, and lay still. She decided against reloading immediately, as she had two bullets left, and only one adversary. She holstered the gun and climbed slowly back to the lip, got her elbows over, and surveyed the scene in front of her.

The eight women were huddled together on the far side of the little plateau, Prudence hugging Charlie in her arms. They were staring at Bream, but now they stared at Vicky as well, uncertain about what had happened in the wadi, uncertain about what was going to happen. David's stretcher was on the ground close by; he was lying still beside it – but to her enormous relief, even as she looked at him he moved. Alison Dobree crouched, quite close at hand, naked, face expressionless as if she had shut her mind to the reality of her situation. And Harry Bream stood a few yards to her left. He had been watching the women, but now he turned his attention to Vicky. He had a knife in his hand, but as he saw her, it slipped from his fingers and hit the ground with a soft thud.

'Victoria?' Alison asked in a low voice, seeming to awaken. 'Those men . . .'

'Are all dead, milady.' Vicky got one knee over the lip, and climbed out. Bream stared at her as she stood up.

'Shoot 'im too,' Nathalie shouted. 'Shoot 'im.'

Vicky took a long breath and levelled the gun.

'I didn't . . .' Bream began, then closed his mouth, and his eyes.

Vicky lowered the gun, trying to breathe. 'I need you,' she said.

'Victoria . . .' Alison stood behind her.

Vicky pressed the gun into her hand. 'Don't shoot him,' she said. 'We need him.'

'Victoria . . .' The other women ran forward.

'Are you all right, Victoria?' Alison asked.

'No, milady,' Vicky said. 'I'm not all right.' She dropped to her knees and vomited.

CHAPTER 8

Vicky could bring up nothing but bile; her head was spinning, and she wanted to scream and scream and scream.

The women stood around her, all except Mary, who went to look over the edge first. 'Oh Good Lord,' she said to Elizabeth in one of her penetrating whispers. 'She shot them all. She shot *four* men. Dead. Just like that.'

Yes, Vicky thought. I have just killed four men. Just like that. The widow of James Lang.

'Victoria.' Alison knelt beside her. 'You really are . . . well, I don't know what to say. You are a most remarkable person. And we owe you our . . . well . . .'

'Your lives, milady,' Vicky said absently. 'I don't think they were going to leave any of you in one piece. Don't you think you could put something on?'

'Oh.' Alison's eyebrows arched as she looked down at herself. 'I'd quite forgotten.' She got up and ran, almost girlishly, towards her discarded nightdress.

'Bang,' Charlie said. 'Bang. You went bang, bang, Victoria. And killed them all. I'd have killed them all, if I'd had a gun.'

Vicky wiped her lips with her sleeve; the morning was beginning to steady, just a little.

'Vicky,' Prudence asked, 'what are we going to do now?'

Vicky glanced at the other women, all waiting for her to speak; she realised she had probably just won the most decisive victory of her life, at any level. Where before they had been prepared to trust her, now they were prepared to worship her. But at what cost?

And she still had to prove herself worthy of their worship.

She scrambled to her feet. 'Bream,' she said. 'I spared you, not because I don't consider you to be as guilty as the rest of them, nor even because you helped me save Mr Whiting's life. Simply because we need you. But if you want to live, you are going to have to damned well work your passage. You understand me?'

His head moved slowly up and down.

'So get down there,' Vicky commanded, 'put those bodies together, and then start digging.'

'A grave, ma'am?' he asked.

'No,' she said. 'The grave can wait. Dig where the wild flowers are. Dig and dig and dig. Just dig.'

'Yes, ma'am.' He slid down the slope.

Alison had returned, as decent as was now possible. 'What is he digging for?' she asked. 'Is there something there?'

'Yes, milady,' Vicky said. 'There's water down there.'

'Water!' They ran for the edge.

'Just wait!' Vicky shouted. 'We stay up here until Bream has found it. It could take some time. You don't want to be down there.' She was thinking of the flies and the bodies. She went to the stretcher, dropped to her knees beside it. David blinked at her and managed a smile, for all the spreading blue bruise on his chin, visible even through the three-day-old stubble.

'Vicky,' he whispered. 'Did you really . . .?'

'I shot to kill,' she said. 'Maybe I left it a little late, but God, I shot to kill. David . . .' She touched his face, and he winced. 'Are you all right?'

'I don't think my jaw's broken, even if I may have a couple of loose teeth. Vicky, I feel such a helpless fool . . .'

'You were helping me pull the trigger,' she said. 'Every time.' She kissed him on the lips.

His arm went round her shoulders, tightly. 'And now?' he asked.

'We're going to be all right,' she said. 'For a while. There's water down there, David, there has to be. There's a tree growing out of the side of the ravine, and there are flies . . . and flowers. There has to be water. Soon.'

She left him to kneel beside Phyllis Smart. The woman's breathing was stertorous, and her flesh was hot to the touch.

'What do you think?' Alison was following her around like a pet dog.

Vicky sighed. She had encountered scorpions in Kenya. James had in fact once been stung by one. Just one, and he had been a strong and healthy man. Yet his temperature had soared to a hundred and four, and for three days he had been prostrate. Phyllis Smart had been at the last extremity of weakness from hunger and thirst and exhaustion, and she had been stung at least six times. 'If there was some way we could get the poison out,' she said.

'But there isn't.'

'No, milady, it's right through her system now. If we had drugs . . . quinine . . . but we don't. So we can just wait, and pray that she throws it off. We stay right here, milady, until she either dies or pulls through.'

'Of course,' Alison agreed. 'Especially if there is water. There is water, isn't there, Victoria?'

'Yes, milady. If we keep looking long enough, we'll find water.'

She stood up, and gazed at Alison, who gazed back. And licked her lips. She so obviously, and desperately, wanted to talk. 'I . . . that man was going to . . . well . . .'

'He was going to rape you, milady. You mean he couldn't?'

'Couldn't? Oh, you mean . . .' Alison blushed. 'I don't know. He made me kneel, you see, and took his trousers down, and then I felt him . . . his . . . well . . .'

'It's called a penis, milady.'

Alison's eyebrows arched. 'I know that. It's a ghastly word.'

'It's a word, milady, with a meaning. If you felt him, then he probably did it.'

'Oh. But . . . I wouldn't have thought it was possible to do it, like that. Is it? I mean, we aren't dogs.'

'It is entirely possible to do it like that, milady,' Vicky told her. 'And more ways than you might think.'

'My God,' Alison said. 'William . . . General Dobree . . . well . . .' Her flush deepened. 'Of course, I don't know about these things. Well, it's not my place, is it?'

Vicky scratched her head, pushing both her hands into her

164

hair; she thought some of the flies had probably settled in it.

'I mean . . . one doesn't, well . . . watch, does one?' Alison asked.

Vicky scratched.

'Did you ever . . . with your husband . . . well, watch?'

Vicky sighed. 'Yes, milady. I believe we have five senses. Maybe six. I can't see any point in not using them all, every time you can.'

'Good heavens,' Alison said, thoughtfully. 'Well . . . obviously I closed my eyes just now. I mean, those men, staring at me . . . ugh. But . . . I'd only just felt him when that other man screamed from down the hill there. And there's . . . well, that horrible sticky stuff on my leg.'

'Well, I think you were probably lucky, milady.'

Alison didn't seem entirely convinced. 'Victoria?' she asked. 'What did you do to that man, down the hill, to make him scream like that?'

'I stuck a knife into his chest, milady.'

'Oh.' Alison assumed one of those expressions of hers which indicated total incomprehension of a mind which could conceive such an act; but maybe keeping one's eyes open during sexual intercourse was also totally incomprehensible. And that was still her primary concern. 'What amazes me, is how he could want to do it anyway. I mean, in such circumstances . . .' She looked around her. 'And in front of all these people . . . and with *me*. I'm absolutely filthy, from head to toe.'

'I don't think that was bothering him, milady,' Vicky said. 'He was starving, for more than food.'

'I . . . I just never knew men could be like that. I mean . . . William . . .' Her flush was back. 'And the language . . . I just never knew people actually used words like that.'

'They do, milady.' Vicky assured her.

'Oh, Vicky,' Alison said. 'It's all been so *ghastly*.' And to Vicky's total surprise, she took her in her arms and began to weep.

'Hey,' Harry Bream was shouting. 'Hey! Mrs Lang!'

Vicky gently disengaged herself from Alison's arms and ran to the lip. Bream had used his knife to attack the soft earth and was in fact standing in a hole only just over eighteen inches deep – and water was bubbling around his ankles.

'Holy Hallelujah!' Mary shouted, kneeling beside her.

'Water!' Prudence shouted with unique excitement.

'Let's get down there!' Elizabeth cried, dropping her legs over the edge.

'Just wait,' Vicky said. The sun was high now, and although its beams had not yet reached the floor of the wadi, she could *hear* the buzz from down there. 'I'll tell you when. Bream,' she called, 'move those bodies a good distance away, and bury them. Make sure you strip them first.'

'Oh, Vicky,' Prudence said. 'Do we have to?'

'Do you really want to reach civilisation with your bottom hanging out, Prudence?' Vicky asked. 'Your nightie's torn right across. Now everyone,' she said, 'come away from the edge until Bream is finished. You won't enjoy it.' She went back to David.

'You found water,' he said. 'You made it, Vicky. Oh, I am so proud of you.'

'Well,' she said, 'don't be. It was an accident, and there certainly isn't any food to go with it. How long can people last without food, David?'

'If they have water? A long time.'

'Trying to walk thirty miles a day?'

'Ah. Well . . . maybe ten days. Maybe even more.'

'Ten days? Could we really last ten days?' Because surely, in ten days, they must reach somewhere.

But they had already, in real terms, been three days without food; two biscuits a day could hardly equal a square meal.

'Victoria . . .' Alison stood above her.

'Yes, milady.' She stood up.

'David is going to be all right, isn't he?'

'Yes, milady. We are all going to be all right. Well . . .' She looked at Phyllis Smart. But she had to believe that. And she wasn't even worrying about Phyllis Smart. No one had looked at David's leg since they left the beach. In fact, she had been afraid to. Yet she was sure the pain was easing, which had to mean the bone was knitting. Her real fear was gangrene. But there again, she had always understood that gangrene would smell horrible. And that hadn't happened yet. She just *had* to believe.

'I'm sure you're right,' Alison agreed. 'So I was wondering . . . do you think I could have a bath? I'd like to well . . . wash everything off.'

Vicky nodded. 'Yes, milady. I think we should all have a bath. As soon as Bream is finished.'

She took the empty water barrel and slid down the slope to see how he was getting on. She found he had all but filled in the grave, while the other pit he had dug was now overflowing with a splendid gush of water, beginning to trickle down the wadi, forming little pools. She slapped flies. 'That was good work, Bream.'

'Thank you, ma'am.' He continued to scrape earth over the naked bodies of his four fellow seamen.

'Would you have helped them rape us, Bream?' she asked.

He raised his head. 'I don't know, Mrs Lang, and that's a fact. If they'd all been at it . . . if you hadn't resisted . . . well, if anyone was going to have you, ma'am, I'd have wanted it to be me.'

They gazed at each other.

'Are you going to kill me?' he asked.

'For saying that? No,' she said. 'Not unless you make me. I guess you just paid me a compliment. But Bream, Harry . . . you understand that I had to kill them. They would have murdered us, if not now, then later, as we got near civilisation. They couldn't have let us live.'

'I understand that, Mrs Lang. Let me say, you're an extraordinary woman.'

Vicky smiled. 'My day for compliments. Well, Harry, as you've done all the hard work, you can have first drink of the water.'

She waited while he lay down and buried his face and head in the pool, and then drank long and deep. 'God,' he said, 'that tastes so good.'

'Right,' she said. 'Now fill this barrel, and take it up, and give water to Mr Whiting and Mrs Smart. Then stay with them, and tell the ladies they can come down here. And Harry . . . if you so much as peep over that edge up there, I am going to blow your head off.'

'Yes, ma'am,' he said.

They took off their clothing, lay on their bellies shoulder to shoulder to drink, and then bathed in the gathering pools, splashing and screaming and cavorting like a most unlikely collection of nereids, Vicky thought. But it was heavenly, to kneel in the water, and scoop the cool liquid over her shoulders and feel it trickle down her back and between her breasts, to soak her hair, to feel almost clean. And to watch the others do the same, watch the energy almost visibly flowing through their veins again. They knew each other too well, now, to be embarrassed by their mutual nudity. She supposed they were nine women who would never be embarrassed again.

She wondered if Charlie, splashing about with each of them in turn, would ever remember this adventure. And what he would think of it; he was, after all, Alison's son.

'Oh, that was just wonderful,' Mary said, spreading her nightie and lying on it, allowing her thick black hair to trail on the ground.

'Not so fast,' Vicky said. 'Let's get these clothes in. All of them.'

'Wash day,' Prudence giggled happily.

They were all hovering on the very edge of hysteria.

They put all the clothes into the pool and trampled on them and rubbed them together, then did the same for the trousers and shirts taken from the sailors, and spread them all out to dry. Vicky, however, put on one of the seaman's shirts; it was a jersey, in horizontal stripes, and wet, fitted her like a second skin, but it stretched almost to her knees and was actually a far more respectable garment than her tattered dressing gown.

She climbed back up the ravine wall to be with David. She and Bream poured water on to his face and shoulders, let him drink as much as possible. 'Would you like to have an all-over wash?' she asked. 'Bream could help you.'

He grinned. 'Why? Do I stink?'

'Sure you do. But I can stand it, if you can. I just wondered if . . .' She looked at his leg.

He nodded. 'I think maybe we should leave well enough alone, until we get to the grassland.'

She knew he was as afraid as she of what they might find when they took off that bandage. Nor could she argue with postponing it, because if there *was* gangrene under there, there was nothing any of them could do about it.

'I've been trying to give water to that woman, ma'am,' Bream said. 'But she won't take it.'

Vicky went over to kneel beside Phyllis Smart. Phyllis was dying. Vicky suspected her temperature had gone up. That could have been partly the increasing heat of the day. But she was still dying. Their only blessing was that she was quite unconscious.

Vicky sighed, and sat down with her back against a rock, after she and Bream had arranged shelters of soaking clothes for both David and the woman. Of course it would be best for Phyllis to die, and quickly. Because even with water, they couldn't stay here. They had to get on, and find food . . . and they couldn't carry her. She didn't even know how they were going to carry David, although she was determined that they would.

She was asleep before she knew it. She was utterly exhausted, at once from the night's march and from the terrible events of the morning. And now there was hope again, to relax her . . . and an ever-increasing fear again, about David.

But the exhaustion mattered most. Not even the sun could disturb her, although in fact when she awoke she discovered that someone – almost certainly the devoted Harry Bream – had thrown a wet nightdress over her head to protect her. But her legs had been left exposed, and the pale flesh was already bright red. Victoria Lang, sleeping in a man's jersey, with her legs exposed to the public gaze. But there were so many things

169

that had happened during the last few days to make this Victoria Lang no one that Mrs Payne, just for instance, would recognise.

What really mattered was, would she recognise herself the next time she looked in a mirror? Or would she turn away from the eyes of a woman who had killed four men?

Her eyes opened, and she gazed at Mary, kneeling beside her. She too wore a seaman's jersey, and she had copied her in leaving her legs bare as well. She had magnificent legs, almost as perfect as her stepmother's. 'Vicky,' she said. 'The water's drying up.' Vicky blinked at her. She had never expected to hear Mary Dobree call her Vicky. 'It'll still be there,' she said, and sat up. Most of the women had followed the routine which had become second nature to them, and retired to their pits; they all had to be as exhausted as she was. Nathalie had dug a pit for David and herself. Well, that was all right. Nathalie was just trying to help. 'Bream,' she said. 'Harry.'

'Yes, ma'am.' He had been lying by himself, close to her. Now he got up and knelt beside her.

'You'll have to get down there and dig a little deeper.'

'Yes, ma'am.' He went to the slope.

'Where is Elizabeth?' Vicky asked.

'She's down there. We were both down there, bathing. It felt so good.'

'Then you'd better get her up.'

'She'll be all right. Bream won't touch her. Not with you around.'

Vicky gave her a quick glance; that remark could be taken two ways.

Mary flushed, and sat beside her. 'And if he did . . . Vicky . . . what was that man trying to do to Mother?'

Vicky frowned. 'You mean you don't know?'

'Well . . .' Mary bit her lip, and her flush deepened. 'Well,' she said again, 'do men really do that to women?'

'Mrs Chandler never spoke of it?'

Mary shook her head.

'How did she explain your monthlies?'

Mary looked mystified, obviously not seeing the connection.

170

'She said those were a curse women had to bear.'

'My God!' Vicky exclaimed, suddenly alarmed by another imminent crisis. 'What *about* monthlies? When are you due?'

'We had them on the ship, both of us, only a week or so before she struck.'

'Oh.' Vicky gave a sigh of relief. She wasn't due for another week either, and she reckoned Alison and the rest of them could look after themselves. 'Well, Mary, I guess you could say that is what men do to women.'

'You mean Father . . . and Mother?' She was incredulous, and added, 'Stepmother?' just so Vicky couldn't possibly suppose anything like that of the first Lady Dobree.

'If they hadn't done it, Charlie wouldn't be about, now would he?' She could work out where *she* came from on her own.

But Mary was thinking of other things. 'And you and Mr Lang?' She seemed to find that even more difficult to imagine.

'No,' Vicky said thoughtfully. However enthusiastic, James had possessed very orthodox view on sex. 'And not your father and stepmother either, I shouldn't think. That is . . .' She had been going to say, the wrong way, but she had never been sure about that. It was certainly in many ways the more natural position. 'That was something brutal,' she said. 'Not necessarily the way, but . . . there is all the difference in the world between when two people do it because they both want it, because they love each other, and when a man is just determined to do it regardless of how the woman feels. When two people love each other, or at least want each other, it doesn't matter how they do it because it is an act of love. And when one of them doesn't want it, and is being forced, I guess it still doesn't matter how they do it, because it is still an act of violence.'

'But . . .' Again Mary bit her lip; obviously she had arrived at the question which was really bothering her. 'What that man was going to do to Mother . . . was it that bad, that he, and all the others, had to die for it?'

Vicky gazed at her. That wasn't a question she truly wished to face, right this minute.

'I mean . . . they weren't going to kill her, or anything,' Mary said, 'were they?'

Vicky sighed. 'As a matter of fact,' she said, 'I think they probably would have killed her. And you and Liz, and all of us. Once they had done . . . that . . . to all of us.'

'But you would have killed them anyway,' Mary said.

Vicky hesitated, and then nodded. 'Yes,' she said. 'I would have killed them anyway, because, don't you see, rape *is* a form of murder. It is taking away of humanity, of what we are, just as much as depriving us of our lives. Making love with a man who loves you, Mary, and whom you love back, is the most beautiful experience in the world. But it's not possible to love anyone that much, if you've ever been raped. Or maybe . . .' She didn't really know. 'Maybe it is, but it's surely a damned sight more difficult.'

Mary's turn to sigh. 'I wish I had your certainty,' she said. 'About things.'

'My certainty?' Vicky's laugh was almost harsh.

'Well, you know so much about the desert, and you knew just what to do about David's leg, and you knew that you had to kill those men before they killed us, and . . .'

'I don't *know* anything,' Vicky said. 'I'm just as frightened as you are, believe me, by everything that has happened, by the thought of everything that may still be going to happen. And I want to cry every time I think of those men. But I'm going to be *me*, until the moment I die. And nobody is going to make me anything else. Can you understand that, Mary Dobree?'

Mary gazed at her for several seconds. Then she stood up. 'I want to understand that,' she said. 'Oh, God, Vicky, how I want to understand that.' She went in search of her sister.

Vicky let them rest there the night. She had no choice, anyway. Quite apart from Phyllis Smart, there was the question of David. She thought she could put two women to one end of the stretcher – for very brief spells – but she wasn't sure even Bream still had the strength to undertake another long walk carrying so much weight. He was basically as strong as an ox, but even oxen needed to eat, every so often.

Having spent the night, it was necessary to spend another day. Bream had deepened the well, and there was all the water they could use. They bathed, and drank, and tried to forget the hunger pains by filling their bellies with water. Above all, they rested. 'But we have to have food, Vicky,' Alison said, sitting beside her.

'I know, milady,' Vicky said. 'We move out again, this evening.'

'Where?'

'We head south-east, as we did before. There's water here. We're across the stony desert. We're going to find water often enough from here on, believe me. And sooner or later we'll find food as well.'

'But what about . . .?' Alison looked to where Phyllis Smart lay.

Vicky looked too, watched Prudence coming towards them. The big, happy face was at once solemn and paler than usual. 'Vicky . . . she's dead.'

Alison looked at Vicky. 'You knew.'

'Yes, milady. I checked her as soon as I woke up, an hour ago. She was dead then. I'm just waiting for Bream to finish his rest. We move on tonight.'

They buried Phyllis Smart in a separate grave from that of the seamen, and made their preparations. From the five pairs of trousers they were able to make five pairs of very serviceable breeches, by cutting the legs off at the knees – the knees were the most torn, anyway. These were apportioned to Prudence, whose nightdress really had disintegrated; to Alison, whose nightdress had been torn when she had taken it off for Curly; to Mary, whose nightdress was in tatters; to Joanna Cartwright, in a similar state; and to Vicky herself, as her dressing gown had been ripped apart in her tumble down the cliff into the ravine. The remnants of their nightclothes made very serviceable shirts, although Vicky retained the seaman's jersey and allowed Mary to do the same. The other seaman's shirts were useful additions to the nightdresses of the remaining women, and at last Vicky thought they looked

173

almost decent – when it was no longer necessary.

'Now,' she told them. 'We can be pretty sure we're going to find water, from here on. And we're not likely to drop dead of starvation for a day or two yet. So all we need is one more big effort. I'll need one woman to help me carry the front end of the stretcher. I'm sorry, Harry, but you're stuck with the back.'

'That's fine with me, Mrs Lang,' Bream said happily.

'Well, then . . .'

'Forget that.' David threw the satin bindings aside, and pushed himself up, with the aid of the remaining oar, which he had obtained while she slept and now apparently proposed to use as a crutch. His face twisted with pain as he inadvertently allowed some weight to fall on to his broken leg, but he regained his balance, and stood straight. 'No one is carrying me another step,' he announced.

'Now David,' Alison protested. 'Do behave as Vicky wants.' She obviously was not prepared to consider any other course of action.

David managed a grin. 'But I'm in command of this expedition,' he said. 'Your husband said so, Alison, and I think Vicky acknowledges that.'

'Of course you are, you great silly man,' Vicky said. 'But . . . can you really walk all right?'

'I can damned well try,' he said.

'Well,' she said. 'You'd better have your gun back.'

He shook his head. 'That's yours, Vicky. You've earned it. Now let's move out.'

Another straggling line of scarecrows, Vicky thought, but with a difference. Now she and David led the way, because she did not have to fear any of the people behind them. Bream followed immediately behind, to catch the officer if he fell; he also carried the full water cask. Joanna Cartwright and Alice Marker walked together behind Bream, followed by Margaret Pilling and Nathalie. Prudence and Alison shared Charlie. Mary and Elizabeth brought up the rear, carrying the stretcher between them. Vicky had no idea if and when they might need it again, but she certainly had no intention of leaving it behind. She had left nothing behind, she thought grimly, save the discarded biscuit barrel . . . and eleven dead bodies. So far.

As for having the girls as back markers, she could think of no one better. They were as tough as anyone, now. And they were prepared to follow her anywhere.

It was David's toughness which surprised and reassured her. He was obviously in considerable pain, especially when, as happened regularly enough, he stepped into an unexpected hole or dip and his left leg brushed the ground, and she knew the immense strain being put on his muscles by having to take the weight of his body on the oar with every other step. But he never complained, only occasionally grunted when taken by surprise, and kept going.

On into the night. On all night. Nobody spoke any more. They had too much to think about. Yet Vicky was pretty sure they were not remembering the horrible events at the wadi. They were thinking only of food.

She prayed for the dawn, but was again afraid of what it might bring. Because when she remembered what the last dawn had brought . . . She watched the sky lightening, and then the huge red sun begin to peep above the eastern horizon, and halted, David at her side, and stared. At nothing but empty desert. No ravines were visible, although she knew they had to be there, could they but be found, no wild flowers . . . she had said they could not now run out of water. But she had forgotten that they had found their last water entirely by accident.

'God.' Alison fell to her knees. 'Nothing. God!'

'Pass round the water, Harry,' Vicky said, and also sat down.

Nathalie knelt beside them. 'We are going to die,' she said. 'Oh, we are all going to die. Just like those men.'

'Oh, do be quiet, Nathalie,' Mary said, also kneeling. 'Are we going to die, Vicky?'

Vicky didn't reply. She didn't think she could reply, right that minute.

Charlie was weeping, sensing the grown-up's despondency, as Prudence bounced him on her knees.

Elizabeth sprawled on the ground. 'Oh, for a vanilla ice,' she said. 'I would give everything I possess for a vanilla ice.'

'You don't possess anything,' her sister reminded her. 'And anyway, why a vanilla ice? What rubbish. I want a slice of roast lamb. No, two slices. A whole rack. Yes, a whole rack . . .'

Vicky got up and went to David, who had remained standing, as if too bemused and disappointed to sit. 'You must rest,' she said.

He didn't reply, remained staring at the horizon.

'So we're not as close as I thought,' she said. 'We'll get there, David. We have to.'

'We're there now, Vicky,' he said.

'What?' Oh, God, she thought, he's going mad.

'There.' He pointed. 'I can see trees.'

Slowly she turned to look in the direction he was pointing, approximately due south. But she couldn't see anything except desert, already starting to shimmer in the heat. 'David,' she said, 'that's a mirage. We've seen those already.'

'I can see trees, my darling,' he said. 'I tell you, I can see trees.'

He stood at least a foot taller than she, and therefore had to be able to see that much farther. Could it be possible? Heart pounding, she went back to the women, stopped beside Alison. 'Milady,' she whispered. 'Can you come a moment?'

Alison's eyebrows arched, but she obediently got up and went to join David; she was very nearly as tall as he.

'Can you see anything out there, milady?' Vicky asked.

Alison stared into the distance. 'Well,' she said. 'There's something moving out there . . . waving . . . oh, Vicky, do you think it can be people?'

'No,' David said. 'Those are trees. That's an oasis.'

'An oasis? You mean water . . . and food? Oh, my God!' A tear rolled down Alison's cheeks as she hastily corrected herself. 'Oh, thank God!'

Bream joined them. 'Shall I start digging pits for resting, Mrs Lang?' he asked, obviously prepared to dig all six that might be necessary, himself.

'No, Harry,' Vicky said, keeping her voice under control with an effort. 'We'll not rest today. If you're agreeable,

176

milady, we'll keep going. How far do you think those trees are, David?'

'The horizon is visible at just over four miles, at ground level,' he said. 'Supposing those trees are twelve feet tall, and we can just see them . . . maybe six miles. Perhaps a shade more.'

'Six miles, Oh, six miles,' Alison shouted. 'Come on.'

The news spread, and the women came to life. Shouting and chattering they fell in once more, their exhaustion and near despair seeming to drop away like excess clothing. Six miles. 'Three hours,' Vicky reminded them. 'There's no use going crazy. Three hours at our normal rate of march. Just remember, now, one foot in front of the other, for three hours.'

Otherwise she thought they would have wished to run. And despite her stricture they did set off at a much faster rate than usual, which soon slowed to a slower rate than usual as they got tired, and their feet hurt even more from the number of stones they kicked or tripped over – and as the sun grew hotter and hotter. Soon Vicky doubted the wisdom of continuing instead of resting – except that none of them would have been able to rest, knowing that succour was so close. And now she could see the palm trees herself, waving gently in the breeze. They were no mirage. They were there.

Joanna Cartwright fell and bruised her knees so badly she could hardly walk. Vicky and Prudence took one of her arms each and helped to carry her, while she protested that she could manage as well as anyone, tears streaming down her face. Alison and Mary shared carrying Charlie, while Elizabeth shared the stretcher with Margaret Pilling. They all fell down fairly regularly, because they were no longer watching where they placed their feet, as they usually did, but looked only at the trees, rising higher and higher out of the empty landscape, until they topped a shallow rise and looked down on the oasis, upon the trees, not fifty yards away, upon bushes, which they had almost forgotten existed, and upon a bubbling stream, perhaps the same stream they had found the previous day, here coming to the surface.

Then there was no holding them. Screaming and shouting, they ran down the last slope: Vicky was reminded of Xenophon's description of the Ten Thousand reaching the sea. It never seemed to occur to them that there might be people down there – and that none of them would wish to be seen dead in the odd assortment of clothes they were wearing. Even Prudence ran, half carrying Joanna, and followed by David, hobbling on his oar. Vicky let them go. She just wanted to kneel and weep, allowing herself, at last, to be aware of just how much her feet hurt – the slippers were now hardly more than soles, with a few strips of tattered felt, while she was covered in bloody scratches on her toes and heels. But she couldn't collapse until she had made sure of their safety. The oasis wasn't very big, hardly more than two acres in extent, she estimated, and she could see no sign of life; certainly anyone using it would have been alarmed by the cries of the women. Her other responsibility was to feed them, but she could see, by looking up into the trees, the clusters of fruit.

She glanced at Bream, who had remained standing beside her. 'I think those are date palms, Harry,' she said.

'Yes, ma'am.'

'Do you think you could climb them?'

Bream grinned. 'I can climb anything, ma'am.'

He held her hand to help her down the last part of the slope, and they stood before the first tree, looking up at the fruit. Alison joined them, soaked from the waist up, hair wet, water still dripping from her chin; Vicky had a sudden delicious vision of her appearing like this in Sloane Square. Or even before Bestwick the butler.

'Is that really food?' Alison asked. 'Oh, God, is it really?'

'The best food in the world,' Vicky told her. 'Harry?'

'Yes, *ma'am*.' He went up like the sailor he was, arms round the trunk, feet curved inwards to grip the rough bark with his insteps, swarming up it until he reached the crown, when he anchored himself with one hand wrapped in a frond while he tore off bunches of dates with the other. 'Coming down,' he bawled.

The women ran to stand beneath the tree and catch the fruit

as it fell. Soon they each had a bunch, and there was one for Bream himself as he came down.

'I adore dates,' Elizabeth said.

'Well remember, chew each one nice and slow,' Vicky warned them. 'Make sure each one is thoroughly digested, otherwise you'll have the worst stomach cramps you've ever felt.' She supposed they would anyway. But there were lots more dates. She limped towards David, a bunch in each hand. 'Breakfast,' she said.

They chewed their dates slowly, sitting facing each other. Saliva filled their mouths almost painfully, and they could feel each carefully masticated morsel of food tracing its way down their gullets.

They gazed at each other, neither really able to believe their ordeal was over – if it was.

'A Boston Belle,' he said, 'leading a party of English aristocrats across the desert. That must be unique.'

'A Boston castaway,' she reminded him, 'who happened to know something of Africa. Do you know that I don't know that much about you?'

'Oh, I'm a Cumberland castaway. If you listen carefully you'll discern the accent, even after Eton and Sandhurst.'

'Eton and Sandhurst doesn't sound too castaway to me,' she remarked.

'I'm a younger son. Younger sons are always castaways, into the army, or the church, or, dreaded word, the professions.'

'Then you *are* an aristocrat,' she said, somehow disappointed.

He shook his head. 'My people farm. Have done for generations.'

'I'm glad.'

He gazed at her. 'I'm glad you're glad, Vicky. You'll love Cumberland. It's cooler than Africa.'

She raised her eyebrows, but his eyes were already drooping shut.

'Vicky,' David said. 'Do you suppose I could have a bath?'

Vicky belched, and raised her head. She had fallen into a deep sleep after eating and drinking, sprawled on the ground, careless of the flies which clustered about her. Here in the shelter of the palms it was no longer necessary to dig pits to stay cool. Here they could enjoy the breeze, in the shade. Here they could stop worrying about tomorrow. Tomorrow would most certainly arrive, which was itself reassuring, but it could be faced when it came. And she had already made up her mind about one thing: *tomorrow* didn't matter. Maybe not even the day after tomorrow. No day was going to count until they had regained some of their strength and lost some of their blisters.

She kept remembering Omar Khayyam: 'A loaf of bread, a flask of wine, and thou, . . . is paradise enow . . .' That had of course been Fitzgerald's translation: she couldn't read Arabic, although she had picked up enough of the language in Zanzibar and Kenya to be able to hold a simple conversation. The words had always puzzled her, as surely Khayyam had been sufficiently devout a Moslem not to touch wine. But of course, what he had really said was, a bunch of dates, a pool of clear water . . . and David.

'A bath seems like a good idea to me,' she said. 'Want me to call Bream?'

'No,' he said. 'I thought you could help me. I'd like to take a look at my leg.'

Vicky sat up as her heart constricted. Tomorrow had arrived sooner than she had imagined it would, and she could not postpone this particular duty.

She helped him over the edge of the pool, and they sat on the ground. They were quite alone; the rest of the party were scattered throughout the oasis, sleeping, enjoying this first reminder that it was possible to eat and drink in this world, and be reasonably cool, and even to have some privacy. She smiled at him. 'Well,' she said. 'Here we go. I'm afraid it may hurt a little.'

He nodded; he was just as tense as she.

Holding her breath, she released the first belt buckle and then the next. He hardly winced. The pieces of blood-stained

180

wood fell to either side, and she was left only with crushed white flesh and the bloodsoaked bandage. But at least the blood had long since dried, and there was no offensive smell. She untied the cloth, found it was stuck to his flesh. She scooped water from the pool and bathed it; gradually it came free. She gazed at a pus-filled scar, but the pus was forming a scab, and still the horrible smell of putrefying flesh was absent.

Then she looked at the leg itself . . . and took a sharp breath.

He grinned, his mouth twisted. 'Looks a little crooked.'

'Oh, David . . .'

'They'll have to retire me,' he said. 'I'll go and manage my father's farm. He's been wanting me to do that for years, ever since he worked out I was never going to be Commander-in-Chief. It's a hell of a long way from anywhere, Vicky . . .'

She supposed he was talking to stop himself from screaming in despair. She felt close to that herself, even though she knew she had done the best she, or anyone except a qualified surgeon, could have done in the circumstances. She kept on bathing the leg, to stop having to look at him. Besides, she didn't want to think about Cumberland, about anywhere she might eventually end up, at this moment. Only here and now mattered. She had to keep reminding herself that although the leg hadn't set straight, they had been enormously lucky. If there had been no life out in the stony desert – probably *because* there had been no life – there had also obviously been nothing to cause the wound to putrefy. And perhaps it had now gone far enough into the healing process to withstand anything that might attack it in the future. But she couldn't be sure about that: the future was again clouded.

'You said something about a bath,' she reminded him. 'I'll leave you to it.' She got up.

'I'd like you to stay,' he said.

She looked down at him.

He smiled at her. 'Don't you feel like a bath, too?'

Before, it had seemed natural to speak endearments to him, to talk to him of love – even, on the beach, to let him touch her. He had needed her, to pull him out of the depths, mentally as

181

well as physically. And she had needed him, as a mentor, someone who, even if she could not ask him what to do at any precise moment, she had yet been able to use as a guide. What would David do now? had been her watchword. She had not lied when she told him he had been pulling the trigger of the revolver with her.

But now it was necessary either to kill their strange, circumstantial relationship, here and immediately, or allow it to develop. Develop! Give herself to a man, when she had promised herself she would never do so again, save to another James. But wasn't this man another James, even if there was little physical resemblance? Here was the same courage, the same gentleness allied to the same determination. She had not failed him. She was sure he would never fail her.

She took off the gun belt, laid it on the ground. 'I've become so used to that,' she said. 'I feel odd without it.'

'This could be unpleasant,' he said, and began taking off his boots and socks.

Vicky hesitated; she stood up, released the other belt, and allowed the seaman's breeches to slide over her thighs to the ground. She was, in fact, still perfectly covered by the shirt she had retained for her own use.

David took off his own shirt, and then slowly, carefully, rose to his feet, cautiously allowing just a little weight on to his injured leg, and hastily transferring it to the other as the pain struck him.

She caught his arm to help him keep his balance.

'Are you all right?'

'Just over optimistic, I'm afraid. You'll have to help me.'

She nodded, released his waistband in turn, slid the torn trousers and the drawers down to the earth. 'Come into the water,' she said.

He hopped forward, still holding her arm, and sank into the stream below the pool. 'My God,' he said, 'that feels good.' He ducked his head, soaked his hair, sat down, water coursing past his shoulders. 'Whoever thought life could have nothing more to offer than this . . . and that this could be so wonderful!'

She stood above him, dripping water, waiting, wondering . . . then she lifted the shirt over her head and threw it on the bank.

She knelt beside him, allowed him to caress her breasts, slip his hands down her sides to hold her buttocks, kiss her mouth and her neck and her nipples, slide down her to kiss her stomach and then bury his head between her legs. She kept still with an effort; no man had ever done that to her before, and in fact she was astonished by his lack of inhibition, and then remembered that he had served in India. Still, a great many men who had served overseas, certainly officers, were careful never to demand such freedom from their English lady friends – General Dobree was a case in point. She wondered if she should be angry, as he was perhaps treating her as less of a lady than he should – or whether it was because she wasn't English at all, and he might suppose American women were different. What would his reaction be to discovering that American women, at least those in Massachusetts, were far more reserved than the most inhibited of their English counterparts?

But the fact was, she knew, that he wanted, just as badly as any of the sailors. And didn't she want, just as badly? At his first touch she had nearly exploded with long suppressed passion, as she had come so close to doing on the beach. But she wanted only him, and he wanted only her.

She laughed.

His head came up. 'Do you know that's the first time I have ever heard you laugh?'

'Oh? I guess since we met there hasn't been much to laugh about. Do you like my laugh?'

'I think it's the most marvellous sound I ever heard. But I'd hate to think it was something I did that amused you.'

'Why not? It could have been pure happiness. But actually, I suddenly thought, I'm keeping my eyes open. Lady Dobree wouldn't approve at all.' She kissed him, sent her hand down to hold him, because she had wanted to do that, too, for a long time. 'Do you want to make love to me, David?'

183

'Want to . . . oh Vicky, if you knew . . .'

'You'll have to lie on your back. Your leg won't take any weight.'

'That's the best thing I've heard in years.'

They crawled out of the water, and he lay down. She lowered her body on to his, kissed his mouth, nuzzled his beard, worked herself against him, felt him become hard against her. How long was it since she had felt a man against her body. And she had never lain naked, in the open air, beneath soughing palm trees . . .

'Oh, damn,' he said, and came.

She rolled off him to watch. She had never actually seen it happen before, but she wanted to see it now. After her conversation with Alison Dobree, she was determined to look at everything, for the rest of her life. Never to shut her eyes again.

'Oh, Vicky,' he said, and kissed her lips. 'I'm so sorry. I suppose . . . being surrounded by all that nubile femininity had more effect on me than I thought.'

'I suspect it had an effect on everybody,' she said, 'even on the nubile femininity. But those men . . . I almost feel sorry for them.'

He drew her back down to his chest. 'I've an idea, if you have the time, that it won't be long before we can restore the status quo.'

She kissed his mouth, slowly, then held him and played with him. 'I have the time,' she said. 'I want you in me. Oh, how I want you in me!'

'Now and always?'

'Yes. That would be nice. But I'm not asking for any promises from you, David. This last week has been pretty strange.'

'I loved you before we ever set foot on that ship,' he told her. 'I think I fell in love with you the moment I first saw you. And you knew that.'

'I knew you wanted to get your hands on these,' she said, and guided him.

'But you wouldn't take my height, then.'

'I had a lot on my mind.' She sat astride his thighs, tossing

184

her hair from her eyes, and wanted to laugh again; this was something else she had never done before. James would have been shocked. But what would James have made of her killing four men?

'And you don't have anything on your mind now?' David asked.

'It's different. Now, I think simply, what must I do to keep alive, keep us all alive. That is actually much simpler than trying to decide how to reply when someone is rude to you in civilised society, or when there isn't enough money to pay the bills, or even what to wear when you know everything you own has been seen before. Those are decisions. Trying to keep alive is ninety per cent instinct.'

He was in, and moving, despite the pain it must be causing him as his body surged from the ground. But she was moving too. After fifteen months she felt like a virgin again. And she had been telling the truth when she confessed that she had been as affected as anyone by the circumstances of their march. By the knowledge, even if she had not actually seen them, that she was entirely surrounded by hardened penises, and by the thoughts which went with them. By Bream's devotion, which she knew had been, and remained, largely a sexual devotion; he had confessed to that. And even by the beauty of Alison and Mary. But now she was happy, and because he had already spent once, it took him longer this time. If it was fifteen months since she had had a man at all, it was getting on for two years since she had had an orgasm, with a man. Before James had first started to complain of the stomach pains which eventually killed him. For all of that time, she had had only herself. But now she had David, and he had her. They had each other.

The nine women and the two men, and Charlie, sat together that evening, eating dates, drinking water, and relaxing. They were all as fully dressed as they could be, and as polite as they could be as well. They were, after all, Vicky reminded herself, English ladies and gentlemen; only she and Bream were outsiders – even Nathalie was now wholly absorbed into the society in which she had lived for several years. Thus there could be no suggestion, no risk, of any lowering of the essential standards of public propriety – and as for private propriety, she felt that even David was a little shocked at what had happened that afternoon. Yet they had achieved a rare level of democratic intimacy through their experiences, exemplified by the mere fact that Alison Dobree would sit down at all with her maid and her children's nurse and governess, and even more by the manner in which they inspected each other's bare and sore feet, and offered advice, while Nathalie used her fingers to comb through and untangle Alison's hair, before doing the same for Mary and Elizabeth, and Prudence bounced Charlie on her knee . . . they might have been on a huge picnic.

But they weren't, and just before dusk she went to stand on the far side of the oasis, and look south, across the desert, slapping flies as she did so.

Alison joined her. 'Don't you feel a sense of unreality?' she asked. 'That we should be here? That . . . my God, when I think of the solemnity of an English funeral, the sanctity of life . . . and we have walked away from . . .?'

'Eleven corpses, milady,' Vicky said.

Alison glanced at her, then looked away again. 'Without a backward glance,' she said. 'I suppose I never truly understood how human nature can adapt to circumstances so readily. However horrible the circumstances. Please don't think I'm criticising you in any way, Victoria. I know, we all know, that we wouldn't have got this far without your leadership. But I suppose I'm a little . . . I don't know what the right word would be . . .'

'I would say, shocked, milady,' Vicky told her, and smiled. 'I understand exactly what you mean. I guess I wasn't the right material to be a governess after all.'

'Oh, goodness gracious, I didn't mean *that*,' Alison protested. 'Good Lord, suppose that Chandler woman hadn't resigned, but had made the journey? We'd all be dead by now. But Victoria . . . are we going to be all right now?'

Vicky sighed. This was the question she had been dreading. But it would be pointless to paint too rosy a picture; she still needed all their determination if she was going to get them to safety. She took refuge in the facts, as she knew them. 'We've walked for four nights, and for another three hours this morning, milady. We should've covered something like a hundred and thirty miles. I know we didn't do that much, but I still reckon we've covered a good hundred miles. We're half-way, at the very least, milady.' She glanced at her. 'Half-way to the grassland, at any rate.'

'Four more nights,' Alison said softly.

'Well, we'll rest up here for at least forty-eight hours, until our feet are better. It'll give David more time to recover and get his strength back, too. And when we do go, it'll be with a full water barrel, and we'll load the stretcher with dates. We'll be much better equipped, milady, and we'll be moving towards less arid country all the time. We'll make it.'

'To the grassland. But that's not the end, is it?'

'I'm afraid not, milady.'

'How far is it from the grassland to the coast? Or at least, civilisation?'

Vicky looked away, at the horizon. 'I don't know. Maybe . . . maybe five hundred miles.'

'Five hundred *miles?* But on the beach, you said it was five hundred miles to Cape Verde.'

'I did, milady.'

'And now you say we've come at least a hundred, so . . .?'

'I didn't say we'd find civilisation at Cape Verde, milady,' Vicky pointed out.

'But . . . another five hundred miles after we reach the grassland? Is there grass right down to the coast?'

'Well, no. It becomes tropical rain forest a couple of hundred miles from the coast.'

'Oh, my God!' Alison sat down, as if her knees had given way. 'But . . . what about people? Surely to goodness there are people in the forest, in the grassland? People who will help us?'

Vicky sat beside her. 'I'm pretty sure there are. It's even possible that there are mission stations down there. But it'll be pure chance if we happen to stumble on one. As for the natives, well . . . I'm not sure bumping into them will necessarily be to our advantage.'

'Because they're black people, you mean? But you've lived amongst black people in Kenya, haven't you?'

'Yes, milady.'

'Well, then, surely they can't be as bad as people say.'

'I don't know what people say, milady. I do know that the people I lived among were wonderful, unless they were angry for any reason. But milady, to suggest I know what the people here are like because I knew those in Kenya is like saying you have to know just what the Russians are like because you've lived in France.'

Alison gazed at her, eyebrows arched.

'The only thing I know for sure that's common to them all,' Vicky went on, 'and it's something that's pretty common to all people, black, white, yellow or brown, is that they don't like being conquered. In East Africa the process was pretty near complete, and to some extent they were becoming resigned to it. Here, so far as I know, it's still going on.'

'My God,' Alison said again.

Vicky gave her an encouraging smile. 'But if we're at all lucky, we'll only meet up with those who have accepted British rule. And I'm sure we're going to find that conditions in the desert were the worst we'll encounter. We'll reach the coast, milady. We'll make it before the ship is ever reported overdue.'

'Some of us will make it, you mean.'

'I hope all of us, now, milady.'

Alison was quiet for a few minutes. Then she said, staring into the gathering dusk. 'Do you care, Vicky?'

Vicky turned her head, sharply.

Alison's cheeks were pink with more than sunburn. 'I . . . I felt like a drink of water, this afternoon.'

'Oh,' Vicky said, looking at the darkness in turn.

'I . . . I didn't know what to do. Whether I should come and help you. Rescue you.'

'I'm glad you didn't do that, milady.'

'But . . . you mean you were actually enjoying it? I must say, you seemed to be doing so. I thought I heard you laughing.'

'I'm afraid I was laughing, milady. I guess because I was

enjoying it. David and I have been getting close to that for a long time.'

Alison's eyebrows were arched. 'I never saw anything so . . . *abandoned* in my life,' she said, and got up to rejoin the others.

It was impossible to tell whether she had been admiring, envious, or disgusted. Vicky rather felt that the last was the most likely.

It was strange, she thought, how sometimes she almost felt she was getting through to Alison, that they might even be able to be friends, and then at other times that it was an impossible task, because they were just too far apart in their outlook and upbringing. But it was *her* outlook and upbringing which had brought them this far, and would take them to safety. Alison's form of determination and courage, though in no way inferior to hers, she was sure, was entirely passive. Alison would endure as long as she lived, without breaking, but she lacked the will to initiate. Had Alison been in command they would all still have been on the beach, waiting for help which would never arrive . . . and be dead by now. She had to keep reminding herself of that, and believing it, too. It was too easy to doubt.

She slept in David's arms, the sleep of utter relaxation, for the first time in a very long time. Now even the fear was gone. He would be all right. They would be all right. There was so much to look forward to.

Perhaps even Cumberland . . .

She was awakened by Prudence, gently shaking her arm. She opened her eyes, discovered it was just dawn.

Prudence's face was a mixture of solemnity and excitement. 'Vicky,' she whispered. 'Can you come?'

Vicky moved David's arm and got up, followed Prudence to the southern edge of the oasis, and gazed out at the desert. The empty desert, last night, when she and Alison had sat here. Now she looked at some score of camels, each camel carrying a rider, robes fluttering in the dawn breeze, as they topped a rise perhaps a mile distant. And she knew instinctively that those men were merely the advance guard of a much larger force.

'People,' Prudence said. 'Oh, at last, people! We're going to be all right, Vicky. We're going to be all right.'

Vicky continued to stare at the men, who were too far off to be properly identified. But she could tell that they were men of the desert, and that they carried rifles and spears, and that they were slowly increasing in number, and spreading out so as entirely to surround the oasis. Her heart beat fast because from behind the men there now came sound, drifting on the wind. It was principally the sound of many hooves, many tramping feet, and of clanking accoutrements. There were a great many people out there. But there was also a kind of singing sound, a mournful dirge which rose and fell with a regular cadence, punctuated by short, sharp snaps. Those were sounds she had heard before, in the slave kingdom of Zanzibar.

'Oh, my God,' she muttered.

'Vicky?' Prudence frowned at her consternation. 'What's the matter? Don't you want me to wake the others?'

'Oh, yes,' Vicky said. 'We must wake the others. Quickly. Those aren't just people out there, Prudence. Those are Touaregs. And that is a slave caravan.'

CHAPTER 9

Prudence obviously had no idea of what Vicky was speaking. 'But . . . don't you want to signal those people?' she asked in bewilderment.

'It doesn't make any difference whether we signal them or not,' Vicky told her. 'They are coming here anyway.' She hurried through the trees, shook David awake. 'We have trouble,' she said. 'Serious trouble. We have to bluff our way out. Can you tidy yourself? Comb your hair? There's no time to shave, but here, you must wear this, now.' She gave him the gun belt, while he blinked at her uncertainly. Her brain raced as she tried to think of everything, and anything, that might provide a solution to their plight. 'Mary,' she snapped. 'You and Liz take that stretcher apart. We need David's red jacket.'

'But it's all torn up,' Mary explained. 'The sailors cut the sleeves into strips to make it easier to tie to the oars.'

'Can't be helped. It's still better than nothing. Do it.'

'Would you mind telling us what is going on?' Alison inquired.

'There is a slave caravan approaching, milady,' Vicky explained. 'I don't know if somehow they have worked out the oasis is occupied or if they're always this cautious, but right now they're approaching very slowly. So we have a little time to prepare ourselves. However, they'll be here in half an hour. Now, everybody, please listen very carefully.'

'A caravan?' Joanna Cartwright cried. 'But doesn't that mean people? People who will help us?'

'I said a *slave* caravan, Joanna,' Vicky said. 'They'll have been on a raid down into the grassland, and will be on their way

191

back to – well, wherever it is they're going.'

'But they'll help *us*, surely,' Alison protested. 'Certainly when they learn that I am Lady Dobree.'

'Milady, it won't matter to them who you are. The only way they are going to help us is if there's some very big reason, either some profit in it for them, or some retribution if they don't. Because shall I tell you what they are going to see when they get here? They are going to see a group of attractive white women wearing almost nothing. They will have us upside down before you can say heavens to Betsy, and find out that we aren't virgins. As that will make us valueless to them, except for a bit of fun, what they will then do to us will make Curly seem like the vicar of Little Wissing. David and Harry will already have been murdered. And when they're through with us, they'll cut our throats as well.'

'You can't be serious,' Alison said.

'They'll keep the girls alive, and Charlie,' Vicky went on. 'The girls will be put up for auction, to be taken into some harem or other, because they are virgins, you see, and Charlie will be castrated and sold as a eunuch.'

'Victoria,' Alison snapped. 'You are being disgusting. And obscene.' She looked at David. 'David, please tell your . . . your . . . Victoria to behave herself and stop having hysterics.'

'What's being castrated?' Elizabeth whispered to Mary.

Vicky wanted to stamp her foot in desperation, but she looked at David as well.

'I'm afraid Vicky is very probably right, Alison,' he said, and Vicky gave a sigh of relief. 'This is a different world to the one you're used to.'

'But what are we to do?' Margaret Pilling asked, her voice high. 'Can we hide?'

The question was so patently absurd it wasn't worth answering, but Mary did so anyway. 'Where do you suggest, Mrs Pilling?' she asked. 'Up a tree?'

'What's castrating?' Elizabeth whispered again, anxiously.

'Well, can't we hold them off with the gun?' Alice Marker asked.

192

That was no less absurd, to anyone who had seen what was approaching; but the rest of them hadn't, yet.

'You'd better come with me,' Vicky said. 'All of you. But stay in the trees.'

She led them to where they could look to the south, and caught her own breath. The twenty-odd men of the advance guard had been joined by their comrades, and she estimated close on two hundred warriors were slowly approaching the oasis. Behind them could now be seen the rest of the caravan, flags waving, camels carrying miniature *howdahs*, heavily draped to conceal the occupants, people walking, brightly coloured robes brilliant in the morning sunlight, horsemen galloping to and fro. She thought there could be five hundred people out there. This was a huge caravan. And a good third of the people could be seen to be naked, even at this distance, shackled together and stumbling along, singing their mournful dirge, being driven by the whips of the slave masters, those snaps of sound which had first alerted her to the true nature of the caravan.

'Oh, my God,' Alison whispered.

''Oly Mother,' Nathalie commented.

Charlie started to cry.

Vicky couldn't tell whether their reactions were prompted by the size of the caravan or the sight of the slaves.

'Christ Almighty,' David muttered, forgetting his manners. But he was certainly considering the strength of the opposition. 'What can we do?'

Vicky licked her lips. 'There's only one way we can hope to make them help us,' she said. 'Or at least, not murder us. Listen. As I said, they're only interested in profit. The more profit they think they can be made out of us, the more they'll help us. If the profit is only to be Mary and Elizabeth and Charlie, then they'll certainly kill the rest of us.'

'I wish you'd stop saying that,' Mary grumbled. 'It gives me goose pimples.'

'What's castration?' Elizabeth asked a third time, pinching her sister's arm. 'Why don't you ever tell me anything?'

'But if they think there's a lot to be made out of us all,' Vicky went on, ignoring the pair of them, 'then they might just go for it. Milady, as you said just now, you have to be Lady Dobree.'

Alison's eyebrows arched. 'I *am* Lady Dobree.'

'But you must *be* her, in such a way that they can have no doubt you are a lady. I mean,' she hurried on as Alison shot her a glance, 'that you are what they call an Agha, a great personage. David, you have to be General Dobree. You too must act the part to the hilt. And we are your personal servants, all of us. You are the most famous general in the British Army, David. Don't let them forget that. If you are killed, you will most certainly be avenged by the whole strength of the British Empire. But more important, the British government will pay an enormous reward to the man who returns you and your family safe and sound. The Arabs will know you are actually talking about a ransom, but they are used to double talk. The important thing is to make them believe such a ransom will be paid.'

He bit his lip. 'It might just work.'

'But then what?' Mary asked; her stepmother was apparently speechless. 'They still won't let us go, without the ransom being paid.'

'They'll send to the coast,' Vicky told her. 'And they'll keep us alive, and probably well cared for, until a reply arrives. If we can get them to accept us as guests, we're almost home and dry. No Arab will ever harm a guest, without extreme provocation.'

'But they won't ransom us,' Elizabeth said. 'The Government, I mean. Because they'll know Daddy isn't with us.'

'They *won't* know that!' Vicky cried, nearing despair. 'Even when the *Doncaster* is reported overdue, and that can't be for another month yet, so far as anyone will know, everyone was either lost with the ship or is with our party. They'll send a ransom or they'll send help. Either way, it's our only chance, for God's sake!'

'I agree with Vicky,' David said, and put on his red jacket.

'That looks ridiculous,' Alison pointed out. 'With the sleeve cut into strips like that.'

'It'll have to do.' He strapped the gun belt round his waist.

Vicky turned to Alison. 'Milady, this entire plan depends on you. You have to be utterly convincing, both that you are Lady Dobree, and that David is your husband. You have to be absolutely confident, absolutely arrogant. You have to be . . .'

'I don't see how David can possibly impersonate General Dobree,' Alison complained. 'He's just not old enough.'

'They won't know how old the General really is, milady,' Vicky said. 'He's certainly old enough to be your husband.'

'I must say, I don't like that part of the plan at all,' Alison went on. 'I mean, it's not decent, is it? I mean, suppose we are confined in the same room?' Her eyebrows arched.

'That is entirely possible, milady. That is part of the plan.'

'I don't think I could accept that,' Alison said. 'I mean, well, really, Victoria . . .' She gazed at Vicky, eyebrows still apexing. She wouldn't say it out loud in front of the other women, but she was obviously thinking of what she had seen the previous afternoon, and certainly concluding that she couldn't allow herself to be confined with a man who could indulge in something as 'abandoned' as that. 'I don't see why we don't tell them the truth, that my husband is dead, drowned in the shipwreck. I mean, I'll still be Lady Dobree. I'll still be ransomed.'

'Milady,' Vicky begged, when what she wanted to do was take the woman by the hair and shake some sense into her – the horsemen were not four hundred yards away now, and were clearly massing to overwhelm the oasis in a single charge. When they started that, there would be no stopping them. 'With respect, milady,' she said. 'They won't feel that is at all certain. You just have to accept that women don't count for much in this world. No Arab would pay a ransom for one of his wives; he would simply go out and get another one. Milady, our only hope is for David to be accepted as the General, and for you to support him in that role.'

'I couldn't,' Alison said. 'Not if it meant . . .' she looked at David, who was flushing. 'You must understand, David. I just couldn't. Anyway,' she said, brightly. 'I don't know anything about Arabs and things, I don't speak the language or anything.'

'I know some Arabic, milady,' Vicky said. 'I will interpret for you.'

'If you know Arabic,' Alison said, triumphantly, 'then I know what we'll do. We'll say *you* are Lady Dobree. I'm sure you can act the part. You seem able to do everything else. And if you and David are locked up together, well . . . it won't matter, will it?'

Vicky realised everyone was staring at them, listening to the strange conversation. As was David, even if he also had no idea what they were really saying to each other; she hadn't told him how they had been overlooked. But Vicky had no doubt that she could portray an Arab concept of Lady Dobree, far better indeed than Alison herself, and was in any event thoroughly exhausted by the wrangling, when time was so short. 'Very well,' she said, 'very well, milady. If that's how you want it, that's how it's going to be. But if I am going to be Lady Dobree, then by God I am going to *be* Lady Dobree. And you all . . .' she looked from face to face, 'will just do exactly as I say. And *be* what I say, too. I haven't the time to explain everything now. Just listen, and *obey* me.'

'But we've been doing that anyway, for days and days,' Mary pointed out.

'Here they come, ma'am,' Bream said, urgently.

'Give me your engagement ring, milady,' Vicky said.

'My ring? Now, really, Victoria . . .'

'I need that ring,' Vicky snapped, seizing Alison's hand and pulling the diamond solitaire off, to slip it on her own finger, next to her plain wedding band. Then she looked from face to face a last time, turned away from them, and stepped out from the trees. She checked for a moment at the sight of the camels racing towards her, at the rifles and swords being waved, then went on walking.

'Vicky!' David gasped.

'I want you here beside me, David,' she said.

She heard his feet crunching the sand at her shoulder, but kept on watching the warriors. She held up her hand, and they drew rein, sending dust clouding into the air, staring at the two ragged figures in amazement, but although Vicky didn't doubt that she must make a most interesting picture, obviously a woman despite her male garb, and with her titian hair blowing across her face, she was pleased to note that they were more inclined to look at David. However tattered his clothing, it was obviously part of a uniform, and she had an idea these men knew which uniform – they must have encountered a red jacket before. Not, she reminded herself, that that was necessarily reassuring.

'Can you speak any language?' she asked.

'Only English,' he said. 'And a bit of Hindustani.'

'I don't think that's going to be of much use here,' she said, desperately trying to remember all the Arabic she had once known. 'You!' she shouted at the nearest man as the dust cleared. 'Who is your commander?'

He gazed at her, then looked left and right at his companions. Then he fired his rifle. She did not suppose he had actually aimed it, but the bullet ploughed into the sand only four feet in front of her.

It took a great effort of will not to leap three feet into the air and then take to her heels.

'By Christ!' David's hand moved to his holster.

'Don't draw it,' she snapped in English. 'You,' she shouted again, reverting to Arabic, 'will be flogged! Summon your commander! Tell him General Dobree of the British Army wishes to speak with him.'

The camels snorted and the men looked at each other uncertainly as they considered the situation; the total confidence she was projecting was certainly having an effect. And now, to her great relief, she heard the sound of horse's hooves, and a moment later a man, even his face entirely concealed beneath his white robes, appeared, the camel riders moving left and right to give him passage, their beasts well under control – camels and horses do not as a rule take to each other.

The newcomer stared at Vicky, and she stared back into his eyes, as imperiously as she could, praying that David was doing the same.

He was, magnificently. 'Who is this fellow?' he demanded, loudly, with a toss of his head.

'General Dobree is tired of waiting,' Vicky said in Arabic.

'Are you the commander of these brigands?'

The man gave a brief bow, which could have meant either yes or no. 'You are General Dobree?' He addressed David.

'My husband speaks only English,' Vicky informed him. 'He is very angry at this attack.'

The man's gaze returned to her. 'Is it permitted to ask what you are doing here, in the desert?' He made a gesture as if to indicate that the British had no business in this land.

'Are you the commander?' Vicky asked again.

'No, lady, I speak for him.'

'And I will speak only with him,' Vicky insisted. 'Send him to see my husband. And tell him that we require food and clothing.'

Perhaps the man smiled behind his veil as he inspected her. 'Yes,' he said. ' I will tell my commander.' He looked past them to the fluttering clothes of the rest of the party. 'And those?'

'Our family and servants,' Vicky said.

The man looked at them a few moments longer. No doubt he was making mental notes, of Alison's stature and magnificent hair, and the hardly less striking dark looks of Mary. Then he nodded. 'I will inform my commander.'

'He comes,' said the man on his left.

The horseman hesitated, half turned his head, then rose in his stirrups. 'All kneel,' he bellowed. 'All kneel, for His Excellency, the Commander of the Faithful of the Mahdi, the illustrious Emir, Zobeir ibn Rubayr ibn Walid ibn Ali ibn Muhammad, Ruler of the World.'

'Oh, God *damn*,' Vicky muttered in English.

The exhortation was obviously directed at them, for the camel riders clearly could not obey, and indeed merely came to attention.

'Do we kneel?' David whispered.

'No,' Vicky said. 'We stand straight.'

'But you know this character?'

'I've heard of him.' Her heart was pounding so hard she thought it might burst its way out of her chest. Zobeir? What

198

could he be doing here, at the wrong end of the Sahara? But of course he would be here, with a caravan this size. Zobeir conducted a moving court, like the old kinds of England and France, roaming the length and breadth of North Africa, commanding, defeating, rewarding, punishing . . . a man of whom she had heard so much, and not merely from Sejm. Of whose handiwork she had seen so much. But now was not the time to think of that: if she did she would certainly kneel, and beg for mercy.

Instead she kept her shoulders back and her chin up, pushed the hair from her eyes to gaze at the rise and the group of horsemen now approaching, a green flag waving above their heads. They all wore white burnouses, and glittered with jewels, from the hilts of their scimitars to the brooches in their headdresses. But there was only one who mattered. He rode a pure white stallion, and was some distance in front of the others. His breeches and tunic were also white, but his belt was cloth of gold, and she could swear that the scabbard which hung at his side, no less than his horse's bit and bridle, or the stirrups in which his brown kid boots were encased, were all at least gold plated. His veil was thrown across the lower part of his face, but even at a distance she could make out his dark and fathomless eyes.

Zobeir ibn Rubayr walked his horse through the ranks of his silent soldiers, until he was some thirty feet in front of them, and thus only thirty-odd feet away from Vicky and David. He gazed at them for several seconds, then looked past them at the waiting women and children.

'Zobeir Pasha,' Vicky said, 'my husband bids you welcome.'

His gaze came back to fix on her face. Then he dismounted, and she discovered she had been holding her breath. He walked forward, his boots crunching on the sand, and stood immediately in front of them. Again he stared at them, then he saluted David, crisply, in the British fashion, before giving a brief bow. 'General Dobree,' he said. 'I have heard of you. Milady.' He bowed again, and took Vicky's hand – her left hand, and she had no doubt that he was inspecting the rings.

Then he allowed the veil to droop, as he kissed her fingers. And only then did she realise that he had spoken English, perfectly.

Zobeir straightened. 'No doubt your army is camped close by, General,' he remarked to David.

Vicky couldn't reply for him now. But she prayed he would not attempt to lie to this man – at least, not where the lie could be so easily disproved.

'I have no army,' David said. 'I was on my way to South Africa, with my staff, to take command of the army there. But my ship was wrecked, on the coast.'

Zobeir frowned. 'You are a long way from the coast, General.'

'We have walked for five days,' David said, looking him in the eye.

Zobeir's frown deepened, and he glanced at David's obviously injured leg. 'You have hurt yourself?'

'The leg was broken in getting ashore after the wreck,' David explained.

Zoebier looked into his eyes in turn. 'You have walked across the desert? With a broken leg, and . . .' He looked at the oasis again.

'With my wife, and six other women, three children, and some men,' David said. 'Most of the men have died.'

'I see,' Zoebir said thoughtfully. Clearly he was thinking very hard. But he could hardly doubt the evidence of his own eyes; there was simply no other way for the General to have got here.

'You say you have heard of me?' David asked.

'Indeed, General. There are few more famous soldiers in the British Army.'

'Then you will understand that the War Office will handsomely reward the man who sends me, and my family, to safety,' David said. 'I dislike asking a favour of you, Zobeir Pasha, but it is one a general can ask of another.'

'That I send you to the coast,' Zobeir mused. He continued to gaze at David for several seconds, then he looked at Vicky, gave another bow, and dropped his veil. She gave a little gasp.

200

He wore a beard, of course, and a heavy moustache, but neither could hide the great slash of a mouth, curving slightly downwards beneath the huge, beaked nose. It was a face of immense strength, immense power . . . but she did not doubt it also hid an utterly ruthless character, as well.

Zobeir smiled. 'I am sure that before we make any plans, you would like to be refreshed, and clothed. I will have my people pitch a camp, and make accommodation ready for you. They shall endeavour to provide you with adequate clothing. Poor stuff, you understand . . .' He flicked his own linen cloak. 'But still, better than the rags you wear. And then, when you have bathed and changed, you shall be my guests for dinner. And you will tell me about your shipwreck and your remarkable walk. And we will see what can be done about restoring you to your rightful place.'

Vicky gasped again, but this time it was with relief.

'Dinner? We have been invited to dine with this . . . this Zobeir person?' Alison asked. 'Oh, good heavens.'

'I think he actually means lunch,' Vicky said. 'And do please remember that he is an Emir. That is something like a king, in English. And I am sure he does regard himself as a king.'

'You mean we're going to be fed?' Mary cried. 'Real food?'

'Steaks,' Elizabeth muttered. 'Ice cream.'

'I don't think it'll be either steaks or ice cream, somehow,' Vicky told them. 'But I'm sure that whatever it is will be very nice.'

'I told you they'd help us, Vicky,' Prudence said. 'I told you.' It was almost the first word of reproach she had offered since their ordeal had begun.

'Yes,' Vicky said. 'You did.'

Alison was less convinced. 'Is this man really going to help us, Vicky?' she asked in a low voice, looking past her to the sudden activity as the Arabs prepared to camp, an activity into which Zobeir had disappeared with most of his men.

'So far,' Vicky said. 'I think he hopes to gain that profit we were speaking of, milady. And just at this minute he considers it

201

may be a substantial one. We've been fortunate in that he has actually heard of your husband.'

'Oh? I never realised William was so famous. But of course, he did win the Victoria Cross.' She frowned. 'Although it was a long time ago.'

Vicky made no comment. She was suddenly discovering herself to be very uneasy. Perhaps she had subconsciously been uneasy since she discovered she would be dealing with Zobeir himself; Alison's comment had only served to make her aware of it. There were several hundred holders of the Victoria Cross; Zobeir would hardly have made a study of them all. She wondered if William Dobree had ever served in Egypt. It was possible. In that case they might actually have met.

But Zobeir had accepted David as the General. So they had never met. Yet he knew of him. A great deal would depend on just how much he knew.

And equally, on how much David knew of his late employer's military past.

'Still, he has invited us to lunch,' Alison said. 'But . . . what shall I wear?'

'The Pasha will provide us with clothes, milady, as soon as the camp is pitched. But you must remember the subterfuge we are practising. We cannot change our story now, without making him distrust us. You are now Mrs Lang.'

'The governess?' Alison frowned.

Vicky smiled. 'I would not inflict such a fate on you, milady. You are my dearest friend and travelling companion.'

Alison gazed at her.

'If you are not that, milady, you will be considered a servant, and treated as one. However, I'm afraid that from now I shall have to stop addressing you as milady.'

'Yes,' Alison said, drily. 'Perhaps you would like me to call *you* milady.'

'I don't think that will be necessary. We are friends, remember, and therefore presumably of an equal social standing.'

Once again Alison gazed at her for some seconds, for the first time beginning to realise just what she had let herself in for by her refusal to take the lead. 'And is my name now Victoria?'

'No,' Vicky decided. 'I think it would be safer to keep our own Christian names, otherwise we might make a mistake.'

'And Charlie is now your son?'

Vicky considered again. But she had no wish to make their situation more precarious that it was by upsetting Alison too much, and besides, she didn't really want to have the care of the boy. 'He will remain your son.'

'Why, thank you,' Alison said, sarcastically. 'What about the girls?'

'Ah. Well . . . I'm afraid I don't look old enough to be their mother, and David obviously isn't old enough to be their father, even by a former wife. Mary, Elizabeth, you will have to be our nieces. The daughters of David's dead brother. Understood?'

'Yes, Vicky,' Mary agreed.

'The rest of you . . .' Vicky glanced over the other five women, 'will be yourselves.'

They nodded.

Bream coughed.

'You will be my personal servant, Bream,' David said.

'Thank you, sir.'

'Well, then . . . David, you and I must have a little chat, and get our backgrounds absolutely straight.'

'It'll have to keep,' he warned.

Vicky turned, to see one of Zobeir's officers approaching them.

He gave a low bow, and said in Arabic, 'Your quarters are awaiting you, lady.'

'Thank you,' Vicky said. She hesitated, but decided not to delay. There should still be time to put David in the picture regarding her apprehensions before they met Zobeir again, and she couldn't take a chance on this man understanding English. 'I think we've a bath and a change of clothing awaiting us,' she told them. 'So let's go.'

They walked out from the trees to gaze at a scene of amazing industry, as the tents were being pitched, in a huge circle, around another tent erected in the centre, this one twice the size of any of the others, and judging by its various roofs, obviously containing several canvas-walled chambers. The slaves had been herded together in a vast mass, downwind of the encampment; there were no tents to shelter *them* from the sun. Guards had been posted on the rising ground to oversee the desert, and detachments of men were forming goatskin brigades to convey water to the various tents. Other men were lighting fires, some for heating the water; while the smell of cooking meat was already starting to make their saliva flow.

But not all was civilisation. Vicky checked as she saw, some distance to their right, four stakes being driven into the sand, and a man, stripped naked, being spreadeagled on his face between them.

'Oh, my! Don't look,' Alison commanded her children.

'Is he going to be castrated?' Elizabeth inquired.

'A runaway?' Vicky asked their guide.

'No, no, lady,' he replied. 'He is the man who shot at you.'

'Oh . . . but he didn't hit me. I don't think he meant to hit me.'

'That is of no importance. The captain of the advance guard informed the Emir that you wished that man flogged. He is to receive a hundred strokes of the bastinado.'

'A hundred . . . oh, Lord.' She hurried on, mind spinning. But what else could she expect, of Zobeir? They were in the hands of the most feared man in all Africa. And as with the desert, she would have to be the one to extricate them, if it could be done. She knew she had so far brought them very little but time; even if her fears were unfounded, she had very little faith in a ransom ever being paid.

The guide stopped before one of the tents. 'The General and his servant will go in here,' he said. 'Attendants await them.'

'Oh.' Vicky hesitated, then nodded. There was no way she could argue without revealing those apprehensions she had to conceal. 'Here's where we split up, David,' she said. 'We'll have to have that chat later on. Just remember to be careful what you say. And be the boss at all times.'

'I will do that,' David agreed, and gave the guide the most

arrogant stare he could command. 'Ask him where you are being taken.'

'My husband wishes to know why I do not remain at his side,' Vicky said.

The man gave the inevitable bow. 'Because there is a tent waiting for you and your ladies as well, lady. It would not be seemly for the General to be encumbered with women while he is dressing.'

'I understand,' Vicky said, and translated.

'It's a backwards world, isn't it?' David commented, and limped into the tent, the doorway of which – it could hardly be called a flap in so elaborate a structure – was being held for him by one of the Arabs.

'Did you *know* that you were going to be segregated?' Alison asked, clearly supposing that she had been made the victim of a plot.

'No,' Vicky said, only just in time stopping herself from adding milady. 'And I'm sure it's only temporary, anyway.'

'Lady.' Their guide gestured them on.

Their tent was actually next door, and was somewhat larger. Here the door was again held open by a man who, although not young, had a completely hairless face. For about the third time that day, so far, Vicky's heart skipped a beat.

He bowed very low. 'Welcome, great lady,' he said. 'I am the Harem Agha, Saeed. I am to obey your every wish.'

Vicky gave him a nod, went inside and found herself in a large and really luxurious chamber. The inner walls of the tent were hung with magnificent drapes, a Persian carpet covered the sand, there were tables and piles of cushions to either side, and in the very centre of the carpet four steaming tin tubs of water, from which emanated a delightful aroma. The room also contained a large number of people; some dozen young women, and four other eunuchs.

'Oh, that smells good,' Prudence said, and ruffled Charlie's hair. 'We are going to get you clean at last.'

Charlie was actually being remarkably quiet, clearly overawed by the men and weapons with which he was surrounded.

205

'Victoria,' Alison said in an uneasy whisper, 'those men aren't going to stay here while we bathe, are they?'

'I'm afraid they are,' Vicky told her. 'They are even going to assist us, I fancy.'

'But . . . good Lord! I can't permit that. I mean, the girls . . .' She gazed at Mary, eyebrows arched.

Mary was looking delighted.

'But actually, they aren't men,' Vicky explained. 'Not any more. They're eunuchs.'

'Eunuchs?'

'Good Lord,' Mary remarked. 'You don't mean they've been . . .' She flushed.

'Exactly,' Vicky said. 'So there's nothing to worry about, is there?'

'What has happened to them? What?' Elizabeth was very excited.

'They're the ones who've been castrated, stupid,' Mary told her.

'Oh, but . . .?'

'They've had their dingdongs cut off.'

'Oh!' Elizabeth turned bright red. 'That's just horrible.'

'You wanted to know,' her sister pointed out.

'It's not true,' Elizabeth said. 'Vicky, say it's not true.'

Vicky sighed. 'I'm afraid it is true, Elizabeth.'

'They'll never be the same again,' Alison said, sadly.

Vicky assumed she was referring to her stepdaughters and not stating the obvious. 'But you are not going to object to *anything* that happens,' she told her, told them all. 'The one thing we must not do is show any discourtesy or lack of appreciation for the help they are offering.'

'Vicky,' Nathalie was squealing even as she spoke, for two of the girls were beginning to strip her of her torn and filthy garments.

Vicky crossed the carpet in two strides, and slapped her face.

Nathalie's head jerked, and her mouth sagged open, while tears filled her eyes.

'You must call me milady,' Vicky insisted. 'And I must be as harsh as any Arab lady. Please believe that, and play the part, *please*, Nathalie, or we will all be treated like that poor man outside.'

Nathalie gulped and swallowed. 'Yes, milady,' she whispered.

'Am I still permitted to call you Victoria?' Alison asked, somewhat coldly.

Vicky glared at her. 'Of course you are. You're pretending to be my friend. And I'd be grateful if you wouldn't make things tougher than they are.'

'What do we call you?' Elizabeth wanted to know.

'Why, Auntie, of course.'

'Lady will permit?' asked a liquid voice, in Arabic.

It was the first opportunity Vicky had had to study any of their hostesses. This was a slender, dark-haired young woman of medium height. As she was indoors she was not wearing her yashmak – the veil which covered the lower half of her face whenever she would appear in public – and her features were well formed and could even have been pretty, but for the utter docility of eyes and expression. She wore her hair loose, in a black cloud drifting down her back from beneath a tiny jewelled cap on the crown of her head, and there were paste jewels decorating the hem of her bolero jacket and her pantaloons, as well as the leather straps of her toethong sandals. And these four garments, Vicky realised, were all she *was* wearing. There was no blouse beneath the bolero, which swung to and fro as she moved to reveal entrancing glimpses of the small breasts beneath, and, if the pantaloons were of mauve silk, and sufficiently voluminous to gather in folds at every available place, they were also entirely sheer, to reveal that she wore nothing underneath them, either.

As Mary had already observed. 'Vicky,' she whispered. 'Oops, Auntie . . . they've nothing *on*.'

'Nonsense,' Vicky said. 'They're every bit as properly dressed as we were in our nighties.'

'Yes, but . . . these aren't their nighties, are they?' she pointed out with maddening logic.

'Vicky,' Alison said. 'We aren't going to have to wear things like that, are we?'

Vicky sighed. They had just walked across a hundred miles of desert, with death at their elbows every step of the way, wearing nothing but nightclothes – and now they were going to start worrying about being a trifle underdressed? 'I'm afraid we are,' she said, and closed her ears to their complaints. She had problems of her own, as the girl, now assisted by another, began removing her clothing, with a most distasteful expresion, handing each article to Saeed, who received it with an equally distasteful expression. But all the time he gazed at Vicky. Did he really feel nothing at all? She could not believe that, had the greatest difficulty in stopping herself placing her hands across her breasts and crotch – and yet at the same time knew a most remarkable feeling of relaxation . . . of abandonment, she supposed Alison would call it. But she dared not look at Alison right this minute, as she was led to the scented water, and allowed to sink into its warmed embrace. She had to do absolutely nothing for herself, even if she was relieved to discover that the washing of her body was to be done by two of the girls; Saeed continued to attend her, but his responsibility was her hair, which he lovingly soaked and soaped and rinsed and soaked and rinsed, and then began to brush when she was at last taken from the tub and wrapped in an enormous soft towel.

Yet the whole experience, from the soft touch of the girls' fingers sliding over her flesh, finding their way into every nook and cranny, no less than the gentle ministrations of the man, induced the most sensuous feeling she had ever known. She thought she could have lain in the water forever, had known a tremendous temptation to spread her legs . . . she clutched the towel tightly and shook her head to empty her mind of such remarkable thoughts, while the girls stared at her in alarm.

She looked round to see how the other women were getting on. Alison had already been bathed and, cheeks pink, was similarly being dried, as were Mary and Elizabeth, giggling at each other; the Arab girls had correctly interpreted the order of precedence. Now the rest of them were also being bathed, while Prudence shared a tub with Charlie, who was having the time of his life, splashing water and playing games with the eunuch who was washing him.

'I have *never* known anything like that in my life,' Alison confided to Vicky. 'I would not have supposed such . . . such . . .'

'Abandonment?' Vicky suggested, helpfully.

'Call it what you will. I would never have supposed it possible, had I not seen it with my own eyes. And felt it.' Her eyebrows arched. 'Are we always going to be bathed by these people?'

As usual, it was impossible to be sure whether she had enjoyed herself, or had hated it.

'I think that's very likely,' Vicky said. 'So we may as well get used to it.'

'Aunty Vicky,' Mary whispered. 'These girls . . . well . . . they've been *shaved*.'

'Yes,' Vicky agreed, having also observed.

'Heavens above,' Alison commented. No doubt she had kept her eyes shut throughout the bath.

'I have an idea it's mainly to do with cleanliness,' Vicky pointed out. 'In this climate it's very easy to get bugs.'

'Bugs?' Mary screamed. ' In there?'

'And anyway, the men prefer it,' Vicky hurried on, wondering why she was continually getting involved in these absurd conversations.

'They're not going to want to do that to *us*, are they?' Elizabeth begged.

'You're speaking as if *you* had a problem,' Mary remarked scornfully.

'I think they'll leave us alone,' Vicky said, as reassuringly as she could. 'At least as long as we are their guests.'

The girl who had first attended her was standing beside her. 'If lady pleases,' she said.

Vicky stepped into the pantaloons she was holding, and had a bolero pulled over her arms and settled on her shoulders. The silk felt superb against her flesh, but boleros, she realised, had never been designed for women with thirty-seven-inch busts.

Or even less; the garment wasn't going to do a lot of good for Alison, either.

'Victoria,' Alison said, 'if you think I am going to walk out of that doorway into the midst of a lot of Arabs, much less sit down to lunch with them, dressed like this . . .'

'Relax,' Vicky said. 'The Arabs are the most perfect gentlemen in the world, when they are being gentlemen. Our haiks!' she commanded the girl.

Who bowed, and produced the voluminous white linen robes worn by Arab women in public, in which they were each wrapped, instantly being as totally concealed as nuns, even their wet hair being lost to view. The girls also produced yashmaks, but Vicky waved these away. They were not Arab women, and she wanted Zobeir to be in no doubt about that.

'Oh, this is much better. Indeed, it's rather grand,' Alison agreed, giving herself a little twirl. 'I wish we had a mirror. An outfit like this could become quite a sensation in London.'

Vicky inspected the rest of them. 'You look very nice,' she told them. 'Let's go and eat.'

Their guide was waiting for them outside, where the morning was well advanced, and the camp seethed with noise and activity, people talking at each other in voices loud enough to suggest a perpetual argument, camels belching and spitting, horses neighing and stamping, while a variety of odours, not all of them pleasant, rose into the still air. Vicky listened, but could hear neither the sound of the cane nor the cries of the man suffering the bastinado. She gave a sigh of relief; if the punishment had been delayed, she might yet be able to intercede with Zobeir.

'The man who was to be punished,' she said. 'When will it happen?'

'The punishment has already been carried out. A hundred strokes does not take long. The bastinado is a continuous flogging by two men, you understand. The culprit is now being revived.' He smiled. 'But he will not walk for the next few days, I do assure you.'

'Oh,' Vicky said. 'I . . . I did not know. I heard nothing.'

The man continued to smile, grimly. 'Soldiers of the Emir do not cry out, lady. However severe the pain.'

They had arrived before the Emir's tent, the one in the centre of the circle. Here, as Vicky had expected, there were several chambers. They passed through what appeared to be a guardroom, for it contained six soldiers, standing rigidly to attention, and then went into a reception room, where Zobeir and David were waiting to greet them – to Vicky's alarm. She wondered just how long the pair had had alone together, and what had been said. But they both looked happy enough, and David had been fitted out in breeches and tunic and boots similar to those worn by the Emir, although his head had been left bare while Zobeir continued to wear a burnous. He was unarmed, but then, Zobeir had also discarded his scimitar.

The Emir hurried forward. 'Welcome,' he said, 'oh, welcome to my humble abode, Lady Dobree. May I say . . .' Having kissed her fingers, he held her at arms' length, 'that you look more beautiful now than on the occasion of our first meeting. And you were beautiful then, believe me.'

'Your excellency understands that a woman's heart will always be melted by flattery,' Vicky answered. 'May I present Mrs Alison Lang, my closest friend.'

Zobeir had discarded his veil, and Alison was staring at him as if hypnotised, while he smiled at her. 'But', he remarked, 'is England populated by nothing but women of extreme beauty?'

For a moment, Vicky thought Alison was inadvertently going to curtsey. Certainly she simpered.

'My nieces, Mary and Elizabeth Dobree,' Vicky went on.

'Two more beauties.' Zobeir kissed their knuckles. 'I am entranced.'

Mary looked about to comment, but fortunately caught Vicky's eye and kept her mouth shut; Elizabeth looked on the verge of a fainting fit.

'Mrs Cartwright, Mrs Marker, and Mrs Pilling,' Vicky said. 'Wives of my husband's staff officers.'

'Alas, ladies, that we meet in such unhappy circumstances,' Zobeir said sadly, kissing their hands.

'My maid, Nathalie Prudhomme.'

Zobeir did not offer to kiss Nathalie's hand, but merely nodded.

'And Mrs Lang's son Charles, with his nurse, Prudence Brown.'

Prudence made a small curtsey.

'A fine-looking boy,' Zobeir commented. 'I am sure he will be happier eating by himself.' He snapped his fingers, and the guide, who had remained at the door, probably in anticipation of this development, Vicky decided, saluted and touched Prudence on the arm.

'Milady?' Prudence asked in alarm.

She was probably addressing Alison, but Vicky replied. 'You may go with him, Prudence. And you, Nathalie. I am sure Bream will be there to look after you.'

They hesitated, and then left.

'And now, ladies, shall we eat?' Zobeir invited.

'Oh, yes,' Mary said.

Vicky frowned at her, but Zobeir smiled indulgently, and led them into another chamber, this one much larger, where there waited several servants, one standing behind each of a series of cushions placed on the rich carpet which covered the sand. The cushions were arranged in a circle around several steaming pots of food; hungry as she was, however, Vicky could not help but be interested in her surroundings, in the richness of the drapes and, even more, in the obvious fact that they had only seen about half of this palace-like tent. Obviously there were the Emir's sleeping quarters beyond . . . and also his travelling harem? She could not forget the closed howdahs she had seen as the caravan had approached the oasis, and she could not believe the girls who had attended them had been so protected and mollycoddled.

'Oh, how good that smells!' Elizabeth said, clapping her hands.

'Elizabeth,' Vicky said severely. 'Do please mind your manners. My nieces are very hungry,' she explained to Zobeir.

'I am sure you are all hungry, madam,' Zobeir said, gesturing her to the cushion on his immediate right. David he motioned to sit on his left. Alison sat next to David, Mary and Elizabeth next to Vicky. Joanna sat beside the girls and Margaret and Alice completed the circle. The ladies, apart from Vicky, took some time to get settled, apparently quite unable to decide what to do with their legs, but eventually they all, even Alison, followed her example of squatting cross-legged, the folds of their haiks being gathered on top of their calves and heels.

Zobeir waited and watched with polite patience.

'Can we begin?' Mary asked.

'Mary!' Vicky admonished.

Zobeir continued to smile. 'May the Great Allah, who rules all things, and *knows* all things . . .' He gazed at Vicky as he spoke, 'bless this our food and increase our enjoyment of it, even as we pray that he will increase our wisdom.'

She wondered why she suddenly seemed to have indigestion. There was no way he could have seen through their deception. Surely. Unless David had said something careless. But how much did he *know?*

The servants were presenting gold-plated finger bowls filled with warm and very faintly scented water. As soon as their fingers were rinsed, the first pot was presented to the Emir.

'Auntie,' Mary whispered, 'they've forgotten the plates.'

'And the knives and forks,' Elizabeth added.

'Ssh,' Vicky begged.

Zobeir flicked back his sleeve, reached into the pot, and took out a chunk of meat attached to what looked like a somewhat soggy biscuit. 'Couscous,' he said. 'It is made from goats' meat, you understand.'

'We use fingers?' Mary whispered, even more loudly than the last time.

'Goats' meat?' Alison asked in consternation.

'And cooked on a platter of unleavened bread.' Zobeir placed the morsel in his mouth and chewed, while the servants watched him anxiously, and his guests watched him with equal apprehension. 'Excellent.'

The dish was offered to David, and then to Vicky and the girls, before it got to Alison, who was biting her lip and flushing

213

furiously, partly, Vicky supposed, because she was being so pointedly excluded from a part in the Dobree family, but equally because she was just realising that they were all dipping into the same pot – with their fingers. But she dutifully followed suit – she was too hungry to consider doing otherwise. The meat was actually extraordinarily tough and very high, but nevertheless it tasted better than anything Vicky had ever eaten before.

'Be sure you chew it well,' she warned the girls. 'And don't overeat, or you'll have upset stomachs.'

If they didn't already.

Another dish was being offered to the Emir, and once again he dipped his fingers in, to remove a morsel. 'These are the eyeballs of the goat,' he said. 'A great delicacy.'

Elizabeth suddenly choked, and Mary had to slap her on the back. 'Ooh,' she said. 'My fingers are all sticky; they've left a mark.'

'You haven't?' Elizabeth gasped.

A servant hurried forward with a fresh bowl of warm water and a napkin.

'What lively . . . nieces you have, Lady Dobree,' Zobeir remarked. 'They make my heart warm to them.'

'They are usually better mannered than this,' Vicky explained. 'But they haven't eaten anything except dates for some time.'

'Of course. Your husband has been telling me of your adventures. How you set his leg. My dear lady, I am overwhelmed with admiration for you.'

Vicky tried desperately to catch David's eye, to attempt to gain some idea of just what he had told the Emir. And David gazed back. But there was nothing he could do more than waggle his eyebrows.

She had to play the whole thing by ear, literally, and rely on the likelihood that he would have told the exact truth, wherever possible.

'It's not quite right,' she said. The bowl was back and she had some more couscous, but this time she passed the goats' eyeballs – she had swallowed the last one without chewing, and could feel it sitting in the centre of her oesophagus – apparently permanently.

'You do not like the food?' Zobeir inquired, anxiously.

'Oh, I do, I do,' Vicky said. 'It's just that after fasting for so long I think I should eat very little until my digestion returns to normal.'

'Very wise. But then, you are clearly as wise as you are courageous. Did you really shoot four men?'

'Well . . . it was them. Or us. My nieces . . .'

'Of course. The protection of one's family is one's most sacred duty. I have observed your husband's leg. Do not fret about it, madam. As soon as we reach Timbuktu, I will have my own surgeons reset it. The General has agreed to this.'

'Timbuktu?' she cried. 'Is that where you are going?'

'That is where *we* are going,' Zobeir explained. 'I could not leave you here, in the desert, with your . . .' His gaze drifted over Mary and Elizabeth, who were whispering together and giggling, 'adorable nieces, at the mercy of any marauder who might come along.'

'Ah,' Vicky said. 'Of course you couldn't. I've always wanted to see Timbuktu. But . . . isn't it a long way away?'

'A week's march,' Zobeir said carelessly. And smiled. '*You* will not march, Lady Dobree. You will be borne.'

'Of course,' Vicky said. 'But . . . we would like news of our susrvival to be sent to the coast. I am sure General Dobree has explained this.'

General Dobree was now engaged in conversation with Alison, his head turned away.

'Indeed,' Zobeir agreed. 'We have discussed the situation, and have decided to send the General's man, Bream, accompanied by one of the women, down to Kumassi to acquaint the British governor there of your present position. Do you know this governor? He is a man called Hodgson. He is also a sir, like your husband.'

'No,' Vicky said, 'we've never met. There are an awful lot of sirs in England. But . . . Bream, and a woman? Is that necessary?'

'I think so,' Zobeir said. 'This Hodgson is not a man like your husband, Lady Dobree. He is a distrustful fellow, and he is most distrustful of me. I believe it is one of his dearest ambitions one day to hang me, an old British custom for those with whom they do not see eye to eye. But of course, you know this. So I think the more convincing our messengers, the quicker you will be returned to your loved ones.'

All the food Vicky had eaten was turning to lead in her stomach. This man knew they were feeding him a pack of lies. Yet if that were so, why was he humouring them at all? Or were they about to be murdered, when they had finished dinner? But that too made no sense, from what she had heard of the Arabs. They had eaten with this man. He would not now harm them, certainly as long as they were in his care.

'We shall send the nurse, the woman Brown,' Zobeir said.

'Prudence! Oh . . . but what will Alison, Mrs Lang, do without her?'

'I am sure she will wish to care for her son herself, for the brief while it will take us to reach Timbuktu. There, I will provide her with a new nurse. But why choose the woman, Prudence, you asked? Because she is big and strong, and it is a very arduous journey from here to Kumassi. And a dangerous one, I might add. My people will of course escort them as far as they can, and we will see that they are equipped with food and arms, but there will still be a lengthy distance to be covered on their own, through the land of the Ashanti – a most barbarous people – before Kumassi can be reached. Do not be alarmed,' he hurried on, as Vicky obviously *was* alarmed. 'When I described the Ashanti as barbarous, I meant that they were uncouth and uncivilised in their habits. However, they are British subjects. Oh, indeed, they had the misfortune to be conquered by the great Sir Garnet Wolseley, about twenty years ago. Do you know, I fought against Wolseley, in Egypt, just after that campaign? I was with Arabi Pasha. We were defeated . . .' He gazed at the bowl being offered for several seconds before taking some more meat. 'But that is in the past. The important point is that once Bream and the woman reach the kraals of the Ashanti, they will be safe, whereas my men would be regarded as enemies. But even with Ashanti aid, it is still a journey which will require much stamina and I am afraid that your other servant, the little French girl, Nathalie, does not seem to have the required strength.'

'No, she doesn't,' Vicky said absently, brain doing handsprings. She had always accepted the Ashanti as hostile, because she had understood that they had never truly accepted British rule. But if Zobeir was right . . .

'You are still distressed at sending the nurse?' he asked. 'But you would hardly wish to send one of your . . . dear friends, would you, Lady Dobree?'

Vicky bit her lip. 'No, of course not, your excellency. But . . . would it not make more sense for us all to go? Together? I mean, if your people can provide us with an escort to the land of the Ashanti, and the Ashanti are well disposed to us . . .'

'I could not dream of it,' Zobeir protested. 'It is far too arduous a journey for your husband to undertake with a broken leg, and I would never forgive myself if any misfortune were to overtake a lady like yourself. Even a lady like yourself, I may say, who has so proved her ability to withstand hardship. No, no, I am honoured to have you as my guest.'

'But . . .' Vicky persisted, 'we will have to make that journey eventually, won't we?'

'Eventually. When all has been prepared, and your husband is fully restored to strength. For the time being, believe me, it is better to send your servants.' Another smile. 'After all, that is what servants are for, do you not agree?'

'Of course,' she said. 'But you make it sound as if they might not reach Kumassi at all, for all the help they will be given.'

'I am afraid that is always a possibility. But there is nothing for you to worry about, milady. You will be very comfortable, in Timbuktu. I have a house there, which you are welcome to use for as long as you desire.'

'But . . . supposing they *don't* get through, and no message comes back from this man Hodgson?'

'I have said, my home is yours.'

Vicky opened her mouth, and then shut it again.

'And your husband's, of course,' Zobeir went on.

Vicky felt as if someone had kicked her in the stomach.

'There is just one remaining point,' Zobeir continued. 'I feel it would be best if your messengers were to take with them some proof of your identity, that Hodgson may be in no doubt who is awaiting their return.'

'Yes,' Vicky gasped. 'That would be a good idea. Unfortunately, everything I own went down with the ship.'

'Except for the ring you wear,' Zobeir said. 'It is clearly a very beautiful, valuable ring, such as must belong to a great lady. Would you trust your servants with it? I am sure it would confirm the truth of what they have to tell Hodgson.'

'Oh. Oh, yes.' She pulled the ring from her finger. It took a considerable effort, as her fingers were somewhat larger – being so much stronger – than Alison's; she had not noticed that when forcing the ring on in so much haste that morning.

Alison's head jerked. She had been listening after all, and now appeared ready to spit.

'You have been exposed to so many hardships, my dear Lady Dobree,' Zobeir observed. 'Thus it is most reassuring to see that you have not lost as much weight as one might have supposed. You could even have put some on, at least in your hands. But do not worry, my cooks will restore you, restore you all, to your best health. And if the ring is never returned to you, why, I shall provide you with another. One which fits you properly,' he smiled. 'That is the word of Zobeir ibn Rubayr, never broken.'

He kissed her finger, and handed the ring to the servant at his shoulder.

Alison appeared to choke on a sheep's eyeball.

CHAPTER 10

Remarkably, the meal ended with ices, or at least sherbets, as dreamed of by Elizabeth. But what was remarkable about that, Vicky wondered? The Emir obviously travelled with all the churning equipment he could possibly use, and there was no lack of salt in the desert. Although all he would really have had to do, she thought, was place the churn on her stomach, for it to be thoroughly shaken up. She had known, from the moment she first watched the caravan approaching the oasis, that they were in more danger than even when subject to assault by Curly and his friends, and she had chosen the only way out that had occurred to her in the brief time at her disposal. Now she wondered if she might not have landed them in far deeper waters than if they had just thrown themselves on the Arabs' mercy.

But that would have been to commit suicide. She had to believe she had made the right decision. Because, whatever happened now, it was the *only* decision.

'Um, that was very good,' Mary said. 'Mr Zobeir, what was that last meat dish, the one with the faintly sweetish flavour?'

'It felt like some kind of nut,' Elizabeth volunteered. 'Only it was soft.'

Zobeir smiled at them. 'The goat's testicles,' he explained.

'Oh, good Lord,' Mary said.

Elizabeth made a strangled sound which was not actually a word at all.

'They are not sweet in themselves, of course,' Zobeir went on. 'But my cooks prepare a special sauce to serve with it. I am glad you liked them. We will have them again. I am afraid,

219

until we reach Timbuktu, goat is our staple diet.'

'I'm going to be sick,' Mary said in a sepulchral tone. 'I know I'm going to be sick.'

'Well, don't,' Vicky snapped, she was feeling somewhat queasy herself.

'Now, General, Lady Dobree,' Zobeir said. 'It is our custom to rest after our meal, while the sun is at its hottest. I must tell you that when we are on the march like this, it is the only time we do rest. Our journey will be resumed this evening. We will despatch your messengers and their escort to the south this evening as well.' He smiled at Vicky. 'But I am aware that it is the English custom for a man to wish to rest with his wife, madam. Your chamber has been prepared.' He stood up, and they all hastily scrambled to their feet. 'I look forward to your company when the sun begins to set.'

They were ushered to the door, where servants waited for them.

'Victoria,' Alison said, in a voice suggestive of a volcano about to erupt. 'Do you think I could have a word with you?'

Vicky gave her a sweet smile. 'I'm afraid not just now, Alison, my dear. I really am most awfully tired after that delicious meal.' She yawned, patting her lips delicately. 'I cannot wait to put my head down. Do you think you could possibly acquaint Prudence with the journey she is going to make? Be nice about it; she may be a trifle upset. But she is your nanny, isn't she? Tell her I will have a word with her before she leaves.'

'You . . .' Now the volcano was seething.

Zobeir loomed over them. 'Rest, my dear Mrs Lang,' he said. 'Rest. It will bring back the bloom to those beautiful cheeks.'

Alison gazed at him with her mouth open.

'I think he likes you,' Mary whispered as the Emir stepped past them. 'And I'm sure he does it differently from Curly.'

'She is absolutely livid,' David said, as they found themselves in their tent, the one to which he and Bream had been taken to be bathed. Bream was now absent, but two eunuchs were waiting eagerly to assist them. 'I have no idea how long she is going to

220

be able to keep it up. Do you think we could get rid of these fellows?'

'I think we must,' Vicky agreed. 'We have no need of you,' she said in Arabic. 'You may leave us now.'

The men exchanged glances, but their business was to obey, however odd the behaviour of their guests. They bowed and left. The door dropped into place.

David took off his haik. 'Certainly keeps a fellow warm. And how they wear these tunics all the time . . .'

'They bath all the time.'

'Yes. I was thinking earlier that they must just about drink an oasis like this dry.' He lay down with a sigh on the thick pile of blankets which, laid on the carpet and covered with a linen sheet, was apparently to be their bed.

'Painful?' she asked.

'It comes and goes.'

'Did you really agree to have it reset in Timbuktu? It'll mean breaking it again first, you know.'

'Oh, I know, believe me. But his nibs suggested it so casually I couldn't let our side down by appearing afraid of the idea.' He sat up again as Vicky also took off her haik and dropped to her knees beside him. 'My God, Vicky. You are the most magnificent woman I have ever seen.' He parted the bolero to kiss her.

'It's the clothes. Lie down.'

'I'd rather sit up for a while.' He caressed her. 'It'll be better for the digestion.'

'Just do it.' She pushed him down, lay on her stomach beside him, lips close to his ear. 'Listen, David. We are in terrible trouble.'

'Oh? I thought things were going rather well. I'm sorry about having to send poor old Prudence off into the bush, but I gather it's not all that dangerous. Zobeir promised to have them escorted as far as he dared without starting a war.'

'Prudence is at least getting out of here,' Vicky reminded him. 'Oh, sure, she'll be upset. I mean, going off into the bush alone with a man . . . she's a *very* respectable woman.'

'There comes a time when respectability has to take a back

221

seat to expedience. And as you say, she'll be first out. So what's bothering you?'

'The rest of us. David . . . and keep your voice down, because we don't know if he has an English-speaking Arab listening just outside that wall . . . David, Zobeir knows.'

David frowned. 'Knows what?'

'I don't know. That's the trouble. He knows we're not quite who or what we say we are.'

'What makes you say that? He hasn't questioned any aspect of our story.'

'I know that. And I don't *know* what he knows. It's a hundred and one things. The remarks he makes. He must've spotted right off that the ring didn't fit. And then, the way he looks at Mary . . .'

'Well, she's a lovely girl. She seems to have got a great deal more lovely since this jaunt began, as if the life totally agrees with her.'

'I wish you'd be serious.'

'I am being serious, my darling. I think you're just being over-anxious. Fair enough after what you've been through, but this time we really have fallen on our feet. Believe me, Zobeir wouldn't be taking all this trouble, treating us virtually like royalty, if he didn't entirely believe us.'

'He knows a great deal about Dobree's background.'

'So do I.'

'Like his Egyptian service?'

'Dobree never served in Egypt, Vicky. You're just imagining things.'

'Am I? Do you realise that Zobeir fought with Arabi Pasha against Wolseley at Tel-el-Kebir? Just about the time Sir William was earning his reputation? Are you positive he wasn't with Wolseley's army?'

'Absolutely positive, my darling. That same year, of 1882, was the year Sir William won his V.C., taking on the Afghans single handed in the Khyber Pass.' He kissed her. 'And Zobeir knows that. There is no way the pair of them could ever have seen each other.'

'Oh. That's a relief. But if he knows that . . . then he knows Dobree's age. And you . . .'

'He does not know Dobree's age,' David said, patiently. 'We got on the subject of the V.C., and I reminisced happily – the General has told me all about it often enough – throwing in that I was so young, foolish, and brave, at eighteen. That makes me thirty-five now. Don't tell me I don't look thirty-five, with this beard.'

'Um.'

'He swallowed it, Vicky. Believe me.'

'All right. Maybe he did. But try this: Zobeir was also one of the Mahdi's chief lieutenants. And the Mahdi's people, the Dervishes, were smashed by your General Kitchener at Omdurman just a year ago. Right?'

'You are a mine of information.'

'I read the newspapers. Especially items about Africa. I adore the place, at least, I used to until this last fortnight. What I am trying to say is that Zobeir was almost certainly at that battle, which is why he's had to flee the Sudan. Either way, he is still at war with the British. And you are a British officer.'

'I had worked that out for myself, my dearest girl. But in that case, he will surely be more anxious than ever to ransom me, us . . . or at least use us for some *quid pro quo*. And in the meanwhile, he will accord us the respect due an officer who is also a prisoner of war. He may be an Arab, but he is also very obviously a gentleman. Surely even you must agree with that? Now come along, I think I'm digested.'

'I don't think I could concentrate,' she said. His arguments were impeccable . . . but altogether too sanguine, she was positive.

'You must try.' He smiled, and eased the bolero from her shoulders. 'As you say, we must put up a good show, as we don't know who may be listening. Or even watching.'

'That's doesn't bother you either?'

'It's not going to turn me into a monk, if that's what you mean. I have never felt so, well . . . so contentedly alive in my life. Tell me something, were you bathed by a eunuch?'

'Yes,' she said, and allowed herself to be taken into his arms. Because, despite her fears, she knew just how he felt. And besides, she didn't know when would be the last time.

'Prudence,' Vicky said, hugging the big woman. 'Oh, Prudence.'

Prudence was dressed as they were, in a haik over her silks, and she had also been given a burnous. As had Bream; they both looked quite Arab. Now she smiled. 'I am quite happy to go, Vi . . . milady,' she said.

'We shouldn't have any trouble, ma'am,' Bream assured her. 'These fellows are apparently going to take us to the river, and even arrange for us to be escorted down it. We'll be almost within shouting distance of Kumassi before we know it.'

'And you feel all right . . . I mean . . . setting off with Bream like this?'

'I'm sure Mr Bream and I will get on very well together, milady,' she said. 'I have no doubt at all he is a perfect gentleman.' She squeezed Vicky's hand reassuringly. 'And now you've shown us how to survive, we'll make it easily. It's you, and . . .' She glanced at Alison, 'Mrs Lang, and Charlie and the girls that I worry about.'

'What, living in the lap of luxury?' Vicky asked, forcing a smile of her own.

'We'll get back to you, ma'am,' Bream promised. 'With all the soldiers in Africa.' He gave a nervous glance at Zobeir.

Who also smiled, as usual. 'I am sure General Dobree would prefer it if you were merely to bring the cost of a package home, for himself and Lady Dobree, and their companions. It will also be much cheaper for the British Government. One hundred thousand pounds sterling will be sufficient.'

'One hundred thousand . . .' Vicky stared at David. He hadn't mentioned anything about agreeing a ransom amount.

But he looked equally astonished. 'I say, old man,' he remarked, 'are you holding us for ransom?'

'My dear General, I am distressed that you should suppose such a thing. But looking after you, feeding and clothing you, and then escorting you to the coast when the time comes, is going to be very expensive. And then there is your leg . . . I am not a rich man, General. It grieves me to have to admit this, but since your General Kitchener has appropriated all my estates in the Sudan, why, I am stricken with poverty.'

'Oh, quite,' David agreed, drily. 'But you know, a hundred thousand is a little steep, even for a general.'

'But you are not *a* General,' Zobeir pointed out. 'You are General Dobree. And you are accompanied by your wife, and so many . . .' He smiled at them all, 'beautiful ladies.'

'Mr Zobeir is quite right,' Alison said. 'I am sure I, we, are worth every penny of a hundred thousand. Now, you be very careful with that ring, Prudence. I . . . I'm sure Lady Dobree would like it back.'

Had Zobeir not been standing beside her, Vicky would have kicked her on the ankle.

'I'll bring it back, milady,' Prudence said, not actually addressing anyone. 'Or I'll have it waiting for you when we get to this place . . . Ku . . . Ku?'

'Kumassi,' Zobeir said. 'And now it is time for you to leave. We will wish you a safe journey, and a speedy return.' He gestured them towards the waiting camels.

'Oh, Lord,' Prudence said. 'What awful-looking beasts.'

'They bite, too,' Mary said.

But with some assistance from her escort Prudence was safely settled, as was Bream, and they rode off, south from the encampment, looking back for a last wave. Vicky felt almost weepy. But Prudence *was* getting out.

'We don't have to ride on one of those things, do we?' Elilzabeth asked anxiously.

'Of course,' Zobeir said. 'But in a special chair.' He pointed to where howdahs were being made ready, as indeed the entire camp was bring struck; the sun was beginning its droop towards the western horizon.

' I think I would rather ride,' Vicky said. 'If it can be on a horse.'

'Alas, madam,' Zobeir said, 'I have no side-saddles.'

'That's all right with me. I'm just as happy astride.'

'And you will ride all night?'

'I'm sure it'll make a change to walking all night, your excellency.' In any event, she had so much on her mind she knew she wasn't going to sleep.

'Of course,' he said. 'I keep forgetting, that you are as wise in the ways of the desert as myself. A horse will be provided.'

'Oh, and for me,' David said. 'I will ride with my wife.'

'I think I'd like to do that too,' Alison said.

Zobeir nodded. 'As you wish.'

'And us,' Mary said.

'Good heavens, no,' Alison said. 'I mean . . .' She looked at Vicky. 'Victoria, you cannot permit that.'

When Victoria hesitated, Zobeir came to Alison's support. 'I'm afraid Mrs Lang is quite right, madam. It would be most unseemly for young ladies like your nieces to ride astride.'

'Oh,' Vicky said, understanding what they were driving at. 'Yes. I'm afraid you'll have to go in a howdah, girls.'

'Oh, bother,' Mary said.

'Why can't we ride?' Elizabeth asked. 'Why can't we?'

'Because we might lose our virginity, stupid,' Mary said.

'Mary!' Alison admonished.

'It would certainly be a catastrophe,' Zobeir observed, gently.

'Oh, well . . .' Mary sighed.

'What's our virginity?' Elizabeth asked.

'Explain it to her, Mary, there's a dear,' Vicky said. 'In the howdah,' she hastily added.

Nathalie and the three other women were quite content to ride in howdahs, although Vicky didn't see how any of them could avoid being seasick as the camels jerked and stumbled along. But on horseback it was heavenly, as the moon rose to bathe the desert in its brilliant white light. Moving along in the midst of such a vast assembly of people, utterly secure from anything that might exist beyond the ring of outriders, they were even able, for this brief spell, to forget the perils of their situation within that ring.

They rode all night, and then for several hours into the next morning, to reach the next oasis. Zobeir, or his caravan master, seemed to know exactly where each was to be found, and also able to navigate their way across the desert with remarkable accuracy, although they did not appear to use any instruments.

The oasis they now came to was larger than the last, and was occupied by a group of Bedouin, who hastily evacuated and camped some distance away when they learned that it was the great Zobeir ibn Rubayr who was approaching them.

'It must be marvellous to have such a reputation,' Vicky remarked at lunch.

Zobeir gave one of his half-contemptuous smiles. 'It was earned, Lady Dobree. And must be maintained.'

'I must say, this is all rather fun, now,' Alison said, after the meal. 'Of course, it would be so much nicer if William actually were with us . . . poor William.'

It was almost the first time she had mentioned her late husband since they had reached the beach. But Vicky reckoned that even now it was only a passing thought. Alison had a lot to do without Prudence, but she naturally made Mary and Elizabeth share her duties, as well as Joanna Cartwright, who willingly had the boy in the howdah with her during the night. They had all made a rapid and indeed amazing recovery, but Vicky feared it was also only a temporary recovery. After the living death of the desert, this was indeed like being transported to heaven, with the girls and the eunuchs anxious to perform the smallest task for them, with all they could wish to eat or drink – although there was, of course, no wine ever offered, as Zobeir was a devout Muslim – and with a succession of fascinating landscapes constantly unfolding before them. Even crossing the various stony deserts that they came to was now nothing less than enjoyable, surrounded as they were by people who were experts at it.

But she knew they were all still suffering from shock. So much had happened in the week since they had come ashore, that the true facts of their situation, of their widowhood, of their being prisoners of the Arabs, of their having sent Prudence and Bream into the jungle, of the unimaginable fate which would be theirs if neither of them reached Kumassi, had not yet had the opportunity to sink in. But it would.

If they ever wanted a true estimate of the misery that could

227

exist in their exotic world, they had only to look over their shoulders at the slaves who trailed dolefully along behind the caravan, behind even the herd of goats, diminishing every day, often falling several miles behind the main group, and thus having to walk longer during the daylight hours to reach the next encampment. 'I wonder you do not take more care of the poor things,' Vicky ventured to Zobeir. 'Do you not intend to make a profit out of them?'

'Of course,' he said. 'But they are stronger than they look. Most will survive. And those that do not, why, they will hardly survive slavery itself, as will be seen at a glance when they are placed on the block, so they will not attract a good price anyway.'

'Have you no feelings for them, as fellow human beings?'

His frown suggested genuine bewilderment. 'Would they have feelings for me, if I were back there and they up here? They are Fulani, hardy warriors. They ruled an empire in West Africa up until comparatively recent times, and were as cruel as the Turks.' He smiled. 'Or the Arabs, you might say. Or as I might say, as the British and the French, with their cannon and their machine guns. They are hereditary enemies of the Touareg.'

'And you are a Touareg?'

Another smile. 'No, madam. But my men are.'

Obviously he was not going to tell her anything about himself at this moment. 'I see you have only men back there,' she remarked. 'I had supposed girls and young boys were also of importance.'

'They are. But only of the right stock. The Fulani, no. There is little market for their women; they are too proud, too eager to resist. They have to be broken, and this often makes them unusable. The men are no less proud, but they are born soldiers. They will be employed as household guards. Once they understand that there is no escape, most of them prove remarkably faithful, and as they are big, strong men, they are ideal for the purpose.'

'Then what sort of person do you regard as the ideal stock for domestics, or for the harem?' she asked.

228

He raised his eyebrows, as if surprised that she should wish to delve into so delicate a subject. 'Well, of course, black men make ideal eunuchs. But they have to be taken young, not only because a eunuch must be trained in docility from an early age, but because castration is less dangerous when performed on a small boy. The incidence of survival is far higher. It can be a dangerous operation, you understand, madam, both from the risk of infection, and because for as much as three days no water can be passed.' He gazed at her as he spoke.

And she gazed back. 'I can understand that, your excellency,' she agreed.

'There are of course boys who are wanted, for other purposes,' he went on, still watching her.

'Of course.'

'But for these we tend to look among certain of the desert peoples, which are more comely, to our eyes, and more pliable, too. Naturally, were it possible to secure a constant supply of white-skinned boys . . .' At last he looked away from her. They were in camp on the fourth day since leaving the first oasis, and were seated outside his tent while luncheon was being prepared. A short distance away Charlie was playing a game of tag with his stepsisters; their laughter drifted on the breeze, as did the girls' haiks, to allow glimpses of silk pantaloons beneath. It would not be difficult to imagine what the boleros were doing beneath the haiks, and Vicky had no doubt that Zobeir, as she watched his expression, had a very powerful imagination.

She kept her voice even. 'But they are hard to come by.'

'Oh, indeed. One needs exceptional circumstances. As for white-skinned girls, who are also virgins, my dear Lady Dobree, they are worth their weight in gold.'

She could no longer doubt that he intended to take possession of Mary the moment he was ready – her only hope was that he would not make the decision until after the ransom arrived, or after he was sure it was never going to arrive: he was clearly a man who calculated every step, even when it involved satisfying his lust. His lust. The concept was sufficiently horrifying by itself, but when related to the utter callousness he had shown regarding the slaves, the way he had talked about castration, it quite made her stomach roll.

And there was simply no one to whom she could confide her increasing apprehensions. Not even David. In fact, she placed David in the same category as the women. He too had not had the chance to sit back and evaluate his situation, which extended far beyond his present captivity. He had shrugged off her failure at setting his leg, with the courage she now knew he possessed in enormous depths. But he would eventually have to come to terms with the fact that his military career was over, however many more weeks of excruciating agony lay ahead of him as the Arab doctors broke the leg and tried to reset it: she had no faith in their ability to do so properly. But for the time being he was content that he seemed to be successfully playing the role she had given him, and that they were safe. When she did raise the point, at the first opportunity after the departure of Prudence and Bream, that Zobeir had finally come out into the open and revealed himself to be their captor rather than their host by naming a ransom, and that a ransom set so high was hardly likely to be paid, David had merely said, 'I don't agree at all. I think Alison was probably right when she said that Her Majesty's Government might consider a hundred thousand quite a reasonable sum for a man like Dobree. Especially when his family and several other women are involved. And actually, I must say I'm rather relieved that Zobeir is settling for cash. I'd hate to think we were being used for some political purpose. I'm not sure I could accept that.'

That had frightened her, the thought that he might be prepared to put his duty as an English officer before their safety. She believed that she was in love with him, but she still did not know him well enough, and his background was as different to hers as was Alison's. To tell him she feared that for all his fine manners Zobeir might have designs on the two girls might be to make him draw his revolver and attempt to act the gallant British gentleman.

And she did not even know if she was right, or if she was, as he said, being over-anxious. After all, there was no law against

Zobeir looking, and dreaming of what might have been.

Remarkably, she felt that the safest person with whom to discuss the situation was probably Mary herself, who was revealing qualities of maturity and resilience she was not sure even Alison possessed, and who was, in fact, coming across as a most sterling character. But she couldn't risk that either, because again she didn't *know* what Mary's reactions might be.

So she smiled, and appeared as cheerful as everyone else. And retired to her couch with David every afternoon, and did nothing but make love. After so long it was something she wanted, anyway, and at least while in his arms she was unable to brood on her problems. He was growing stronger by the day, and had secured a razor to trim his beard, although she would not let him shave it off, just in case he appeared too young. Besides, she had fallen in love with him while he was wearing the beard. Time enough for him to shave it off when this adventure was over, if it was ever to be over.

She clung to him during those midday rendezvous with an almost desperate intensity. She had not envisaged anything like this. If she had dreamed of another James, it had been in the context of a Devon village, not the Sahara. Perhaps she even hoped for pregnancy, because however severe the complications which would result, it would at least put her beyond the reach of recall, in any direction. Because she understood that of them all, she was walking the narrowest path between mental collapse to either side. She was at least as exhausted as anyone else. She was the one who had killed the four sailors. She was the one who had driven them across the desert, and thus in fact driven poor Phyllis Smart to her death. And thus she was the one who had landed them in their present situation. That the alternative might have led them to an even quicker disaster was neither here nor there. However it turned out now, it was her responsibility . . . and as they were handed over to the Arab soldiery, when Zobeir was tired of humouring them or had realised whatever objective he truly had in mind, they would turn their faces towards her in a last reproach.

But before that happened, they must come to Timbuktu. On the fourth day since leaving the oasis, they had scarcely commenced their evening march when they saw trees, and came to the grassland.

'Well, Victoria, I must congratulate you,' Alison remarked. 'I never really supposed it was there.'

She had remained relentlessly cool since the episode of the ring, and even more, Vicky knew, her own relegation to a position of unimportance beside Lady Dobree. But the choice had been hers, however much she might now regret it. 'I suspect this is a bit farther north than the grassland I was aiming at,' she confessed. 'We've been travelling virtually due east.'

That afternoon they sighted the river. But it was only a river. 'I thought the Niger was one of the great rivers of the world,' Vicky remarked to Zobeir, as they looked at the meandering streams which seemed to run in every direction, creating a huge area of swamp, and soon debouching into a large lake.

'It is,' he told her. 'This is but a branch of it. The main stream is some miles south of Timbuktu itself, but easily reached by water, you understand. It is an age-old battle, this, between the river and the desert. Because of it, the Touaregs and the men from the forests met here, and Timbuktu came to greatness. It began as a trading post, for the exchange of slaves for salt. Then the Touaregs fortified it, and built mosques and a castle. Then the men from the forests assaulted it and took it for themselves. I am talking now of some three or four centuries ago. Then the Touaregs took it back. Now . . . it is but a shadow of its former glory. Yet it is immortal. Timbuktu is the Rome of Africa.'

When he spoke like that, with so evident a knowledge of history, and with so much feeling for the past, for the receded glory of his people, it was difficult to relate him to the ruthless slave driver which she knew he was.

'When do we see the city?' she asked.

'Soon,' he told her. 'It is only a few hours off, so we will not rest today, but keep going. Now, you must excuse me.' He rode away from her side to await the return of a patrol he had sent out the previous evening, and which was now approaching beneath a dust cloud from the north, as the sun rose above the eastern horizon. They galloped up to the Emir and told him their story, but they were out of her earshot. He was clearly not pleased with what they had to say, however, as they could tell as he walked his horse back to them. 'I have changed my mind,' he said. 'We will, after all, camp here for today, and enter the city tonight.'

'Is there trouble, your excellency?' David asked.

Zobeir smiled. 'It is my desire to avoid what you may call trouble, General. In view of my precious cargo, you might say. There is a French column out there.' He pointed at the desert.

'French?' Vicky cried, while she could feel the quickening of interest in her companions.

'Oh, indeed. They probe to the south, always, from their stronghold in Algiers. I know the commander of this column, a Major Joffre. He is a bull-headed fellow. He was in Timbuktu but a few years ago, announcing, if you please, that it was now a French protectorate, in retaliation for the murder of a French officer who had earlier visited the city, and was unfortunate enough to die there. Well, as he was supported by a regiment of soldiers, and at that time there were few fighting men in the city, everyone bowed and accepted what he had to say. Then he left and the people of Timbuktu forgot about him. Now it seems he is back.'

'And has he, also, sworn to hang Zobeir ibn Rubayr?' David asked.

Zobeir bowed. 'I am an incredibly popular fellow, General. Absurdly so. The French and the British wish to place me beyond the law, because I deal in slaves. But I at least select my slaves with a purpose in mind. They seek to enslave entire peoples, for no apparent reason whatsoever, save to paint certain parts of the map red or blue. Ah well, in any event, it would be best to enter the city clandestinely. I have no wish to start a full scale war at this moment.'

'But . . .' Vicky looked at David.

'Oh, quite,' he agreed. 'It seems to me that in these circumstances, we might be of some assistance to you, your excellency. If you were to send us to this man Joffre, we would certainly tell him how we were rescued by you and your people, and how courteously we have been treated, and therefore . . .'

Zobeir smiled. 'And then you would be hurried back to civilisation, home and beauty,' he agreed, 'having escaped my clutches.'

'My dear fellow, we do not for one moment suppose that we are in your clutches . . .'

'I am glad of that,' Zobeir said. 'You would be acting hastily, and ungenerously. What of the two faithful servants you have sent into the jungles to inform Governor Hodgson of your situation? Besides, you would not like Joffre; he is an uncouth fellow. And you would be faced with another long journey across the desert. No, no, it is far better that you stay with me, for the time being.'

David had ceased smiling, and Vicky indeed recognised that he was close to losing his temper. 'What you mean, you villain,' he snapped, 'is that we are your prisoners, for all your fine talk, and that the real reason you are waiting until darkness to enter the city is that Joffre will not discover our presence.'

Zobeir gazed at him for some seconds, and then bowed. 'You are a man who chooses to call a spade a spade, General. I admire that. Now I would beg you to be a sensible man. Are you not being treated like a prince? And your ladies?' He shook his head as David's hand dropped to his revolver holster. 'That would be extremely foolish. In any event, I have had the bullets removed. Please believe that.' His face hardened. 'Please believe also, General, that if any member of your entourage attempts to steal away from my camp to reach the French position, he or she will be shot dead.' He turned to Vicky. 'May the Great Allah forgive me, Lady Dobree, but I'm afraid that law will also apply to any of your women, the children . . . and even to yourself.'

CHAPTER 11

'Well,' Mary remarked, as they had their morning bath, the camp having been pitched beside the river. 'I really am quite shocked. I thought he was such a nice man.'

'You knew he was going to become unpleasant all along, didn't you, Victoria?' Alison asked.

'I thought it likely,' Vicky said. 'I had no idea the French arms would turn up to complicate matters, though. Forgive me for saying it, but life would be a darned sight simpler if you British and French, and the Germans, the Belgians and the Dutch or whoever, would just leave these people alone to get on with living their lives.'

'Is that Lady Dobree speaking?' Alison inquired, coldly.

'I thought perhaps we were going to be rescued,' Joanna Cartwright ventured.

'With our throats cut,' Vicky said bitterly.

'But Vi . . . milady,' Nathalie said. 'Those are Frenchmen. If I could get away, and reach them . . . they could mount a surprise attack, maybe, and seize us . . .' Her face fell as she gazed at Vicky's expression.

'Nathalie,' Vicky said. 'You heard the man. You try to escape, and we are all finished. Just forget it. We'll sit this one out, as we sat all the others out. All right, we're being used as pawns. That must mean we're valuable, as long as we stay pawns. Just sit tight, for God's sake.'

'I am sure,' Alison said, 'that General Dobree . . .' She paused to let there be no doubt which General Dobree she was speaking about, 'would hardly agree with such a philosophy.'

'And I am sure,' Vicky retorted, 'that whatever the

circumstances, General Dobree would behave like a sensible man.'

She abandoned them, and fled to the comfort of her own General Dobree. Who had little to offer, being in a thoroughly depressed mood. 'God damn it,' he said. 'I completely overlooked checking my revolver. I mean, that's the sort of thing a batman does for you. What a stupid mistake to make.'

'What a lucky escape, you mean. If it had been loaded you might just have been tempted to try some heroics, and we'd all be dead.'

'He threatened our lives, God damn it.'

'Don't you suppose our lives have been on the line since we became his guests?' But now was not the time for I-told-you-so's. 'Please, David. We just have to sit tight and wait and see. *Please.*'

He sighed. 'I suppose you're right. But what wouldn't I give to see a British column appearing south of that river! While a French column lies north of it. By God, we'd squeeze him like a nut in a cracker.'

Vicky snapped her fingers. 'That's it!'

'What do you mean?'

'I mean, I'm beginning to understand what Zobeir is aiming at. Listen. Didn't Great Britain and France nearly come to blows, last year?'

'Well, there was a diplomatic crisis, certainly.'

'Simply because an English expedition, led by your General Kitchener, followed the Battle of Omdurman by ascending the Nile, and arrived at the same place as a French expedition, led by Colonel Marchand, at the same time?'

'Yes. Well, Egypt and the Sudan are in the British sphere of influence, don't you see? The French had no business there at all.'

'I do see. And is the Western Sahara not in the French sphere of influence?'

'Of course. That's why this fellow Joffre can march his columns around the desert without worrying about anyone objecting, save a few Arabs like Zobeir.'

'Exactly. And what would the French do if a British column

appeared south of the river? Especially a British column with every intention of crossing the river and seizing Timbuktu?'

He frowned. 'That would be tantamount to an act of war. I mean, that fellow Marchand wanted to make a fight of it, but was told to apologise and withdraw by his government.'

'I remember,' Vicky said. 'But would a British column, commanded by this Sir Francis Hodgson, apologise and withdraw if he was sure it was a matter of rescuing General and Lady Dobree? No matter what Major Joffre might say?'

'Good God,' David said. 'That could be rather sticky.'

'Very,' Vicky agreed. 'But I'll wager it's what Zobeir has in mind. Maybe he didn't anticipate having a French column on his doorstep. But he must know that Timbuktu is regarded as a French protectorate, and equally he knows that the British and the French hate each other. So he has meant to start something ever since he laid eyes on us. I thought he was pitching that ransom far too steeply. He knows it'll hardly be paid. But he also knows that this Hodgson man, who apparently hates him, when he learns that Zobeir is holding English women and children, as well as General and Lady Dobree, captive in Timbuktu, is going to mount a rescue expedition, even if it means moving into the French sphere of influence. Zobeir knows he can't take on the French, any more than he could take on Kitchener and the British. But if he can get the British and the French fighting each other over various bits of North Africa, he may be able to pull a few choice chestnuts out of the fire.'

'He'd be in the middle.'

'No, he wouldn't. Because I'll wager he'll just sidle off and leave them to it when the shooting starts.'

'And us?'

'I suspect we could be in even more of a mess than we thought.'

'So could the whole world, if Britain and France come to blows. We just have to get away, and get south, before Hodgson arrives.'

'I couldn't agree with you more.' Because despite what she had told the women, if that was Zobeir's plan, then if it came off they would be of no more value to him anyway. 'But for God's sake, take it easy. We'll have to find a way out of Timbuktu. We'll never get out of this camp.'

'Vicky,' he said. 'Oh, my Vicky . . . you are just magnificent. I'd never have realised what that scoundrel is up to.'

'I tell you what,' she said, 'let's pray I'm wrong. And meanwhile . . . not a word to a soul.'

Because although she wouldn't say so to David, *her* idea was to get away to the north, and the French. If they could do that, surely it would be possible for the French to get a message to the British, however much the two nations disliked and distrusted each other, to the effect that a punitive expedition was no longer necessary. And escaping north of Timbuktu to a military force strong enough to protect them and only a few miles away, had to be simpler, and safer, than plunging into the rain forest, pursued by Zobeir's cut-throats.

But she didn't know what might be David's reaction to putting himself at the mercy of the French.

Anyway, nothing could be done until they entered Timbuktu itself, at which time she hoped and prayed some of Zobeir's vigilance might be relaxed. The caravan moved on again at dusk, and only a couple of hours later, as the moon rose, the towers of Timbuktu also rose before them. In view of Zobeir's remarks as to the decay of the famous old city, Vicky supposed they were actually seeing it for the first time in the best possible light. They looked at high, mud-brick walls, the enormous towers of a mosque, the remains of an old fort, crumbling into dust, and then entered a maze of narrow streets, overhung with shuttered windows. Even in the gloom it was possible to make out that the houses were painted in brilliant pastel shades of pink and blue and green and yellow. The streets were unevenly paved, and were also crowded with people; the *souk*, or open-air market, was still trading vigorously; noise and odours rose into the air to match the dust; and veiled men and women stood in their narrow doorways and watched the caravan go by, while their dogs barked and howled.

But the whispered rumour spread quickly among the people. 'Zobeir comes'. Vicky really did not see that he had gained a great deal of concealment by postponing his arrival.

'Isn't it grand?' David said, walking his horse beside Vicky's. 'I feel as if I'm stepping back a thousand years.'

'Well, you are stepping back. At least, three hundred or so.'

'It's a frightfully smelly place,' Alison remarked from behind them. 'I'm amazed they don't all die of cholera, constantly.'

'They do,' Vicky told her. 'Constantly.'

Alison drew her haik tighter about her.

'The people looked like a lot of cut-throats to me,' David growled, glancing right and left.

'I suppose they are that too,' Vicky agreed, and realised that the caravan was splitting up. The slaves, under a strong escort of soldiers, were being led into an open area by the market, where they would spend another miserable night, she supposed, before being offered for sale in the morning. But the front section of the caravan, in which they were, continued on its way, to turn down another narrow side street and approach a high mud-brick wall, blank except for a narrow archway. Through this opening Zobeir walked his horse, and they followed him, urged on by their guards, to find themselves in a spacious courtyard entirely surrounded by buildings, which were all obviously part of the same establishment. The courtyard was crowded with people, all busily engaged in greeting the Emir, but compared with the street outside it smelt relatively clean – the air even had a vague scent of perfume.

Zobeir himself helped Vicky to dismount. 'Welcome to my home, Lady Dobree,' he said. 'One of them. But at least your travels are over.'

'For a while,' Vicky reminded him.

'Of course. But I would hope a considerable while. Come.' He himself led them through an arched doorway, on to a rough-floored hallway, at the end of which there was a heavy wooden door bound in iron. This was opened as he approached, and they stepped into another world. For here was another courtyard, in which water bubbled from a fountain in the centre, palm trees rustled gracefully as they swayed to the night wind, and there were even flower beds to either side.

'Oh, how lovely,' Alison commented. It was the most

pleasing aspect of her character, Vicky thought, that she reacted almost like a child to either pleasure or displeasure, but, again like a child, never let the mood of one moment affect those reactions.

'It must be the harem,' Mary said.

'What's a harem?' Elizabeth asked.

'No, Miss Dobree,' Zobeir said. 'This is not the harem. Those who enter the harem . . .' He smiled at her, 'very seldom emerge. And I know you ladies wish to be free, to explore the city, and enjoy yourselves. Captain Chardin will show you to your apartments.'

Vicky looked at an enormous black man, who stood well over six feet tall, a mountain of ebony muscle with an intensely handsome face. But . . . muscle? And he also carried a scimitar at his side and wore the white tunic and breeches, and brown boots, of an officer in the Emir's guard.

She glanced at Zobeir, who smiled. 'Oh, Chardin is not a eunuch, madam. He is too valuable a fighting man to be destroyed. I have placed him in charge of your arrangements because he speaks both French and English with some fluency. He is from the East, and once served with the British Army, believe it or not.'

'You mean he is our gaoler,' Vicky said.

'I mean he is in charge of your comfort and safety, Lady Dobree.'

They gazed at each other, but as he seemed determined to continue the charade for as long as possible, she shrugged and followed the captain. Chardin led them up a flight of stairs to an open balcony, overlooking the fountain and the garden, and thence through a succession of bead curtains and apartments, all floored in marble, and sumptuously furnished with priceless carpets and divans and drapes, until they entered a large room which overloooked yet another interior garden, this one with a pool of clear water in the centre instead of a fountain.

'The Lord Zobeir hopes you will be comfortable here,' Chardin said in English, bowing to David. 'There are six sleeping chambers adjacent . . .' He indicated the various bead curtains, 'and these girls will be pleased to take care of your every need.' He nodded to the six young women, dressed as immodestly as all the others owned or employed by Zobeir – or as themselves beneath their haiks, Vicky thought – who were anxiously awaiting instructions.

'A supper will be provided,' Chardin said, and left.

'Well,' Alison said, 'Zobeir may be a thug, but he's obviously a very *rich* thug.' This clearly made a lot of difference. 'I only wish he'd dress his people a little more carefully. I mean, David . . . well, you shouldn't really be here at all, much less looking at them.'

'Why not?' Vicky asked. 'Isn't he going to look at us? Or are you going to spend the rest of your life wrapped in a haik?'

'Good heavens,' Alison said, obviously not having considered the matter before. 'Well, really, I don't see how we can allow this.'

'We will allow it, Alison,' Vicky told her, 'simply because to do otherwise would be to make a fuss with Zobeir, and that we have to avoid.'

'Is *this* a harem?' Elizabeth asked, hopefully.

'Of course it isn't, stupid,' Mary said. And then looked doubtful.

'I think it very probably is,' Vicky told them. 'A visitors' harem. Zobeir obviously imagines we are all David's women.'

'Lucky David,' Mary commented.

'I find that quite disgusting,' Alison said.

'It's a different world,' Vicky said wearily. 'And I am sure David isn't going to take advantage of the situation.'

He looked decidedly uncertain as to *what* was the correct way to behave under the circumstances, so she decided she had better take charge again.

'So we may as well make the best of it,' she went on. 'I think, Alison, that if you would be prepared to share one of the bedrooms with Charlie, then Mary and Elizabeth could share a second, Nathalie can have one to herself, and if, Joanna, you and Alice would share, then Margaret can also have one to herself. Unless she'd like to move in with Nathalie.'

'That would be best,' Alison decided. 'Then you and David could have one each.'

241

'You mean we'll have one spare,' Vicky pointed out. 'David and I will share.'

'Now really, Victoria, I simply cannot permit that,' Alison said. 'It is quite immoral, disgusting, and a *very* bad example for Mary and Elizabeth. I quite understand that you are a person of low moral standards, although I find that most disturbing in the wife of a missionary, and I was prepared not to say anything while we were in the desert and surrounded by Arabs, but now that we are back in a civilised community, well, I hate to be blunt, but . . .'

'One day, maybe one day very soon,' Vicky said evenly, 'I am going to slap your face so hard it'll make your teeth rattle. Until then, when I decide I need a lesson in morals, I will ask you for it.'

Alison stared at her with her mouth open.

'And just in case you haven't noticed,' Vicky went on, 'we are still surrounded by Arabs, who are watching our every movement, probably right this moment. May I also remind you, my dear Alison, that as Lady Dobree, I make the decisions.'

Alison's mouth closed, sharply.

'Do you really think we are being watched?' Joanna Cartwright asked hastily, anxious to avoid an explosion.

'I would be very surprised if we are not,' Vicky said. 'We are his prisoners, you know. He has made that perfectly clear.'

'You are without a doubt', Alison said, 'quite the most pessimistic woman I have ever met, not to mention the rudest.' She appeared able to forget that Vicky had been the only optimist in the party at the beginning. 'However, I am sure it would be self-defeating for us to quarrel. Come along, Charlie. Let's get some of these girls to prepare you a bath before supper. And see if they have some of that bark for our teeth.' One of the greatest luxuries provided by Zobeir's caravan had been the means of cleaning their teeth after a week, not with brushes and tooh powder, but by rubbing the teeth with the bark of a selected bush, which left them as bright and clean as if they had been polished.

Vicky merely sat down and allowed her muscles slowly to

242

relax. She wished she could do the same for the muscles of her mind. She knew she had snapped at Alison, even if the woman had been most unpleasantly rude. But her nerves were stretched almost to breaking point, a tension which had increased with Zobeir's warning in the desert. There simply was no time for relaxing, however easy Alison and the girls and the other women seemed to find it. But even she began to feel a little calmer as they were served a delicious meal, in which sherbets and small cakes and sweetmeats abounded. Afterwards it seemed entirely natural to retire to the bedchamber with David, and actually lie on a soft divan, with sheets and even pillowcases. 'I don't suppose I shall sleep a wink, mind,' she said. 'It's just too comfortable.'

'I don't suppose you will sleep a wink either,' he promised her. 'You are just too beautiful. And after the way you stood up to Alison . . . mind you, she isn't ever going to forgive you, you know. Or me either,' he added thoughtfully.

'Does that matter so very much?'

'Compared with holding you in my arms? Oh, my darling girl! But . . . suppose she becomes sufficiently annoyed to go to Zobeir and tells him who she really is?'

'He won't believe her, now. And he'll probably resent her lying. She could finish up with some bastinadoing herself.' She stifled a shriek of laughter. 'That would be a sight for sore eyes. But it would probably do her a world of good. Oh, I'm sorry,' she said, watching his expression. 'I don't mean it. But it would, you know.'

'I agree with you,' he said. 'But the thought of it . . .'

She placed her hands on his chest as he came down on her; his leg was now strong enough to bear his weight without too much discomfort. 'We have to talk, first. Because afterwards I am going to be in no fit state. Getting out of here isn't going to be easy. Especially with an English-speaking guard in charge of us.'

'The first rule of any campaign is accurate reconnaissance,' he said. 'And we can't do that until tomorrow.'

'But we will do it tomorrow,' she told him. 'Because it is now becoming a matter of life and death.'

'Now, Vicky, my darling, he said, 'it really isn't all that urgent. It's going to take Prudence and Bream a good fortnight to reach the coast and, if I know our colonial governors, it'll take Hodgson a week of telegraphing London to have anyone arrive at a decision as to what to do next. In fact, now I think about it, there's every possibility that before then the French will have returned to Algiers and the immediate problem will be over. And besides I think it is essential for us all to rest up thoroughly before we start undertaking any more adventures or long treks.'

'The immediate problem?' she demanded. 'David . . . the immediate problem is right here. It's us. Zobeir has got us here, wrapped up neatly in the very centre of this place. And he's taken off the gloves, remember? Now he just has to decide on the order he wants us.'

'Wants us?'

'Oh, David, surely you've seen the way he looks at Mary and Elizabeth. And Alison too.'

'Come now, Vicky, if I may say so, you are expressing a typically irrational feminine point of view, suspecting every man who looks at a woman twice of wanting to rape her. Do you really suppose a man like Zobeir, surrounded as he is by the last word in beautiful young women who are all his slaves, is going to be foaming at the mouth to get his hands on you?'

Vicky sighed. 'It's not me I'm worrying about, right now,' she said. 'Tomorrow we start looking for a way out. If they'll let us.'

To her utter surprise, when the next morning, after the best night's sleep she had had since first going up to the Dobree Mansion in Little Wissing, she mentioned the idea of a stroll through the city to Chardin, the captain readily agreed. 'I will accompany you,' he said, 'with an escort. But Lady Dobree, I am afraid I must ask you and your ladies to wear the yashmak on the streets of Timbuktu. Otherwise you may attract attention.'

'And the French may learn we are here,' Vicky said. 'Very

well. I was just joking,' she added hastily. 'We'll wear our yashmaks.'

'A walk in the city,' Mary said. 'Oh, good.'

'Will we see a harem?' Elizabeth asked.

'I should hope not,' Alison declared, clearly having made up her mind that it was time she resumed control at least of her stepdaughters. 'And we must be very careful to stay close together.'

'You will remain here, Mrs Lang,' Chardin said.

They all turned to look at him.

'What did you say?' Vicky asked.

'It is the Emir's command that Mrs Lang should remain within the palace, madam,' Chardin said.

'It is, is it? May we ask why?' As if she didn't know.

Chardin shrugged. 'I am not in his excellency's confidence, madam.'

'Well, in that case, you may forget the walk,' Vicky told him. 'When we go, we go all together.'

'Oh, really, Victoria,' Alison said, 'you are being absurd. I am quite happy to remain here if the Emir wishes me to. I imagine he wishes to speak with me.'

She suddenly looked her old arrogant self, Vicky realised. She was clearly delighted, because she was supposing that Zobeir did indeed wish to speak her, privately; and that he had singled her out above anyone else, including Vicky, had to mean that he had discerned her superior breeding and social standing. And she was so desperate to regain her rightful position, the poor, silly innocent woman.

But if it was Alison whom Zobeir wanted – and she could understand that, as Alison was by far the best looking of them all – well then . . . at least it would preserve Mary and Elizabeth for a while.

But Alison's reactions to what was going to happen to her . . . although Vicky wondered if it might not even do her a bit of good, providing she didn't go and get herself executed or something by refusing to surrender.

She looked at David. 'If she's happy to stay,' he said.

245

Vicky could tell what *he* was thinking – that there would be less friction if Alison wasn't with them. He also clearly had no idea what was going to happen to her, and probably thought that she might be able to pick up some information, or at least discover what Zobeir really wanted. Oh, she would do that all right.

She still felt the silly girl should be warned, both of what to expect and of what not to attempt. But there was nothing worthwhile she could say with Chardin standing there.

'Well, Alison,' she said, 'if you're sure you don't mind . . . do remember, well, all the things you should.'

'Of course I will,' Alison said. 'Have a nice walk. And look after the girls.'

Alison watched them filing through the door, Chardin waiting for the last. They really were, she supposed, a helpless and confused bunch of people. David was certainly confused, but then, David had always been confused. William had often said that he lacked the true decisiveness ever to command any large numbers of troops.

But even Vicky had lost her way. Because of course, she had never truly had a way. She had instinctively fought for survival because she was that kind of person; she possessed no breeding, no dignity, only the determination of the cornered animal. Alison conceded that in the circumstances they had experienced, Vicky had revealed a courage and tenacity she herself . . . well, she did not think she actually lacked it. But she was less willing to put it to work, except as a very last resource. And she was prepared to admit, if only to herself, that her nerve had failed her when this Zobeir person had first appeared. But now that she understood he meant them no harm, was merely anxious to realise his profit or such like, she no longer feared him in the least. And he had chosen her, out of them all, to have a private conversation with. She did not doubt she could hold her own in that. And through that, she also had no doubt she would be on her way to regaining the ascendancy over the rest of them, thus resuming her proper place.

While Vicky had chosen to use the ascendancy she had

246

earned by her leadership to wallow in a slough of sexual despond. That would be pitiful were it not so despicable. But there, she supposed, character will out in the end. And actually, she was not the least bit concerned about Vicky's morals or habits, or what she did with herself. She was only concerned about the effect it might have on the girls. And of course, poor David. But it was David's own fault for having allowed himself to be seduced.

She stood before the wall mirror – it was such a luxury to have a mirror again – and threw the haik from her head. Nathalie had combed and brushed her hair as usual that morning, but lacking the requisite pins and pads had been unable to dress it as usual and thus the golden tresses lay neatly on her shoulders and down her back – but actually, she thought loose hair went best with this Arabian outfit. But she wished the girl had done more with her eyebrows, which she often thought of as two of her most attractive features. But still . . .

She heard a sound, and turned. 'Oh!' she said. She had expected Zobeir to come to call, and instead found herself looking at the eunuch Saeed, the Harem Agha. 'Am I to go with you?' she asked.

He bowed, although she did not suppose he understood what she had said. But he moved to the door, and opened it.

Heart pounding, she crossed the carpet and stepped into the corridor, to discover there were three other eunuchs waiting there. Did they think she was going to try to break out?

Saeed led her a short way down the corridor, then turned on to a gallery which led off at right angles to the main hall, and then descended a flight of stairs. They had turned away from the enclosed garden, and were obviously in the bowels of the palace itself. She thought she even heard a tinkle of laughter, and a low cooing sound, as of a lot of voices whispering together. The harem! It had to be the harem. And how happy they sounded.

She was being taken to the harem! She was sure of it. There would be a tale of privilege to tell the others!

Then she remembered Zobeir's somewhat sinister remark as they had entered the palace, that once a woman entered the harem, she never left it again. Well, she would soon disabuse him of that idea, even if it meant telling him the truth about who she was. That would make him stop and think!

They walked for several minutes, in and out of corridors, without seeing anyone else, not even a servant, then Saeed opened a door on his left, and waited for her to enter. Alison hesitated, then stepped inside, and stopped in surprise and more than a little apprehension. While she had expected some kind of reception room, in which Zobeir would be waiting, this was clearly a bathing chamber – although it was unlike any bathroom she had ever seen in her life.

She stood on a slight dais, the walls of which were lined by magnificently draped divans. A shallow flight of steps led down to another level, also with a marble floor, in the centre of which there was a large, raised marble slab, rather like pictures she had seen of sacrificial altars. Then another three steps led down to a third floor, still in marble, although covered with wooden gratings, and off which there led several large drains. On each level there was a doorway, but the entire room was at the moment empty except for herself and her escorts, for all four of the eunuchs had entered the room behind her, and had closed the door. Now she realised to her surprise that although it was a warm morning, there was a fire burning in an open grate on the second level, almost as if they were intending to cook a meal, for above the glowing embers there waited a spit.

Alison became aware of a peculiar feeling, as if the hairs on the back of her neck were standing on end, even as her heartbeat seemed to quicken and she could feel the blood racing through her arteries. I must keep calm, she told herself. I am Lady Dobree. I must keep calm.

'Lady will disrobe,' Saeed said, in French.

Her head turned, sharply. 'I didn't know you could speak French,' she snapped, in the same language.

Saeed bowed.

'My God,' Alison muttered. Because if he could speak French . . . but most of their conversations had been in English. On the other hand, perhaps the sly devil spoke English as well.

'You must disrobe,' he said again.

248

'No, no,' Alison said. 'You do not understand the situation. I will take my bath with the others, when they return from their walk. If this is all you have kept me in for, then I am really very angry with you, and be sure I will report this to the Emir. Now I shall return to my apartment.'

She faced the door, and the eunuch who stood there, arms folded. Her knees touched in sudden shudder. 'If you attempt to manhandle me . . .' she warned.

Saeed gave another bow. 'Lady, I am empowered to use force, if it should be required. But I should warn you that if, as a result, you become injured or tarnished in any way, then you will have to be discarded.'

Alison stared at him. The unutterable impertinence of the man! Discarded? What did he mean by that? Oh, my God, she thought: what *does* he mean by that?

Certainly he seemed to assume that she was entirely in his power. As she was, in real terms, until she could seek help. And what could they do to her? she asked herself; they were not even men. Equally, why should she be afraid of undressing in front of them, when she had already done so, at least before Saeed, several times?

But always in the company of others. Of Vicky. Oh, Vicky, she thought; what would I give to see you opening that door. But that was absurd. She didn't need someone like Vicky to cope with the situation. She had simply to be patient and preserve her dignity, no matter what happened, until she could complain to Zobeir.

She regarded Saeed with the most venomously contemptuous expression she could manage, and removed her haik. Then she shrugged off her bolero, and released her pantaloons to allow them to slip to the floor, and stepped out of her slippers. There, she thought, look your fill. But they were not doing that; they were undressing themselves. Oh, Lord, she thought. They cannot be going to strip. I don't want to have to look at *them*.

In fact they only stripped as far as a piece of cloth which they each wore wrapped round their waists and passed between their legs, and she found she was breathing normally again. It was time to regain control of the situation. 'There is no water,' she remarked, icily.

Saeed bowed. 'Lady will lie down.' He pointed at the marble altar on the second level.

'Whatever for?' she demanded.

'Lady's body hair must be removed,' he explained.

She stared at him, realised her jaw had sagged, and hastily brought it up again. She thought of the girls who attended them, of Mary's first scandalised remark. But she wasn't a harem girl. She was a lady. Lady Dobree.

Only these idiots didn't know that.

The eunuchs were waiting, standing in a row, and looking at her face, she realised, rather than her body. Somehow their impersonality was harder to bear than if they had been visibly aroused. She turned away from them, went down the three steps, lay on the slab, legs straight and pressed together, arms at her sides. She had never felt so *exposed* in her life, had to keep remembering that these weren't men. That was what mattered.

But the marble was cold on her flesh and brought it up in goose pimples. She heard a door open and close, but refused to turn her head to see who it might be. Yet she was holding her breath again. Zobeir? Come to look at his victim?

Saeed stood beside her, raised her head, and gathered her hair, scooping it out so that it flowed over the edge of the altar. Then she saw the new arrival – obviously also a eunuch – standing on her other side, and this man carried a tray, on which there lay a variety of unpleasant-looking instruments. Saeed now lifted her right arm, extending it above her head. 'Lady must lie absolutely still,' he said. 'I am very skilful, but even I may not be able to cope with a sudden movement.'

Alison sucked air into her lungs, slowly, as he began to hone a curved knife, perhaps eight inches long, which he had taken from the tray. Meanwhile, another of the eunuchs was powdering her armpit, coating it thickly and then gently pulling the hairs through it. What was she afraid of? She had always shaved her armpits; it was only since the shipwreck that they had been neglected. And these men were probably every bit as efficient as Nathalie.

It was what might be coming after that frightened her.

The blade scraped with the utmost care across her flesh, and her left arm was being equally treated. 'Now, lady, spread your legs,' Saeed commanded.

She tensed her muscles, pressing her legs together, then slowly relaxed and allowed them to be pulled apart. She could not believe this was happening to her. She did not know what she would think, or feel, or do, when it was over. She had never imagined a situation like this in her wildest nightmares. Yet she was obeying him, because there was nothing else she could do. English gentlewomen did not disgrace themselves by screaming and fighting and begging for mercy. They remained, to the end, English gentlewomen.

She shut her eyes, tightly, as the fingers began to sift the powder into her groin, to pull the hairs through it. There was nothing gentle or enticing about these fingers, and yet, because they were the first fingers ever to touch her there – it was an area she even avoided herself – it was all she could do to keep still as a succession of most peculiar feelings seemed to surge upwards through her belly.

Now Saeed was again scraping away. She recognised his touch, and opened her eyes to look at the top of his head as he bent over her stomach. 'Those ladies who prove recalcitrant,' he remarked conversationally, 'are depilated by having the hairs plucked from their flesh. It is very painful, and often leaves a considerable inflammation for some time. But you are too sensible for that, lady.'

Alison closed her eyes again. She had no concept of what might be going to happen next; her imagination could not rise to such heights. For now the knife was moving between her legs, guided and assisted by those so knowledgeable and yet so disinterested fingers. It required all her willpower to lie still, and before he was finished she became distracted by a peculiar smell which began to seep through the bathroom, a sweet, titillating odour which had her nostrils dilating.

'Lady will stand,' Saeed said.

She opened her eyes, sat up, and looked down at herself, realised that it was almost the first time she had ever done that,

that she had previously had no idea what she truly looked like. She felt the heat in her cheeks and looked up anxiously as she swung her legs to the floor, but the eunuchs continued to be politely disinterested, busy now with an enormous pot, which two were stirring with great endeavour, the pot itself being suspended from the spit over the fire; it was from the pot that the smell was arising.

Now one of them nodded to Saeed.

'This may feel hot on the flesh, lady,' Saeed said. 'But it will only be a temporary discomfort. Now kneel, and stretch your arms across the table.'

Alison obeyed, amazed at her subservience. But in fact she was now curious as to what was to happen next, watched in terror as the heavy pot was carried across the room and placed on the table between her arms, and then with a mixture of fear and disgust as a giant ladle was used to lift out a molten brown mess. Some of this was carefully dripped on to her left arm, bringing an immediate gasp of pain, because it was extremely hot. She gasped again as more of the mixture was heaped on her right arm, and now one of the eunuchs was smearing the mess over her flesh, coating every inch from her wrist to her shoulder, while another was doing the same to her other arm.

'It is a mixture of sugar and lemon,' Saeed explained, standing at her shoulder. 'Brought to a molten state. Is it cooling?'

Her head jerked as she nodded.

'Well, now you must remain absolutely still, lady. What I am about to do requires enormous skill. The skill is mine, to be sure, but I cannot be responsible for damage if you move. The slightest mistake in applying pressure will result in your skin being removed.'

'Oh, my God, she thought. Saeed had come round the table to face her, and now he used one knee to kneel upon the marble surface, while he took a length of silken thread between his hands. This thread he placed on her shoulder, where it joined the upper arm. Face contorted with effort, he pressed gently, until the thread cut into the toffee-like mixture covering her skin, and then, slowly and carefully, watched with intense

252

interest by his subordinates, he drew the thread down the length of Alison's arm, removing the main part of the smothering mess as he did so, but also, she discovered to her fascination, removing every trace of hair. The golden down which normally covered her forearm was entirely gone by the time he reached her wrist, leaving her flesh absolutely white and clear.

She discovered that her mouth had dropped open, as she watched him turn his attention to the other arm. All manner of thoughts were chasing themselves through her mind. She did not only have hair on her arms, thus the shaving process, so apparently carelessly done, could have been no more than a preliminary.

She had no time properly to consider the situation. Her arms completed, Saeed made her lie down again while her legs were attended to. Then she was made to kneel again while her back was coated and cleaned, and to lie down while her armpits received another scouring.

Saeed smiled at her. 'Now comes the truly difficult part, lady. I can only warn you again, lie still.'

She closed her eyes. She could not bear to look at their faces, so close, so eager now, although still without the slightest suggestion of sexual interest. The mess was smeared over her chest and breasts – she had never known she had hair there, she thought desperately – then coated on her stomach and belly, and reached her groin and between her legs. How could they avoid skinning her down there, she thought in sudden terror. Especially as the heat now induced another series of sexual urges, causing her body to quiver, which brought her an admonishing slap on the buttock from Saeed.

'Lie still, lady,' he commanded. 'I am commencing.'

She attempted to hold her breath, then abandoned that in favour of slow and careful breathing. She felt the cord sliding over her skin, slipping between her breasts, and discovered that a subordinate had taken each nipple, firmly but gently holding the mounds of flesh apart to permit his master's thread to pass between. Then her breasts were released as the cord passed over her stomach. She tensed her muscles, made herself keep still, and felt the thread coursing over her groin. She felt fingers once again upon the insides of her thighs, stretching them so wide she thought she must be torn in two. She wanted to cry out in anticipated pain, but there was none, and suddenly she was released, and received another gentle pat, and looked up to see Saeed smiling at her.

'You are well disciplined, lady,' he said. 'Now come, it is time for your bath.'

She sat up, slipped from the table, and all but fell – her muscles seemed totally devoid of strength. No one offered to assist her, so she held on to the table until she regained her balance. The eunuchs had already descended to the lower level, where two bowls were waiting, filled with water, the large one steaming and the small one still, beside two even larger buckets of water; she realised to her surprise that the bowls were actually made of beaten silver.

She was first of all made to kneel, while Saeed carefully soaked and then washed her hair, using a soap the scent of which was strange to her, but unbelievably fragrant. Her hair was rinsed, also by Saeed, and again with great care, then it was bound on the top of her head with a piece of ribbon, and she was made to stand on one of the slatted wooden boards, while the larger bowl was emptied over her, then refilled again and again until seven had been used. The water, she discovered, was already soapy. Then the smaller bowl was used to rinse her, obtaining water from a fresh tub, and this was clean.

'Now, if you will lie down, lady,' Saeed commanded.

Alison lay on the wet grating, and the eunuchs each armed himself with a loofah and commenced soaping her from neck to her toes. The water was warmed, and the feeling of cleanliness and well-being which spread through her system was overwhelming. She discovered she had quite lost both her horror of them as creatures and her embarrassment at being so intimately manhandled by them. There seemed nothing more they could possibly do to her which could in any way transcend what they had already done.

The soaping process completed, she was made to stand again, and the rinsing began all over again, once more repeated seven times with soapy and seven times with fresh water.

'Now, lady,' Saeed said, holding a large towelled robe, in which he proceeded to wrap her, following which he released the ribbon holding her hair. He then escorted her back up the steps to the top level, where she was made to sit on a divan. Once again she felt absolutely exhausted, and wondered for the first time how long she had been in the steamy confines of the bathchamber.

But her toilette was far from being completed. While she sat on the divan, feeling her body slowly drying and cooling, the eunuchs continued to fuss about her, extending both arms and both legs first to trim and then to paint her fingernails and toenails with henna, while Saeed supervised. He himself was gently rubbing her hair dry, seeming to work from strand to strand.

'In most cases,' he remarked, 'we henna the hair as well. But for you, it could do nothing but detract from your own beauty. Yellow hair is an uncommon blessing, in Africa. Sometimes the Lord Zobeir obtains slaves from Circassia, and they are often fair haired, but their hair is coarse as string compared with yours. Nor do they have such a colour.'

He was paying her a compliment! Her nails were now completed, and a eunuch was offering her a tray on which were steaming cups of black coffee, so strong it made her gasp, to be followed immediately with a mouth-watering sherbet which seemed to trace its way through her digestive system like a cascading waterfall.

Saeed continued to busy himself with her hair, brushing it and combing it, smoothing it with his fingers, endeavouring to remove the very last suspicion of a damp-induced curl, to have it lie absolutely straight on her shoulders and down her back. Once he was satisfied, he removed her robe and made her lie down on the divan again, following which she was vigorously massaged by all four of them, legs, arms, back and front, with an unguent which gave off the same delicious fragrance as her hair, and left her smelling sweeter than she would have imagined possible – and also even more sexually aware than during the depilation.

'You are ready, lady,' Saeed said. 'Will you dress?'

A eunuch waited with another tray, on which there lay a clean set of silk pantaloons, matching bolero and slippers, together with a little jewelled cap like those worn by the maidservants. The prevailing motif was crimson, with gold thread intertwined at the hem and shoulders. To her surprise, Saeed finally added a white yashmak to conceal the lower half of her face, following which he clapped his hands, and one of his aides produced a large brass mirror, which he held up for her inspection.

She supposed she looked quite magnificent. The heat and the bath had induced a faintly pinkish tinge to all her flesh, to match the sunburn on her face and arms, and in addition she seemed to glow after her massage. The crimson of the sheer trousers did no more than outline the shape of her legs, and provide a titillating shadow to the shaven groin. Her nipples peeped out from the inner hems of her bolero, as her breasts rose and fell to her breathing. And to cap it all, the half-concealed face, from which the pale blue eyes stared at herself, and the long golden hair flowing out from beneath the crimson cap. Why, she thought, I could fall in love with me. But what an utterly wanton thought! To go with such utterly wanton clothes. What would William have said, had he ever seen her like this? What would he have *done?*

'Well, lady, you are satisfied?' Saeed inquired.

'I am amazed,' she confessed. 'How often must I suffer such a metamorphosis?'

'That depends on how well you please your master, lady. He awaits you now.'

CHAPTER 12

Alison's head jerked. She had, in fact, forgotten the reason for what had just been done to her. Indeed, she had never actually allowed herself to consider that there had to be a reason. The thought that she might have been prepared for a man, rather as a chef prepared a special dish for the table, was quite horrifying. And yet, such an effect had the bathing and massaging had, not less than the actual depilation, that it wasn't quite as inconceivable a thought as it might have been only an hour earlier. She found herself thinking thoughts such as that she couldn't escape what was going to happen to her anyway, and that it could be nothing worse than William had ever done – Zobeir was so obviously a gentleman – and that it was her duty to preserve her calm dignity as an English lady no matter what happened.

Then she must commence now. 'Where is my haik?' she demanded, getting as much ice into her voice as she could.

Saeed shook his head. 'You do not need a haik, lady. That is for outdoor wear, and you are not leaving the palace.'

Alison hesitated, knowing a strong desire to scream. But that was not practical either, and could only end in her humiliation. 'Be sure', she said, 'that I will report your insolence to the Emir.'

Saeed bowed. 'If lady will follow me.'

Alison followed him, down a succession of corridors, up flights of stairs, and along more corridors, all in marble, until they arrived at an antechamber in which there waited two black guards, armed with scimitars. Alison checked. There were so many things she suddenly wanted to do with her hands.

Because where she had ceased to feel any embarrassment in front of the eunuchs, these were whole men.

On the other hand, she was wearing her yashmak, and they seemed no more interested in her than the eunuchs. One of them opened the door.

Saeed stepped inside. 'The lady, Madame Lang,' he said in French, no doubt for her benefit, and bowed.

Then he straightened. 'Lady,' he invited.

Alison took a deep breath, and stepped through the doorway. She blinked in the sudden light, and for a moment quite lost her bearings, then realised she was in a huge, high-ceilinged room, which, in strong contrast to most of the rest of the palace, had windows opened to the east, so that the still rising sun could flood the chamber with light. As the prevailing motif, in the carpets and on the divans, was cloth of gold, while the incidental tables and their ornaments were at least brass, the effect was that of stepping into the centre of a kaleidoscope. Yet the room was not hot; ceiling fans turned vigorously, no doubt propelled by an army of punkah wallahs in some adjoining compartment.

She blinked again, and gazed at a large desk, made of polished wood inlaid with gold, behind which Zobeir had been sitting, apparently reading a huge book. The desk was some distance away from her, perhaps twenty feet, and was reached by a length of carpet. Behind it was a series of divans, and then an arched doorway, beyond which she could see an enormous bed. She caught her breath: she was in Zobeir's bedroom.

But what else had she expected?

Zobeir got up and came round his desk. He wore a cloth of gold robe, but his feet and ankles were bare. 'Mrs Lang,' he said. 'How very nice to see you.' As if this call had been her idea. 'Or may I call you Alison?'

Alison listened to the double doors closing behind her. She was alone with him. 'You may,' she said, her voice breathless. 'If you wish.'

'I do wish,' he said, coming right up to her. 'Will you not take off the yashmak?'

She released the cord with some relief; it was difficult to

breathe properly with the linen pressing against her nose and mouth every time she inhaled.

'I cannot tell you how pleased I am that you have come to call,' Zobeir said.

He was a man who lived in a series of charades. She knew this. Just as she knew she had to fight the insidious feelings of sexual relaxation which kept creeping over her. Otherwise she would lie on the floor at his feet.

She made herself snap. 'I? Come to call on you? Do you believe I would even consider such a thing? I have been dragged here, after having been subjected to the most vicious and unpleasant and indecent of assaults by your . . . your creatures.'

Zobeir frowned, as he slowly inspected her, from head to foot. 'You have been assaulted? Are you then injured, Mrs Lang? I do not see any bruises.'

'Oh . . . that is not the point. And now, bringing me here like this, virtually naked . . .'

'But you are a beautiful woman, Mrs Lang. Quite the most beautiful woman I have ever seen, and believe me, I have seen a lot of women. Come.' He took her hand, led her across the room. For a moment she thought they were going directly to the bed. She was about to be subjected to a sexual assault. By someone who was not even English, who might seek to take the most dreadful liberties . . . yet she was more angry than afraid, at his arrogance, his unutterable impertinence. Yet she understood that she could not fight him with any hope of success, even if he did not have his guards and eunuchs to summon to his aid. More important, to fight would mean casting dignity to the wind. That was unthinkable.

To her relief, he stopped at the divans, released her, and sat down, lounging on his elbow. 'Sit. Beauty should never be concealed. Except just sufficiently for the purpose of awakening the senses.'

'My late husband would have had you hanged,' Alison said. But she sat down. With her legs crossed she felt easier.

'Was he too a soldier?' Zobeir inquired. 'Of course he must have been, as you are with Lady Dobree. And now you are a widow. This is the most difficult of positions for a woman, I know. You are not a virgin, and therefore can neither command a good price nor be taken as a wife. Yet you obviously consider yourself above the station of a concubine.'

'Command a price?' Eyebrows arched, Alison gave him her coldest stare. 'Be a concubine? I am nobody's concubine, Zobeir.'

'Not yet,' he agreed, with an easy smile, refusing to be offended by the informality of her address. 'As I said, it is a difficult position, and for me, as well. I find you intensely attractive, as I have told you. I desire you. But Zobeir ibn Rubayr has never taken any used woman to his bed before. However, in your case . . .'

'*Used!*' Alison stood up. 'I demand to be returned to my apartment. Or do you intend to force yourself upon me?'

'Force? My dear Alison, I have never forced myself on a woman in my life. They have always been happy to accommodate my wishes. As I am sure you will be, when you have considered the matter. In any event, I did not go to all the trouble of bringing you here merely to return you to your apartment. I wish to speak with you, upon a very serious matter. And an important one, to you. Sit.'

Slowly Alison lowered herself back to the divan. 'What matter?'

'I wish you to unravel the web of falsehood and deception that Lady Dobree is attempting to weave about herself, and about me. And explain to me why she is doing this.'

Alison frowned, even as her heart began to pound. She knew she had to think very seriously, to concentrate, so as not to make a mistake which might ruin their entire situation. 'Falsehood?' she asked. 'Deceit? What makes you think she is doing that?'

'Timbuktu, Khartoum: to you English they are the ends of the earth, Alison. I know this. But to us Arabs, these cities are the very centre of the earth. It is all a point of view. You think we are ignorant savages. But we think that *you* are ignorant savages. And do you know, I suspect there is more justice in our claim. For instance, have you ever seen an Arabic newspaper in England?'

'Good heavens, no.'

'You see? You are so ignorant, and so arrogant, you do not even wish to know about the world beyond the English Channel. We are not so limited.' He got up, walked to his desk. 'Come,' he said.

Alison hesitated, then followed him. He waited, without speaking, while she glanced at the desk, in the first instance without interest, then catching her breath. Because what he had been reading when she entered the room had not been a book, as such, but rather an enormous wooden binder, which lay open to reveal that it consisted of copies of *The Times*, in English.

'I have them sent to me,' Zobeir explained. 'It keeps me abreast with world affairs, shall I say.'

'Oh, my God!' Alison muttered, hastily scanning the page he had been studying, and arriving at the photograph. The date on the page was 13 December 1897.

'They arrive very late, of course,' Zobeir went on. 'Sometimes several months late, and owing to my other preoccupations it is sometimes more months yet before I have the time to read them. Nevertheless, they are a record of what the English are thinking, and saying, and doing. I take *Le Figaro* as well.'

Alison bent over the desk to look more closely at the picture. She could remember only too well that ghastly little man with his cape and his exploding bulb. She had been furious at the time, at such an invasion of privacy. Now . . . it was a terribly bad print, but there was no mistaking William. She was unrecognisable, mainly because she had turned her head away, but Mary was quite discernible, even if Elizabeth was only a blur.

'Read the caption,' Zobeir invited.

Alison held her breath. '*General Sir William Dobree returns from India*,' it said. And beneath: '*General Sir William Dobree, V.C., D.S.O., M.C. and bar, arrived back in England last Tuesday afternoon*

261

from three exacting years on the North West Frontier. Here we see the General at Victoria Station, being greeted by his charming wife and his equally charming daughters.'

Alison sat down on the chair before the desk.

'I felt . . . my instincts told me that there was something not quite right with Lady Dobree's manner,' Zobeir said. 'I felt sure she was lying to me, but then I thought . . . how can a lady like Dobree tell a lie? And of course I could not do anything to prove, or disprove, my apprehensions, out there in the desert. I had to reach my home, and gain access to my library. But now I realise that my instincts were correct. I would be deeply appreciative if you would tell me what she wishes to achieve.'

Alison licked her lips. He knew everything. Vicky's marvellous plan had landed them squarely in the soup. Because it hadn't been a marvellous plan after all. The stupid woman had presumed she was dealing with a fool. Well, she thought, there is only one thing to do. She felt Zobeir's hands sliding across her shoulders, gently. 'I should have thought it was obvious,' she said, quietly. 'She is not really Lady Dobree.'

'Alison,' Zobeir warned. 'Lady Dobree may suppose she is capable of making a fool of me, but I do assure you that I will permit no one else to.'

Alison turned on the chair and jumped to her feet, out of his reach. 'Of course she isn't Lady Dobree. Oh, for heaven's sake, how could you be taken in like that? I am the real Lady Dobree.'

Zobeir raised his eyebrows.

'I!' Alison shouted. 'Me! For goodness' sake, can't you tell? That woman . . . she is my stepdaughters' governess.'

Zobeir returned to the divan and sat down.

Alison followed him. 'All you need to do is look at that photograph.'

'I have studied that photograph, Alison. For some time. That photograph tells me very little. The woman certainly does not look like you.'

'All right,' Alison agreed. 'I looked away from the camera. But it doesn't look like Victoria either, does it? I mean, she isn't that tall.' She paused, realised he was not convinced, because the blurred figure in the photograph actually gave no impression of height. She decided to try a different approach. 'I mean, how on earth could she be the mother of Mary and Elizabeth? She's not old enough.'

'And you are?'

'Of course not. They're my stepdaughters.'

'The trouble with lying', Zobeir said mildly, 'is the difficulty one experiences in avoiding trapping oneself. Are the girls not actually Lady Dobree's stepdaughters? I have read somewhere else that she is the General's second wife. I think you should know that I regard lying as a most iniquitous crime, deserving of severe punishment. Now tell me, truthfully, why is her ladyship pretending that this man is her husband? Because I can see that he is not Sir William; the photograph does tell me that. And why is she pretending that her stepdaughters are her nieces? I have to admit that I can see no object in it. Quite apart from the fact that she is wantonly committing adultery. In Islamic law, adultery by a woman is an even greater crime than lying.'

Alison stood in front of him. 'Cannot you understand? She has committed adultery because she isn't Lady Dobree,' she shouted, feeling close to tears with frustration. 'She isn't Lady anything. She isn't even a lady. She's just a common slut. For heaven's sake, man, she's an *American*. Can't you tell that from the way she speaks?'

'Ah. I thought she had an unusual accent. An American. How very interesting. What a delightful people they must be. But what is so strange about it? According to that newspaper, many members of the British upper classes regularly marry them.'

'Oh, good God!' Alison sat down, beside him. 'What can I say . . .' She raised her hand. 'The ring. You saw how the ring was too small for her.' She thrust her hand under his gaze, allowing him to look at the long, slender fingers. 'That was my ring.'

Zobeir regarded her for a moment. Then he placed his hands on her shoulders and slipped the bolero from her arms. She did not even notice what he was doing, she was so upset. 'So beautiful,' he said. 'And so determined to protect your friend. But you must not try my patience, Alison, or I will become angry, and then I will hurt you. And it would be a shame to tarnish so much beauty.' He stroked her breast.

'Oh, God, oh, God, oh God!' Alison screamed. '*Why* won't you believe me? Why? Listen to me, Zobeir. My husband, General Sir William Dobree, was drowned on the *Doncaster* when she sank after striking that rock. We . . . I led the survivors across the desert until we met you. But then I felt that you might not agree to send to the coast and demand a ransom unless you thought you had captured Sir William Dobree. Well, apart from the seaman, Bream, the only man with our party was David Whiting, my husband's aide-de-camp, so he had to pretend he was Sir William. He had to have a wife, so I chose Victoria. I mean, *I* wasn't going to pretend to be another man's wife.'

Zobeir nodded, and her heart began to settle down. 'Yes,' he said. 'Now it is all starting to make sense. Apart of course from your absurd lies. I am astonished that you persist.'

Alison stared at him, a huge lump of lead beginning to form in her stomach. 'You . . .'

Zobeir was smiling, and pulling his beard. 'A remarkable woman,' he said, apparently to himself. 'Truly, a remarkable woman. Well, of course this changes the entire situation. The only object of any value I seem to have brought out of the desert is Lady Dobree herself. And her stepdaughters of course. Her ladyship has indeed committed a most serious crime in lying, of course, but perhaps with an almost justifiable purpose. I shall have to consider . . . but that man, that broken-legged cur –' his voice changed – 'by Allah, I shall have him sit on a sharp stick and watch him wriggle to death.'

Alison felt sick; she had never seen a face so contorted with anger.

'Her daughters,' Zobeir mused. 'Hm. I shall have to think about them. But the rest of you are worthless flesh, that is obvious. Yes, that is very disappointing. But you . . .' He suddenly closed his fingers on her neck, forcing her head upwards. 'You are so riddled with lies I doubt you understand the meaning of the word, truth.'

'I have not lied,' she gasped. 'I have not lied,' she sobbed as he released her.

'You have not claimed to be Lady Dobree?' he asked contemptuously. 'You have not tried to take the credit for this scheme, where you obviously lack the intelligence for it?'

'You . . .' Her eyes blazed at him. 'How *dare* you speak to me like that! You . . . you desert hyena.'

Zobeir gazed at her for a moment, then got up, walked to a table in the corner, and picked up a thin-switched riding crop. 'You have tried my patience too far.'

Alison leapt to her feet. 'I . . . you wouldn't dare to hit me. You wouldn't. *I* am Lady Dobree. I *am* Lady Dobree!'

Zobeir came closer. 'My dear Alison, it is always a grave mistake to compound a lie by insisting upon it. It is always best to confess, and accept one's fate, with courage.'

'Oh, *God!*' She fell to her knees. 'I *am* Alison Dobree. Please believe me. Oh, please believe me!'

He stood above her, and smiled at her. 'There is no way that you can be Lady Dobree. I am not a fool.'

'No way . . . but . . .' She seized his left hand. 'How can you say that? Surely you just have to look at me?'

'I have told you already, a liar always confounds herself out of her own mouth,' Zobeir said. 'And you have just done so. Indeed, I have to do no more than look. A woman like Lady Dobree,' he explained, 'married to so famous a man, and a baronet, would have to possess certain qualities, intangible, perhaps, but yet to be observed by the careful student, which set her apart from other women. I have already observed this in women who are married to greatness, and upon whom some of that greatness has necessarily been imposed. Alas, my poor Alison, you entirely lack that quality.'

'You . . . I . . .' She licked her lips. 'And you think *Victoria* possesses such qualities?'

'Certainly she does. Lady Dobree is the most striking, the most forceful, woman I have ever met. She has the true aura of greatness about her, whatever her crimes. But it is a well-known fact that the greater the person, the greater the crimes they are capable of. And of course, if her husband is truly dead, then she is not actually guilty of adultery. Only of lying and fornicating with an inferior. A dog, who will suffer for it. But she . . . what would I give to have her here before me, instead of you! To possess such a woman would be the greatest experience of my life. Such poise, such elegance, such arrogance . . . but she is Lady Dobree.' He sighed. 'You will have to do.' The hand holding the riding crop twitched.

'What do you think?' David asked in a low voice, as they walked back towards the palace.

'Um,' Vicky replied. It had been an intensely interesting morning, however she had worried about him. But Chardin had produced a pair of well-made crutches, and David had as usual revealed enormous qualities of endurance, although she could tell from his face how exhausted and uncomfortable he was.

Yet even he had been fascinated by what they had seen. Timbuktu had to be the most cosmopolitan city Vicky had ever known. It was cosmopolitan in itself, in its buildings, representing so many different styles, from the graceful Moorish arches of the Touaregs to the narrow window slits of the Bedouins to the low, featureless huts of the indigenous Arabs, all huddled together higgledy-piggledy. There were Muslim mosques close by temples of various obscure religions, together with, amazingly, a small church, from the front steps of which a black-robed priest smiled at them as they walked by, obviously unaware that they were Europeans – for even David was wearing the burnous and haik of the Arab.

But it was the people who most interested her. They seemed to represent every race and colour under the sun, for some of the women were definitely so fair-haired and skinned, even when concealed beneath a yashmak, that they had to be of Caucasian stock – their blue eyes, peering out from the almost concealed faces, were quite startling. Then there were statuesque black men from the Sudan, like Chardin himself, smaller black men from the forests, white-skinned Touaregs, also hidden behind their veils – men and women – dusky Bedouins and Moors, and more than one obvious Caucasian, complete with sun helmet and gold watch chain. But no French soldiers: Major Joffre was keeping his men outside the city to avoid any risk of confrontation – if indeed he was still there at all.

She asked Chardin how the various races and religions got on, so huddled together, and he seemed surprised that she could suppose they would not. 'All are welcome,' he told her.

'It is a Muslim city,' she said. 'Yet other religions are tolerated?'

'Should they not be? Those insufficiently wise to worship the One True God must be pitied, not abhorred. They pay a tax, and are left in peace.'

Certainly everyone seemed remarkably free and relaxed – and yet she knew that a large proportion of the people she saw at the market were slaves, acting for their masters and mistresses, and indeed, at the market, as she had supposed would be the case, Zobeir's Fulani prisoners were being placed on auction. But that Zobeir himself was a feared and respected man was obvious from the deference shown to Chardin, and to their entire party once it was realised they belonged to the great warlord. Thus there could be no doubt that every man's, and every woman's, hand would be against them if it was supposed they were doing anything opposed to the Emir's wishes. And the city was walled. Even on the river side it was walled, the boat exit being through a water gate, that would obviously have to be opened for them. Which seemed a pretty hopeless prospect.

'Grim,' David commented, reading her thoughts.

'Um,' she said again. It was indeed grim, with one little exception. Chardin apparently much preferred to speak French than English, and thus it had been obvious for him to attach himself to Nathalie more than the rest of them. But Vicky had a feeling that his attraction to the French girl lay in more than a mutually acceptable grammar. On the other hand, to try to make something of that would demand an enormous effort on Nathalie's part. And Vicky did not know if she could ask that of her, for a variety of reasons. 'We'll have to brood on it,' she decided.

'I'm inclined to go back to your original idea, that we should sit it out,' David said. 'Our paramount concern must be your safety, yours and all the girls'. There'd be no point in stopping a confrontation between England and France if you got all your heads chopped off in the process.'

'The local way of execution is impalement,' she muttered. Which was a pretty horrifying thought. Just as it was reassuring to feel that David had at last got his priorities right. But it was she who now felt they really didn't have the time to spare.

And as they entered their apartment, having been taken straight there and seeing scarcely another soul in the palace, she knew she was right.

'That was really splendid,' Mary said to their guide, as he bowed before leaving them at the door. 'I did enjoy it so, Mr Chardin. We must do it again.' She hurried inside. 'Mother!' she said. 'It's such a shame you couldn't come. Why it was like a page from the *Arabian Nights*.' She paused in the doorway to her stepmother's bedroom. 'Mother? Are you all right?'

Alison, wearing only crimson pantaloons, was sprawled across her bed with the curtains not even drawn.

'I say,' David began.

'You'd better stay out here,' Vicky snapped, and ran inside. 'Alison!' She shook her arm, then gasped as she saw the thin weals beneath the silk.

'Oh my God!' Mary stood beside her. 'She's been . . .'

'Shut up,' Vicky snapped.

'What is it? Let me see. Let me see.' Elizabeth crowded into the doorway.

Vicky turned. 'Joanna! Will you please take the girls away. Please!'

'Of course.' Joanna had given one horrified glance at the woman on the bed, and that had been enough.

Vicky drew the curtain, returned to the bed, sat beside the inert body. 'Alison . . .'

'Go away,' Alison muttered. 'Go away, and leave me alone.'

'You must tell me what happened to you,' Vicky said.

Alison rolled on to her back, winced, and rolled on to her stomach again. But Vicky felt an enormous sense of relief at her glimpse of the slender white body – for a moment her fears had ranged as far as mutilation.

'Tell me,' she said again. Because even without mutilation she guessed it was going to be bad.

Alison sighed. 'He knows, everything,' she said.

'What do you mean?' For a moment Vicky's brain would not accept the truth.

'He takes *The Times*,' Alison said. 'He had a photograph of William. He knows we have been lying to him, about David.'

The words affected Vicky almost like separate blows from a hammer. She couldn't think for a moment, was surprised to hear the sound of her own calm voice. 'What did you tell him?'

'Nothing.' Alison rose to her knees. 'I told him nothing, Victoria. I swear it.'

'Very well,' Vicky said. 'Very well, I believe you. And he beat you?'

'He caned me.' She shuddered. 'He *whipped* me. There was nothing I could do, he was so strong. And then . . .'

Her shoulders drooped and she lay down again. But Vicky had been slowly taking in what had been done to her, before she had ever got to Zobeir's bed.

'My God,' she whispered.

'Oh, yes,' Alison said. 'I was *prepared*. And then . . . when he had beaten me . . . oh, Vicky.' She rolled over and Vicky took her in her arms, holding her close and smoothing the silky texture of her hair as if she had been a child. 'Oh, Vicky . . . he made me touch it. Oh, Vicky!'

Vicky said nothing. There was nothing she could say, on a subject like that and to someone like Alison.

'And then he . . . oh, Vicky, it was quite horrible.'

'Was it?' Vicky asked.

Alison's head came up. Her cheeks were pink. She lay down again, staying on her back this time. 'Yes,' she said. 'It was . . . disgusting. But I never told him anything, Victoria. I swear that.'

269

Vicky nodded. 'You already did. All right, you've been raped.'

'And again and again,' Alison said. 'First . . . oh, it was too ghastly for words.'

'And he told you he knows all about us. What about us, apart from the fact that David isn't Sir William?'

'Everything,' Alison insisted. 'That the girls are your stepdaughters, that . . . oh everything. He considers only you to be of importance, now, because you are Lady Dobree. He's still convinced you are me. Would you believe it? I tried . . . I didn't know what to say. Oh, my *God*.'

'So he thinks the rest of you are unimportant,' Vicky said, fighting against the terror which was lapping at her mind. 'What does that mean? What is he going to do? Did he tell you?'

'Oh . . . he says he's going to send for me again. I shall go mad, Vicky. I know I shall go mad. Or I will have to kill myself.'

'Relax,' Vicky said. 'It won't be so bad the second time. What about the others? What about David?'

'Oh, he means to execute David,' Alison said. 'He said something about a sharp stake. He was really furious about David impersonating William. After he showed me the photograph, as it couldn't possibly have been David, I had to confess that William was really dead, don't you see?'

'I see,' Vicky said, wondering just what else she had felt called upon to confess, for all her repeated disclaimers.

'So he is angry. He is angry with you for pretending David is your husband, and he is livid, as I said, with David for acting the part. For sleeping with you. My God . . .' She gave a humourless laugh. 'Do you realise that Zobeir really wants *you*? I believe he's in love with you! He positively drools every time he mentions your name. He talks of your strength, your determination, your courage, your arrogance. It was perfectly sickening. But he's afraid to touch you because you are Lady Dobree. I sometimes think the whole thing has to be a ghastly nightmare. And the thought that David *has* touched you nearly drives him mad. I always knew your lechery was going to cause a catastrophe.'

Vicky let her run on. She was trying to assimilate what had just been told her, and finding it difficult. Because if it was true . . . 'What about the girls?' she asked.

'I think he's going to take them as concubines. Poor Margaret and Alice and Joanna will be sold as slaves. Nathalie too, I suppose. But Charlie . . . oh, Vicky, he's going to sell Charlie as well. After . . .' Once again the tears.

'After castration,' Vicky said. 'Yes. Well . . . you'd better have a good rest, Alison. And try not to brood. He hasn't . . . well, if you think about it, you'll realise he hasn't actually hurt you in any way. Not permanently. Remember that. Your bruises will disappear, and the rest of you . . . you're only hurt by something like that if you want to be.'

'Oh, you . . . you would have lain back and enjoyed it, you mean.'

Vicky gazed at her. 'Maybe I would,' she agreed. 'It would have to be better than collapsing in despair. None of us can afford to do that, Alison, until we are all safely out of here. Maybe not even then.'

Alison caught her hand. 'Vicky! What are we going to do? If he takes Charlie . . .'

'He's not going to take Charlie,' Vicky promised her. 'We'll think of something.' She dropped the curtain into place behind her, gazed at the women, huddled in the centre of the room. Chardin had left. David had gone into their bedroom to lie down.

'Is she . . .' Joanna began. 'Was she . . .?'

'Yes,' Vicky told her. 'Things are a little more serious than we had supposed.'

'What does she mean?' Elizabeth asked her sister. 'What's happened to Mother?'

'She's been raped, stupid,' Mary said.

'What's being raped?' Elizabeth asked.

Vicky tried to ignore them. 'Zobeir knows,' she told the women. 'Apparently he takes *The Times*. Isn't that ridiculous? Now please,' she shouted, as they all started talking at once. 'Please don't panic. He hasn't decided what to do yet, and it seems certain that he means to wait for the arrival of the

271

ransom, or at least for word whether or not it's going to be paid, before he does anything. So we have time to think, and plan what we're going to do.'

'Is that true?' David muttered, when she went to him.

'Yes. Except maybe I didn't tell them all of it.' She sat on the divan beside him, shoulders hunched. Thoughts were racing through her mind. It was all very well to ask Nathalie to seduce Chardin, but even supposing it could be done at all, it would certainly take time. And Zobeir might decide to execute David and hand the women over to his soldiers at any moment. As for the girls and Charlie . . .

'Then what is all of it?' David asked, quietly.

She could not look at him, any more than she dared tell him the truth, either. 'Apparently he means to sell everyone into slavery. Except me. He knows that you're not really Dobree, but as I am still Dobree's widow, I'm the only one worth ransoming.'

He frowned. 'You mean he still thinks you're Lady Dobree? Alison didn't tell the truth? I say, don't you think that was rather splendid of her, especially when he began to knock her about?'

'Yes,' Vicky said thoughtfully. If only she could be certain just how much of what Alison had told her was true. Yet the evidence was there. She had certainly been caned, and Vicky was equally certain that she *had* been raped . . . if it had been rape. But the things she had said . . . it was like some dreadful misplaced comedy.

David sat up to be beside her. 'So what are we going to do?'

'It's me he really wants,' she said. 'Only me.' Because the fact that Zobeir still thought she was Lady Dobree, and that, if Alison was telling the truth, he had managed to get himself into a frame of mind where he had fallen for her, was their only hope.

Their only hope. She got up, and went to the window, which looked down on the garden. That too was like some dreadful comedy. She had set out to impress the man, to the limits of her ability. She hadn't considered what might be the result of so impressing a man. Any man. But a man who held the power of

272

life and death over them . . . because that was what it came down to. Her life and her death.

She had accepted, deep in her mind, almost from the moment they had walked away from the beach, that it was her responsibility to die, if need be, to save the rest of them. At the time it had seemed the natural thing to do; she had had no doubt she had less to live for than any of the others. She had abandoned everything for one last trip to Africa, knowing that she would return to absolutely nothing – not even her job, after the way she had walked away from it. Well, she had had her trip to Africa.

But those thoughts, that understanding, perhaps even that determination, had been before David. Yet did that alter her situation at all? Or rather, did it not accentuate her situation? She could keep reaching for life and David, knowing that he was going to be executed, horribly; knowing Zobeir, she might even have to watch. Impalement *was* the method of execution here, where anger was involved. Or she could die herself. Only she wouldn't actually die. It would be a living death, down there in that garden. When she thought of what had been done to Alison, both before and during her meeting with Zobeir, her blood ran cold. And he had only been playing with Alison. If he were ever to learn of her deception . . . but she had to believe that he could not do that now, that she could maintain this pose no matter what it entailed.

That Alison, Mary and Elizabeth, Nathalie, Joanna, Alice, Margaret and Charlie might escape. Back to the society which wanted them, to resume their idle lives. And love and be happy. And perhaps remember, although she doubted that; they would be only too eager to forget. But she had taken the responsibility for that, too. She had promised Sir William.

And that David also would live. That *had* to be her responsibility.

'Vicky?' He came to stand beside her. 'What are you brooding on?'

'A lot of things. David . . .' She held his hand and led him back to the divan, sat down. 'Do you trust me?'

'Trust you? Oh, good heavens, what a question! I'd trust you with my life, my darling. I already have.'

'And will you go on trusting me, no matter what happens?'

'Of course. But . . . what are you thinking of doing?'

'I think I know how we can get out of this mess, and pretty quickly,' she said. 'But . . . we may have to travel separately.'

He frowned. 'I'm not sure I understand.'

'Then don't try. Just promise me that if the opportunity presents itself, you'll take it. No matter what.'

'You mean whether you are with us or not? Oh, no, my darling girl. When we go, we go together.'

'David . . .' She held his hands. 'You're a soldier. And you're Willaim Dobree's aide-de-camp. I was there when you accepted the responsibility of taking his wife and family to safety. You cannot abandon that trust, that responsibility, you cannot disobey those orders, now.'

His frown deepened. 'Just what are you thinking of doing?'

'Well . . .' But now he had to be told the truth, or he would merely dig his heels in. 'Well, we know that the only part of our story Zobeir believes is that I am Lady Dobree. I suppose that's rather a sick joke, when he has held Alison in his . . . his arms, don't you think? But he more or less told Alison that he doesn't care what happens to the rest of you. Of course, he talked about selling you as slaves, but I don't imagine he cares about that one way or the other. He doesn't think you're worth anything. I suspect I can use that to get you out of here. I'm sure I can do a deal.'

'That he'll let us go and keep you here?' He shook his head. 'I'm sorry, but that just isn't possible, my darling. The others, maybe. But I stay with you.'

'David, Zobeir isn't going to lay a finger on Lady Dobree. He told Alison that. And I believe him. If he had any intention of treating me the way he treated her, he'd have done that already, wouldn't he? Who was going to stop him? Alison is the only one of us he's interested in, physically. Alison, and maybe Mary. That's going to be the most difficult thing I have to do, getting him to release them along with the rest of you. But if I can do that, then there is nothing to worry about. I will stay here, in the greatest comfort, acting Lady Dobree for all I'm worth, until the ransom is paid.'

'And suppose the ransom isn't paid?'

He had fallen into her trap. To a man like David Whiting there could be no challenge to equal that of rescuing the woman he loved. 'That's why you *have* to go, don't you see?' she said. 'If I thought you wouldn't make sure the ransom was paid, David, I wouldn't be staying here.'

'Oh, Vicky . . .' He squeezed her fingers.

'But you'll get it paid,' she told him. 'And I'll come down the river with an escort of Zobeir's *spahis* riding around me. Believe me, I know the Arabs. They are people of their word. Zobeir will promise me to set you free, and not to lay a finger on me, and I'll be safer than in a nunnery.'

'And if he refuses?'

She shrugged. 'Are we any the worse off than we are now?'

He released her fingers, threw himself back on the bed. 'God, the thought of it . . . of leaving you . . .'

'I am the only one who is *safe*,' she insisted. 'Can't you get that into your head?'

'Oh, Vicky . . . I cannot just ride away . . .'

'Yes, you can,' she said fiercely. 'Firstly because it's your duty, and secondly – and believe me, this is more important to me – because you are the only one who can get me out of this place. Get us all out. Do believe that, David. Do please believe that.'

Captain Chardin escorted her to the antechamber. 'Of course, madam,' he explained, 'I cannot say for certain that his highness will receive you, but your request for an interview has been forwarded.'

Vicky nodded. 'He will see me,' she said.

She was amazed at her calmness. But it was a brittle tranquillity. Her heart was threatening to break loose at any moment and perhaps charge straight out of her chest, and she had acute indigestion, although she had had a light lunch. None of them had eaten well – they were too suddenly conscious of the danger of their position. Alison had not eaten at all, had remained in bed.

'Is it going to be all right, Vicky?' Mary had asked.

'Of course it is. I am going to see Lord Zobeir this afternoon, and tell him just how angry I am about what has happened to your stepmother. Don't worry. I'll see he apologises and makes up for it.'

'Goodness!' Mary said. 'If there is anything I can do to help . . .'

'Nothing,' Vicky said. But it was comforting to feel that from Mary, at least, David would receive one hundred per cent support. Now there was the girl he *should* marry. 'Just do whatever David tells you to.'

'Make her tell me what rape is,' Elizabeth suggested. 'She won't, you know.'

'You explain it to her,' Vicky told Mary.

They didn't really understand, she knew. None of them. There were frontiers of the mind beyond which English gentlewomen did not venture, under any circumstances. That Alison had been across such a frontier was in itself a frontier they could not cross, in their imaginations.

Was it a frontier *she* could cross? She did not know that. Yet she was here. Victoria Lang, sacrificial lamb. Or femme fatale. Or desperate woman engaged upon a suicide mission?

Because the doors were swinging in. 'His highness will see you, milady,' Chardin said.

Vicky went forward, slowly, wrapped in her haik. Zobeir stood behind his desk, waiting to receive her, and now he bowed, very low, as she approached. She glanced from him to the divans, and then the bed. She wondered where he had taken Alison. 'Your Excellency,' she said. 'I believe it is time we discussed the situation, seriously.'

'To speak with you, on any subject that you desire, madam, can be nothing but a pleasure.' He gestured her to the divans. 'Will you take tea?'

'Perhaps later,' she said, and sat down. He sat opposite her. 'To assault Mrs Lang was hardly the act of a gentleman,' Vicky said, severely. 'Or a man of such honour and standing as yourself.'

'I am weak, in matters of the flesh,' Zobeir admitted. 'Besides, the woman angered me, by her lies and prevarications.'

'Indeed?' Vicky asked. 'Had she not already been prepared for your bed?'

'Oh . . .' He waved his hand. 'That was part of, shall we say, preparing her for her interview with me. Putting her in a proper frame of mind to tell me the truth. Which she did, after attempting to lie. That is why I punished her. And, madam, if you are perhaps entitled to be angry with me for whipping one of your women, am I not entitled to be angry with you, for the falsehoods you have told me? Can there be a greater crime than a lie?'

'In English eyes,' Vicky told him, meeting his gaze, 'it is the duty of the person in command of a situation to do everything in his, or her, power, to preserve those lives entrusted to her. No matter what crimes she may have to commit to do so. I killed four men to save the lives of my women. Do you suppose I would shrink from a lie?'

'By Allah,' he said, 'I had forgotten about those four men. Yes, indeed, you are a *woman*.' He pointed. 'But to commit adultery . . .'

'My husband is dead, Zobeir.'

'Well, fornication. A woman like you, and with such a creature. The thought sickens me.'

'Does it? The act of fornication, or the thought that I did so with an inferior? But why should I not take whomever I please to my bed, Zobeir? I am Lady Dobree. Am I interested in petty morals? I seek my pleasures where I choose. If I wished Lieutenant Whiting for my bed, the decision was mine.'

They stared at each other, while she felt sweat trickling down her back. She could not believe she was actually uttering those words, looking so angrily insulted that he should dare question any of her actions. She could have made a fortune on the stage.

Zobeir was the first to lower his eyes. He got up, walked to the window, hands clasped behind his back, looked out. 'So you wish me to apologise to Mrs Lang. And to you, I do so, freely.'

'I am not interested in apologies, Zobeir,' Vicky said.

He turned to look at her.

She stood up. She felt physically sick, because the moment had arrived.

'What do you wish, then, madam?'

'I wish my people set free and sent to the coast. *All* of my people.'

He frowned. 'Why should I do that?'

'Because they are worthless to you.'

'You think so? Oh, I will admit I was disappointed in Mrs Lang. She is a lifeless creature. But your nieces? They are delectable. And suitable for my harem.'

'They are my stepdaughters, as you well know, Zobeir,' Vicky said. 'But even they are worthless to you. Is the satisfaction of your lust to be compared with the obtaining of the ransom?'

He smiled. 'Do you not suppose I can accomplish both those objectives?'

'No,' she said. 'I am the one to be ransomed. Oh, they will pay the ransom, for me.' Another long breath. 'Do not suppose I am just Lady Dobree, Zobeir. My maiden name is . . .' She hesitated. Although she had already chosen the name, on her way here, she was aware that once having said it, she was past the point of no return. 'Carnegie.'

Zobeir's frown was back. 'You are related to Andrew Carnegie?'

'He is my grandfather,' Vicky said. 'My father is his eldest son and, as I have no brothers, I am his heiress. Grandpapa will certainly pay a ransom for me, of whatever sum you may care to name. But I should warn you that if I am harmed, in any way, you will have to face the might of the United States of America.'

'The United States,' he said, attempting contempt.

'You are a student of history, Zobeir,' she said. 'Especially the history of your own people. My country has divorced itself from the politics of the world. But I suggest you think back, to what happened less than a hundred years ago, when the Barbary pirates kidnapped some American citizens. Have you never heard the name, Stephen Decatur? Have you forgotten the smoking ruins of Algiers, as it was left by an American fleet?'

He looked at her for some seconds, then turned away again, to resume gazing out of the window. 'You drag up nightmares from the past. Bah! Decatur had warships. And a seaport to attack. He could not have sailed across the desert, or up the Niger. I could execute you all, here in my palace. I could watch you die, slowly, and listen to you scream, and no one would be any the wiser.'

'Word of what you had done would yet leak out, and summon my people to vengeance,' she said. 'And what would you have gained by such a senseless act?'

He turned again, his gaze seeming to shroud her. 'By Allah, you have courage, so to challenge me.'

'I am Lady Dobree.'

Another long stare, then he walked past her and threw himself on to a divan. 'What is it you wish of me?'

'I have told you. Your assault on one of my closest friends, your threats against my stepdaughters, have convinced me that they are too much at the mercy of your lusts. I wish them, I wish all of my people, sent to the coast. I will remain here as surety. My people will confirm to Governor Hodgson that I am still alive and well, and that the ransom must be paid. But they must all be sent, in safety. My nieces as well. In fact, they are the most important. They may be my stepdaughters, but Grandpapa Carnegie regards them as his great-grand-daughters. They are his favourites. And they, more than anyone else, will convince him the ransom must be paid.'

'You have become a source of trouble to me,' he growled. 'I should have left you in the desert to die of thirst.'

'Then you would surely have been neglecting your fortunes, Zobeir.'

'Hah,' he said, and brooded for a while. 'Very well. I will do as you wish, and release them all, except for the man who defiled your bed. He, I intend to impale upon the sharpest stick in North Africa.'

'You will release them *all*, Zobeir.'

'Hah,' he repeated. 'You think you can come here, and give me orders?'

'I am not giving you orders, your Excellency. I am giving you advice. But it is very good advice, believe me.'

'Hah,' he said a third time. 'Well, I am certainly not releasing the blonde virago. She is useless to anyone . But I want to hear her scream. I will have her bastinadoed every day for a week.'

'You will do no such thing,' Vicky snapped.

'You do not know her as well as I do, madam. She is no true friend of yours. Why, do you know that she claimed to be you?'

'What?' Vicky did not have to fake consternation.

'Oh, yes. She tried to tell me, *me*, that she was Lady Dobree, and convince me that you, Lady Dobree, were merely a governess. I was not fooled for a moment, of course. That is why I whipped her. But I wish to whip her again, and again.'

Oh, Alison, Vicky thought. You *bitch*. You lying bitch. She was almost tempted to agree to Zobeir's wishes. But that would be too dangerous. It would also be quite un-Christian . . . and she had had to do sufficient un-Christian things to get them this far.

'She will accompany the others,' she said.

He got up, impatiently. 'You cannnot bully me, Lady Dobree. I hold you in the palm of my hand. All of you. I can do what I like with your companions. And who will know of it? I have sent the man Bream to the coast, with the woman Brown. The ransom will still be paid.'

'It will only be paid upon the safe delivery of myself,' Vicky pointed out.

'Oh, I will deliver *you* safely, madam.'

'You will not,' she told him. 'Because if you harm any one of my companions, I shall take my own life. And do not think you can prevent my doing so. If I have to, I will starve myself to death.'

Their gazes seemed to spark against each other. Then he said, 'You would do that?'

'Do you suppose that Arab emirs are the only people in this world with honour?' Vicky demanded. 'I am Lady Dobree. My honour demands that my people are safely returned to their homes. I will not live without honour.'

Zobeir came towards her, stood in front of her. She thought for a moment he was going to touch her, and tensed her muscles, but he merely stared at her for some minutes. At last he said, 'And if I do this thing that you wish, can I hope that you will look on me as favourably as you have done on that half man?'

Vicky kept her breath under control with an effort. She had known it must come to this, in the end. 'Perhaps,' she said. 'When we are better acquainted with one another.'

'By Allah!' he said. 'You are a *woman!* To have you ride at my side, across the desert, would be the greatest triumph of my life.'

'You will have other triumphs,' Vicky said. 'Many of them.'

'And then I sometimes think, to have you lying at my feet, begging for mercy as I whipped you, would equally be a great triumph,' Zobeir said.

'I am sure you would be sadly disappointed,' Vicky told him. 'I have never been very good at begging for mercy, convincingly. Now, your Excellency, I will leave you, and prepare my people for their departure. I would like a boat made ready for them to leave by the water gate, at dawn tomorrow morning. I shall count upon it.'

She stepped outside, and had to make an enormous effort to walk at Chardin's side back to the apartment. Her position could now be sustained only as long as she was Lady Dobree. And because she knew that, as she was not related to Andrew Carnegie, and as once Alison gained Kumassi and identified herself Vicky would be totally worthless in the eyes of the British Government, unless David *could* pull the necessary strings and raise the ransom, she would have to lie at this man's feet . . . one of these days. Or indeed kill herself.

281

CHAPTER 13

'Oh, no,' Joanna Cartwright said. 'When we go, we go together. David . . .' She turned to him. 'You surely cannot permit this.'

David chewed his lip.

'I have explained the situation to David, Joanna,' Vicky said quietly. 'I wish you could get it into your heads that I will be in no danger by remaining here. Zobeir appears to have an absurd reverence for the British titled classes, even if the title is only a baronetcy. He will not harm me in any way, as long as he believes the ransom will be paid. But the rest of you . . . I cannot answer for your safety if you remain here one day longer than you have to. And you do *not* have to remain here for even another twenty-four hours,' she said vehemently. 'Zobeir has agreed to put a boat at your disposal and allow you to go down the river. It connects with the Niger, only a few miles away, and will take you right into Kumassi. Don't you see? You simply have to go, and have the ransom made up, and sent up here. Then I'll be directly behind you.'

They looked at her, and then at each other, and then at David.

Who sighed. 'It does make sense, I'm afraid. Believe me, I hate the idea, but it could be the only way we'll all get out of here alive.'

'Oh, Vicky!' Mary said. 'You're awfully *brave* to stay here all by yourself. I mean, if something were to go wrong . . .'

'You'd be *raped*,' Elizabeth said, having obviously at last discovered the meaning of the word.

282

'Then it must be your business to make sure that nothing does go wrong,' Vicky told her.

'May I have a word with you alone, Victoria?' Alison said.

Their heads turned. She had remained in the bedroom during the earlier part of the discussion, but she had obviously been listening. Now she was wrapped in her haik.

'Of course,' Vicky said. 'Will you excuse me?'

She went into the bedroom.

Alison sat on the bed. 'Are you trying to commit suicide?' she inquired.

'I don't think so.' Vicky sat beside her. 'You say he has fallen for me . . .'

'Fallen for you.' Alison shuddered.

'All right, I feel the same way. If it were to come to that . . .' She allowed herself a shudder as well. 'But it won't come to that, if you'll play your part.'

Alison's eyebrows were beginning to arch. 'Have you told David about, well . . . Zobeir's feelings about *him?*'

'Of course I have not. And neither must you. I have told them all nothing, save that Zobeir knows that David is not my husband. You must not let me down, milady, please. Or I am on a hiding to nothing.'

'I will not let you down, Victoria,' Alison said. 'But as Elizabeth said, if anything should go wrong, my God . . . what he would do to you . . .'

'I'm relying on you to make sure nothing does go wrong, milady,' Vicky said.

'On me? Good Lord!' She seemed for the first time to understand the responsibility she was at last being forced to accept.

'Milady,' Vicky told her. 'The only thing that *can* go wrong would be if the British Government, having regained the real Lady Dobree, were to decide that an itinerant American governess was not worth bothering about. Then I would have committed suicide, as you say. So I am relying on you, and David, not to let that happen.'

Now the eyebrows were at full apex. 'I have to agree with

Mary,' Alison remarked, 'that you are a woman of remarkable courage. Do you know . . .?' She peered into Vicky's eyes, 'I simply cannot make up my mind whether I loathe you or adore you.'

Vicky returned her gaze. As I should hate you, she thought, for what you have done to us all. But she thought it best to keep that to herself – and Zobeir would have found out the truth anyway. Alison had tried to betray them, and had failed. She should be pitied for that. 'The quandary is mutual, milady,' she said. 'But I will promise you this; send up that ransom and get me out of here, and I will adore you.'

Alison hesitated, then suddenly leaned forward and kissed her on the cheek; Vicky supposed that was the nearest she would ever come to apologising.

'Vicky . . . milady,' Nathalie whispered, 'I wish to stay 'ere, with you.'

It was next morning, and they were ready to depart; there had been no packing to do, as they possessed only the clothes they were wearing.

Vicky frowned at her. 'That is quite impossible, Nathalie.'

'Why? Who is going to do your 'air? 'Ow can you be a great lady and not 'ave a maid? I will not go. I wish to stay with you.'

And with Chardin? Vicky wondered. Perhaps she had been pessimistic in supposing it might take too long for Nathalie to seduce the big Sudanese. Or in fearing that she might not wish to. Of course, this was much the safer way. Except for her. And Nathalie?

'Well,' she said uncertainly. 'Alison . . . Nathalie wishes to stay.'

'Here?' Alison asked. 'My dear girl, don't be absurd. You are my maid.'

'No, madame,' Nathalie said, tilting her chin. 'I am Lady Dobree's maid.'

'Oh, good Lord . . .' Alison looked at Vicky. 'Doesn't she know how dangerous it could be?'

'What do I care about danger?' Nathalie demanded, stoutly. 'Milady will protect me.'

Vicky scratched her head. Of course she would be truly grateful for even the smallest support – her heart was leaping at the thought of it. And somehow she felt she could accept the French girl where she would not even consider one of the others. Nathalie was not a lady born and bred, and thus surely would be better able to stand up to the sort of catastrophe they might have to face than anyone else. 'The decision must be yours, Alison,' she said.

'Oh . . . very well,' Alison said. 'I suppose I can find another maid in Kumassi. Well . . .' She held out her hand. 'I will wish you good fortune . . . milady. We shall endeavour to get you out of here just as soon as possible.'

'I'll be waiting,' Vicky said, and squeezed her fingers.

Joanna and Alice and Margaret were waiting to hug and kiss her goodbye.

'If you don't get out soon,' Mary told her, 'I am going to mount my own expedition and come and get you. If I have to shoot my way through the whole Arab nation.'

Vicky kissed her. 'I'll look forward to that too.'

'Mind you take care,' Elizabeth begged. 'And don't get yourself raped.' Perhaps, Vicky thought, she still hadn't found out what it meant.

'It's not something I have in mind,' Vicky promised her.

Then there was David. They had clung to each other all night, afraid even to allow an inch of distance between them. But even that had not been enough. Now they must take refuge in commonplaces. 'I feel a total cad,' he confessed.

'I'm looking on you more as my private Lancelot.'

'But Vicky, there's something we've forgotten. Suppose there's a British column already on its way here?'

'Believe me, I'm counting on that,' Vicky said. 'I think that's a much safer bet than hoping there's a ransom on its way.'

'Yes, but what will Zobeir do then?'

'If there's one thing I'm sure of,' Vicky told him, 'it's that Zobeir is terrified of the British Army. Just have the commander of the column utter the most terrible threats he can think of, and make sure they reach Timbuktu, and I'll be perfectly safe.'

'But suppose the French are still encamped outside the city?'

'Well, then, David, you will have to decide what is more important, preserving peace or saving my life.'

He frowned at her, and then smiled as she winked. 'Do you really think I'd waste the time thinking of that? I'll be your Lancelot, Vicky. I swear it. If Mary and I do have to raise that army on our own, I'll be leading it back here to get you. Just the moment I've dropped this lot off in Kumassi. And when we do get back together, we're going to be married, remember?'

'I'm looking forward to that,' she said, and kissed him on the lips.

Then it was just a matter of waiting. Not that she was allowed to be bored. With the departure of the rest of the party, Zobeir suddenly evinced a desire to show off his titled guest, as he chose to call her. Actually she guessed that the reason had nothing to do with her being left on her own – it was simply that the French column had withdrawn to Algiers, having shown the flag and received sufficient guarantees of fealty from the residents of Timbuktu.

Indeed, she wondered if she and David had not been crediting Zobeir with a Machiavellian statecraft way beyond his mental capacity, in supposing he had dreamed of engineering a confrontation between Britain and France. Not only had he shown no reluctance to let the rest of the party go, provided she stayed, but he also seemed to regard the French with total contempt.

'They are such fools,' he remarked, scornfully, riding through the city with her, suitably veiled, at his side. 'They think they can conquer North Africa, an area twice as large as all Europe, with a few columns of soldiers.'

'Did not the British conquer Egypt and the Sudan, and virtually all Africa south of the Vaal, with a few columns of soldiers?' Vicky asked him, and smiled as she saw the flash of anger from his eyes. 'And a few batteries of artillery and Maxim guns, to be sure.'

'Yes,' he said. 'Those are the keys to military success. But we will have them. One day we will have them, and then . . . it will

286

take the Arab nations a long time to forgive the Europeans for the crimes committed against them.'

'When you speak like that, you almost frighten me,' Vicky confessed. 'Just keep remembering that I'm an American.'

Zobeir bowed. 'I do not mean to frighten you, madam. And besides, how could I, a mere desert wanderer, frighten the famous Lady Dobree?'

She wondered if he was poking fun at her, but he seemed sincere enough. And that night he entertained her to dinner, as he did every night from then on. His manners remained impeccable, although their meals were always tête à tête. 'These matters are not understood or appreciated amongst our people,' he explained. 'Men eat together, never in the company of women. Women are confined in the harem.'

'Then I am most privileged,' she acknowledged.

'You are no ordinary woman,' he said.

'I should like to visit your harem.'

He smiled. 'Perhaps, one day. Just before you leave. Were you to enter there now, I might find it too difficult to let you go again.'

She believed that. Just as she also believed it was his dearest dream – as he had told Alison – to make her entirely his, that only the very real fear he had of the power of the British, that power he had seen at the Battle of Omdurman when his people had been savagely beaten by a British army, kept him from making the dream reality. Far more so than any hopes of obtaining a ransom for her. So hurrah for the British Army, she thought. Even for the Kitcheners and the William Dobrees of this world. They were not men who had any place in the heart of a missionary, or a missionary's widow. She had always rather disliked the very thought of soldiers, and especially British soldiers, with their red jackets and their insufferable confidence. But she was now prepared to concede that without them the world would be a more dangerous place.

Besides, she reminded herself, she was going to be married to one of them. Soon. She had to keep reminding herself of this, or sometimes the waiting would have been unbearable. She was

287

engaged to David Whiting. That was her future. Even while she was being courted by another man.

Because Zobeir was definitely courting her. Apart from the rides around the city, the dinner parties, there now began a succession of gifts, mostly jewellery, exquisite filigree work, magnificent stones, superb brooches... however, she endeavoured to refuse them all. 'My dear Zobeir,' she said. 'In English society a lady cannot accept gifts from a gentleman, unless, well . . .'

'Unless she is prepared to look kindly upon him,' he suggested.

'I am a married woman.'

'You are a widow,' he corrected her.

She had kept the gifts. And as the days lengthened into weeks, he became more open in his ambitions. 'I cannot remain forever in Timbuktu,' he told her. 'I have dallied here for too long as it is. There are great things happening in the East, and I am needed there. While those people of yours – I doubt they have even reached Kumassi as yet. I have sent out a patrol into the forests to learn what has become of them. But it could be months before the ransom arrives. I do not know I can wait that long.'

'The decision must be yours,' Vicky said, daintily eating her sherbet in order to avoid having to look at him, and thus give him the opportunity perhaps to observe the fear in her eyes.

'I do not know if I actually wish the ransom to arrive,' he went on. 'Suppose I were to ride east. Would you come with me?'

'I am sure the British Army would regard you as guilty of kidnapping.'

'The British Army. Always the British Army. But what could they do, if you were my wife?'

Now she could allow herself an amazed stare, although she had known such a request was on its way.

'Is that so impossible?' Zobeir asked. 'Are you not a widow, free to wed again?'

'Which also means I am not a virgin,' she pointed out. 'You

are Zobeir the Mighty. Can you seriously consider taking another man's relict to your harem?'

He smiled. 'If I am Zobeir the Mighty, Lady Dobree, can I not do whatever I wish?'

He kept posing these unanswerable questions.

'Of course I am enormously flattered, Zobeir,' she said. 'I have never been so flattered in my life.' She didn't think she was telling a lie, either; William Dobree had only invited her to be his mistress. 'And you are one of the most attractive men I have ever met, and a gentleman. I could easily . . . but you see, I do not *know* my husband is dead.'

His smile changed to a frown. 'He went down with the *Doncaster*. The woman Lang told me this.'

'Well, I very much fear that is the case. But you see, I do not *know*. William, my husband, remained on the ship with his men, as he was bound to do. We were placed in a lifeboat, and drifted away from the ship in the darkness. We never saw the ship or my husband again, and therefore we suppose it must have gone down, and he with it. But still, I do not know that for a fact.'

Zobeir pulled his beard, his expression suggesting that if Sir William were to enter the room at that moment, the matter would immediately be resolved at least to his satisfaction. 'You will never know, for certain, what happened,' he said.

'I know that. But British law says I cannot presume that my husband is dead until seven years have passed.'

'Seven years? Then you are an adulteress, after all,' he growled.

'I do not know that either,' she said. 'I do know I could not possibly ask you to share my crime.'

She received another glare, but he was clearly uncertain as to the ethics of the question, and let the matter drop.

''E really is very nice,' Nathalie commented, as she brushed Vicky's hair. 'And so rich. I 'ave never lived in such a palace.'

'And he employs nice people,' Vicky commented, watching her in the mirror.

Nathalie smiled, lazily. 'Chardin! Now 'e is a *man*.'

'Maybe I'll ask Zobeir to let him come with us,' Vicky said.

'Oh, madame! Could you do that? That would be splendid.' Then she frowned. ''Ow soon are we leaving?'

'Soon,' Vicky promised her.

But clearly Nathalie had no desire for it to be too soon. Lucky Nathalie.

It had to be soon. It was a fortnight since the others had left for Kumassi. In many ways it was a fortnight she had desperately needed, she knew, fourteen days in which she had to do nothing save rest. There were no decisions to be made, no position to maintain – other than that of Lady Dobree, and this came naturally to her, now.

But they were also fourteen entirely empty days. Even had there been no David, and had Zobeir been young and chivalrous and attractive and handsome and everything a woman might want – instead of a cruel, lecherous despot – she still knew she could never consider this life as permanent. She did not know what the ladies of the harem did with their time, but presumably they had each other with whom to gossip and quarrel and love. She was allowed the use of Zobeir's library, but only a few of the books were in English or French. She was bathed every morning by her maid servants, and soon took to prolonging this for as long as possible, just to help fill the day.

Before the midday meal she could walk in the garden, always watched by either Chardin or Saeed, neither of whom offered any conversation. Luncheon was usually taken alone, and she was entirely alone for her siesta. That was when Nathalie clearly sought her lover. And in the evenings sometimes she was taken for a ride by Zobeir. Then it was a matter of being bathed again in readiness for dinner with the Emir. Then bed.

She could feel a blanket of soporific relaxation being spread across her brain, had to keep reminding herself not only of David but of who and what she was, and more important, where and when she was, to maintain that alertness she knew was essential to survival. Why, she realised, it was now five weeks since they had left England. It would be mid-April by now. Five weeks! It seemed like an eternity, while England seemed like another world. It was so long since she had left

America, that had seemed like another world for some time. But the *Doncaster* would have been reported as overdue in Cape Town by now, and the telegraph wires would be humming. And certainly Bream and Prudence would have reached Kumassi some time ago, so the telegraph wires down there would be busy as well. The ransom, or the rescue column, would already be on its way. She had to believe that.

On the fourteenth night after David's departure, as she entered the room where she was invariably entertained to dinner, it occurred to her that Zobeir might also have been counting the days. He rose as usual as she came in, watched her walk across the room towards him, but did not perform his usual elaborate bow, nor did he smile. 'Sit,' he commanded, with less courtesy than usual.

Vicky sat on the cushion, even as her brain began to tighten in company with her muscles. Something had happened.

Zobeir took his place beside her, and the food was brought in, but to her increasing alarm the servants immediately left again, without offering any of the dishes.

'Do you not suppose your *friends* should have gained Kumassi, by now?'

The accented word was another unfavourable straw in the wind. Her only refuge was the arrogant confidence she had portrayed from the moment of their first meeting. 'Unless they have been delayed,' she said. 'Who can tell what problems they may have met with in the forest?'

'Problems. Delays,' he said. 'Oh, indeed, they have been delayed. My patrol has returned.'

Vicky's heart seemed to skip a beat. 'To tell you what?'

'That the Ashanti are in revolt.'

'The . . . oh, my God!'

'Indeed, it is to Him that you should pray,' Zobeir recommended.

'But . . . is there news of my people?'

'No. But their fate is easy enough to decide. The Ashanti are in revolt against British rule. This has been simmering for some time. They are a simple people, the Ashanti. Their lives, their politics, are built around fetishes and, while the revolt has certainly long been planned and prepared, they would not undertake it until they discovered the exact fetish they sought, one which they believe will guarantee them victory. Do you know what that fetish is?'

'I'm afraid not,' Vicky said, beginning to feel vaguely sick.

'The skull of a white woman,' Zobeir said. 'Is that not quaint?'

'The . . .' Her jaw dropped. Now she did feel sick.

'Yes, an interesting concept. The Ashanti have always believed that the skulls of their enemies are powerful juju. Of course British skulls are hard to come by. But many years ago, when the British first started to penetrate inland from the coast, and they encountered the Ashanti for the first time, there was a clash, naturally; the Ashanti were then a very proud and warlike people. They also have their traditions. Very like the British, indeed. British kings are always crowned, are they not, sitting on the Stone of Scone. The Ashanti were somewhat more refined. Their High King, the ruler of the Ashanti Federation, was always crowned on the Golden Stool. Of course, I do not know if the stool really is made of gold; I have never seen it. And I should point out that an Ashanti High King is not crowned in a European sense; he is invested with the Umbrella of State, a much more useful symbol of authority in such a climate. Would you not agree?'

Vicky could only stare at him. He was leading up to something. Something dreadful.

'So the British reasoned, naturally enough, that the way to bring the Ashanti to heel would be to secure the Golden Stool. No Stool, no High King, except in London. They sent a man called McCarthy to secure this Stool from the Ashanti. Unfortunately, they only sent very few soldiers with him, and no cannon or machine guns. Actually, there were no machine guns when this took place. McCarthy was defeated and taken prisoner, his head was cut off and, as he had done enough to convince the Ashanti that the British were foes worth taking seriously, his skull was made into a battle fetish. Under this fetish, they fought, and beat, the British for some years, whenever the British sought to avenge McCarthy's death, or to make another attempt to gain possession of the Stool. So at last the British decided that the Ashanti had to be taken seriously in turn, and they sent their greatest general, Sir Garnet Wolseley, to West Africa, along with a British regiment, rather than native levies. Wolseley marched on Kumaṣsi, and defeated the Ashanti.' He stroked his beard. 'He would almost certainly have beaten them anyway. He had defeated Arabi Pasha and the whole Egyptian army at Tel-el-Kebir, in 1882; and he led the column which invaded Abyssinia, and defeated the Negus, even before then.' He half smiled. 'Do you know what the Emperor of Abyssinia had done? He was holding some English women and children captive. Is that not quaint? But the British have this habit of waging war relentlessly when their nationals, especially their women, are involved. And Wolseley was a great soldier. I fought against him, with Arabi, at Tel-el-Kebir. Of course, I was only a boy then. But I have already told you of this.'

He was deliberately keeping her in suspense, and she could stand it no longer. 'The fetish,' she gasped. 'You were telling me about the fetish.'

'Indeed. Well, after Wolseley defeated the Ashanti, they were forced to accept British suzerainty. But they did so in much the same spirit as we of the desert have accepted French suzerainty, with, shall we say, certain reservations, certain plans, or at least hopes, for the future. And they hid the Golden Stool, claiming it had been lost. They still dreamed of regaining their independence, ruled by a High King seated on his Stool. But of course they knew this was impossible unless they could obtain a fetish powerful enough to defeat a man like Wolseley, or his successor, Kitchener. They have waited a long time, and might have waited forever had it not been pointed out to them that their mistake had lain in going into battle under the skull of this McCarthy. That might have worked when there was a king ruling in Britain, but Wolseley had been fighting for a woman, Queen Victoria. Thus they understood that they had no hope of defeating the British unless they could obtain a *female* British skull.'

Vicky stared at him as a monstrous suspicion crept across

her mind. 'Who pointed that out to them?'

Zobeir smiled. 'I have fought many times against the Ashanti, over trade routes, over escaped slaves. But where they oppose the British or the French, they, or any men, are as my brothers.'

'You!' she shouted. 'And you let my people, my friends, just walk into their arms . . . my God! You *sent* them! First Prudence, and then the others . . .'

'Well,' he said, 'the nurse had been gone some time, and nothing had happened. I realised that she must somehow have reached Kumassi, although my orders had been to turn her and the man Bream loose in the Ashanti country, to be sure. And I could not let such an opportunity to start a new Ashanti war slip by, now could I? I wonder which of the other women they chose,' he said thoughtfully. 'It would have been a shame had it been the girl Mary. But what a tragedy if they have selected Lady Dobree! And she was the most likely candidate, I imagine, with her splendid golden hair.'

'Selected Lady . . .' Vicky gasped; she felt exactly as if a mule had just kicked her in the stomach. But the understanding that something else had gone terribly wrong was overlaid by the horror of imagining Alison, or Mary, in the hands of the Ashanti, her neck stretched to be cut through.

'So you see,' Zobeir went on, 'I would appear to have succeeded in at least one of my objectives of avenging the defeat of Omdurman. Of course the British contribute to their own problems. Instead of leaving well enough alone, it appears they are still looking for the Golden Stool. Would you believe it? This revolt started ten days ago, when the Ashanti attacked and defeated a British column seeking the Stool. Undoubtedly they were inspired by their new fetish. They must have been most gratified. But I . . . I can find no gratification at all. What matters to me is not that I may have achieved a political objective, but that I have been made to look a fool. I do not think there is anything in this life I hate more than being made to look a fool. Indeed, it has never happened before.'

Vicky licked her lips, desperately. 'I . . . I do not understand you.'

Zobeir got up; she watched him as a rabbit might watch a snake.

'Almost at the same time as my patrol returned from the south,' he said, walking to his desk, 'a caravan arrived from the north. Bringing mail. Bringing books for my library. Bringing newspapers.'

Vicky found she was clutching her throat.

'I flicked through the copies of the *Times*. Do you know, they are last year's, more than six months old. I expected to find nothing of interest,' Zobeir said, sitting at the desk, and turning the pages, 'but I was lucky. Or perhaps unlucky.' He smoothed the page in front of him. 'Here it is. I shall read it to you. It is the guest list of those who attended a garden party at Buckingham Palace, last autumn. There is mention of Sir William Dobree, V.C. etcetera. They go on to mention his beautiful wife. But how quaint, her name is given as Alison, not Victoria. And lest there be any mistake, the journal goes on to describe her gown, which so sets off her golden hair. Her golden hair. Nothing about red is mentioned.'

'Oh, Jesus,' Vicky muttered. 'Oh, God.'

'Indeed,' Zobeir agreed, 'I strongly recommend that you call on the name of every saint you can remember. Although as you are in a Muslim country I doubt whether any Christian saint will be of assistance to you. Do you know, I cannot make up my mind what angers me more, your brazen effrontery, the tissue of lies you have been telling me from the beginning, or the fact that I have actually had Lady Dobree here, in my hands, and let her go. Because you persuaded me to. And now she has been murdered by the Ashanti. *I* having sent her to them. I certainly did not intend that to happen.'

'You do not know that she is dead,' Vicky gasped. 'You cannot be certain that it was her. It could have been any member of the party. It . . .'

'Of course you are right,' he agreed. 'But either way, she is still lost to me. Because of you.'

Vicky rose to her knees. She didn't actually mean to beg, but she lacked the strength to stand. 'The ransom will still be paid.'

'Do you really think so? Ah, I was forgetting, of course, that you may not be Lady Dobree, but you are still Andrew Carnegie's granddaughter. Is that not right?'

'Well . . .' Vicky gasped for breath while she tried to think.

Zobeir smiled. 'My mail also included books for my library, as I told you. Again, they were ordered a very long time ago, and have only now reached me. One of them is a volume of biographies of great men, something I have sorely felt the need of in the past. And listed as a great man, presumably because he is one of the richest men in the world, is Andrew Carnegie. However, from the biography, which I read the moment I discovered this item in the Court Circular, I have learned something I never knew about Carnegie: he never married. Therefore he has no sons. No legitimate sons, anyway. Therefore he can hardly have had a legitimate granddaughter.' He stopped smiling, suddenly. 'What is your real name, woman?'

'I . . .' She bit her lip. But the game was up. She could only survive now by making him realise that it was her that he wanted, not her supposed rank or title. 'My name is Victoria Lang.'

'Ah. So you *are* the governess. Yes. Lady Dobree claimed you were, and I whipped her for lying. *I* whipped Lady Dobree. The thought is a scandal to me. She further described you as a common slut. I have no doubt she was telling the truth there as well. And I refused to believe her.'

Vicky drew a long breath. 'I am the same woman as you admired when you thought I was Lady Dobree, Zobeir,' she said. 'I am also still an American citizen. That is no lie.'

'It is also quite unimportant to me,' he replied.

Vicky decided against pressing such a debatable point. It was all or nothing, now. 'I am still the most desirable woman you have ever known. Or I could be, to you. You once told me you wished me to ride at your side across the desert. Well, ask me again.'

He got up, and walked towards her, slowly. Hastily she scrambled to her feet. 'Believe me,' he said, 'since discovering the truth of the matter, I have thought of nothing else but what I should do with you. What would give me the most satisfaction, and at the same time provide you with a punishment equal to your crimes against me.'

'I have eaten at your table,' Vicky gasped, clutching at straws.

'Victoria Lang has not eaten at my table,' he pointed at the untouched food. 'I will concede that I have entertained someone, for several nights. But I do not know who that person was, other than she was pretending to be someone she was not. I owe Victoria Lang *nothing*. And to think that I allowed myself to become fond of her – that is a weakness of the flesh. You are indeed a most desirable creature, and therefore, even after learning the truth of you, I was still tempted to take you to my bed. On the other hand, I quickly realised that was impossible, both because it would compound error upon error, and because you are such a consummate actress I doubt I would achieve any real satisfaction from reducing you to the woman you are.' He stretched out his hand, and she made herself keep still as he flicked the cowl of the haik from her head and let it drop on her shoulders. Now she was holding her breath.

'I would be good to you, Zobeir,' she whispered. 'I swear I would give you everything you seek in a woman.' So she was begging, after all. She had nothing left. And David would have to forgive her.

'Then I thought,' Zobeir went on as if she hadn't spoken, while continuing slowly to remove the haik, 'that I might obtain pleasure from giving you to my men, one after the other, out there in the courtyard, while I watched.'

Slowly Vicky released her breath and then caught it again; the haik slipped from her shoulders and fell around her ankles. She knew she was very close to, at the least, a savage attack.

'Then I thought I would prefer to strangle you with my hands,' he said.

'Would that not be a waste?' she gasped, as her bolero followed the haik. If he could not keep his hands off her, she still had a chance.

'A waste.' He held her breasts, one in each hand. 'That is the greatest crime of all, waste. Do you know for how long I have dreamed of holding these? Now I would like to cut them off.'

He released her left breast to draw the exquisitely carved knife from his waistband. She could only stare at it in horror as it came closer, almost touching her flesh, while she tried to hold her breath again to stop herself moving.

Zobeir's face distorted. 'Slut!' he shouted, and threw her away from him. Taken by surprise, she lost her balance, staggered a few feet, and fell over a cushion. She kept on going, deliberately, and landed on her hands and knees, facing him. 'Female demon!' Zobeir screamed, reaching for her. She could not make up her mind whether to fight him, attempt to escape him – neither promised success – or just let him work out his anger and pray she avoided injury. Her hesitation enabled him to seize her again, and he shook her like a dog, tearing the pantaloons from her thighs, throwing her again to the floor and kicking her several times in the buttocks as she rolled away from him to shelter her groin.

She lay on her face and panted, while he stood above her. 'So beautiful,' he said. 'No doubt you hope that if I were to plunge into you I would be unable to hurt you, afterwards. Who knows, you may be right. And I wish to hurt you, governess. Oh, I wish to hurt you, and watch you suffer.' He snapped his fingers. 'You will be impaled.'

Vicky regained her knees. 'Impaled?' Her brain seemed to coagulate.

'Do you know of this? Ha.' He threw himself on to the cushions, staring at her. 'It will be a sight no one in Timbuktu will ever forget, and I promise you, all Timbuktu will gather to watch you die. Tomorrow morning at dawn you will be paraded. You and that French whore you call a maid. You will be stripped as naked as you are now, and marched round the market place, that the people of Timbuktu may look upon your secrets. The day after tomorrow, the maid will be despatched, before your eyes. And the day after that will be your turn. We will see how your arrogant acting stands up to impalement. Do you know of it?'

Vicky closed her eyes; her body seemed to be seized in an ice-cold vice.

'In men,' Zobeir told her, 'the point of the stake is inserted into the anus, and he is left to wriggle to death.' He smiled. 'In women, we use the alternative orifice. But where the executioner is kind, the stake is greased, that it may enter and travel the more easily.' He sat up, pointing again. 'Your stake will not be greased, governess. You will not die for at least an hour. Perhaps longer, as you are strong, and will clench your muscles. Oh, you will scream, and you will rue the day you sought to make a fool of Zobeir ibn Rubayr. But I make you a promise. I promise I will personally insert the stake into you. It will be my first, and my last, act of sex with you. And then I will stand before you and watch you die.' He got up, and she tensed her muscles for another assault. 'Guards!' he bawled.

The doors opened, and the soldiers came in.

'Take this wretched thing away,' Zobeir said. 'Throw her into a cell, and put the other one beside her. Not into the same cell, mind. And make sure their hands are bound, behind their backs. We wish no accidents. Now take her away, before I slit her belly.'

Vicky only vaguely heard the door slam shut behind her. She had been thrust into the tiny, noisome room so violently that she had staggered against the far wall, and from there had slowly subsided into a kneeling position, head against the wall. She was bruised and battered from the manhandling she had received on the way as she had been dragged down here, but her external discomfort was nothing. Her brain still seemed to be atrophied, and she knew that if she really attempted to think she would scream and scream and scream, and then go mad. It was utterly impossible for her to imagine what was going to happen to her, as so graphically described by Zobeir; what it would feel like, what it would *be* like. She could only believe that it could not be happening, that this had to be some terrible nightmare from which she would awaken with a gasp of relief. If she had understood the risk she was taking in staying behind, she had supposed the worst fate that could overtake her would be rape by Zobeir. That his anger could find such an unthinkable way of expressing itself . . .

She heard a sound and, raising her head, saw the guard

looking at her through the small barred window set in the door. They were down in the cellars beneath the palace, and a single torch guttered outside in the corridor. She was in blessed gloom, and he would be able to see nothing more than a white shadow huddled in the corner, although she could make out his features quite clearly.

Then she heard a lot of noise, principally Nathalie screaming, men cursing as she obviously fought them, followed by the sound of another door slamming shut. The voices of the men faded, and for a few minutes there was silence, then Nathalie said, 'Milady? Milady?'

She was on the other side of the wall.

'Milady?' she asked again. 'Vicky?'

'Yes,' Vicky said.

'Oh! I am so glad. I did not know where you were. I . . . milady.'

'You can call me Vicky,' Vicky said. 'Now.'

Nathalie was silent for a few minutes as she digested this. Then she said, 'What 'as 'appened, Vicky? They dragged me from my bed, and brought me down 'ere . . . they took away my clothes and they pinched me so. Oh, Vicky, what 'as 'appened? Are they going to cut off our 'eads?'

Vicky sighed. If only they were going to cut off their heads. But she couldn't tell Nathalie the truth. 'Yes,' she said. 'I believe they may be going to cut off our heads.'

Another brief silence. 'But why will they do this?' Nathalie asked.

'I guess Zobeir has found out exactly who we are,' Vicky sighed. She didn't want to talk about it. Every time she opened her mouth she thought she was going to vomit, and every time she spoke she could feel the tears gathering. Far from leading them anywhere, she had led, or sent, them all to their deaths. All. Every one. Mary, or Alison, or one of the others, to have her head cut off, the hair and flesh scraped away, and the skull mounted on a spear as a fetish. The others . . . imagination could not suggest what might have happened, what might still be happening, to them.

But then, imagination could not cope with what was going to

happen to Nathalie, and herself. They would be the very last survivors of the *Doncaster*, reserved for the most terrible fate of all. They would be paraded round the market place, naked, and they would be pointed at and jeered at by the onlookers, undergoing the greatest humiliation a woman could suffer, especially in this world of secluded sexuality, that of exposure. That their secret places, as Zobeir had put it, might be seen.

And then . . . but her brain simply dared not grasp the enormity of what would be done to Nathalie, and then to her. She dared not let it. That way indeed lay madness.

She awoke with a start, surprised at having slept. And certainly she had not slept for more than an hour. Yet the door of her cell was opening. She sat up, pushed herself against the wall. It could not be dawn already. It could not! She had prayed for this dawn never to come.

She stared at the white uniformed figure which stood there, gazing at her in the gloom. 'Lady,' Chardin said. 'It is time to leave this place.'

CHAPTER 14

Using her leg muscles only, her bound hands scraping the wall behind her as she slowly propelled herself to her feet, Vicky watched Chardin enter the cell, silhouetted against the light in the corridor. He wore his full uniform of white tunic and breeches, brown boots, and his desert burnous, and carried a knife in his hand. 'Turn round, lady,' he commanded.

Vicky hesitated, unable to believe he had really come to help her, muscles instinctively tensing against the possibility of some new assault. But she obeyed, because there was nothing else to do, and felt his fingers on her arm as he located the cords in the gloom, and then sliced through them. Her hands flopped to her sides, devoid of feeling for a moment, and then bringing a moan of pain from her lips as the blood started to flow, creating pins and needles in every finger and even in her palm.

'There are clothes for you outside,' Chardin said. 'You must make haste.'

He left her, to go next door, while she tried to control the wild spinning of her mind. Dared she move? Or was she not going to step into an even worse fate than that already promised? Should she not just curl up into a ball on the floor and pray that tomorrow would never come?

But tomorrow would come. And there could be no fate worse than impalement. Cautiously she walked across the cell, listening to a cooing sound from next door. Thank God for Nathalie. And Chardin. She knelt in the doorway, and recoiled; in the torchlight she made out the guard lying at her feet, the blood still seeping from his cut throat. Biting her lip, she picked up the various garments Chardin had left for her. There were

302

only three; a tunic to slip over her arms and shoulders and button in the front, then a piece of cloth which she could not understand for a moment, before recalling that it was one of the loin cloths worn by the eunuchs or the common household slaves – she passed it between her legs and then round her waist, and fastened the two ends together with a knot. There was also a haik in which to wrap herself and, best of all, a pair of soft kid boots. She sat down to drag them over her feet, and looked up at Nathalie, who was similarly dressed. With the tunics secured they could have been men, or at least boys – save for their hair, and the length of slender white legs revealed when the haiks moved.

'Come,' Chardin commanded, and held Nathalie's hand. Vicky scrambled to her feet, dragging her haik round her, and followed. Now was not the time for questions. Chardin was heavily armed, with a scimitar hanging at his side and a revolver holster on his right hip, while he carried a new repeating rifle in his hand, and slung over his shoulder was an obviously well-filled bandolier. She did not think he would allow them to be recaptured, even if he had to shoot them. She had to rely on that.

They made their way down more of the interminable corridors of this palace, as usual without seeing a soul, or, at this time of night, hearing a sound; their own footfalls were deadened by the soft leather of their boots. Finally they reached a postern gate. 'Wait here,' Chardin said. 'Do not move until I return for you.'

Vicky pressed herself against the wall as he opened the door and stepped through. 'Did you know he would help us?' she whispered to Nathalie.

'I 'oped 'e would,' Nathalie replied.

'I hadn't realised you and he . . . well, had become so attached to each other.'

Nathalie giggled. 'What else would you 'ave me do, these two weeks, while you 'ave been enjoying the Emir?'

'Enjoying him!' Vicky gave a shudder.

The door opened, and Chardin reappeared. 'Come,' he said. They stepped over another body, found themselves in an alleyway behind the palace. Vicky did not even look down this time. She seemed to have left, to be still leaving, a trail of death across West Africa. Because there was no sanctity of life here.

They hurried through the deserted streets of Timbuktu, chased only by the occasional yelp of an awakened dog, the grunt of a camel, the bray of an ass, and finally reached the river front. 'Where are we going?' Vicky asked. She had expected them to make for the desert.

'Away from here,' Chardin said simply. He pointed at the boat, a small vessel hardly larger than a canoe, waiting on the outside of a raft of larger craft all moored together. 'Be careful,' he told them and climbed across, kneeling in his boat to hold it steady. Vicky, cautiously crawling from boat to boat, followed closely by Nathalie, gasping and panting with anxiety, observed that there were already some bags in the bottom of their boat; this was no spur of the moment act of knight errantry.

'You go forward, lady,' Chardin commanded as she reached him.

Vicky obeyed, crouching in the bow. Nathalie took her position in the stern; Chardin released the painter and with a few deft strokes of his paddle moved them into midstream.

In front of them loomed the water gate, and a guard, leaning over the parapet to look down on them. 'Who is that?' he asked in Arabic.

'Captain Chardin of the Emir Zobeir ibn Rubayr's guard,' Chardin replied. 'I am on private business for the Emir.'

The guard raised a lantern, and Chardin allowed it to play on his face and uniform. Then the man nodded, and began winding the portcullis-like gate up from the water. He paid no attention to the two other people in the boat.

A moment later they were through, listening to the creaking of the portcullis as it dropped back into place. But already Chardin was driving them through the water at speed, with deft flicks of his paddle, which he used alternately on each side of the boat, giving little grunts as he did so.

'Where are we going?' Vicky asked again.

'Into the forest,' he replied. 'To Kumassi. Is that not where you wish to go, lady?'

'Kumassi? But . . . have you not heard the Ashanti are in revolt?'

'I have heard that they are at war,' he corrected her. 'We will not fight with the Ashanti.'

'Yes, but they may wish to fight with us. Should we not make for the desert? For Algiers?'

'Algiers is nearly two thousand miles to the north, lady. Besides, the Emir will follow us to the very gates of the city. He knows the desert better than I. But I know the forest and the rivers better than he. I know the Ashanti, and they know me. I have been to their kraals before, in peace. They will welcome me. They will not harm us. Their quarrel is with the British. But we are not British.'

There was unanswerable logic. And she had had enough of the desert, anyway. But the forest, and the Ashanti . . .

But wasn't that where she wanted to go? she wondered. Where she *had* to go, now. The news of the revolt had been overtaken last night by such a dreadful threat to herself that she had not properly assimilated it. Now that her personal safety seemed more secure, the thought of what might have happened to the others was banging inside her brain. Zobeir had let David lead the women into a trap. They could all be dead. David . . .

But they could also be in captivity. Most of them. If the Ashanti had only wanted one woman's head . . . that was a sufficiently dreadful thought, but it offered the hope that the others might have survived. To be rescued by her? Could she possibly persuade Chardin to risk his life again, for people he did not know and probably did not like? She had to believe that, too, might be possible.

Her head drooped with exhaustion. Perhaps she had not known how tired she was. The mental strain had wearied her, though for the past fortnight she had been physically rested. But the strain had been there, and yesterday . . . she still felt a sense of shock when she recalled Zobeir's anger. She had never seen a man that angry before, had never actually encountered anyone with whom she had not been able to cope, been in a position where there had been nothing she could do to avert catastrophe. Even when the gigantic waves had rolled her up the beach, she had never doubted her ability to survive. Last night had been the most shattering experience of her life. And even now she was no longer in command of her destiny. Chardin had assumed that responsibility, and she found that a most comforting thought. She dozed.

And awoke with the first light. In the darkness there had been only the river. Now she looked at trees and bushes, not thick as yet, but forming an avenue on either side of the river. She attempted to move, her muscles being painfully cramped, and the boat rocked dangerously. She looked over her shoulder, gazed at Chardin, who continued to paddle with unceasing energy. Sweat dribbled down his cheeks and soaked his white uniform, but his movements never changed, as the paddle was switched from side to side. It was an economic movement. He did not drive the blade into the water with any great force, just a quick stab and then out. More to steer and give them way through the water than to cover the bottom, because, as she realised, the current was doing that for them.

'You must be exhausted,' she said. 'Can I not do that while you rest?'

'Later,' he said briefly. 'We cannot delay. The Emir will have found that you are missing, by now.'

She gave a little shiver, and watched the morning mist begin to dissipate as the sun rose. 'I have not expressed my gratitude to you for saving my life. You are risking your own. If you are taken . . .'

His smile was grim. 'We would mount the stake together, lady. But we will not be taken, alive. So you see, I have not yet saved your life.'

'I am still grateful, and will remain so.'

'I could not let my woman be exposed, and then impaled,' Chardin said. 'It is not a worthy fate for a woman, even had she committed a crime.'

'And I?'

'You are my woman's lady,' Chardin said.

Vicky looked past him to the stern, where Nathalie still slept, snoring faintly. She was totally relaxed. And why should she not be? She was with her man.

'Will Zobeir send after us?' she asked. As if she did not know the answer.

Chardin nodded.

'Do you think we will get away?'

'As Allah wills it, lady,' He nodded at the bags in the bottom of the boat. 'Eat.'

She reckoned he wanted her to shut up. That was fair enough; she had only been asking stupid questions from fear. She found that the bag contained dates. The food of the travelling desert man. Here helping them on their way into the forest.

She ate, and tried to think, but was still too tired, and too reluctant, to consider the future, too frightened to remember the past. She wanted to follow Nathalie's example and leave the thinking to Chardin, for a while. She needed that.

She dozed again, and awoke with a start as Chardin suddenly altered his stroke, concentrating on the right side of the boat to turn it from midstream into the left-hand bank.

'Quickly,' he said. 'You must get ashore.'

Vicky obeyed without question, stepping over the bow as it nosed against the earth.

'What is 'appening?' Nathalie demanded, also awakening with a start.

'No noise,' Chardin said, and took her hand to assist her to the land as well. He handed Vicky the bag of dates and his rifle, then stooped, and with a succession of heaves of his powerful shoulders dragged the boat from the water. 'Help me,' he said.

They assisted him to drag the boat into the bushes. 'Stay here,' he commanded, and went back to the bank, scuffing the earth with his boots to cover all trace of the boat's keel. Then he rejoined them. 'Down,' he said.

Vicky lay on the earth beside the boat, peering through the bushes. Now she heard sound, but coming from further down the river, instead of from up-river, behind them, as she would have expected. She listened to men singing, or rather, chanting.

'No one must move,' Chardin commanded.

She held her breath, and watched a large boat coming round the bend in the river, perhaps a quarter of a mile away. The boat was not less than fifty feet long, and was crammed with people, apart from the men who paddled along either side. They were the ones chanting, and were naked. The men amidships and in the stern wore the robes of prosperous Arabs, and the forward section was packed with bales and boxes.

'You heard them?' she whispered. 'So far away?'

'My ears are trained to listen, lady,' he said.

The boat drew level, and went on its way. No one even looked at the bank where they lay.

'We will rest here, for a few hours,' Chardin said.

'But . . . Zobeir's men . . .'

'Will encounter that boat, and learn that they have not seen us. They will then suppose we have gone ashore before here. It will at any rate delay them, lady, while they consider the situation, and it is necessary to rest.' He ate two dates, took a drink of water from the river, lay down, closed his eyes, and appeared to be asleep within seconds.

''E is a great man,' Nathalie commented, and lay down beside him, apparently content to accept his judgement in everything.

And should she not also accept his judgement? Vicky scratched her head. It was a strange feeling, since this trek had begun, not only to be no longer making the decisions, but even to be the outsider. She walked down to the river, took off her haik and boots and tunic, and stepped into the water, kneeling in the shallows to feel it flowing past her and round her and under her. She even soaked her hair. This was a far cry from the perfumed loofahs of the slave girls in Zobeir's palace, but it was so much cleaner and fresher . . . and besides, she wanted to wash all memory of Zobeir's palace out of her system, just as rapidly as possible.

She bathed for nearly half an hour, then ate two more dates, and sat with her back against a tree, turned away from Chardin and Nathalie, while she let her skin dry in the sunlight filtering through the trees. She did not want to look at them, because it made her feel so lonely. For the past five weeks she had never been lonely, even though on occasions she might not have appreciated her company. And for three weeks she had supposed she would never be lonely again. Even now, the possibility of David's death had not properly sunk into her consciousness. As she did not know for sure whether he was dead or not, it was obvious to hope, to believe, that he had somehow survived. But how could he have survived? He would have died to save the women, if he could.

She sat up at the sound of paddles! She looked at Chardin, but he had heard it too, even while apparently asleep. Now he moved like a huge cat, quickly but silently, to kneel in the bushes by the river bank. Vicky dragged on her tunic and crouched beside him, watching the boat coming downstream. She caught her breath as she saw the white uniforms and the robes, the sun glinting from the swords and rifle barrels. Their pursuers. But there were only six of them – although even that was six too many.

Chardin smiled. 'As I thought,' he said. 'They have divided their force, because of what the traders told them. We will have no trouble, now.'

Vicky watched the men go by. They were concentrating on the river itself, not the banks. 'But they will be downstream of us,' she said.

'They are Arabs,' Chardin pointed out, simply. 'They will rest, when the sun becomes hot.'

'There are six of them.'

He looked at her. 'Are you not the great lady who slew four men?'

Vicky opened her mouth and then closed it again.

'Arabs . . . pouf,' Chardin remarked, expressively.

'I was also very angry at the time.'

'And are you not angry now? Those men would have impaled you, lady. They would do so yet, could they but catch you. You should hate them.'

They were his erstwhile comrades. 'Do you hate the Arabs, Chardin?'

'My people hate the Arabs.'

'I thought the Sudanese supported the Mahdi?'

'I am not Sudanese, lady. It pleased my *master* so to describe me. I am from Ethiopia – that country which your people call Abyssinia. I was with an Ethiopian force which was defeated by Zobeir. I was taken prisoner, but because I had fought well and I showed him that I was not afraid to die, he made me a captain in his guard. He came to trust me.' The statement was simple, yet it was redolent of contempt. And Chardin clearly found nothing deceitful in the way he had nursed his hatred, probably for several years – rather would it have been unnatural for him not to do so.

'But you served him faithfully, until last night.'

'I served the Emir, because I had nowhere else to go, and nothing to do with my life,' Chardin said. 'As a defeated soldier I would not be welcome with my own people. But now . . .' He looked over his shoulder at the still sleeping Nathalie, pillowed on her hair. 'I have found something that I wish to do.'

'Do you love her?' Vicky asked.

'She is my woman. I have never had a woman, before. The Emir sent women to me, once a week, to serve the demands of my flesh. But they were his women, not mine. Nathalie is mine. I will take her with me, wherever Fate leads me. Now, lady, will you help me to destroy those six men? It is necessary, for our survival.'

How many times during the past five weeks had she thought that! But of course he was right. 'I will help you, Chardin,' she promised.

With Chardin in command, the business was made quite frighteningly simple. They waited another half-hour, then relaunched the boat. 'Now, lady,' he said. 'You may paddle if you wish.'

Vicky readily took off her haik and knelt amidships. Nathalie was in the stern as before, highly nervous and excited, as she gathered what they were about to do. Chardin knelt in the bows, carrying his rifle; the revolver he gave to Vicky. 'But it should not be necessary,' he said. 'Now, remember, just keep the boat in midstream, and leave the rest to the current.'

She obeyed, and for the next few minutes they went round and round in a circle. Chardin waited patiently, and Vicky slowly got the hang of it, and could keep the bow pointing down river, although equally soon her shoulders began to ache from the constant changing from side to side, while, with the sun now directly overhead and no longer shaded by the trees, she poured sweat. But the boat slipped quietly through the water, as she gazed at Chardin's sweat-soaked back, where he knelt in front of her, the rifle across his thighs. They had travelled for just an hour when he said, 'Stop now,' just before they came to a bend.

He had calculated the time lapse to perfection. As she ceased using the paddle they drifted round the corner, and saw the pursuit boat anchored just off the bank. A cloth awning had been erected to keep off the heat of the sun, and one man sat in the stern, gazing idly to and fro while his comrades rested. He saw them at the same moment they saw him, and gave a shout, but Chardin had already levelled his rifle and opened fire, with a startling accuracy pumping three shots into the hull of the boat itself, then raising the sight and sending two more into the man, who was only then raising his own weapon. The Arab fell overboard with a scream, too badly hurt to do more than drift away, slowly drowning, while the boat itself immediately began to fill, and then to capsize as the other five men woke up and reached for their weapons, shouting in alarm as they did so.

Without any hesitation Chardin ejected the last of his spent cartridges and fitted a new clip of five into his magazine, then opened fire again, now aiming at the men floundering in the water. Vicky gasped and Nathalie gave a low moan of horror as the bullets slashed into the living flesh and the river discoloured with blood. Three of the men were hit and left to drown. The other two managed to reach the bank, but Chardin had fitted a third clip to his rifle and brought them down as they floundered through the shallows. The whole episode was over in under three minutes, and then the only sound was the continuing echo of the rifle fusillade; it had been the most perfect job of execution Vicky could have imagined possible. She didn't

311

know what to do, what to think, as she watched the men's struggles grow weaker, before they slowly disappeared beneath the surface . . . and then remembered, as Chardin had suggested she do, that these were the men who would have impaled her. Then she thought the only pity was that Zobeir had not been amongst them.

'Now, lady,' Chardin said, 'we will change places, and I will resume paddling.' He smiled at her as he held her arm to assist her past him into the bow. 'As I said earlier, now we will escape. At least from the Emir.'

Vicky still had no doubt that Zobeir would count as the most dangerous of their problems, especially if Chardin *could* reach some agreement with his fellow blacks in the forest. But she soon revised her opinion, because of course first they had to survive the forest itself. The next day the stream they followed debouched into the Niger, and they gazed in awe at the huge brown waterway, drifting inexorably towards the sea. Now the trees were thicker, and they even saw game, a herd of antelope, one of which Chardin brought down with his superb marksmanship, and then butchered for them so that they had succulent steaks for dinner, roasted on the fire he constructed and lit with equal expertise. 'Oh, if only we'd had you with us from the beginning,' Vicky told him, to his obvious pleasure.

'Oh, yes,' Nathalie said. 'That would have been ver' good.'

The most remarkable, and enjoyable thing about him, Vicky thought, was the way he treated Nathalie almost as a mother might treat her babe. Even his somewhat grim features became instantly gentle when he regarded the French girl, while as for the sensuous manner in which he took her in his arms when they rested . . . Nathalie's reactions were no less heart-warming, as she seemed to bask in his affection. If he had at last found a woman of his own, there could be no doubt that she felt she had at last found a man. The pair of them made Vicky feel distinctly like the fifth wheel to a coach, and this was a situation totally strange to her. She had never doubted her own beauty and, however low down on the social or masculine scale a missionary might have been regarded, the stalwarts of

Zanzibar and Nairobi, white, black or brown, had never failed to cast a second glance at James Lang's wife. As had William Dobree, David, and Zobeir himself, whatever the feminine pulchritude with which she had been surrounded. Yet apparently she meant nothing at all to Chardin, compared with Nathalie. Although he continued to treat her with the utmost respect, she knew it was because, in his eyes, she remained Nathalie's 'lady' – if he undoubtedly knew that she wasn't actually Lady Dobree, he had not yet got her true station right in his mind. Well, she reflected, she had to be lucky; she did not see herself being able to resist the big black man should he ever decide to establish a harem of his own. She knew now that he was a far tougher proposition than even Zobeir, in that where Zobeir planned and schemed and fumed when things went wrong, Chardin merely acted, with a deadly intensity. While she also knew that there was a mood of almost nihilistic despair lurking on the edges of her consciousness: the fear that David might be dead, the very real feeling of emptiness that thought induced, was tinted with the realisation that once again there stretched before her a lifetime of nothing. No, resisting would not be easy, just at that moment.

Now that the trees gave them shelter from the sun, they abandoned the desert techniques, and resumed a more normal life, resting at night and travelling during the day. They slept in the boat anchored off the bank to keep them safe from snakes and reasonably free of insects, awoke cramped but rested, bathed off the boat as well, and ate the food Chardin was so adept at procuring for them – for in one of his bags he had fishing line and hooks, and the river teemed with life.

On the second day after their encounter with the Arabs, it rained. The sky became obliterated by huge black clouds, almost without warning; there were vivid flashes of lightning and tremendous peals of thunder almost overhead, and then the sky seemed to open and an ocean of water poured down on them. In a matter of seconds they were soaked to the skin, and the boat began to fill, so that Vicky and Nathalie had to use their cupped hands to bail it out, while the surface of the river was pitted as the drops bit into it. The rain lasted only about an hour, but it was a portent of what lay ahead, when Chardin pointed and said, 'The forest.'

Now the trees clustered close to each other, and reached upwards to heights they had not previously seen in their search for light; the bushes formed an almost impenetrable thicket, and liana vines trailed from the branches above their heads. Now there was on a sudden more life than Vicky would have thought possible. Monkeys swung through the trees and hyenas screamed at each other; baboons chattered to huge crocodiles gazing sleepily at them from the banks or peering at them as they drifted by, motionless as logs; there were sudden flurries of activity just below the surface as a shoal of fish closed on some morsel of food, while often in the background there would be loud roaring noises. 'Lion?' Vicky asked. She had heard lions in Kenya, and this sound was at least as loud, if of a slightly different timbre.

'Gorillas,' Chardin replied.

'Ooh, là la,' Nathalie said. 'They will kill us all.'

'They will not harm you,' Chardin said, with total certainty. Obviously nothing was going to harm them, as long as he had care of them. If *only* he had been with them from the moment of the shipwreck, Vicky thought.

Now it rained twice a day, at dawn and dusk, and the nights were loud with the croaking of the bullfrogs. To either side the forest steamed, and rotting branches snapped with the sound of rifle shots. Next morning Chardin varied their diet by bringing down two monkeys for their breakfast. Vicky could hardly bring herself to eat, so like babies did the skinned creatures appear as they cooked, but the meat itself was tender, if with a faintly sweetish taste.

''Ow much further?' Nathalie asked.

'Tomorrow we leave the boat,' he replied.

'We 'ave arrived? Oh, I am so 'appy,' she cried, and clapped her hands.

'No, no,' Chardin explained. 'The river does not go near Kumassi. We must walk across country. And now that the wet

314

season has started the way will be difficult. But this is where you wish to go, is it not?' He looked at Vicky.

'Well . . . I guess it has to be. Would the others have left their boats here?'

'They would have left the boat somewhere in this vicinity,' he agreed. 'Here is where the river is at its closest to Kumassi.' He pointed to the south-west. 'Over there is the land of the Ashanti.'

Vicky shivered.

The following morning they pulled in to the bank and dragged the boat ashore, carefully concealing it beneath some bushes. Vicky wondered why, wondered if Chardin meant to return, and realised with some surprise that he had not attempted to discuss the future with her, to ascertain what would be his reward for taking her to safety. No doubt he had talked about it with Nathalie. Or was he acting entirely on trust?

Or did he really mean what he had told her, to go wherever Fate took him – trailing Nathalie behind him? But was there anywhere in Africa that he could count himself safe from Zobeir's vengeance?

Well, she certainly intended to see that he was rewarded just as handsomely as she could manage, when they got to Kumassi.

If they got to Kumassi. They walked into a steady downpour. There was not an inch of their bodies which was not soaked, and their clothes were only of value to stop their flesh being torn by the bushes. And she had imagined the desert the most arduous part of their journey!

Chardin went first, using his scimitar as a machete to hack a path through the vines and bushes which reared in front of them like walls. Nathalie came next, and Vicky brought up the rear; she was the junior partner, and began to understand something of how Alison must have felt when they had fallen into the hands of the Arabs. The ground was soft from the rain, and became softer with every downpour; often they sank to their ankles and knees and had painfully to drag themselves

315

out. They clambered across fallen tree trunks and dislodged ants and spiders and the occasional snake, but Chardin had invariably dispersed or disposed of these before the women got to them. Low branches reached out to tear at their haiks, bushes caught at their feet. When it did finally stop raining, the forest as usual steamed, but now they were steaming with it. Vicky soon took the haik from her head, and let her hair hang in sodden rats' tails down her back, while the once white tunic was stained with brown and green, and already torn in several places. She thanked God for the boots, which at least protected her feet, but nothing could stop the swarms of insects from attacking her exposed legs and arms. These were bad, but could be slapped away. Far more unpleasant were the bush ticks which sought lodgements wherever possible; their preference was for damp crevices in the human body. Within twenty-four hours it seemed the most natural thing in the world to bend this way and that while Chardin thrust his fingers into her hair, or examined the soft flesh behind her knees or where her buttocks joined her thighs, to extract the horrible creatures, touching them, and therefore her, with a glowing piece of wood taken from the fire, in order to make them relax their grip – if merely pulled from the flesh their legs would break off and remain embedded, to cause festering sores. Having removed the tick, he would then squash it between his thumb nails, while blood – her blood – spurted.

' 'Ow much further?' Nathalie as usual wanted to know, having undergone a similar experience as they camped on the third night, listening to the patter of a steady drizzle which threatened to extinguish their fire.

'Several days yet,' he told her.

'Ooh, là la,' she commented. 'We will drown first.'

Certainly it was often difficult to decide where the forest ended and swamp began. Often they were trudging waist deep and once the water came up to their shoulders, forcing Chardin to carry the rifle above his head while Vicky bore the revolver similarly aloft. Walking through swamp was a hundred times more unpleasant than walking through the forest, because it was impossible to tell what lay beneath the surface. There was the usual accumulation of rotting tree trunks, and when one moved beneath the feet it was difficult not to imagine it was a crocodile or a snake. They saw sufficient of these, but were not attacked. 'The creatures of the forest', Chardin said wisely, 'do not make war, wantonly. Their powers are reserved only for obtaining food and for self-defence. Only man is wantonly vicious.'

Vicky was quite prepared to concede that point, but she was so glad she had him with her. It was quite impossible to imagine Alison and Mary and Elizabeth, much less the three older women, coping with these conditions.

But there were other things even more difficult to imagine, for three mornings later they heard drums. Chardin held up his hand and, without a word, both Vicky and Nathalie sank to their knees, regardless of the fact that they immediately sank into the soft earth up to their thighs. Vicky had never been so exhausted in her life. The desert had been brutal to her feet and, because of the heat and the thirst, terrible. Here the heat was no less intense, but at least they were not thirsty, or hungry, either, thanks to Chardin's skill, and his knowledge of which fruits they could eat and which were poisonous. However, the labour of dragging each foot out of a glutinous mess and placing it in front of the other, step after step after step, made her feel she had red-hot pincers running through her thigh and calf muscles.

Chardin stood above them. 'Come,' he commanded.

Vicky dragged herself up; he had to lift Nathalie.

'Can you understand what they are saying?' Vicky asked.

'It is a call to arms,' he told her. 'A call to battle. The Ashanti are being assembled from all over their land to fight the British. This time of year is the best for them, because of the rain. The British, those not born to the forest, cannot survive here, in the wet season.'

Vicky nodded. There was no point in reminding him that neither she nor Nathalie had been born in the forest. 'Will we get past them?' she asked.

'No,' he said simply.

Her head jerked.

'They will soon know we are here,' he said. 'We will have to go through them. We will do it.'

They continued on their way, resting at midday, as usual, for an hour, and then staggering onwards until, about an hour before dusk, Chardin held up his hand again. He did not turn his head, but spoke quietly. 'Now lady, I must ask you to obey me in all things. I am Chardin. I am known in these parts, at least by name. You and Nathalie are my slaves. Is this understood?'

'Yes,' Vicky said. 'Yes. Does that mean . . .?'

'Do not speak,' Chardin commanded.

Vicky stood very still, glancing from left to right without actually turning her head, and saw men.

She caught her breath, and Nathalie instinctively stepped back to hold her hand. 'Ooh, là là,' she whispered.

They were entirely surrounded by the men, who carried bows and arrows and spears, all made of wood, but with sharpened and fire-hardened tips to the missiles. The men were tall and well built, although somewhat thin, naked except for fringes of grass or hair at knee and shoulder, and a grass belt round their waists from which hung either a knife or a very serviceable-looking wooden club. Their faces were painted with streaks of white, and their naturally frizzy hair was dressed in ringlets. Their expressions, aided by the paint, were entirely hostile.

But Chardin was addressing them, his voice resonant. If he was apprehensive, and it was impossible to believe that he was not apprehensive, he gave no sign of it. But as we are only slaves, Vicky thought, there is nothing wrong in our showing fear. She had, in fact, never been so terrified in her life; these men looked far more dangerous than the Kikuyu in Kenya, and the thought of being manhandled by them was more repellent than even Zobeir and his people.

One of the men now replied to Chardin, and she could almost

sense an air of relaxation amongst the other warriors. Chardin turned to them. 'Kneel,' he said in French. 'Kneel.'

Vicky and Nathalie hastily dropped to their knees, gazing at the man who approached. He was obviously some kind of a chieftain, because he wore a necklace, of bones. Human bones, Vicky was positive, trying to suppress a shudder.

She knew she must look a sight. She hadn't bathed since leaving the river, however often she had been soaked with rain, and her face was streaked with dirt, while her hair was stiff with grease and sweat. But she obviously fascinated the man, for he stood immediately in front of her, stretched out his hand, and thrust it into her hair, raising the strands and allowing them to trail through his fingers. As with when Zobeir had touched her, it required an immense effort to keep still, especially when he took her chin in his hand and tilted her head this way and that. She supposed he might be intending to continue his examination lower, and did not know if she was going to be able to stand that, but Chardin made a remark and the hand fell away. The two men exchanged some further words, then the chieftain addressed his men, and they formed a kind of guard of honour to either side – or were they actually preventing any attempt at escape, Vicky wondered? – before leading them into the forest.

'They are taking us to their king,' Chardin told her.

'Oh,' she said. 'I thought *he* was their king.'

'No,' Chardin said. 'He is but a petty chieftain. But one with much ambition. He wishes to buy you from me.'

Vicky's head jerked, and she stopped walking. She could think of no good reason why Chardin should not trade her, if it meant he could more certainly preserve the lives of Nathalie and himself.

He observed her concern, and allowed himself one of his grim smiles. 'It is your hair which attracts him. He has never seen hair like yours.'

'But . . .' Her heart gave such a sudden leap it was almost painful. Alison's hair was yellow, and hers was tinted with red, but no one, having seen Alison, would say that he had never seen hair like hers before. That meant that David must have got through.

Or had he, and all the women, perished before even reaching the land of the Ashanti?

'I have told him you are not for sale, lady,' Chardin said. 'But there may be other offers. From the king himself. We must consider these matters.'

Vicky said nothing, and resumed walking. She seemed to be leaping out of a succession of frying pans into a succession of fires. Would Chardin also refuse the king? Would he be able to?

But if David and Alison and Mary and Elizabeth *had* survived . . . oh, if only she could believe that. She had to believe it. And thus she had to believe also that she couldn't possibly fall by the wayside, now.

The Ashanti were apparently not concerned by light or dark, and weary as the fugitives were, they were forced to keep walking until well into the night, when they heard the sounds of a large number of people, and inhaled the odours, too, of humanity and cooking meat. Soon they caught sight of a huge fire, around which were built the huts of the kraal.

'This is their main village,' Chardin explained, 'where the king – his name is Kuno – is assembling his people.'

'Is there news of what is happening?' Vicky asked.

'There has been fighting, with a British column which has been forced to retreat,' he told her, 'and the Ashanti plan to invade Kumassi itself.'

'Oh, my God!' she said.

'We can still reach there, if we can escape these people soon enough,' he said. 'The town is not yet fully surrounded, partly because the British keep launching probes to keep their communication with the coast open, and partly because Kuno has not as yet completed his mobilisation. I have said, the Ashanti do not regard time as important, because of the rains. The rains have just started, but now will grow steadily worse, right up to November, and they know that the British cannot manoeuvre in the rain. The situation will therefore steadily improve from the Ashanti point of view, and as long as

Kumassi falls by the next dry season, which is more than six months away, Kuno is sure his revolt will succeed, and his people will have regained their independence.'

Vicky licked her lips. 'Is there . . . is there news of my people?' she asked.

'This man has not spoken of them, and I have considered it unwise to ask him,' Chardin said. 'Now look to yourself, lady. Cover your head. We are to go before the king.'

Nathalie squeezed her hand, as they draped their tattered haiks over their heads and across their faces. ''E will protect us,' she promised.

Vicky did not doubt he would, to the limit of his ability. But he was one man, and suddenly they were in the midst of several hundred people, of whom a good half were warriors very like those surrounding them, only many of these men carried rifles – mostly old single-shot pieces but obviously serviceable enough – as well as spears. These men, and their women and children, looked scarcely less demoniac in the flickering light of the fire; nor were they less disturbing in the manner they clustered around the three strangers, allowed by the men surrounding them to come right up close, to finger their arms and hair and clothes, and chatter at them in an unintelligible tongue – but perhaps being unable to understand what was being said was a blessing.

'I think they are cannibals,' Nathalie whispered fearfully. 'They 'ave bones. I am so 'appy Chardin is with us.'

It was true that nearly all the ornaments worn by both men and women seemed to be made of bone and, while Vicky was no anatomist, she suspected a large proportion of them were indeed human.

'They are only cannibal when it is required of their religion,' Chardin told them, no doubt meaning to be reassuring. 'But their religion involves much human sacrifice. They have a scant regard for human life.'

Chardin said so! A scant regard for human life, Vicky thought, her knees touching – and he belonged to a society which she, or any European, would have supposed had an even more scant regard for human life.

Yet not even her fear could entirely subdue her interest in her surroundings, in the kraal itself – the huts, so neatly made of mud and untreated timber, yet so clearly sturdy, despite the fact that they were subjected to the daily downpours; the domestic animals, the cattle and hens no less than the dogs, which clustered around; and most of all the people, who, she was realising, were very far from as hostile as they had first appeared. Indeed, they seemed to be inordinately happy, laughing and shouting with good-natured enthusiasm.

But there was nothing good about the group of men towards whom they were being led. These scowled at the approaching strangers, and in their centre the short, squat, black man, who sat on a wooden stool beneath an elaborate, eight-panelled umbrella held above him by one of his people, looked grimmest of all. He leaned forward, his left elbow on his knee, his chin on the hand, to stare at them as they came closer. He carried an elaborately fashioned fly whisk in his right hand, which he flicked impatiently, and wore a white robe, embroidered in various designs, in what Vicky was sure was gold thread, as well as a curious dome-shaped cloth cap, covered with equally elaborate embroidery, which reminded her of pictures she had seen of the ancient Persians. A long dagger was thrust through his waistband, and at his side there lay on the ground a most remarkable sword, which grew from a small but exquisitely fashioned haft into a blade almost as wide as an axehead. She would have sworn that both the weapons were also made of gold, and thus had to be purely ornamental, but indicative of enormous wealth, even if, clearly, little was shared with his subjects.

Zobeir had spoken of a Golden Stool. She had actually not taken the concept very seriously – but could it possibly exist?

The king spoke, in a guttural tone.

Chardin answered quietly enough, but invested his voice with a ring of authority. Indeed, he even managed to impart some suggestion of criticism, and King Kuno, for Vicky guessed that this had to be the famous man, did not look very pleased. He spoke again, and then stood up, and the warriors to either side gave a rustle as they came to attention.

Kuno moved forward, up to Chardin, and past him, to gaze at the two shrouded figures. Then he spoke again, and Chardin replied even more brusquely than before. The King hesitated, then spoke in a quieter tone. Chardin also lowered his voice, and the two men spoke quite softly for a few minutes. Chardin was obviously explaining who they were, for Vicky heard the words 'Nathalie' and 'Victoria' more than once. To her consternation, the King, having repeated the name 'Victoria', again turned to stare at her. Once again his tone became brusque, indeed demanding. This time Chardin hesitated, then turned to Vicky, while her heart pounded and her knees banged together. 'The King wishes to look on you,' Chardin said, and himself took the haik from her head.

The King certainly wished to look at her. He came closer, peered at her, and then, as his general had done, touched her hair, speaking as he did so, addressing Chardin, but also, she felt, herself, even if she could not understand what he was saying. But she certainly felt the nearness of him, almost as if he were a black cloud threatening to overwhelm her.

Chardin was shaking his head, and replying. The King made a more imperative demand, and again Vicky caught her name. But Chardin continued to refuse.

The King commenced to scowl.

'I think 'e wants you,' Nathalie whispered, unhelpfully.

Vicky could only watch Chardin, who seemed to be getting the better of the argument, at least for the moment. Oh, thank God for Chardin!

The King glared at him, then at her, then turned and stamped away, shouting orders as he did so.

'Oh, Lord!' Vicky muttered. Were they about to be murdered, for defying him?

But while the warriors moved restlessly around them, and thudded their rifle and spear butts on the earth, Chardin stood his ground as confidently as ever, and after a moment two of the men standing around the stool hurried off into the large hut immediately behind the King, to return a moment later, bearing two spears. Vicky gave a gasp of horror, and Nathalie clutched her arm, because each spear was surmounted by a human head. One was already a naked skull, having been scraped free of flesh and hair, and treated in some fashion, Vicky thought, as it had a somewhat glazed appearance. The other had not been preserved, and was a rotting, decomposing mass of horror – but even so Vicky could recognise that it had once been Harry Bream.

Nathalie dropped to her knees and retched, and Vicky instinctively knelt also to put her arms round the French girl's shoulders. Because if one of the heads was Bream's, then the other . . .

Kuno was bellowing and almost thumping his chest like a gorilla, clearly telling Chardin, who must have cast some doubts upon his power, that with such fetishes he could not be defeated, while his warriors supported him with great shouts. And Chardin certainly revealed great interest, walking forward to examine the skulls, while Vicky and Nathalie continued to cling to each other, discovering that they were being surrounded by women. 'Chardin!' Vicky gasped.

He turned, looked at them, and spoke with the King, who grunted a reply, once again staring at Victoria.

Chardin came back to them. 'These women will take you to a house,' he said, 'where we will spend the night. Do not be afraid. They will not harm you, and I will come as soon as I can.'

Vicky hesitated, then allowed Nathalie and herself to be led away into a hut, where as many women and children as possible pressed into the doorway to watch them. The women who took them inside were in authority, however; young, wearing only aprons, with splendid figures and imperious carriage – she supposed they were either the King's wives or his daughters. These girls produced a pot of some kind of stew for them to eat, and a bowl of liquid to drink. Vicky certainly could not eat anything after what she had just seen, but she was terribly thirsty, and gulped at the liquid, to discover that it was not water, nor anything she had ever tasted before, but a fermentation of some sort which made her quite dizzy.

There was no furniture, and the pair of them sat on the floor, joined by three of the girls, while the spectators continued to cluster in the doorway.

'Are they going to eat us?' Nathalie whispered.

Vicky did not reply. The beer she had just drunk was making her head spin, and her stomach was spinning anyway. Huge leaps of relief that somehow David and Alison and the girls had managed to avoid these people were confounded with great surges of horror at what had happened to Bream and Prudence. They had scarcely given the pair a thought since their departure, so sure had they been that they would be delivered to the very gates of Kumassi, as Zobeir had promised. But Zobeir had instead sent them straight to the Ashanti, to start the war he wanted. Prudence and Bream had never had a chance. They, far more than the others, had been despatched to a dreadful death. And Prudence would have accepted it, accepted all the horror and humiliation that must have preceded her execution, with that massive calm of hers, that almost peaceful determination to do her duty and die like a lady when the time came.

Prudence had been her only real friend, throughout the voyage and the walk.

The women kept pushing the pot of stew at her, and at last she took a morsel, fighting back the urge to spit it out. Indeed, she was as hungry as she had been thirsty, and the stew was very tasty – she did not dare allow herself to consider what might be its ingredients. But what a relief it was to see Chardin's figure bending to enter the doorway, from which the onlookers had hastily withdrawn.

The three girls also filed out, at his command. He sat between Nathalie and Vicky, drank some of the beer, sighed, and ate some stew. 'It is bad,' he said in English.

They waited.

'This Kuno wishes to obtain possession of you, lady,' Chardin explained, looking at Vicky. 'I believe it must be for his harem.'

Vicky frowned. There could hardly be a more unpleasant

fate for her than that . . . and yet she was sure Chardin was not telling her the truth. But why should he lie about something as unthinkable?

'I have refused him,' Chardin went on. 'I have told him that I am on a mission from Lord Zobeir, to deliver you two white slave women to the King of the Fulani, and that we became lost in the forest. I have asked him to provide us with an escort that we may continue on our way, and I have told him further that should he fail to help us, or attempt to seize you, lady, he will arouse the wrath of both the Fulani and Lord Zobeir. This has made him hesitate, as he can hardly risk war with the Fulani while he is fighting the British, and in addition he knows and fears the wrath of Zobeir. He has therefore let the matter rest for tonight, while he considers the situation. But I am afraid that his wish to possess you may overcome his common sense by morning. It is the hair, lady. No one here has ever seen hair like yours. He thinks it is made of gold. Real gold, I mean. And he is very greedy for gold, as you will have observed.'

Vicky gazed at him.

'We cannot let 'im do this,' Nathalie said.

'You must kill me first,' Vicky said.

Chardin shook his head. 'I will not do that, lady. I have sworn to take you, take you both, to the safety of your own people. Besides, it will not be necessary if we can delay his decision – and this can be done. If he does not, or cannot, take you to his bed tomorrow, then we are safe for several days. He is in haste, because the day after he must leave to join his armies near Kumassi. He dreams of gaining a great victory there, because of the fetish he now possesses. It is even possible that he sees you also as some kind of fetish, because of your hair and your name. Your name was important to him.'

Vicky drank some more beer. She knew, instinctively, that Chardin had just told her something of great importance, but she couldn't decide what it was. Nor did she want to. She felt that to get as drunk as possible as rapidly as possible was the only way to prevent herself from going mad.

'My first idea', Chardin went on, 'was to explain to him that you are not a virgin. But this does not seem to be important to

326

him. Thus there is only one thing left to do, one way in which he can be prevented from taking you to his bed. When did you last pass blood?'

Vicky opened her mouth and then closed it again. There was certainly nothing inappropriate in the question, even when asked by Chardin, after everything that had happened. 'A week before we left Timbuktu,' she said.

'That is two weeks ago. That is a pity. Then we must pretend. A woman is regarded as taboo during that period when she is unclean. The taboo lasts for ten days. Not even a king will break taboo.'

'Pretend?' Nathalie asked. ''Ow can we pretend?'

'I will do it, if lady will permit me.'

'You?'

'Take off your cloth, lady. Do not remove it altogether, but release it so that you sit on it.'

Vicky obeyed him; there was nothing else to do. Besides, she felt she was in the hands of a doctor.

'Now spread your legs,' he said, and drew his knife. She gave a gasp of apprehension, having no idea what he intended. Chardin reached to the very top of her thigh and slit the flesh on the inside with a single sweep of the razor-sharp blade. She felt no pain for a moment, but blood immediately oozed from the cut.

'Haste now,' he said. 'Retie the cloth again.'

Vicky obeyed.

'Now lie down and sleep,' Chardin commanded. 'And tomorrow, after he has seen you, be sure to tear the scab off the wound so that it will bleed again.'

'You want me to do that for *ten days?*'

He shook his head. 'That will not be necessary. Tomorrow will be sufficient. The king knows that you are exhausted and weakened by our walk, and therefore will not have a normal flow. But the mere fact of your having passed blood at all will place you in taboo for ten days, and that is all we need.'

'But . . . suppose he has me examined, and discovers the subterfuge?'

Chardin gave one of his grim smiles. 'Then we will all die.

327

But there is no reason for him to do this.' Then he did something he had never done before: he reached out and squeezed her hand. 'Courage, lady. Did I not tell you? We are to accompany the army. He knows I am a skilled general, and intends that I should advise him on the best way to attack the fortress at Kumassi. Tomorrow, we march towards the British.'

CHAPTER 15

Vicky awoke to a great deal of noise surrounding the hut. Just as in Zobeir's cell, she was surprised she had slept at all, but the combination of being warm and dry after the damp eternity of the forest and the effects of the beer she had drunk, proved too much for her exhausted body, and even the earth floor of the hut proved comfortable.

She sat up, as did Nathalie. She too had slept the sleep of utter exhaustion, and neither of them had even dreamed, for which she supposed they should be truly grateful. But now it was dawn, and the crisis of King Kuno's intentions was upon them. Vicky gazed at Chardin, standing in the doorway of the hut with two men. They were looking at her, and Chardin came forward and pointed to her loin cloth. She wore nothing else, and it could easily be seen to be stained with blood.

The two men were not pleased, while Chardin shrugged. Then one of the men snapped an order, and instantly the hut was crowded with others, who seized Vicky's arms and dragged her to her feet.

'Chardin!' she gasped.

'Be patient,' he told her, equipping himself with his weapons, and signalling Nathalie to gather up their clothes and to follow. Then they were behind Vicky as she was dragged outside, to blink in the sudden light, and at the people who gathered round her, staring at her – they were not smiling this morning.

Be patient, he had said. And to attempt to resist would in any event be futile. She allowed herself to be dragged across the compound towards the large hut, outside which several armed men waited. She was taken through the doorway, and had to blink again, this time at the sudden gloom within. And at King Kuno.

He sat on his wooden stool, as usual, in the centre of the large room, which contained no other furniture at all, save that behind him, and some distance away, the two spears with their ghastly heads had been driven into the beaten earth, and behind them, against the far wall, there was a low table of some sort, shrouded in an embroidered cloth and impossible to identify. These things Vicky observed at a glance, but it was necessary to concentrate on the King, as he stared at her, and she was pushed to her knees in front of him. One of the men was explaining the situation, and the king glared at her blood-stained cloth, before standing up and stamping his foot in anger.

Chardin and Nathalie had now entered the hut, both fully dressed and Chardin also fully armed. He spoke soothingly to the King, but Kuno was not to be placated, stamped his foot again, and began shouting.

One of his aides hurried forward, carrying what appeared to be the lid of a biscuit tin. Vicky wondered if the king intended to use it as a mirror, when he suddenly stepped right up to her, continuing to shout, and repeating the name 'Victoria' over and over again, while holding the tin lid next to her.

Vicky stared at it in consternation, which slowly changed to horror, as she realised the truth of her situation. For on the lid there was a picture, of the youthful Queen Victoria, sitting on her throne, wearing the robes of state and holding the orb and sceptre. It was a very bad representation, and could have been almost any young woman . . . but her hair had been given a reddish gold tint. And she was undoubtedly a queen. And her name was undoubtedly Victoria.

'Oh, my God!' she whispered.

The King stepped away from her, almost threw the lid at Chardin for him to inspect in turn, and then gave more orders. Two of his men seemed to hesitate, as if they had just been commanded to do something most unusual, then they walked across the room, past the spears, and with great reverence slowly lifted the drape from over what Vicky had supposed to be a low table when she had first entered the room. Now she caught her breath, as she saw that the object was in fact a stool, exactly like the one on which Kuno was at this moment resuming his seat . . . but that it shone, even in the dull light within the hut. She was looking at the Golden Stool of the Ashanti.

Kuno spoke again, in a lower tone, and the two men lifted the Stool forward, and placed it beside him. Kuno addressed Chardin, speaking now in an almost oratorical manner, waving his arms, and every so often pointing at Victoria.

Chardin was obviously attempting to present an opposite point of view, but the King would not be persuaded, and suddenly he clapped his hands, three times. Vicky looked at the doorway, and watched a very big man step through it. Naked like his compatriots, he was also unarmed save for an enormous, scimitar-like sword which he carried in his right hand, the reverse of the blade resting on his shoulder. Instinctively, Vicky rose to her feet and backed against the wall, scarcely breathing, choking back the scream which was threatening to rise into her throat.

The man with the sword advanced into the centre of the room and bowed before his monarch, asking a question. Kuno replied, and at the same time pointed at the floor in front of him. She was to be executed, here and now. And her head, the head of Queen Victoria, stuck on a pole, to lead the Ashanti to victory over the British.

The man with the sword came towards her.

'No,' she gasped. 'For God's sake! Chardin, help me.'

Chardin was remonstrating with the King, who replied in a series of snaps.

The executioner seized Vicky's arm and jerked her forward, then twined the fingers of his left hand in her hair. She gasped, and fell to her knees, tried to strike at him with her nails, but could not reach him, felt her head being pulled forward to expose her neck and knew she was about to die, listened to Nathalie screaming . . . and then the morning exploded into sound, as it had done on the river when Chardin had been eliminating the Arabs. His revolver exploded again and again,

331

blood flew, the smell of cordite filled the room. The man holding Vicky's hair slumped to the ground, still retaining his grip so that she went with him, rolled in his blood, regained her knees and tugged herself free. On the other side of the room Nathalie was still screaming, and the shots still echoed, but outside the hut a terrifying hush had fallen on the people assembled there, as they had heard the noise without knowing the cause.

The four men in the room were dead, shot at close range with Chardin's usual accuracy. The King had attempted to reach the door, but had been checked by Chardin, who had thrown his left arm round Kuno's neck and had the revolver muzzle pressed to his temple. The King was clearly stunned and totally confused.

'We must make haste,' Chardin said. 'Dress yourself, lady, and we will leave.'

Nathalie had brought her clothes as well, and Vicky dragged on her boots and tunic, realising that Chardin must have planned this, probably since last night. That was why he had advised patience; they could only escape with the King as their hostage.

She picked up the haik, then let it fall again; it was too tattered to be of any use. But she found herself gazing at the Golden Stool.

'Are you ready, lady?' Chardin asked. The doorway was crowded with warriors, staring at them, muttering to each other, but afraid to move in case their king should be killed.

'We must take the Stool,' Vicky said.

'Of what use is gold to us, lady?' Chardin inquired. 'It will but slow us down.'

'It is what this war is about,' Vicky told him. 'If we take it, there may be no war.'

'It is heavy,' he warned.

'Help me, Nathalie,' Vicky said.

Between them they lifted the stool, which was actually much lighter than Vicky had expected; it could not possibly be made of pure gold. Perhaps the Ashanti had been the victims of a confidence trick. Certainly, when, with Nathalie's aid, she

332

hoisted it on to her shoulder, she found she could carry it quite easily. In any event, there was no time to investigate more closely, for Chardin was already waving the men away from the doorway, and forcing the King towards them. Every few seconds Kuno gave a convulsive wriggle, and Chardin's grip tightened to force him back into surrender.

They stepped out into the morning. Vicky caught her breath as she gazed at what seemed to be the entire village – women, children and dogs, but above all men, armed with every conceivable weapon, staring at them.

'Ooh, là là,' Nathalie muttered.

'Nathalie,' Vicky whispered. 'Go back and fetch Prudence's head.'

'Oh, I could not,' Nathalie protested.

'You must,' Vicky insisted. 'With that, and the Stool, and the King, we will be safe.'

Nathalie hesitated, then obeyed, running back into the hut and returning a moment later with her ghastly trophy held above her head. At the sight of that, added to their king being held a captive and the Golden Stool on Vicky's shoulder, the assembled warriors gave a great shout, and gathered closer together, as if about to receive an onslaught, while the women and children ran for the shelter of their huts.

Chardin was speaking to the King, urgently. Kuno bit his lip in rage, but after a moment's hesitation shouted orders at his men. The warriors hesitated in turn, and then lowered their weapons, and separated into two groups, leaving an avenue down the centre, towards the gate of the kraal.

'Take the rifle from my shoulder, lady,' Chardin said, 'and make them believe that you will use it. And stay close to me.' Then he walked the King into the gap left by the Ashanti army.

Vicky had taken the rifle as commanded, and glared right and left with suitable determination, she hoped, as she and Nathalie, together with the Stool and Prudence's head, walked immediately behind the two men. The warriors seemed to rustle as they passed them, and several of them drummed their rifle butts or spear hafts on the earth.

Chardin spoke to the King again, and once more, after a brief hesitation, Kuno gave his people an order. Then they stood still, staring at their enemies, as Chardin led the King away from the kraal and into the trees. There he released his hold on Kuno's neck, but spoke to him more brusquely than before, at the same time exchanging his revolver for the rifle Vicky carried; if the King knew anything at all about Chardin – and he seemed to know the big Ethiopian very well – then he would certainly know that to try to escape while Chardin held a high-powered rifle in his hands would be suicide.

'Now let us make haste,' Chardin told the women, and prodded Kuno in the back with the rifle muzzle.

Vicky and Nathalie hurried after them. Vicky carried the revolver in her left hand, using her right to steady the Stool on her shoulder, but it was growing heavier by the moment. 'Will those people not follow?' she gasped.

'At a safe distance. The King has warned them that if I see any of them too close I will kill him.'

They hurried through the morning rain storm and then through the steaming forest as the sun returned. They listened to drums, and looked left and right into the jungle, knowing that Kuno's warriors were all around them. Vicky's brain still seemed to open and shut with the enormity of what she had escaped, what these people had wanted, as Zobeir's scornful words on the last dreadful night in Timbuktu came back to her. She, and Chardin, had instinctively assumed that she was going to be forcibly married to the King. But they had been dreadfully wrong. The Ashanti had been going to war with soldiers ruled by a woman; they had needed a woman's skull as a fetish. They had therefore murdered the first white woman who had fallen into their hands: Prudence. But then another white woman had come along, and her name had not only been Victoria – the Queen for whom the white soldiers fought – she had also borne a passing resemblance to the woman portrayed in Kuno's sixty-year-old biscuit tin. No wonder he had been determined to have her head, no matter whom he angered by doing so.

And she had wanted a last trip to Africa!

''Ow far?' Nathalie asked her usual question.

'To Kumassi? Not more than a few days.'

'It is always a few days,' she grumbled.

Chardin smiled. 'This is the last few days. Those soldiers have told me there is a British column probing into the forest. The King had intended to ambush and destroy it, under the protection of your head, lady. If we can find this column, and take Kuno to it as a prisoner, together with the Golden Stool, as you have said, it may be possible to end this war before it has properly begun. In any event, we will then be safe.'

'But . . . when we stop to rest,' Vicky asked, 'will the warriors not attempt to rescue their king?' She was determined that she would kill herself before she would allow that to happen.

'They are a strange people,' Chardin said. 'They prefer to stalk their game than to kill it. They will not approach us as long as they know their king will die. But we must keep watch.'

He made them walk, with only brief rests, until late into the night, revealing his consummate forest craft by taking advantage of every rain shower to change their direction slightly, although he never seemed to doubt the direction they should be taking. At first, Vicky was afraid that by these abrupt turns they might stumble right into the arms of one of the Ashanti parties, but that never happened. Their only real problem was hunger, for there was no time to seek game, but they managed to gather some wild fruit and there was always water. And at midnight he called a halt, spending several moments listening before nodding his satisfaction. 'They are several hours behind us,' he said, 'so we can rest for a while. Now, lady, you will take the first watch, while we are safest. Count to ten thousand, slowly and regularly; it will help to keep you awake. Because you must not sleep, or we will all die. At the count of ten thousand, awake me.'

He trusted her for that rather than Nathalie; she formed the impression that he regarded her as no mere woman, where he was content that Nathalie should be nothing more than that. Which was very flattering, but when he just lay down and apparently went straight to sleep, Nathalie at his side, she knew she had never been so frightened in her life. She sat and stared at Kuno as she slowly counted. Kuno stared back. He had a disconcerting habit of running his tongue round his lips when he looked at her, and every so often he would move, slowly, seeming to uncoil like a waking snake. But every time he did so, she levelled the revolver, and he subsided again. He had no wish to commit suicide, that was clear.

So he contented himself with speaking to her, although she could understand nothing of what he was saying, other than the word Victoria. She was glad of that. She did not doubt he was telling her exactly what he was going to do with her when his men caught up with them. She had had enough of that from Zobeir.

He wondered if he had any idea how terrified she was, sitting there, facing her prisoner, while Chardin slept and all around her the forest filled with rustling sounds. The forest had always rustled before, and it had not frightened her like this. But now she knew the most deadly of animals, the human, was stalking her. She wanted to scream with joy when she finally reached ten thousand and, on nudging Chardin, saw him instantly awake and alert.

Then it was her turn to fall into a deep and dreamless sleep, knowing she was safe. When she awoke at dawn, even the sound of the drums had ceased.

' 'Ave they stopped following?' Nathalie wanted to know.

'No,' Chardin said. 'They will follow us to the gates of Kumassi, if they have to, awaiting their opportunity.'

The forest was strangely silent, and disturbingly so. But Chardin kept them moving onwards, making the King walk immediately in front of him, while Vicky, still armed with the revolver, and Nathalie came behind, each still carrying her burden. That day, again, the Ethiopian was reluctant to stop and search for food, and their hunger grew. Vicky supposed it was the lack of food that was making her so lightheaded, but in fact she had never felt so unwell in her life. Sometimes she lost all perception of where she was or what she was doing, and she began to have the strangest delusions. Then she thought she was floating through the air, and found herself lying on the ground, while Nathalie peered at her in alarm.

Chardin was also concerned. He made the King lie down, also, several feet away, and kept the rifle pointed at him while he placed his fingers on Vicky's neck, and then her forehead. 'You are hot,' he told her. 'You have malaria, I think. White people are subject to this, in the rain forests, especially in the wet season.' He smiled. 'So are black people. But they are more used to it.'

'Will she die?' Nathalie wanted to know, reverting to her favourite topic.

'I hope not, if we can reach Kumassi. They will have medicine there, to bring down the fever. Lady,' he said, at last looking directly at her, for a brief moment, 'you must walk. I cannot carry you and watch Kuno.'

'I will walk,' Vicky vowed. She used the Stool to regain her feet, then clutched it in her arms, and concentrated upon placing one foot in front of the other, making herself totally oblivious of everything else, so much so that when Nathalie stopped moving she walked into her and almost fell down again. And then realised that Chardin and the King had also stopped.

'Listen,' Chardin said.

Vicky listened, and heard a chattering sound, like a million monkeys all competing against each other.

'That is a Maxim gun,' Chardin said. 'We have found the British column.' He pointed his rifle in the air and fired three times.

'The British,' Vicky sighed, and sank to her knees, just before the morning went mad. Vaguely she realised that Chardin, his attention at last distracted from his prisoner by the proximity of the British, had been pushed to one side, so hard that he had lost his balance and fallen, and that the King was grabbing at her, armed with the knife he had whipped from Chardin's belt. She fell over, kicking her legs and waving the Stool at him, and at the same time fired the revolver. She was so weak that the bullet merely screamed into the air, but the triple defence she was putting up disconcerted Kuno, and he jumped away from her, as Chardin sat up and found his rifle. Nathalie was screaming at the very top of her voice, and the King, after a quick glance left and right, realised that the French girl was his only hope, now. He seized her round the waist and held her in front of him, the knife against her throat. Chardin, levelling his rifle, slowly lowered it.

"Elp me!' Nathalie shouted. 'Oh, 'elp me, Chardin!' She had dropped the skull-topped spear, but seemed too terrified even to wriggle.

Vicky sat up, the revolver thrust forward, and Kuno instantly half turned to face her. She knew she could not fire without hitting Nathalie, and glanced at Chardin for a lead. But Chardin was equally hesitant, although his face had settled into a most terrifying mask of angry hatred.

Kuno grinned, and spoke, and slowly retreated towards the trees, knife still held to Nathalie's throat.

'Oh, 'elp me,' Nathalie wailed. "elp me.'

Kuno spoke again, and then disappeared into the foliage, still dragging his victim.

'Oh, God,' Vicky moaned. 'Oh *God!*'

Chardin stood up. 'Lady,' he said. 'The British are less than a mile away. In that direction.' He pointed. 'Go to them. Take the Stool and the skull. And fire the revolver every five minutes.' He reached into his bandolier and gave her a handful of cartridges.

'While you go after Nathalie? But . . .' She didn't know what to say. He had saved her life, so often now that she had lost count. And however terrible the thought, he must know that Kuno would cut Nathalie's throat the moment he approached. Yet Nathalie was her friend. Together they had gone through more than any women should have been exposed to. She could not just be abandoned. 'Oh, God,' she muttered. 'Can you save her, Chardin? Can you?'

'She is my woman,' Chardin said simply, and ran into the forest.

With his departure, all reality left the morning. She knelt to watch him disappear, into the trees, every instinct calling on her to go with him, yet aware that she could hardly crawl another yard, much less run as he was doing. He was running to certain death. But was not to stay here, without Chardin, equally certain death? The Ashanti were probably as close as the British.

As she thought that, she heard shots again, closer at hand. Rifle shots, not machine gun. The British, replying to Chardin? She pushed herself up, her mind spinning, the ground heaving beneath her feet as if she were in the middle of an earthquake, and fired her revolver in the air. Then she stooped to pick up the Stool and the spear, and overbalanced, falling to the earth, shivering despite the midday heat, clutching one leg of the Stool.

She did not know how long she lay there, but slowly she became aware of feet surrounding her. Black feet. Oh, my God, she thought. After all, I have fallen into the hands of the Ashanti, and my head will be cut off and mounted on a pole . . . then she realised that these feet, if bare, were surmounted by leggings, and blue uniform trousers, and then blue jackets with silver buttons, and black caps, set rakishly at angles on their heads. They carried rifles and bandoliers, wore bayonets at their sides. And the faces beneath the caps were not hostile, but rather amazed.

And were now replaced by a white face, surmounted by a high-domed khaki topee. This face was not startled; it was difficult to imagine anything startling such a hatchet-like countenance, so obviously experienced a mind, certainly in African affairs, as indicated by the mahogany-brown suntan. The face could look concerned, and yet pleased. 'Major Norton McClarrie,' it said. 'And I've a notion you'll be Mrs Victoria Lang. Now there's a remarkable thing. But not so remarkable as that wee bauble you're clutching. If you knew how long and hard we've searched for that . . .' His voice drifted away. It kept speaking to her, that was obvious because she could see the lips moving, but she had no idea what it was saying. But she knew he meant well; she thought he had to be a colleague of David.

She would ask him about David when she woke up. Vicky closed her eyes.

★ ★ ★

She was aware of movement, that she was being jolted to and fro. But it did not involve her exhausted and tortured limbs; she was being carried in some kind of a litter. Occasionally the jolting ceased, and then there were hands, raising her head, and holding cooling drinks to her lips. Sometimes there was rain, but she was used to that, although it made her shiver violently. But after each rain shower she was wrapped in a fresh, warm blanket. It seemed absurd, to be wrapped in a blanket in a tropical jungle, but it felt so good.

Then the jolting would start all over again.

Once she was aware of concern. She was placed on the ground, and felt people hurrying to and fro around her. Then all movement stopped, but the rifles started firing, and the machine gun chattered, close by her head, it seemed. She could hear McClarrie giving orders. But surely he was making a terrible mistake. 'It'll be Chardin,' she explained, 'with Nathalie. Please don't shoot at Chardin. He'll be here any moment now.'

A black man gave her something to drink.

The firing ceased, and the jolting started again. How long it went on she had no idea. Sometimes it was dark, and sometimes light. Mostly she was so cold she shivered, even beneath her blanket, feeling a total fool as she did so. But then it was darker for longer than usual, and the next liquid they gave her tasted bitter. She understood that they were poisoning her before cutting off her head, and determined to fight them to the last ounce of strength in her body, and shout, and try to get McClarrie back, because she was sure he wouldn't try to poison her, as he was a soldier, like David. But of course she was helpless, and they held her arms and legs, trying to soothe her with soft, cooing voices, while more of the bitter liquid was dripped into her mouth.

'Don't cut off my head,' she begged. 'Oh, please don't cut off my head.'

'My dear Victoria,' Alison said. 'Of course we are not going to cut off your head. We are trying to help you get well.'

It was a trick, of course. Alison was dead, somewhere in the jungle, her head cut off and raised on a pole. She fought the hands more angrily than ever, and then felt a soft touch on her forehead, and a drip of something wet as her face was washed. 'Oh, Vicky,' Mary Dobree sobbed. 'Don't die. Please don't die.'

Eventually the turmoil in her brain, the continuous night-mares, were replaced by an utter silence. There was sound, always, but it was distant sound and did not seem to emanate from her own fears. Besides, it was familiar sound, either the pounding of rain or the crack of rifles. When she opened her eyes, she discovered it was still dark, but the darkness was punctuated by little flickers of light. And it was hot. So very hot.

Before, she had been cold.

Her first thought was that she must have died and gone to hell. But then she realised it was raining; not only was the air, even where she was, sheltered and dry, filled with damp, but now the drumming on the roof above her head was very loud. Surely it didn't rain in hell.

But she was certainly thirsty enough to be in hell. Painfully she found her tongue, and scraped it round her encrusted lips. 'Water,' she whispered. She was not sure any sound came out, but it made a loud noise in her brain.

'Victoria,' someone said softly, and a moment later a cup of water was held to her lips while her head was pillowed in a woman's arms to raise her from the bed. 'Oh, Victoria.'

Vicky blinked into the darkness while the water trickled down her throat. She had never tasted anything so good. 'Margaret?' she asked, as her eyes began to focus. 'Margaret Pilling? Is it really you?'

'Oh, Vicky,' Margaret said. 'Are you really going to be all right?'

That seemed an absurd question; she had never been seriously ill in her life. And the cup was empty. 'Is there any more?' she asked.

'Oh, yes. Dr Graham said you were to have as much liquid as you wished.' Again the cup was held to her. Vicky drank this too, then lay back with a sigh. 'Where am I?' she asked.

'In the fortress at Kumassi,' Margaret told her.

341

'Kumassi!' She sighed again. 'Is Chardin here? And Nathalie?'

'Chardin?'

'You remember Chardin? The black man who was guarding us? He brought us out. He and Nathalie were with me, until yesterday . . .' Her voice trailed away as she began to remember.

'Vicky . . . you have been in Kumassi a fortnight.'

'A . . .' Vicky rose to her elbow, and fell back again. She was too weak to support her own weight.

'You rest,' Margaret said. 'You sleep. We'll talk about it when you have slept. Alison will explain.'

The rain had stopped, and sunshine streamed through the windows of the room in which Vicky lay. It was still hot and damp, and every so often it rained, but lying in bed beneath cool white sheets and wearing a freshly laundered linen nightdress – she was given a clean one every day as she still sweated profusely – was almost pleasant. Compared with her experiences of the past five weeks it was indeed heavenly. Only the noise disturbed her tranquillity. The noise was too familiar, a constant drumming, some distance off, louder than the rain but not the less incessant, or disturbing, for that. And every so often the drumming was punctuated by a rifle shot, or several shots, or a burst of machine gun fire.

The noise, and memory. But memory could not be risked, right this minute.

She opened her eyes, and gazed at Alison. An Alison she had almost forgotten existed, for Lady Dobree wore a white linen gown – not a perfect fit, but elegant enough – and her hair was dressed in the huge, loose pompadour she had used in England; she looked as perfectly groomed and totally confident as on the occasion of their first meeting. She might, indeed, just have stepped off the ship from Southampton – save for the still sunburned face . . . and the curious hairlessness of her arms.

And save that she had only just dried her eyes. And looked ready to start weeping again at any moment. 'Vicky,' she said. 'Oh, my dearest Vicky.' She kissed Vicky on the forehead.

Vicky licked her lips – she was still constantly thirsty – and Alison herself held the cup of water for her to drink.

'You've been so ill,' Alison explained. 'You've had a high temperature, and at times you've been quite delirious. Dr Graham says you have malaria. We despaired of you. But we should have known better. You are too strong to die, Vicky.'

Vicky wasn't all that interested in her own health. 'Did Chardin get here?' she whispered. 'With Nathalie?'

Alison shook her head. 'You spoke of them, while you were delirious. Were they really with you in the forest?'

Vicky nodded. 'Chardin helped us escape from Timbuktu. Then we were captured by the Ashanti, but he helped us escape from them too. But then . . .' She sighed.

Alison raised her head to look at the other woman in the room. Vicky followed the direction of her gaze, looked at a woman dressed and coiffured almost exactly like Alison herself, but considerably older, and with somewhat severe features.

'Vicky,' Alison said, 'this is Lady Hodgson.'

'Lady Dobree has told me a great deal about you, Mrs Lang,' Sylvia Hodgson said. 'About the way you led them across the desert, and then volunteered to remain behind with the Touareg as a hostage, that they might escape. I must say, I am proud to make your acquaintance. And now, actually to bring in the Golden Stool . . .'

'The Stool,' Vicky muttered. She had forgotten about the Stool.

'My husband is delighted. Of course he knows that has brought the Ashanti down on us. But we will hold them until reinforcements arrive from the coast, which will be any day now. Oh, indeed, you have done a splendid thing.' She frowned. 'I must confess, my dear, that I don't altogether understand about the skull, though.' She gave an encouraging smile. 'We buried it, of course.'

The skull. 'Prudence,' Vicky said. 'Oh, Prudence.'

'Prudence!' Alison cried. 'Oh, my *God!*'

'Was it someone you know?' Lady Hodgson asked, concerned.

'My Charlie's nanny,' Alison said. 'She went on ahead. Oh, good heavens.'

'They wanted her skull as a fetish,' Vicky explained.

'Ugh!' Alison exclaimed. 'How *dreadful!*'

'And so you brought it in,' Lady Hodgson mused. 'That too showed excellent judgement, Mrs Lang. Excellent. Oh, Francis will be pleased to learn about that.'

But memory, once released, was too incessant now to be rejected. 'David!' Vicky gasped, clutching Alison's hand. 'Where is David?'

'My dear, he's gone down to the coast to get help,' Alison explained, and looked at Lady Hodgson for support.

'He volunteered, Mrs Lang. He too is a very gallant young man. After leading the six ladies to safety, and acquainting us that an Ashanti war was almost certainly on our hands, he volunteered to make the trek to the coast, with just a single guide, to acquaint our people down there with what is happening. The telegraph wires have been cut, you see.'

'Then you mean . . .' Vicky sat up with an immense effort. 'You don't know what has happened to him? He could be dead.' Panic gnawed at her mind.

'Not David,' Alison asserted confidently. 'He's only been gone three weeks. We expect him back with the troops at any moment. Why, he must know the forest better than any white man, now. He led us through it, you know. And besides, Vicky, he was really anxious to get down and see about arranging either a ransom, or a rescue, for you.'

It was marvellous to lie in bed and feel strength slowly coming back to her muscles, to be bathed once a day in cool water, to be given European food to eat, to have the use of a brush and comb, to know there were no insects nesting in her body or her hair. Only the twice daily doses of quinine, administered by Dr Graham, were unpleasant – but they were doing her good.

And above everything else was the feeling that everyone around her was a friend. More than a friend, now. She was a heroine, on several counts.

The Governor, Sir Francis Hodgson, came to her room to

visit, and sat in obvious embarrassment as he listened to her story. 'Remarkable,' he commented. 'Quite remarkable. What you have said entirely corroborates Lady Dobree's account, of course. We shall have to do something about that scoundrel Zobeir. Alas, until the French are willing to co-operate . . . but we will get the fellow, Mrs Lang. Oh, we shall, and we shall make him pay for his insults and mistreatment of you . . . and of Lady Dobree. As for the Ashanti, when the relief column gets here we are going to teach them such a lesson they will never forget. I promise you that.'

It occurred to Vicky that he was less angry than frightened.

Major McClarrie came to call, and squeezed her hand when she tried to thank him for saving her life. 'You're a very gallant lady,' he said. 'A very gallant lady.'

Mary and Elizabeth took on the duties of being her nurses, while Sylvia Hodgson called to see her at least once a day, as did Margaret Pilling and Joanna Cartwright and Alice Marker. But her most constant companion was Alison, who spent several hours a day with her, often accompanied by Charlie. Charlie seemed to have stood up to his experiences very well, although he was less noisy than before, for which Vicky was thankful. He did not seem the least afraid to be in a small fort surrounded by thousands of people thirsting for his blood, and in fact projected his mother's supreme confidence in the certain triumph of British arms. Because quite remarkably, Alison seemed to have totally reverted to the utter certainty and somewhat slightly contemptuous view of life she had held in the safety of Little Wissing, as though she had never been forced to kneel naked before a lusting sailor, or staggered barefoot through a desert, or been depilated by four eunuchs or whipped by an Arab emir. Even her almost doting admiration for Vicky was more in the spirit of, 'See what my protégée has accomplished?' rather than a true regard, Vicky felt.

'Did Kuno really think you were Queen Victoria, suddenly popped up in the middle of his kraal?' Alison asked, and gave a shriek of laughter. 'That is the most remarkable thing I have heard in all my life.'

'I am sure Her Majesty would be amused to hear it,' Sylvia

Hodgson agreed, being present at the time.

'And I shall make sure she does,' Alison promised. 'I think everyone should hear that story.'

Vicky wondered if she would ever admit to having betrayed them to Zobeir, and decided that, as with the other unpleasantnesses she had had to undergo during the preceding couple of months, Lady Dobree had resolutely put the incident out of her mind.

As she grew stronger, Vicky was helped by the sisters on to the verandah which looked out across the parade ground behind the fortress proper. The garrison continued to exercise despite being under siege, for the parade ground was safe from attack, being fronted by the fort and backed by a huge swamp, into which not even the Ashanti were apparently prepared to venture.

But their intention of taking Kumassi and murdering everyone inside the fort could hardly be doubted. If it was hard for Vicky to accept that she had lain in a delirious coma for nearly a fortnight, it had apparently been a fortnight during which a great deal had happened, all of it bad, from the point of view of the British. The Ashanti had not been put off by the loss of their Golden Stool – rather they intended to regain it as soon as possible. Nor had they been distracted by the stealing of their fetish, because they had found another. McClarrie's patrols, retreating before the ever gathering African army, had not only identified King Kuno at their enemies' head – proving that Chardin had not succeeded in avenging Nathalie – but had observed that the King marched beneath two new skulls.

Poor, poor Nathalie. And poor, poor Chardin, who must certainly be the other one. It was hardly believable that two people with whom she had shared so much, and one of them a man who had seemed able to achieve the impossible, could have died, so horribly . . . one of those skulls could so easily have been hers.

And might yet be. The Ashanti had now completely invested Kumassi on the land side, penetrating into the town in several places, but prevented by the swamp from getting close enough to launch an all-out attack. But that they controlled the entire countryside could not be doubted. The various missionaries had all been brought in, as well as the Christian or loyal blacks, to the number of some two thousand people, mostly women, children, and old men; while the garrison, if totally cut off from the coast, had been reinforced to some six hundred men by the arrival of all the northern outposts, which had been mobilised and marched in retreat to the capital by Major Morris. These were policemen rather than soldiers, members of the Haussa Gold Coast Constabulary – in fact, there were no soldiers at all in the fort, although McClarrie and Morris and their junior officers had received military training. But they all hated and feared the Ashanti, and under their white officers were prepared to fight to the last.

The total complement of the fortress was thus nearly three thousand people, of whom only some thirty were white: Governor Hodgson and his wife and secretary, a dozen officers, eight missionaries – four men and their wives – and the seven women who were the sole survivors of the wreck of the *Doncaster*. This was a vast number of souls to be sustained. There was no shortage of water, because of the swamp – but food was already becoming a problem.

And there continued to be no news from the coast. One day there was the magnificently comforting sound of gunfire from the south, and McClarrie asserted, 'The column has reached Bekwai.' But next day the firing had stopped, and it was not heard again; they had to face the unacceptable fact that if it had been a British column, it had been defeated.

'That was probably just an advance guard,' Governor Hodgson declared reassuringly, when Vicky was well enough to get up and join them for dinner. 'And I have no doubt at all that Lieutenant Whiting was probably with them. After what he has surmounted in the past he can have found few difficulties in traversing the forest to the coast – it is only a matter of a hundred miles, you know. But mobilising a sufficient force to relieve us here, which involves taking on the whole Ashanti nation, that is the difficult part of the business. It takes time. So that was probably a probe; now they will be preparing the main assault. But they may be delayed by the rains . . . and all sorts of unforeseen obstacles. We must be patient.' He beamed down the length of the mahogany dining table, daring anyone to disagree.

In fact the rest of the white people, and especially Alison and the girls, were hardly less confident. Apparently David had been a tower of strength during their journey from Timbuktu, quite the equal of Chardin, as they told it. Zobeir's men had accompanied them down-river to a point approximately equal to where Chardin had abandoned the water, and there left them to their own devices. They had fought and slashed and pushed their way through the same jungle as Vicky and Nathalie and Chardin had encountered, waded the same swamps and suffered the same agonies, but had kept on their way, carried along by David's unfailing optimism and determination. Eventually they too had come to the land of the Ashanti, but by careful scouting and a good deal of patience, which had involved sometimes lying in hiding for as many as twelve hours, David had led them through without a confrontation, without, Alison was sure, the Ashanti even knowing of their presence. It had taken them a long time, and indeed they had only been in the fortress a week before Vicky appeared herself, but they had made it without loss.

'He was just magnificent,' Mary told her. 'There were so many times when we felt we just couldn't go on, but he wouldn't let us give up. He kept telling us, now this is what Vicky would have done; so we'll do it too.'

Vicky wanted to weep. The story gave her an enormous sense of personal failure, because perhaps if she had not been so quick to abdicate all responsibility to Chardin she might have been able to bring the three of them through with equal success. Chardin had actually wanted to be found by the Ashanti, sure that they could not avoid it. As a result, he and Nathalie were both dead.

'But their deaths were not in vain,' Governor Hodgson insisted, as usual trying to reassure her. 'Thanks to them, and to you, of course, Mrs Lang, we have the Stool. Without the Stool, Kuno cannot call himself High King and treat with the other black nations. He must either fight his way in here and

348

kill us all before our reinforcements arrive, or take his people home. And in addition, you brought us the fetish under which they hoped to achieve victory.'

'But they have another fetish, Francis,' Alison pointed out, ignoring his frowns and head shakings. 'Of course it's not as effective as if they actually had obtained Victoria, but still . . .' She shuddered. 'Poor Nathalie.'

'You said Nathalie would soon be here,' Charlie protested. 'And Nanny.'

'Yes, my dear,' Alison said. 'But I'm afraid they may be a little delayed.'

Vicky had the strangest feeling that she was living in an upside-down world. Out there, not half a mile away, were all the terrors, human, animal, reptile and vegetable, with which she had contended for two months and more. Within this tiny area, perhaps half a mile square, were all the politenesses and refinements of English society, where manners were everything, and for dinner the men wore mess kit and the women were expected to appear in evening gowns, even if borrowed or sorely in need of refurbishing. Where one never spoke directly of death, or mentioned needing a lavatory, and where, just for example, offering to examine someone else's sore feet would be regarded as the height of bad taste.

The trouble was, out there was the reality; in here was an artificial world which one or two fortunate nations on this earth had been able to create for themselves.

But her own world was equally upside down, a mixture of happiness and misery. Every time she lay on her bed, or had a bath, or changed her borrowed clothing, she wanted to weep with relief. And every time she remembered Nathalie and Bream and Prudence – and Chardin – she wanted to weep with misery. Added to that was the continuing fear of what might have befallen David, and the anxiety of their own situation. Yet she could bask in the adulation of the girls, and enjoy the development of their personalities from the shallow, bored, over-wealthy and unpleasant young women she had first met, to these competent, and confident, creatures, prepared to work as hard as anyone; they shared entirely Charlie's care, as well as Vicky's, although there were many black women in the fortress who would have been happy to act either the nanny or the nurse. She wondered if she could take any credit for the metamorphosis, and then thought, in an abstract fashion, what a shame it would be if all they had experienced and accomplished should, after all, end on the altar of Ashanti determination to regain their independence.

She also wondered what, if any, effect her experiences had truly had on Alison, whether she too was acting all the time, pretending that the world outside was not really there, her adventures only a long bad dream. Or whether she truly believed in the permanence and inevitability of British rule and manners and civilisation, accepting only that from time to time she and her family and friends might have to undergo a little 'unpleasantness' at the hands of the unwashed masses, unpleasantnesses which had to be borne with equanimity and then forgotten as rapidly as possible.

With every day that passed, it became more and more likely that she would have to resume her acquaintance with those masses. The garrison had little fear of being defeated, militarily. They possessed four Maxim guns and a two-pounder cannon, and were amply supplied with powder and shot. The six hundred black constables were sufficient to maintain the walls of the fortress, while neither Major Morris nor Major McClarrie were the men to remain entirely on the defensive; whenever the Ashanti attempted to occupy the houses too close to the fort, they would lead an assault of some forty picked men and drive them out again. Ashanti efforts to retaliate by burning the town failed because of the continuous rain storms, which kept all the wooden houses too sodden to fire.

These constant assaults and counter-attacks of course involved casualties, and as soon as she was well enough to leave her bed Vicky joined the other white women in staffing the little hospital. This was unpleasant work – although, thanks to her years in Kenya when amongst her duties had been the care of the sick around the mission, she was a more experienced nurse than any of the others – but it served to occupy their time and their minds. Because one inexorable fact daily crept closer: they were running out of food. The rations had been reduced time and again, and by the beginning of June were down to what Governor Hodgson regarded as the absolute minimum – a biscuit and five ounces of meat for the policemen who had to fight, and a biscuit and a pound of tinned meat for the white people. If this seemed illogical to Vicky, as the white ladies, at least, did not have to fight, everyone else, including the policemen, seemed to regard it as an equitable division of what was available.

There was some other food to be had. At the beginning of the siege the local black traders had of course all fled to the protection of the fortress, and had brought as many of their goods as they could with them. As Sir Francis would not hear of requisitioning these goods, which were, after all, personal possessions, they had been enabled to continue a brisk trade within the walls for as long as their supplies, and their customers' money, lasted. But now even they were reaching rock bottom. Single biscuits were selling for ten shillings each, a small tin of corned beef cost two pounds sixteen shillings, matches were two shillings a box, while a spoonful of whisky cost the same. These prices were not, of course, problems to the *Doncaster* survivors, as they had no money anyway, but the Hodgsons insisted on treating them all as guests, and would have nothing themselves that was not shared.

And if the garrison itself was on the verge of starvation, such a fate had already overtaken the two thousand-odd refugees, to whom no rations were issued at all. Their suffering was almost unbearable to watch. They dug and redug the ground in search of roots, they made an unbelievable soup out of gathered leaves, and for their meat they depended on a daily scouring of rats and lizards. And they died, daily.

Eventually Sir Francis felt called upon to summon a meeting of all the white people. 'I'm afraid I have to regard the situation as extremely grave,' he said. 'With so many mouths to feed, I do not see how we can hold out here another week. I really had expected that the relief column would have arrived by now, especially after they must have reached Bekwai a fortnight ago, but as there has been no sign of them, we must accept that they have been forced to retreat.'

'Does that mean you think David . . . Lieutenant Whiting, didn't get through?' Mary asked.

Hogdson gave Vicky an uneasy glance; he had been told by Alison that she and David were unofficially engaged. 'I am sure he must have got through, Miss Dobree, or we would not have heard that gunfire at all. But the fact is, no matter what he has accomplished, or what is happening out there, our relief is taking far longer than I had anticipated.'

'I'd say it's because our people are having to fight every step of the way,' McClarrie said. 'Kuno's no fool. He'll have his men across the road, building their beastly blockhouses, each one having to be destroyed before any advance can be made. But that firing came from Bekwai all right. I'd say the relief column is right, there, two days' march away, preparing a new attack.'

'I thought so too,' Hodgson agreed. 'But surely we would have heard *some* gunfire from down there. I'm sorry, Major, but we simply have to conclude that, for whatever reason, the relief column has been forced to retreat, and that therefore there is nothing, nothing at all, out there. So . . .' He looked from face to face. 'I am going to have to ask you all to accept even smaller rations. And then, well . . . to pray.'

'If we could gain the road and pass Bekwai, could we reach the coast?' Elizabeth asked.

'Oh, undoubtedly. Once on the road, why . . . we could be at the coast in three days. But as that is impossible . . .'

'Why don't we just leave?' Elizabeth asked. 'We can walk for three days.'

Heads turned to stare at her.

'Well . . .' She flushed, 'wouldn't it be better than staying here, to starve?'

Hogdson gave her a quiet smile. 'My dear Miss Dobree,' he said, 'you are missing the point. We cannot reach the road, because we are entirely surrounded by the Ashanti.'

'No, we're not,' Mary cried, taking up her sister's point. 'Not entirely. There's the swamp. There are no Ashanti in the swamp. And if we could cross the swamp, surely we could find the road afterwards and, as Lizzie says, simply walk away. It's only a hundred miles to the coast. That's nothing.'

'There are no Ashanti in the swamp, Miss Dobree,' Hodgson said wearily, 'because that swamp is impenetrable. It stretches . . . how far does it stretch, Major McClarrie?'

'Two, three miles, Sir Francis.'

'You see? No one can walk across a swamp three miles wide. Certainly no white woman.'

'That's rubbish,' Alison declared, supporting her step-daughters.

It was her turn to be the target of confounded stares.

'Now, Lady Dobree, please,' Hodgson protested. 'I do think you should leave these matters to those who know about them. You simply have no idea of what you are speaking. There are snakes, and alligators, and disease, and heaven knows what else out there. Leeches,' he added gloomily, as if they would be the last straw. 'Not to mention water. After all this rain, why, that swamp is probably over six feet deep in places. Why . . .'

'Actually, it will contain crocodiles, not alligators,' Alison pointed out. 'We know all about crocodiles, Sir Francis. And snakes and leeches. And disease. And water. We've walked through it all before. And by heaven, we can do it again. If you wish, we'll *lead* you out. *Vicky* will lead you out.' She looked at Vicky. 'Won't you, Vicky? You'll lead us out.'

Vicky gazed at her in total consternation. She realised that she had, perhaps, underestimated Alison's regard for her, at least, her trust in her abilities . . . or was it merely Alison's nature to delegate authority with total confidence? But the thought of leaving this relatively clean and dry place, once again to plunge into the living hell of the forest, was quite impossible. Yet, following Alison's lead, all of these people, soldiers and empire builders and their women, were looking to her. Because she had done it already.

All these people. But what did she have to lose? To stay here would be to lose everything. Besides, David was out there, somewhere. Waiting for her. Without David, this nightmare would never end.

'Sure,' she said. 'I always said we'd walk right to the coast, if we had to.'

CHAPTER 16

'But even if we get through the swamp and reach the road,' Lady Hodgson said, 'will not the Ashanti follow, once they realise the fortress has been abandoned?'

'My God, yes!' her husband said. 'If they catch us on the road . . .'

'They must not be allowed to know that the fortress has been abandoned,' Vicky said. 'Because it cannot be abandoned, entirely.' She looked at McClarrie.

Who nodded. 'You're right, Mrs Lang. Leave me a hundred men, the cannon, and two Maxims, Sir Francis, and I'll hold Kumassi for you until Christmas. I'll pick the men.'

'A hundred men? Now really McClarrie . . . what will you live on?'

'I can hold this place with a hundred men,' McClarrie insisted. 'We've rations for all six hundred of us for maybe another fortnight, at the present rate of consumption. If you march out of here with five hundred, and rations for three days, then my hundred will have two months' food left. Surely you'll have a column up here by then.'

'Can we make the coast in three days?' Lady Hodgson asked.

'You'll get within one march of it, milady. And there's game to be found out there. But I don't think you'll have to make the coast. I'm sure the relief column is somewhere along the road.'

Hodgson looked from his wife to Alison and then back to Vicky. 'Are you sure you can do it?'

Vicky shrugged. 'No, Sir Francis. I can only do what we've done before.'

He stroked his chin, pensively.

'It's your best chance, man,' McClarrie said. 'When you link up with the column, you can hurry them up.'

'When!' Hodgson shuddered.

'What about the Golden Stool?' Mary Dobree asked.

'Ah . . . I'm going to destroy that. It isn't really gold, you know. Just wood, covered in gold paint.'

'I thought it was something like that,' Vicky said. 'Wouldn't it be better just to peel off the paint?'

'By Jove, that might shake them a bit.'

'Leave it with me, Sir Francis,' McClarrie said. 'Mind you, I don't mean to let any of them in here to look at it, except as a last resort.'

'Well . . .' Hodgson looked at the assembled people.

'What about the African non-combatants?' Lady Hodgson asked.

'They can't stay here,' McClarrie said. 'If I'm to hold this place with a hundred men, I can't have two thousand civilians underfoot.'

'They'll have to come with us,' Hodgson decided.

'Two thousand women and children?' Alison was shocked.

'Oh, we'll make it plain we've nothing to share with them . . .'

We've shared nothing with them since the siege began, Vicky thought.

'. . . but they'll be better off with us than staying in Kumassi to be chopped up by Kuno's men. We'll have to tell them the choice is theirs, but we can no longer offer them protection.'

Which is going to give them a marvellous insight into the true value of British rule, Vicky thought.

'Well . . .' Sir Francis stood up. 'It seems that we are going to follow your advice, Mrs Lang. How soon would you wish us to depart?'

She almost felt like telling him. Forget it: I'll stay with the African women and children. But she didn't. 'What time is it now?' she asked.

'Ah . . .' He looked at his fob watch. 'Seven minutes past four. It'll be dark in two hours.'

Vicky considered. She would have preferred to leave at

night, but she knew she would never get these people through the swamp in the dark – she didn't think she'd get them *into* the swamp, in the dark. 'We'll leave at dawn,' she said. 'The very first light.'

'So soon?' Lady Hodgson protested. 'But . . . we have to prepare.'

'Prepare what, milady? We have to walk. We can only take as much as each of us can carry. For a long way,' Vicky told her, feeling an overwhelming sense of déjà vu; she might have been on the beach again, trying to persuade Alison.

But Alison was on her side now. 'Well,' she said brightly, 'I suggest we all get a good night's sleep.'

The doctors prepared their equipment, and the officers who were coming with them assembled their men and briefed the NCOs. Major Morris would lead the retreat, Major McClarrie would hold the fort. The constables were deputed to go amongst the non-combatants and give them their choice of accompanying the retreat, or disappearing into the forest and managing as best they could. Without exception they wanted to accompany the retreat.

Meanwhile, Vicky assembled the ladies, who now totalled twelve, and told them something of what to expect and how to cope. She really didn't know what to recommend as the best dress for the occasion. She personally felt that the lighter they travelled the better, but they were English gentlewomen who had never exposed their ankles save to their husbands; when they went into the bush, as they called it, they believed in wearing more clothes than usual. She therefore told them to go for skirts and blouses, and their thickest boots and stockings, with good hats for their heads – most of them had sun topees anyway. They all wanted to wear veils to protect their complexions, as if they were going on a picnic, and she couldn't object to that, even if she knew the flimsy gauze wouldn't last five minutes in the jungle. She and Alison, the girls and the other shipwrecked survivors were fitted out from amongst the missionaries' wives, as they had been since gaining the fortress, and Alison had devised a special harness for Charlie, so that he could be carried between herself and Mary, his weight evenly divided. The boy himself was supplied with cut-down male clothing.

Then at last it was time for that final precious rest. Not that Vicky supposed many of them would actually sleep. She didn't; her mind was teeming with things to be remembered. And neither did Alison, who after about an hour tiptoed into the room Vicky shared with the other three women, and sat on Vicky's bed. 'It is so splendid to have you with us again, Vicky,' she whispered. 'To be reunited.'

They had actually been reunited for well over a month. 'We'll never be quite reunited,' Vicky said.

Alison sighed. 'I know. I think about Nathalie and Prudence and poor Phyllis Smart as much as you do, believe me. But we have to survive, Vicky. We have to.'

'I'm sure we will,' Vicky said. 'Some of us.'

Alison gazed at her in the gloom. 'That's what you said the first time. Oh, Vicky, I . . .' She bit her lip. 'I'm so afraid. If we're captured, by those . . .'

'Men, milady. They're only men.'

'Yes, but . . .' Alison shuddered.

'I guess they do look at things differently from us,' Vicky conceded.

'There's the girls, too. Vicky . . . do you think . . . well . . .'

'Yes,' Vicky said. 'If you really want me to. But milady . . . once you're dead, you're dead.'

'Don't you think I've thought about that? God, to know what to do . . .' She smiled into the darkness. 'I suppose there have been times when you would have liked to wring my neck.'

Like right now? Vicky wondered. But she smiled back. 'I guess every employee feels like that about the boss, from time to time.'

'Vicky . . .' Alison held her hands. 'I shall never be your employer again. I want to be your friend. I shall be your friend.'

'I'll still need a job.'

'Oh, you shall have whatever you wish. I do promise that.

Why, Mary and Liz would be heartbroken without you. But I shall be your friend.'

'Thank you, milady,' Vicky said. 'But I should tell you that, if we come through, and if David has come through . . . he's asked me to marry him.'

'Has he? You mean really? I mean, I knew . . . well . . . that you were lovers, of course. Oh, Vicky, I am so happy for you. And you must never call me milady again.'

'Very well. If that's what you want. Even in public?'

'Even in public,' Alison insisted. She got up, went to the window and gazed out at the night, then came back and sat down again. 'You know . . . there is something I feel I should confess to you.'

'Something to do with what you told Zobeir?'

Alison's eyebrows arched.

'He told me,' Vicky said. 'He was most upset that he hadn't believed you, had let the real Lady Dobree go. I think he really wanted you, even if he wanted your title more.'

'Oh, my God,' Alison exclaimed. 'What must you think of me?'

'I suspect you were terrified.'

'I . . . I thought that maybe I could save us all. But he just whipped me. And then he . . . God, when I remember . . . Vicky, are all dark men like that? I mean, in what they want from women?'

'All men want that, Alison. Given the chance. Their colour doesn't come into it.'

'I don't believe it. Englishmen? Gentlemen? I mean, no gentleman would even allow a lady to look at it, much less want her to touch it. As for . . . well . . .'

'When it comes to the act of love, Alison, we are none of us ladies, or gentlemen. Or we sure shouldn't be. What you are talking about is the act of two people in passion. Did Sir William never want more than just to lie on your belly while you kept your eyes shut?'

'My God . . . I thought he was a pervert.'

'If you'd realised he was a man, a lot might have been

different. Tell me something, Alison: did you enjoy nothing of what Zobeir did to you? Well, maybe "enjoy" isn't quite the right word. But didn't you feel as if it *might* be enjoyable? With the right man?'

'My God,' Alison said again. But her tone had become thoughtful. 'Vicky . . . what did Zobeir do to you? Did he whip you, too?'

'No,' Vicky said. 'He had other plans for me. But Chardin got me away.'

'Chardin. There was a remarkable thing. I mean . . . a black man . . .'

'A very gallant gentleman,' Vicky said. 'We've met a lot of those.' She was thinking of Harry Bream not less than David Whiting. Or William Dobree, for that matter. 'Milady . . . oops, I mean Alison . . . forget about what you told Zobeir. I always consider one can only do what one thinks is best at the time. And if one doesn't have too much time to think, then it's always possible to make the wrong decision.' She held her shoulders, brought her close, and kissed her on the cheek. 'I think I've been with some very gallant ladies, too, these past few months.'

Alison began to weep.

Vicky awoke to the steady, inevitable, familiar pounding of the rain on the roof, sat up and gazed across the room at Sir Francis Hodgson, who was standing in the doorway, looking terribly embarrassed. She didn't know why; she, and all the others, had slept fully dressed. She got up and tiptoed towards him; he stepped back in the corridor to wait for her. Outside, the darkness was just beginning to pale.

'We'll have to postpone our departure,' he said. 'It's pouring with rain.'

'Sir Francis,' she said, 'that rain is the answer to this woman's prayer. It'll cover us.' She smiled at him. 'Literally.'

He hesitated, then shrugged, obviously realising that he had agreed to go along with a madwoman. But the orders were given, and the retreat assembled. Vicky's heart sagged as she looked at the huge mass of people gathering on the parade ground, patiently, in the downpour. There was simply no way she could take all of those through the forest.

But she had promised to try.

McClarrie stood at her shoulder. 'Mrs Lang,' he said. 'Meeting you has been the only good thing which has come out of this goddamned war. I hope we'll meet again.'

'If I have anything to do with it, Major McClarrie,' she promised, 'we will meet again.'

She went to the back gate of the fort, where Sir Francis and Major Morris were waiting, together with Captain Marshall, who was to lead the advance guard. He was an eager, fresh-faced young man who had only been in the Gold Coast for six months. 'I'm coming with you,' she told him. 'Alison, maybe you'd keep an eye on the ladies. Major Morris, the rearguard doesn't only have to keep stragglers up; it could turn out to be the only thing between us and the Ashanti. We need the best you have.'

He nodded. 'That is arranged, Mrs Lang. I will command the rearguard myself, if that is satisfactory.'

'That was what I'd hoped you'd say. Well, Sir Francis, keep your powder dry, eh? Mr Marshall, let's take a walk.'

Vicky had never doubted that she was taking on the biggest challenge of her life. Nor could she doubt that she would be lucky to bring even half of the refugees through if they had to walk all the way to the coast, even if they did manage to reach the road. There was nothing she could do, she knew, about the horrors which lay before them. Her business was morale. If she could inspire them to keep moving, no matter what cropped up, they stood a chance. With this in mind she had dressed all in white, and tied her hair with a loose bow on the nape of her neck, beneath the sun topee she had procured and which made her look like every picture of what the English lady wore to shoot tiger in India. Hunting through Lady Hodgson's abandoned effects she had also found a large, multi-coloured parasol, and this she now raised above her head just before stepping out of the fortress and on to the parade ground. The waiting people cheered, and she wondered if she had made a mistake – the Ashanti would surely guess that something was up.

But she marched forward resolutely, Captain Marshall at her side. The rain seemed to leap at them like a living creature, welcoming them into its embrace. It fell with a relentless force, and she was soaked to the skin, despite her parasol, long before she reached the swamp, while the thunder rumbled in the background as a kind of accompaniment to the roar of McClarrie's guns, as he opened a distractive barrage on the enemy positions.

Then the swamp. If the rain had welcomed her like an old friend, the swamp welcomed her like an old enemy, eager to regain possession of her. She sank first of all to her ankles, and stuck for a moment, while she pulled her leg free. Captain Marshall was instantly at her side, offering her his arm. 'No, no, Captain,' she said. 'If we ladies cannot manage, we cannot come. We are all equals on this walk.'

Soon she was up to her knees, and then to her waist, thrusting her way through the turgid, evil-smelling liquid, stumbling over fallen branches, pushing ahead, tilting her topee back every time it threatened to slide over her eyes, keeping the parasol resolutely above her head. It was their flag.

After half an hour she allowed herself to look back, at the long, snake-like column which was plodding through the rain and the water behind her; already the white walls of the fortress were almost lost to sight, and the roar of the guns was becoming muffled. The fifty men of the advance guard were immediately behind her, then a gap before the main body and the supply column, then the white women and the doctors, then the hundreds of black women and children, wailing and moaning, and occasionally singing, but moving steadily, and then the rearguard of Captain Morris and another fifty men. She thought of the Israelites escaping Pharaoh. But the waters had opened for the Israelites. Maybe God was fighting for the Ashanti.

But they were all at least still following. And she did not suppose the white people, at any rate, had the slightest doubt for whom God was fighting. Alison saw her looking back and waved, as did Mary; Governor Hodgson marched with the main force, talking vigorously to Captain Leggatt; Lady Hodgson was with the ladies – she carried her pet fox terrier in her arms.

Vicky's attention was recalled to her immediate situation by Captain Marshall tripping and disappearing for a moment. When she helped him up, he spluttered, 'How far across is it, do you think, Mrs Lang?'

'I have no idea. It's just that far,' she promised him. 'Not a step further.'

But her own confidence received a body blow a few minutes later when she stepped into an unsuspected hole and was in turn completely submerged. Actually, she realised as she regained the surface, the hole was more of an ancient river bed, because the same fate had overtaken Captain Marshall and most of the advance guard, and it was only after some desperate splashing and struggling that they regained their depths on the farther side.

'Good heavens,' the captain remarked. 'Do you suppose there are many of those?'

Vicky regained her topee, which had been floating away, and squeezed water from her hair; the only part of her not submerged had been her right wrist and hand, with which she had held the umbrella above the surface – but the umbrella itself was so soaked with rain it was beginning to collapse. 'Very probably,' she said. 'Pass the word back to look out for that one; tell them it's only a few feet across.'

Fifteen minutes later they saw their first crocodile, actually a pair of them, swimming lazily parallel with their march, protruding eyes watching them with what Vicky had to suppose was total amazement. In any event, after she had restrained Captain Marshall from opening volley fire on them, they swam away. She decided against passing *that* piece of information down the line. And compared with the insects which were swarming about her face and head, the reptiles were obviously too bemused by this invasion of their territory to be dangerous.

Conditions actually became worse when the rain stopped

and the sun emerged, for then the mist rose off the surface of the swamp, enveloping them in a thick white cloud and bringing visibility down to about twenty feet. The column disappeared behind them, although it could still be heard, and it was only with the aid of Captain Marshall's compass that they knew the direction to take. Even so Vicky had a sudden terrifying vision of them veering off and walking round and round in the mist, like something out of Dante's *Inferno*, until they all collapsed and drowned.

They waded on. There was no way they could stop to rest, or eat. It was simply a matter of putting those three miles behind them as rapidly as possible, but it was nearly noon before they found the water receding. Soon the advance guard at the least was wading only ankle deep, while water drained from the men's uniforms, and from Vicky's clothes, and as the mist at last began to lift they could even see trees in front of them. But now too the sound of fighting behind them, where McClarrie was keeping up his diversion, was overlaid by the thudding of the drums: the Ashanti had learned of their escape.

'How long will it take them to reach here, going round the swamp?' Captain Marshall asked.

'Not more than a couple of hours. They can travel much faster than we, and they can use the road for at least half the way. But I don't think they'll come into the bush to get us; they'll wait on the road. A lot depends on just where *we* join the road.'

And on how quickly they reached it, she thought, shading her eyes to stare into the mist clouds which still drifted across the surface of the swamp. Out there she could hear shouts of encouragement and cries of fear and despair. But more and more people were coming ashore at every moment, stamping the dry ground and shaking themselves, collapsing to their knees in exhaustion.

'Vicky,' Alison gasped, placing Charlie on the ground and squeezing water from her hair; even the immaculate eyebrows had been disarrayed on one of the occasions she had fallen down. 'That was worse than anything . . . we saw a crocodile.'

'So did we,' Vicky said.

'Bam,' Charlie announced. 'Bam. If I'd had a gun I'd have killed him. But Mummy wouldn't let me.'

'I should think not,' Vicky told him. 'He wasn't bothering you.'

'I saw one of those women just disappear,' Mary said. 'She and her piccaninny just went beneath the surface, and they never came up. And nobody tried to help them. It was just awful.'

'They don't have our strength,' Elizabeth commented.

'Well, they haven't exactly been eating our food, recently,' Vicky reminded her, and stooped beside Lady Hodgson, who was looking utterly exhausted; her dog looked like a rat.

'Don't you think it would be a good idea to camp here for the rest of the day?' Sir Francis asked. 'These people are done in.'

'I think we must get on, Sir Francis,' Vicky said. 'We only have food for three days; we can't waste half of one. And the Ashanti are gathering all the time. Besides, once we reach the road the going will be much easier.'

'The lady's right,' Major Morris said, at last coming ashore with his rearguard, as wet and filthy as the rest of them, and probably as tired as well, but determined not to show it. 'This is no place to have to fight a battle.' He looked over the huge mass of sodden and miserable humanity. 'And no force, either.'

Sir Francis's indecision was relieved at that moment by the arrival of a messenger sent back from Captain Marshall to say that the forest to the south seemed clear of enemies.

'Perhaps they won't follow us at all,' Mary suggested. 'Surely the fort is what they really want.'

'My worry is that they've already gone past us,' Vicky muttered, 'and are waiting on the road someplace. Someplace they know we have to pass.'

'Oh come now, that's hardly likely, what?' Sir Francis protested. 'These people are savages. They can have no idea of strategy.'

'No, Sir Francis,' Vicky told him. 'Here in the jungle, *we* are the savages. They're playing in their own back yard. We'd better get on.'

She went forward with her escort of a Haussa sergeant and

six constables, to find Marshall and the rest of the advance guard waiting for her. 'Let's move to the east,' she suggested.

The machetes came out, and the men hacked their way into the bush. Within an hour the misery of the swamp seemed like paradise – at least it had been cool. Here, following a heavy mid-afternoon shower of rain, the jungle turned into an oven. The policemen hacked, and they followed, stumbling over tree roots, pushing branches from their faces, losing their hats and veils. Clouds of insects continued to buzz around their heads, ants seethed around their feet, birds and monkeys swung to and fro above their heads. Vicky raised no objection when Marshall detached a platoon to kill game; they needed all the food they could find, and the Ashanti knew where they were, anyway. Soon the forest echoed and re-echoed to the sound of rifle shots, and the monkeys, screaming their fear and displeasure, disappeared.

But at last, as the sun began to drop towards the west, they reached the road, to find it deserted, and leading invitingly southward. It was only a beaten earth track, and had in places disintegrated beneath the rain, but it promised an infinitely easier pathway than hacking through the jungle.

'When do you think we should camp?' Sir Francis wanted to know, coming up to join the advance guard. His white jacket was torn and stained with mud where he had fallen, and his once carefully waxed moustaches were drooping to either side of his mouth. 'This would seem an ideal place. I mean, the worst is surely behind us now.'

'The worst is the Ashanti, Sir Francis,' Vicky reminded him. 'And then starvation. I think we should continue until nightfall, at least.'

'These people are exhausted,' he protested, and was distracted by the arrival of another messenger sent by Marshall, behind whom there came a flurry of shots. 'What in the name of God is that?' the Governor demanded.

'I's from the Captain, yo' excellency,' the policeman explained. 'They's got a blockhouse up theah.'

'Oh, God,' Hodgson commented.

'Can we take a look?' Vicky asked.

Cautiously they went forward, until checked by Marshall himself, and then dropped to their stomachs beside him to gaze at a hastily constructed but very solid looking little fort, composed of logs of wood piled against each other, which entirely blocked the roadway. Even at a distance Vicky could tell there was a large number of men behind the barricade, and apparently determined to stay there, although they discharged their rifles at anything they saw moving, with total inaccuracy.

'Well, that's that,' Hodgson said. 'We'll have to go back into the bush, find a place to camp, and then try to get round them tomorrow morning.'

'With respect, Sir Francis,' Vicky protested, 'that is exactly what the Ashanti want you to do. Once you take to the forest, they'll move further down the road and build another blockhouse. They know we'll run out of food long before we can cut our way through the bush. We *have* to keep to the road.'

'But that will mean assaulting that position,' he pointed.

'It will mean destroying that position, Sir Francis. Could we have an opinion from Major Morris?'

The Major was sent for, and arrived twenty minutes later, followed by most of his men. He took in the situation at a glance, then spent five minutes inspecting the blockhouse through his binoculars. 'The lady's right, your excellency,' he decided at last, and as usual. 'You keep the non-combatants back, and leave this to us.'

Vicky felt enormously guilty, not for the first time on this march; she knew what had to be done – but she couldn't do it herself, could only send brave men to their deaths.

But Morris's obvious expertise gave her confidence. 'Now, gentlemen,' he said to his assembled officers, 'we must destroy that blockhouse and disperse those rascals by nightfall, which allows us only just over an hour. We'll use three prongs. Captain Marshall, you'll move into the bush on the right, with a hundred men. Lieutenant Reade, you'll move to the left with a hundred men. Fifteen minutes after you leave, I will launch the main force into an assault. Take a wide sweep now – it matters nothing if you are late. The important thing is that the Ashanti do not know you are there, and that you launch your attacks *after* mine has commenced.' He smiled at them. 'But not too much after, please. Lieutenant Armitage, you'll mount the Maxims, if you please. Captain Leggatt, form up the assault party.'

'Where do you want us?' Vicky asked.

'Well back, Mrs Lang. I'm leaving fifty constables to protect you, but . . .' He drew his revolver, handed it to her along with a box of cartridges. 'I'm told you know how to use this.'

She nodded, suddenly breathless.

'Accidents do happen, Mrs Lang,' he said. 'I don't think you need me to spell out the situation were we to be defeated?'

'No,' she said.

He smiled at her. 'But I do not propose to be. Now, if you will excuse me?'

Vicky returned to the women, who sat or lay amongst the trees, glad of the respite, most of them too exhausted even to watch, while Dr Norman and his colleagues prepared their instruments and their now scanty store of laudanam and bandages. Major Morris meanwhile walked up and down the road in full view of the Ashanti, who sent several shots in his direction, without ever coming close to hitting him. All the while he kept consulting his watch; then, after fifteen minutes, he walked slowly back to stand between the two Maxim guns. 'You may open fire, Mr Leggatt.'

The deadly chattering began, and Vicky could almost hear the bullets thudding into the wooden logs; certainly she could see the splinters whipping into the air, and she could hear the shouts of the Ashanti, even above the murmur of the women, and the shouts of Charlie, who jumped up and down crying 'Bam! Bam!' and even got Lady Hodgson's dog barking. The bombardment lasted for five minutes, while Sir Francis, standing beside Vicky, muttered, 'That'll make the blighters keep their heads down.'

Then Morris spoke in a quiet voice, the chatter of the machine guns ceased, the Major drew his sword, walked in front of the guns again, and pointed at the stockade. 'Tear that down,' he commanded, and set off at a trot, straight at the Ashanti.

Vicky stared in a mixture of horror and admiration. For the entire force of constabulary, hitherto kneeling, rose as a man and charged behind him, bayoneted rifles thrust forward, their officers immediately to the front waving their swords. The Ashanti, who had been crouching behind the logs to avoid the machine-gun fire, now scrambled back on to their barricade and began firing in earnest. Several of the policemen fell, and one of the officers.

'Can't we help those men?' Vicky asked the doctor.

'Not until the shooting stops. To venture up there would be to risk getting hit yourself.'

'Oh, rubbish,' Alison snapped, having joined them. 'We cannot just let those men bleed to death. Come along, Vicky. Come along, girls. Joanna, please look after Charlie.'

She might indeed be as frightened by the jungle, and the Ashanti, as she had claimed, Vicky thought, but she was not going to let fear interfere with her concept of duty. Because she had at last learned what duty was. She tucked her revolver into her waistband and hurried forward, with the girls. Only one of the policemen had been killed outright. The rest they dragged or helped back to the surgeons, while in front of them the rest of the attacking force surged at the barricades, their rifles cracking, their bayonets thrusting, their hurrahs mingling with the cries of the enemy. For several minutes the policemen seemed to be making no impression, and Vicky stopped working to watch, her heart seeming to slow – for all her conversation with Morris, and the weight of the revolver pressing into her stomach, she had not really considered the possibility of a defeat . . . with all that would entail for the women, and for her most of all. But then there came the sound of fresh shooting, and cheers, from behind the stockade: Marshall and Reade and their men had reached the road. A few minutes later the Ashanti broke and fled, throwing away their weapons as they streamed into the forest, chased by the shots of the exultant Haussa.

Then it was necessary to go forward, and see what could be done. And for all the horrors she had experienced on the walk from the wreck, Vicky felt sicker than at any moment since she

369

had fought her own personal battle with the mutineers. A good hundred of the Ashanti had fallen, either to bullet wounds at close range or to bayonet thrusts – Vicky had never imagined that a bayonet could do such terrible things.

Some twenty of the policemen were also dead. And Major Morris had been hit in the arm. 'This is no place for a woman,' he said, as she bound up the wound, blood dribbling over her fingers. 'Not even you, Mrs Lang.'

'I've done it before,' she told him. 'And you won. Would you like your gun back?'

He gazed at her for several seconds. 'No,' he said. 'Hang on to it. We're not there yet.'

His gaze flickered, and she turned to look at Captain Marshall, being carried past her by four of his men; he had been shot through the head at close range. She wanted to weep. She had known him such a short while, really only from that morning, and yet she knew him so well.

'It makes you so angry,' Alison put her arm round Vicky's shoulders to squeeze her. And then looked down at the revolver. 'Were you really going to shoot us, if the policemen had been defeated?'

Vicky raised her head. 'Isn't that what you wanted me to do?' she asked.

They buried their dead by the roadside, Governor Hodgson said a brief prayer, and then they pressed on again, past the blockhouse and into the dusk. It was not merely a matter of taking advantage of their victory to get on while they could; it was also necessary to remove themselves from the dead Ashanti, the stench of blood and the gathering insects and carrion crows.

This was an even more sombre march than earlier. They were exhausted, and their emotions had been stretched to breaking point by the battle and by the loss of so many of their comrades. Lieutenant Reade now led the advance guard, but Vicky had dropped back to be with the wounded and the ladies. Now they were on the road they didn't need her up there any more, and she didn't want to take any chances on getting to know Reade as well as she had known Marshall – she did not think she could stand that again.

At midnight Sir Francis finally called a halt. Sentries were posted, but the rest of the column fell where they stood, and slept. Not even a heavy downpour of rain, followed by the onslaught of thousands of mosquitoes, could keep them awake. 'But tomorrow,' Major Morris said encouragingly, 'tomorrow we'll be at Bekwai. For lunch.'

He was right. Reade and his advance guard left an hour before the main party, and they had not been marching an hour when a runner returned to them. Bekwai was in sight. It was also held in great force by the Ashanti.

Sylvia Hodgson sat on the ground, the picture of despair; her exhausted dog lay in her lap. Her husband hardly looked better. 'Of all the bad luck,' he grumbled. 'Of all the bad luck.'

'Hardly luck, Sir Francis,' Vicky protested. 'We knew it was probably occupied.'

'I was hoping,' he said dolefully.

'Well, we simply have to bust through it, as we did the last one,' Vicky insisted. 'Major Morris . . .'

But even Morris was looking discouraged. 'How many people are holding the village, would you say, Mr Reade?' he asked.

'Well, sir . . . several thousand, in my opinion.'

'And are there blockhouses?'

'Oh, indeed, sir. I counted five.'

Morris sighed. 'Perhaps five thousand warriors, and five blockhouses . . . we have not quite five hundred men. It won't do, Mrs Lang. It simply won't do. There is such a thing as arithmetic.'

'So what *will* do?' Vicky shouted in desperation. 'We can't go back; there are probably even more than five thousand of them behind us. Now you say we can't go forward. Do you mean just to sit here and starve until they're ready to come and get us?'

Morris tilted his topee over his nose and scratched the back of his head.

Vicky looked at Alison.

Who looked back, and shrugged.

Because the men were right, of course. To send five hundred men against five thousand, and those five thousand protected by fortifications, would be sheer suicide. But to stay here was sheer suicide . . .

'It does go against the grain,' Alison confessed. 'To have come so far and be beaten.'

Oh, my God, Vicky thought; she still thinks it's some sort of a game. She looked at Mary, who put her arm round Elizabeth.

'Are you going to have to shoot us, Major Morris?' Elizabeth asked. 'Before the Ashanti take us?'

Joanna Cartwright burst into tears.

Vicky walked away from them, gazed along the road, at the distant rooftops, listened to the noise of the Ashanti shouting at each other, supposing that the crazy British were about to launch an attack even upon so strong a position. But it would be a massacre. Following which, there would be a massacre here, too. Yet she felt less horrified, or afraid, than angry. As Alison had said, to have come so far and endured so much . . . perhaps it was a game, after all. A game with fate. But fate always won such games.

'We'll see the bounders don't lay a finger on you, Mrs Lang,' Lieutenant Reade said encouragingly, having come to stand beside her.

'I think I'd rather do it myself,' she said, and counted the cartridges Morris had given her. 'I have certain responsibilities, to the others.'

'Oh, Mrs Lang . . . ' He bit his lip. 'You are without doubt the bravest woman I have ever met.'

'I am?'

'Well, you're so calm, so certain . . .' He paused in embarrassment as he watched a tear trickle down Vicky's cheek.

'But what's that noise?' one of the Haussa policemen immediately in front of them asked his neighbour.

'Them people killing pigs for they meal,' his friend replied. 'They got plenty food down theah.'

Killing pigs! Vicky slowly turned to look at the village again, as she too heard the noise. 'Mr Reade . . .'

'By God,' the Lieutenant said. 'Listen!'

Vicky was doing that. Accompanying the high-pitched squealing was a steady drumming cadence, not the rhythm of the Ashanti sending messages, but the regular thuds of a military drummer keeping time.

'By God,' Reade said again. 'That's the Gold Coast Constabulary Drum and Fife Band.'

Morris had heard the noise, and come forward as well. 'Well, Mrs Lang, they do say fortune favours the brave. Looks as if you might complete your walk to the coast after all. Mr Reade, prepare your men for an assault on the village.'

Only twenty men remained with the women this time. And if Vicky, so accustomed to disaster, still sat with the revolver and cartridges on her lap, she no longer really expected to have to use them.

The noise of battle seeped across the morning, screams and shouts, explosions, the chatter of the Maxim guns and the deeper explosions of the field pieces. There was a whole army before Bekwai, and the Ashanti were making their last stand.

The battle lasted for hardly an hour. Then they listened to hooves, and the creaking of caissons, and the cheers of the excited visitors. They stood up to gaze, and wave, and cheer as they saw more white faces than they would have believed possible; the policemen had been reinforced by a naval detachment as well as a company of regulars en route to South Africa.

Tears streamed down Vicky's face as she made out David. He threw himself from his horse to hold her in his arms. 'Oh, my darling, girl,' he said. 'My darling girl! I thought you were dead. Two months . . . oh, Vicky . . . and I have the most marvellous news . . .'

She clung to him, incapable of speech, and looked past him . . . at Sir William Dobree.

'It's rather a story,' William Dobree said, as they sat around

373

the camp fire, while all around them the bustle of an army settling down for the night dominated even the sounds of the forest. The dead had been buried, the sentries posted, and tomorrow the column would continue to Kumassi and the relief of Major McClarrie and his gallant men.

But for the women the ordeal was over; tomorrow they would continue to the coast, in wagons. And for four of them, at least, life had taken on a new meaning. Mary and Elizabeth sat beside their father, their arms round his waist, holding him as if they would never let go of him again – as Vicky did with David.

'Although, of course, my adventures cannot compare with yours,' the General continued, magnanimously, looking at his wife while he bounced Charlie on his knee.

Alison sat opposite, gazing at her husband. Her face was expressionless, and Vicky suspected she was the only person in the entire army who had the slightest idea of the thoughts going on behind that beautiful mask.

'But tell us about them, Daddy,' Mary begged. 'Please tell us. We thought you were dead.'

'Well,' Sir William said, 'the ship went down in that squall, as you supposed. Very suddenly. She slipped off the rocks and sank in seconds. There was no time to do anything. I found myself swimming, and grabbed the first piece of anything I could find. It happened to be a liferaft, and I got on to it, with six men. We were knocked about by the waves quite a bit, but we clung on, all night. Next morning, there was nothing. We did hear David's revolver shots, but they were a long way away, and there was no way we could indicate where we were. Then we saw a lifeboat, floating upside down. I suppose that's what happened to all the other boats, capsizing or being swamped . . . I thought we were done, I'll tell you that, just as I thought you were probably all dead, too. I don't know what kept me going. We floated for thirty-six hours, would you believe it? It was quite terrible. There was no food or water . . . three of the chaps died . . . and the sharks . . . ' He sighed at the memory. 'Then a ship came in sight, and their lookouts actually spotted us. We were taken on board. I suppose I was quite done in, because I was

374

apparently unconscious for the next two days, and when I regained my senses the ship, northbound, was already past the Canaries. I was pretty sure some survivors from the *Doncaster* had got through the storm, because of the shots I'd heard, and I wanted the captain to turn back. The scoundrel wouldn't. He wasn't going to take his ship inshore in any event; too dangerous, he said, and he assured me that any people who did make the shore would have died by then anyway. I was so furious that he had to lock me up.'

He paused, and then gazed into the fire, while they waited. Then he sighed again. 'Anyway, as soon as we reached England, I instigated a search. The War Office gave me leave of absence, and I chartered a ship and returned to the spot where the *Doncaster* had struck. We found our way past those rocks, and approached the shore. But we couldn't get closer than two miles, and we didn't dare try to land a boat, because of the enormous surf. My captain reckoned anyone attempting that would surely have been drowned. But I still hoped, so we came down here, to Accra, where I intended to lead an expedition into the interior to see if there was any trace of you. But I'd only just arrived when this business started. I was beginning to go mad because of the delays when David turned up. I could hardly believe my eyes, or the tale he had to tell. Then, of course, there were still more delays . . . we volunteered to accompany the relief force, of course, but meanwhile an advance guard had been despatched immediately, and it actually got to this very village, Bekwai, when it was checked and forced to retreat by a superior Ashanti force . . .'

'We heard the guns,' Sir Francis said. 'When we realised it'd been forced to retreat, we were very disappointed.'

'It was inadequate for the job,' Dobree said. 'So as I say, it retreated, and we then got down to forming an army. This army. All of twelve hundred men, properly equipped . . . but the strain of not knowing what was happening in Kumassi was really severe. But all's well that ends well, eh?'

Not for everyone, Vicky thought. All those people. And now there's only us. Happiness for us, maybe. Death for them. After supper she walked to the perimeter of the encampment to look out at the forest, then heard a soft footfall behind her. She didn't have to turn her head. She knew it wasn't David, who had understood her mood.

'I don't know what to say, Vicky. David has told me everything. I suppose I owe you more than any man can ever hope to repay.'

'I was saving my life as well, Sir William,' she reminded him.

'That might have been easier to do had you thought of nothing else,' he suggested.

'They were all magnificent,' she told him.

'I know. So many people are, when pushed. And now . . .'

She turned to face him.

'David's told me he wants to marry you.'

She nodded.

'He'll be invalided out, of course. Back to Cumberland. You'll be landed gentry. His father is a very wealthy man, you know.'

'Wealthy? Good Lord! No, I didn't know that. He never told me.'

'Well, he's the younger son, of course. Still . . . ah . . .'

'What you are trying to say is it'll be quite a step up, for me,' Vicky said.

'Well, there is that point. I'm going on to South Africa, now, you know. There really could be trouble brewing there. What I meant was, if you ever need anything, anything at all, Vicky, well . . . I shall always be glad to see you. No matter where I am,' He held her hands. 'Do you remember my last words to you, on board the *Doncaster*?'

'I shall never forget them.'

'Well, I did think of you. All the time I was on that life raft. I think dreaming of you was what kept me alive.'

'I'm very flattered, Sir William. But a lot has happened since then. Have you spoken with Alison? I mean, seriously?'

'There hasn't been time. Besides, she's . . . well, she's been behaving rather oddly. Not talking. She's never not talked before. Oh, I can understand that she has a lot on her mind, if even half of what David has told me is true. But the way she looks at me . . . I can't escape the feeling that she's not entirely pleased to find I survived.'

'You say David told you everything that happened, Sir William. Are you pleased that *she* survived?'

'Pleased? Why, of course I am. I'm overjoyed. My God, did you suppose I'd let something, well . . . she was forced. It could happen to any woman, in those circumstances. I . . .'

'If you think about it,' Vicky interrupted, 'you might find that is all true, and not just a matter of saying the right thing. And then, if you were to tell her how you felt . . . well, I've a notion that you could be pleasantly surprised.'

He frowned at her.

Vicky smiled. 'You'll find she's changed a bit. Maybe come more to grips with the business of living, and being a woman. That means loving too, in every way. And it's you she loves, Sir William.'

'By God,' Dobree said. 'I . . .' he released her hands, stepped back, and checked. 'You're a marvellous creature, Victoria Lang. Meeting you was probably the most important event of my life.' He took her hand again, kissed the knuckles. 'Victoria's Walk,' he said. 'Someone ought to write a book about you.'

EPILOGUE

General Sir William Dobree covered himself in glory during the Boer War. But he and Lady Dobree found the time to have three more children.

As for King Kuno: Kumassi relieved, his Golden Stool proved to have been a fake, his armies utterly defeated, he was exiled to Mauritius, and died there; fetish worship was abolished, and the Ashanti had to wait another sixty years to regain their independence.

The Emir Zobeir ibn Rubayr was killed fighting against the French only a year after the relief of Kumassi. In his saddlebag was found a copy of *The Times*, which contained a photograph of Lady Dobree, taken on her triumphant arrival in Accra.

And Captain (retired) and Mrs David Whiting lived happily everafter. David managed, and in course of time inherited his father's farm, and Victoria resumed her earlier profession by founding a school; she found the work much more enjoyable as her own headmistress. She never told the children of her adventures in Africa, however. Indeed, no one ever told the story of that remarkable walk, until now.